Interstellar visitors use their superior technology to free Earth from war, crime, and disease—but their service to mankind comes with a definite catch.

A fetus with superhuman intelligence controls the lives of his reluctant parents.

A time-sphere that allows entrance into the future provides a greedy recluse with an unusual opportunity for murder and gain—and becomes a grisly trap.

A prosthetic man stripped of anger, love, and sorrow finds that there is one emotion he retains—a deep revulsion for all living things.

A little man with a cockatoo-crested head, a white disk that can transform thought into pictures, and a pocketful of diamonds visits New York City one day and unwittingly turns it into a modern Babel.

THE BEST OF DAMON KNIGHT
is an original POCKET BOOK edition.

THE BEST
OF
DAMON KNIGHT

by
DAMON KNIGHT

PUBLISHED BY POCKET BOOKS NEW YORK

THE BEST OF DAMON KNIGHT

POCKET BOOK edition published September, 1976

This original POCKET BOOK edition is printed from brand-new
plates made from newly set, clear, easy-to-read type.
POCKET BOOK editions are published by
POCKET BOOKS,
a division of Simon & Schuster, Inc.,
A GULF+WESTERN COMPANY
630 Fifth Avenue,
New York, N.Y. 10020.
Trademarks registered in the United States
and other countries.

ISBN: 0-671-80699-8.

Printed in the U.S.A.

ACKNOWLEDGMENTS

"Not with a Bang," copyright 1949 by Mercury Press, Inc.
"To Serve Man," copyright 1950 by Galaxy Publishing
Corporation.
"Cabin Boy," copyright 1951 by Galaxy Publishing Cor-
poration.

DARK OF THE KNIGHT

DAMON KNIGHT GREW UP IN HOOD RIVER, Oregon, made himself first known in the science-fiction field via a classic demolition in a fan magazine (despite the fact that the magazine had a circulation of no more than two hundred, the review had significant consequences upon two careers), and, like most bright people of his generation, fled to Manhattan. He worked briefly in a literary agency (the same in which I did almost twenty years later), collaborated with James Blish on "Tiger Ride" for *Astounding,* his first major sale, wrote a few pulp stories under various pseudonyms, became a free-lance illustrator and editor, and began to publish s-f widely. His "Not with a Bang," which leads off this collection, created some talk in the fall of 1949; by the mid-1950s he had established himself at the top of his field by steadily putting out sardonic and elegantly crafted pieces for magazines. He wrote a few novels, too, one of which—*A for Anything*—is probably a masterpiece.

In the mid-fifties Knight's career as a creative writer began to cut back as he became a reviewer, then a critic, and wrote for a number of publications the first body of literate criticism in the history of science fiction. (His criticism was later collected in an important book, *In Search of Wonder.*) Around 1960 he got tired of criticism and turned to editing the *Orbit* series while he got back to fiction on a modest scale. "Down There," the most recent of his stories in this volume, strikes me as being the best he's written, so one can hardly say that Knight has deteriorated in his fifties; in fact, he's a better writer than ever. He lives placidly and happily now with his wife, the distinguished writer Kate Wilhelm, in a big house in Oregon, and he talks of never coming to New York again.

This is a bare enough outline of a working life, yet in the interstices you can see suggestions of the dimensions of the accomplishment. I submit that a good case could be made for Damon Knight's being the most important literary figure to come out of science fiction to date. He has, in the first place, excelled in everything he's done—editing, criticism, novels, short stories, and some extraordinary dirty limericks, too. In the second place, his reputation as critic and editor has obscured to younger writers and readers the fact that the body of fiction he produced in the 1950s was superb. Of all the writers H. L. Gold developed for *Galaxy* as a means of social satire and criticism, Knight was probably the most characteristic and often enough the best. That he was not merely a satirist but a writer of great passion and stylistic range can be seen in stories like "The Handler" and "Masks," which are included here.

Always underrated (even by himself) as a novelist, he has produced several ignored works of quality—of which the aforementioned *A for Anything*, temporarily and unfortunately out of print, stands to last as long as any novel of its decade. (It was published in the late fifties.) A stunning portrait of a feudal society built upon the deliberate repression of abundance, *A for Anything* has the veracity of a political handbook and the conciseness and inevitability of a good scatological joke. It also has characters and a conclusion that strike me as being the most depressing in science-fiction novels. I recommend it to you highly, and I also think you ought to take a look at *The Other Foot* (1964), an extension of his novella *The Visitor in the Zoo;* it strikes me as being the only novel in the manner of Garnett's *Lady into Fox* that has anything new to say.

And of course I recommend *In Search of Wonder*. Knight's original modest proposal was simply that science fiction is a branch of literature to which one can —and has to—apply the same critical standards one would apply to any other branch of literature. Out of reasonable scholarship, a good command of the history of the modern novel, and a shattering wit, Knight produced a critical work that stands by itself and is essentially responsible for any informed criticism by successors in the field today.

In short, Knight is a man of stature and quality, a writer of importance, and a writer whose works will be a new and perhaps jarring experience for many people who were not around when this *oeuvre* was being built block by block over the decades.

Of all the introductions to these "Best of" books, this has probably been the easiest and most pleasant to write. At some basic level I owe almost all the critical apparatus with which I now deal with science fiction to Damon Knight, and I owe practically to him alone my first astonished realization in the early fifties that, by God, science fiction not only was a lot of fun . . . it could be written by its best practitioners so as to correspond to (but never duplicate) the best of work done anywhere.

—BARRY N. MALZBERG

Teaneck, N.J.
September, 1975

CONTENTS

INTRODUCTION

These stories represent a big chunk of my life, from 1949 to 1972. They are certainly not all I wrote during that time, but they *are* most of the best work I did.

In the early stories I was trying to find out who the hell I was as a writer, and in later ones, I think, trying to see who else I was or could be. Actors, con men, and writers choose their careers partly out of a yen to be more than one person.

—DAMON KNIGHT

THIS IS THE FIRST STORY I EVER wrote in my life that was worth a damn. I was twenty-six, and had had eight stories published, and I'd been trying to write well since I was twelve.

I got the idea for "Not with a Bang" during the time it took for a men's-room door to close behind me in a New York restaurant. I wrote the story mostly in the cellar of Jim and Virginia Blish's house on Staten Island, whither I had been banished from the upstairs study because I kept talking to Jim. The story was rejected by every science-fiction market then in existence, and it's possible to suppose that if Anthony Boucher and J. Francis McComas had not founded *The Magazine of Fantasy & Science Fiction* in 1950, it never would have been published. Boucher (may his bones rest in peace) called it "a new kind of catastrophe —the cosmic cocktail mixed with a full jigger of wry."

1

NOT WITH A BANG

<<<<<<<<<<<<<<<<<<<<<<<<<<<<<<<<<<<<

TEN MONTHS AFTER THE LAST PLANE PASSED over, Rolf Smith knew beyond doubt that only one other human being had survived. Her name was Louise Oliver, and he was sitting opposite her in a department-store café in Salt Lake City. They were eating canned Vienna sausages and drinking coffee.

Sunlight struck through a broken pane like a judgment. Inside and outside, there was no sound; only a stifling rumor of absence. The clatter of dishware in the kitchen, the heavy rumble of streetcars: never again. There was sunlight; and silence; and the watery, astonished eyes of Louise Oliver.

He leaned forward, trying to capture the attention of those fishlike eyes for a second. "Darling," he said, "I repect your views, naturally. But I've got to make you see that they're impractical."

She looked at him with faint surprise, then away again. Her head shook slightly. *No. No, Rolf, I will not live with you in sin.*

Smith thought of the women of France, of Russia, of Mexico, of the South Seas. He had spent three months in the ruined studios of a radio station in Rochester, listening to the voices until they stopped. There had been a large colony in Sweden, including an English cabinet minister. They reported that Europe was gone. Simply gone; there was not an acre that had not been swept

2

clean by radioactive dust. They had two planes and enough fuel to take them anywhere on the Continent; but there was nowhere to go. Three of them had the plague; then eleven; then all.

There was a bomber pilot who had fallen near a government radio station in Palestine. He did not last long, because he had broken some bones in the crash; but he had seen the vacant waters where the Pacific Islands should have been. It was his guess that the Arctic ice fields had been bombed.

There were no reports from Washington, from New York, from London, Paris, Moscow, Chungking, Sydney. You could not tell who had been destroyed by disease, who by the dust, who by bombs.

Smith himself had been a laboratory assistant in a team that was trying to find an antibiotic for the plague. His superiors had found one that worked sometimes, but it was a little too late. When he left, Smith took along with him all there was of it—forty ampoules, enough to last him for years.

Louise had been a nurse in a genteel hospital near Denver. According to her, something rather odd had happened to the hospital as she was approaching it the morning of the attack. She was quite calm when she said this, but a vague look came into her eyes and her shattered expression seemed to slip a little more. Smith did not press her for an explanation.

Like himself, she had found a radio station which still functioned, and when Smith discovered that she had not contracted the plague, he agreed to meet her. She was, apparently, naturally immune. There must have been others, a few at least; but the bombs and the dust had not spared them.

It seemed very awkward to Louise that not one Protestant minister was left alive.

The trouble was, she really meant it. It had taken Smith a long time to believe it, but it was true. She would not sleep in the same hotel with him, either; she expected, and received, the utmost courtesy and decorum. Smith had learned his lesson. He walked on the outside of the rubble-heaped sidewalks; he opened doors

3

for her, when there were still doors; he held her chair; he refrained from swearing. He courted her.

Louise was forty or thereabouts, at least five years older than Smith. He often wondered how old she thought she was. The shock of seeing whatever it was that had happened to the hospital, the patients she had cared for, had sent her mind scuttling back to her childhood. She tacitly admitted that everyone else in the world was dead, but she seemed to regard it as something one did not mention.

A hundred times in the last three weeks, Smith had felt an almost irresistible impulse to break her thin neck and go his own way. But there was no help for it; she was the only woman in the world, and he needed her. If she died, or left him, he died. Old bitch! he thought to himself furiously, and carefully kept the thought from showing on his face.

"Louise, honey," he told her gently, "I want to spare your feelings as much as I can. You know that."

"Yes, Rolf," she said, staring at him with the face of a hypnotized chicken.

Smith forced himself to go on. "We've got to face the facts, unpleasant as they may be. Honey, we're the only man and the only woman there are. We're like Adam and Eve in the Garden of Eden."

Louise's face took on a slightly disgusted expression. She was obviously thinking of fig leaves.

"Think of the generations unborn," Smith told her, with a tremor in his voice. Think about me for once. Maybe you're good for another ten years, maybe not. Shuddering, he thought of the second stage of the disease—the helpless rigidity, striking without warning. He'd had one such attack already, and Louise had helped him out of it. Without her, he would have stayed like that till he died, the hypodermic that would save him within inches of his rigid hand. He thought desperately, If I'm lucky, I'll get at least two kids out of you before you croak. Then I'll be safe.

He went on, "God didn't mean for the human race to end like this. He spared us, you and me, to—" he paused; how could he say it without offending her?

4

"parents" wouldn't do—too suggestive—"to carry on the torch of life," he ended. There. That was sticky enough.

Louise was staring vaguely over his shoulder. Her eye-lids blinked regularly, and her mouth made little rabbit-like motions in the same rhythm.

Smith looked down at his wasted thighs under the tabletop. I'm not strong enough to force her, he thought. Christ, if I were strong enough!

He felt the futile rage again, and stifled it. He had to keep his head, because this might be his last chance. Louise had been talking lately, in the cloudy language she used about everything, of going up in the mountains to pray for guidance. She had not said "alone," but it was easy enough to see that she pictured it that way. He had to argue her around before her resolve stiffened. He concentrated furiously and tried once more.

The pattern of words went by like a distant rumbling. Louise heard a phrase here and there; each of them fathered chains of thought, binding her reverie tighter. "Our duty to humanity . . ." Mama had often said— that was in the old house on Waterbury Street, of course, before Mama had taken sick—she had said, "Child, your duty is to be clean, polite, and God-fearing. Pretty doesn't matter. There's plenty of plain women that have got themselves good, Christian husbands."

Husbands . . . To have and to hold . . . Orange blossoms, and the bridesmaids; the organ music. Through the haze, she saw Rolf's lean, wolfish face. Of course, he was the only one she'd ever get: *she* knew that well enough. Gracious, when a girl was past twenty-five, she had to take what she could get.

But I sometimes wonder if he's really a *nice* man, she thought.

". . . in the eyes of God . . ." She remembered the stained-glass windows in the old First Episcopalian Church, and how she always thought God was looking down at her through that brilliant transparency. Perhaps He was still looking at her, though it seemed sometimes that He had forgotten. Well, of course she realized that marriage customs changed, and if you couldn't have a

5

regular minister . . . But it was really a shame, an outrage almost, that if she were actually going to marry this man, she couldn't have all those nice things. . . . There wouldn't even be any wedding presents. Not even that. But of course Rolf would give her anything she wanted. She saw his face again, noticed the narrow black eyes staring at her with ferocious purpose, the thin mouth that jerked in a slow, regular tic, the hairy lobes of the ears below the tangle of black hair.

He oughtn't to let his hair grow so long, she thought. It isn't quite decent. Well, she could change all that. If she did marry him, she'd certainly make him change his ways. It was no more than her duty.

He was talking now about a farm he'd seen outside town—a good big house and a barn. There was no stock, he said, but they could get some later. And they'd plant things, and have their own food to eat, not go to restaurants all the time.

She felt a touch on her hand, lying pale before her on the table. Rolf's brown, stubby fingers, black-haired above and below the knuckles, were touching hers. He had stopped talking for a moment, but now he was speaking again, still more urgently. She drew her hand away.

He was saying, ". . . and you'll have the finest wedding dress you ever saw, with a bouquet. Everything you want, Louise, everything . . ."

A wedding dress! And flowers, even if there couldn't be any minister! Well, why hadn't the fool said so before?

Rolf stopped halfway through a sentence, aware that Louise had said quite clearly, "Yes, Rolf, I will marry you if you wish."

Stunned, he wanted her to repeat it, but dared not ask, "What did you say?" for fear of getting some fantastic answer, or none at all. He breathed deeply. He said, "Today, Louise?"

She said, "Well, *today* . . . I don't know quite . . . Of course, if you think you can make all the arrangements in time, but it does seem . . ."

6

Triumph surged through Smith's body. He had the advantage now, and he'd ride it. "Say you will, dear," he urged her. "Say yes, and make me the happiest man . . ."

Even then, his tongue balked at the rest of it; but it didn't matter. She nodded submissively. "Whatever you think best, Rolf."

He rose, and she allowed him to kiss her pale, sapless cheek. "We'll leave right away," he said. "If you'll excuse me for just a minute, dear?"

He waited for her "Of course" and then left, making footprints in the furred carpet of dust down toward the end of the room. Just a few more hours he'd have to speak to her like that, and then, in her eyes, she'd be committed to him forever. Afterward, he could do with her as he liked—beat her when he pleased, submit her to any proof of his scorn and revulsion, use her. Then it would not be too bad, being the last man on earth— not bad at all. She might even have a daughter. . . .

He found the washroom door and entered. He took a step inside, and froze, balanced by a trick of motion, upright but helpless. Panic struck his throat as he tried to turn his head and failed; tried to scream, and failed. Behind him, he was aware of a tiny click as the door, cushioned by the hydraulic check, shut forever. It was not locked; but its other side bore the warning MEN.

7

TO SERVE MAN" WAS WRITTEN IN 1950, when I was living in Greenwich Village and my unhappy first marriage was breaking up. I wrote it in one afternoon, while my wife was out with another man.

2

TO SERVE MAN

<<<<<<<<<<<<<<<<<<<<<<<<<<<<<<<<<<<<<<

THE KANAMIT WERE NOT VERY PRETTY, IT'S true. They looked something like pigs and something like people, and that is not an attractive combination. Seeing them for the first time shocked you; that was their handicap. When a thing with the countenance of a fiend comes from the stars and offers a gift, you are disinclined to accept.

I don't know what we expected interstellar visitors to look like—those who thought about it at all, that is. Angels, perhaps, or something too alien to be really awful. Maybe that's why we were all so horrified and repelled when they landed in their great ships and we saw what they really were like.

The Kanamit were short and very hairy—thick, bristly brown-gray hair all over their abominably plump bodies. Their noses were snoutlike and their eyes small, and they had thick hands of three fingers each. They wore green leather harness and green shorts, but I think the shorts were a concession to our notions of public decency. The garments were quite modishly cut, with slash pockets and half-belts in the back. The Kanamit had a sense of humor, anyhow.

There were three of them at this session of the U.N., and, lord, I can't tell you how queer it looked to see them there in the middle of a solemn plenary session—three fat piglike creatures in green harness and shorts, sitting

9

at the long table below the podium, surrounded by the packed arcs of delegates from every nation. They sat correctly upright, politely watching each speaker. Their flat ears drooped over the earphones. Later on, I believe, they learned every human language, but at this time they knew only French and English.

They seemed perfectly at ease—and that, along with their humor, was a thing that tended to make me like them. I was in the minority; I didn't think they were trying to put anything over.

The delegate from Argentina got up and said that his government was interested in the demonstration of a new cheap power source, which the Kanamit had made at the previous session, but that the Argentine government could not commit itself as to its future policy without a much more thorough examination.

It was what all the delegates were saying, but I had to pay particular attention to Señor Valdes, because he tended to sputter and his diction was bad. I got through the translation all right, with only one or two momentary hesitations, and then switched to the Polish-English line to hear how Grigori was doing with Janciewicz. Janciewicz was the cross Grigori had to bear, just as Valdes was mine.

Janciewicz repeated the previous remarks with a few ideological variations, and then the Secretary-General recognized the delegate from France, who introduced Dr. Denis Lévêque, the criminologist, and a great deal of complicated equipment was wheeled in.

Dr. Lévêque remarked that the question in many people's minds had been aptly expressed by the delegate from the U.S.S.R. at the preceding session, when he demanded, "What is the motive of the Kanamit? What is their purpose in offering us these unprecedented gifts, while asking nothing in return?"

The doctor then said, "At the request of several delegates and with the full consent of our guests, the Kanamit, my associates and I have made a series of tests upon the Kanamit with the equipment which you see before you. These tests will now be repeated."

A murmur ran through the chamber. There was a fusillade of flashbulbs, and one of the TV cameras moved up to focus on the instrument board of the doctor's equipment. At the same time, the huge television screen behind the podium lighted up, and we saw the blank faces of two dials, each with its pointer resting at zero, and a strip of paper tape with a stylus point resting against it.

The doctor's assistants were fastening wires to the temples of one of the Kanamit, wrapping a canvas-covered rubber tube around his forearm, and taping something to the palm of his right hand.

In the screen, we saw the paper tape begin to move while the stylus traced a slow zigzag pattern along it. One of the needles began to jump rhythmically; the other flipped halfway over and stayed there, wavering slightly.

"These are the standard instruments for testing the truth of a statement," said Dr. Lévêque. "Our first object, since the physiology of the Kanamit is unknown to us, was to determine whether or not they react to these tests as human beings do. We will now repeat one of the many experiments which were made in the endeavor to discover this."

He pointed to the first dial. "This instrument registers the subject's heartbeat. This shows the electrical conductivity of the skin in the palm of his hand, a measure of perspiration, which increases under stress. And this—" pointing to the tape-and-stylus device—"shows the pattern and intensity of the electrical waves emanating from his brain. It has been shown, with human subjects, that all these readings vary markedly depending upon whether the subject is speaking the truth."

He picked up two large pieces of cardboard, one red and one black. The red one was a square about three feet on a side; the black was a rectangle three and a half feet long. He addressed himself to the Kanama.

"Which of these is longer than the other?"

"The red," said the Kanama.

Both needles leaped wildly, and so did the line on the unrolling tape.

"I shall repeat the question," said the doctor. "Which of these is longer than the other?"

"The black," said the creature.

11

This time the instruments continued in their normal rhythm.

"How did you come to this planet?" asked the doctor.

"Walked," replied the Kanama.

Again the instruments responded, and there was a subdued ripple of laughter in the chamber.

"Once more," said the doctor. "How did you come to this planet?"

"In a spaceship," said the Kanama, and the instruments did not jump.

The doctor again faced the delegates. "Many such experiments were made," he said, "and my colleagues and myself are satisfied that the mechanisms are effective. Now—" he turned to the Kanama—"I shall ask our distinguished guest to reply to the question put at the last session by the delegate of the U.S.S.R.—namely, what is the motive of the Kanamit people in offering these great gifts to the people of Earth?"

The Kanama rose. Speaking this time in English, he said, "On my planet there is a saying, 'There are more riddles in a stone than in a philosopher's head.' The motives of intelligent beings, though they may at times appear obscure, are simple things compared to the complex workings of the natural universe. Therefore I hope that the people of Earth will understand, and believe, when I tell you that our mission upon your planet is simply this —to bring to you the peace and plenty which we ourselves enjoy, and which we have in the past brought to other races throughout the galaxy. When your world has no more hunger, no more war, no more needless suffering, that will be our reward."

And the needles had not jumped once.

The delegate from the Ukraine jumped to his feet, asking to be recognized, but the time was up and the Secretary-General closed the session.

I met Grigori as we were leaving the chamber. His face was red with excitement. "Who promoted that circus?" he demanded.

"The tests looked genuine to me," I told him.

"A circus!" he said vehemently. "A second-rate farce! If they were genuine, Peter, why was debate stifled?"

12

"There'll be time for debate tomorrow, surely."

"Tomorrow the doctor and his instruments will be back in Paris. Plenty of things can happen before tomorrow. In the name of sanity, man, how can anybody trust a thing that looks as if it ate the baby?"

I was a little annoyed. I said, "Are you sure you're not more worried about their politics than their appearance?"

He said, "Bah," and went away.

The next day, reports began to come in from government laboratories all over the world where the Kanamit's power source was being tested. They were wildly enthusiastic. I don't understand such things myself, but it seemed that those little metal boxes would give more electrical power than an atomic pile, for next to nothing and nearly forever. And it was said that they were so cheap to manufacture that everybody in the world could have one of his own. In the early afternoon there were reports that seventeen countries had already begun to set up factories to turn them out.

The next day the Kanamit turned up with plans and specimens of a gadget that would increase the fertility of any arable land by 60 to 100 per cent. It speeded the formation of nitrates in the soil, or something. There was nothing in the newscasts any more but stories about the Kanamit. The day after that, they dropped their bombshell.

"You now have potentially unlimited power and increased food supply," said one of them. He pointed with his three-fingered hand to an instrument that stood on the table before him. It was a box on a tripod, with a parabolic reflector on the front of it. "We offer you today a third gift which is at least as important as the first two."

He beckoned to the TV men to roll their cameras into closeup position. Then he picked up a large sheet of cardboard covered with drawings and English lettering. We saw it on the large screen above the podium; it was all clearly legible.

"We are informed that this broadcast is being relayed throughout your world," said the Kanama. "I wish that

13

everyone who has equipment for taking photographs from television screens would use it now."

The Secretary-General leaned forward and asked a question sharply, but the Kanama ignored him.

"This device," he said, "generates a field in which no explosive, of whatever nature, can detonate."

There was an uncomprehending silence.

The Kanama said, "It cannot now be suppressed. If one nation has it, all must have it." When nobody seemed to understand, he explained bluntly, "There will be no more war."

That was the biggest news of the millennium, and it was perfectly true. It turned out that the explosions the Kanama was talking about included gasoline and Diesel explosions. They had simply made it impossible for anybody to mount or equip a modern army.

We could have gone back to bows and arrows, of course, but that wouldn't have satisfied the military. Besides, there wouldn't be any reason to make war. Every nation would soon have everything.

Nobody ever gave another thought to those lie-detector experiments, or asked the Kanamit what their politics were. Grigori was put out; he had nothing to prove his suspicions.

I quit my job with the U.N. a few months later, because I foresaw that it was going to die under me anyhow. U.N. business was booming at the time, but after a year or so there was going to be nothing for it to do. Every nation on Earth was well on the way to being completely self-supporting; they weren't going to need much arbitration.

I accepted a position as translator with the Kanamit Embassy, and it was there that I ran into Grigori again. I was glad to see him, but I couldn't imagine what he was doing there.

"I thought you were on the opposition," I said. "Don't tell me you're convinced the Kanamit are all right."

He looked rather shamefaced. "They're not what they look, anyhow," he said.

It was as much of a concession as he could decently make, and I invited him down to the embassy lounge

14

for a drink. It was an intimate kind of place, and he grew confidential over the second daiquiri.

"They fascinate me," he said. "I hate them instinctively still—that hasn't changed—but I can evaluate it. You were right, obviously; they mean us nothing but good. But do you know—" he leaned across the table—"the question of the Soviet delegate was never answered."

I am afraid I snorted.

"No, really," he said. "They told us what they wanted to do—'to bring to you the peace and plenty which we ourselves enjoy.' But they didn't say *why*."

"Why do missionaries—"

"Missionaries be damned!" he said angrily. "Missionaries have a religious motive. If these creatures have a religion, they haven't once mentioned it. What's more, they didn't send a missionary group; they sent a diplomatic delegation—a group representing the will and policy of their whole people. Now just what have the Kanamit, as a people or a nation, got to gain from our welfare?"

I said, "Cultural—"

"Cultural cabbage soup! No, it's something less obvious than that, something obscure that belongs to their psychology and not to ours. But trust me, Peter, there is no such thing as a completely disinterested altruism. In one way or another, they have something to gain."

"And that's why you're here," I said. "To try to find out what it is."

"Correct. I wanted to get on one of the ten-year exchange groups to their home planet, but I couldn't; the quota was filled a week after they made the announcement. This is the next best thing. I'm studying their language, and you know that language reflects the basic assumptions of the people who use it. I've got a fair command of the spoken lingo already. It's not hard, really, and there are hints in it. Some of the idioms are quite similar to English. I'm sure I'll get the answer eventually."

"More power," I said, and we went back to work.

I saw Grigori frequently from then on, and he kept me posted about his progress. He was highly excited about a month after that first meeting; said he'd got hold of a book of the Kanamit's and was trying to puzzle it out. They wrote in ideographs, worse than Chinese, but he was determined to fathom it if it took him years. He wanted my help.

Well, I was interested in spite of myself, for I knew it would be a long job. We spent some evenings together, working with material from Kanamit bulletin boards and so forth, and with the extremely limited English-Kanamit dictionary they issued to the staff. My conscience bothered me about the stolen book, but gradually I became absorbed by the problem. Languages are my field, after all. I couldn't help being fascinated.

We got the title worked out in a few weeks. It was *How to Serve Man,* evidently a handbook they were giving out to new Kanamit members of the embassy staff. They had new ones in all the time now, a shipload about once a month; they were opening all kinds of research laboratories, clinics and so on. If there was anybody on Earth besides Grigori who still distrusted those people, he must have been somewhere in the middle of Tibet.

It was astonishing to see the changes that had been wrought in less than a year. There were no more standing armies, no more shortages, no unemployment. When you picked up a newspaper you didn't see H-BOMB or SATELLITE leaping out at you; the news was always good. It was a hard thing to get used to. The Kanamit were working on human biochemistry, and it was known around the embassy that they were nearly ready to announce methods of making our race taller and stronger and healthier—practically a race of supermen—and they had a potential cure for heart disease and cancer.

I didn't see Grigori for a fortnight after we finished working out the title of the book; I was on a long-overdue vacation in Canada. When I got back, I was shocked by the change in his appearance.

"What on earth is wrong, Grigori?" I asked. "You look like the very devil."

"Come down to the lounge."

I went with him, and he gulped a stiff Scotch as if he needed it.

"Come on, man, what's the matter?" I urged.

16

"The Kanamit have put me on the passenger list for the next exchange ship," he said. "You, too, otherwise I wouldn't be talking to you."

"Well," I said, "but—"

"They're not altruists."

I tried to reason with him. I pointed out they'd made Earth a paradise compared to what it was before. He only shook his head.

Then I said, "Well, what about those lie-detector tests?"

"A farce," he replied, without heat. "I said so at the time, you fool. They told the truth, though, as far as it went."

"And the book?" I demanded, annoyed. "What about that—*How to Serve Man?* That wasn't put there for you to read. They *mean* it. How do you explain that?"

"I've read the first paragraph of that book," he said. "Why do you suppose I haven't slept for a week?"

I said, "Well?" and he smiled a curious, twisted smile.

"It's a cookbook," he said.

I**N 1951 MY MARITAL TROUBLES WERE**
over (for the time being) and I was feeling
cheerful. "Cabin Boy" is a translation into
science fiction of this quasi-limerick:

> Tommy Loy, the cabin boy,
> The dirty little nipper,
> He filled his ass with broken glass
> And circumcized the skipper.

Horace Gold, who had never heard the
limerick, published the story in *Galaxy*, and
Bob Tucker, who had, chuckled madly.

3

CABIN BOY

<<<<<<<<<<<<<<<<<<<<<<<<<<<<<<<<<<<<<<<<<

I

THE CABIN BOY'S NAME WAS UNSPEAKABLE, and even its meaning would be difficult to convey in any human tongue. For convenience, we may as well call him Tommy Loy.

Please bear in mind that all these terms are approximations. Tommy was not exactly a cabin boy, and even the spaceship he served was not exactly a spaceship, nor was the Captain exactly a captain. But if you think of Tommy as a freckled, scowling, red-haired, willful, prank-playing, thoroughly abhorrent brat, and of the Captain as a crusty, ponderous old man, you may be able to understand their relationship.

A word about Tommy will serve to explain why these approximations have to be made, and just how much they mean. Tommy, to a human being, would have looked like a six-foot egg made of greenish gelatin. Suspended in this were certain dark or radiant shapes which were Tommy's nerve centers and digestive organs, and scattered about its surface were star-shaped and oval markings which were his sensory organs and gripping mechanisms—his "hands." At the lesser end was an orifice which expelled a stream of glowing vapor—Tommy's means of propulsion. It should be clear that if instead of saying, "Tommy ate his lunch," or, "Tommy said to the Captain . . ." we reported what really happened, some pretty complicated explanations would have to be made.

Similarly, the term "cabin boy" is used because it is the closest in human meaning. Some vocations, like seafaring, are so demanding and so complex that they simply cannot be taught in classrooms; they have to be lived. A cabin boy is one who is learning such a vocation and paying for his instruction by performing certain menial, degrading, and unimportant tasks.

That describes Tommy, with one more similarity— the cabin boy of the sailing vessel was traditionally occupied after each whipping with preparing the mischief, or the stupidity, that earned him the next one.

Tommy, at the moment, had a whipping coming to him and was fighting a delaying action. He knew he couldn't escape eventual punishment, but he planned to hold it off as long as he could.

Floating alertly in one of the innumerable corridors of the ship, he watched as a dark wave sprang into being upon the glowing corridor wall and sped toward him. Instantly, Tommy was moving away from it, and at the same rate of speed.

The wave rumbled: "Tommy! Tommy Loy! Where *is* that obscenity boy?"

The wave moved on, rumbling wordlessly, and Tommy moved with it. Ahead of him was another wave, and another beyond that, and it was the same throughout all the corridors of the ship. Abruptly the waves reversed their direction. So did Tommy, barely in time. The waves not only carried the Captain's orders but scanned every corridor and compartment of the ten-mile ship. But as long as Tommy kept between the waves, the Captain could not see him.

The trouble was that Tommy could not keep this up forever, and he was being searched for by other lowly members of the crew. It took a long time to traverse all of those winding, interlaced passages, but it was a mathematical certainty that he would be caught eventually.

Tommy shuddered, and at the same time he squirmed with delight. He had interrupted the Old Man's sleep by a stench of a particularly noisome variety, one of which he had only lately found himself capable. The effect had been beautiful. In human terms, since Tommy's race

20

communicated by odors, it was equivalent to setting off a firecracker beside a sleeper's ear.

Judging by the jerkiness of the scanning waves' motion, the Old Man was still unnerved.

"Tommy!" the waves rumbled. "Come out, you little piece of filth, or I'll smash you into a thousand separate stinks! By Spore, when I get hold of you——"

The corridor intersected another at this point, and Tommy seized his chance to duck into the new one. He had been working his way outward ever since his crime, knowing that the search parties would do the same. When he reached the outermost level of the ship, there would be a slight possibility of slipping back past the hunters—not much of a chance, but better than none.

He kept close to the wall. He was the smallest member of the crew—smaller than any of the other cabin boys, and less than half the size of an Ordinary; it was always possible that when he sighted one of the search party, he could get away before the crewman saw him. He was in a short connecting corridor now, but the scanning waves cycled endlessly, always turning back before he could escape into the next corridor. Tommy followed their movement patiently, while he listened to the torrent of abuse that poured from them. He snickered to himself. When the Old Man was angry, everybody suffered. The ship would be stinking from stem to stern by now.

Eventually the Captain forgot himself and the waves flowed on around the next intersection. Tommy moved on. He was getting close to his goal by now; he could see a faint gleam of starshine up at the end of the corridor.

The next turn took him into it—and what Tommy saw through the semi-transparent skin of the ship nearly made him falter and be caught. Not merely the fiery pinpoints of stars shone there, but a great, furious glow which could only mean that they were passing through a star system. It was the first time this had happened in Tommy's life, but of course it was nothing to the Captain, or even to most of the Ordinaries. Trust them, Tommy thought resentfully, to say nothing to him about it!

Now he knew he was glad he'd tossed that surprise at

21

the Captain. If he hadn't, he wouldn't be here, and if he weren't here . . .

A waste capsule was bumping automatically along the corridor, heading for one of the exit pores in the hull. Tommy let it catch up to him, then englobed it, but it stretched him so tight that he could barely hold it. That was all to the good; the Captain wouldn't be likely to notice that anything had happened.

The hull was sealed, not to keep atmosphere inside, for there was none except by accident, but to prevent loss of liquid by evaporation. Metals and other mineral elements were replaceable; liquids and their constituents, in ordinary circumstances, were not.

Tommy rode the capsule to the exit sphincter, squeezed through, and instantly released it. Being polarized away from the ship's core, it shot into space and was lost. Tommy hugged the outer surface of the hull and gazed at the astonishing panorama that surrounded him.

There was the enormous black half-globe of space— Tommy's sky, the only one he had ever known. It was sprinkled with the familiar yet always changing patterns of the stars. By themselves, these were marvels enough for a child whose normal universe was one of ninety-foot corridors and chambers measuring, at most, three times as much. But Tommy hardly noticed them. Down to his right, reflecting brilliantly from the long, gentle curve of the greenish hull, was a blazing yellow-white glory that he could hardly look at. A star, the first one he had ever seen close at hand. Off to the left was a tiny, milky-blue disk that could only be a planet.

Tommy let go a shout, for the sheer pleasure of its thin, hollow smell. He watched the thin mist of particles spread lazily away from his body, faintly luminous against the jet blackness. He shivered a little, thickening his skin as much as he could. He could not stay long, he knew; he was radiating heat faster than he could absorb it from the sun or the ship's hull.

But he didn't want to go back inside, and not only because it meant being caught and punished. He didn't want to leave that great, dazzling jewel in the sky. For

22

an instant he thought vaguely of the future time when he would be grown, the master of his own vessel, and could see the stars whenever he chose; but the picture was too far away to have any reality. Great Spore, that wouldn't happen for twenty thousand years!

Fifty yards away, an enormous dark spot on the hull, one of the ship's vision devices, swelled and darkened. Tommy looked up with interest. He could see nothing in that direction, but evidently the Captain had spotted something. Tommy watched and waited, growing colder every second, and after a long time he saw a new pinpoint of light spring into being. It grew steadily larger, turned fuzzy at one side, then became two linked dots, one hard and bright, the other misty.

Tommy looked down with sudden understanding, and saw that another wide area of the ship's hull was swollen and protruding. This one showed a pale color under the green and had a dark ring around it: it was a polarizer. The object he had seen must contain metal, and the Captain was bringing it in for fuel. Tommy hoped it was a big one; they had been short of metal ever since he could remember.

When he glanced up again, the object was much larger. He could see now that the bright part was hard and smooth, reflecting the light of the nearby sun. The misty part was a puzzler. It looked like a crewman's voice, seen against space—or the ion trail of a ship in motion. But was it possible for metal to be alive?

II

Leo Roget stared into the rear-view scanner and wiped beads of sweat from his brown, half-bald scalp. Flaming gas from the jets washed up toward him along the hull; he couldn't see much. But the huge dark ovoid they were headed for was still there, and it was getting bigger. He glanced futilely at the control board. The throttle was on full. They were going to crash in a little more than two minutes, and there didn't seem to be a single thing he could do about it.

He looked at Frances McMenamin, strapped into the acceleration harness beside his own. She said, "Try cutting off the jets, why don't you?"

Roget was a short, muscular man with thinning straight black hair and sharp brown eyes. McMenamin was slender and ash-blond, half an inch taller than he was, with one of those pale, exquisitely shaped faces that seem to be distributed equally among the very stupid and the very bright. Roget had never been perfectly sure which she was, although they had been companions for more than three years. That, in a way, was part of the reason they had taken this wild trip: she had made Roget uneasy, and he wanted to break away, and at the same time he didn't. So he had fallen in with her idea of a trip to Mars—"to get off by ourselves and think"—and here, Roget thought, they were, not thinking particularly.

He said, "You want us to crash quicker?"

"How do you know we will?" she countered. "It's the only thing we haven't tried. Anyhow, we'd be able to see where we're going, and that's more than we can do now."

"All right," said Roget, "all *right*." She was perfectly capable of giving him six more reasons, each screwier than the last, and then turning out to be right. He pulled the throttle back to zero, and the half-heard, half-felt roar of the jets died.

The ship jerked backward suddenly, yanking them against the couch straps, and then slowed.

Roget looked into the scanner again. They were approaching the huge object, whatever it was, at about the same rate as before. Maybe, he admitted unwillingly, a little slower. Damn the woman! How could she possibly have figured that one out in advance?

"And," McMenamin added reasonably, "we'll save fuel for the takeoff."

Roget scowled at her. "If there is a takeoff," he said. "Whatever is pulling us down there isn't doing it to show off. What do we do—tell them that was a very impressive trick and we enjoyed it, but we've got to be leaving now?"

"We'll find out what's doing it," said McMenamin,

"and stop it if we can. If we can't, the fuel won't do us any good anyway."

That was, if not Frances' most exasperating trick, at least high on the list. She had a habit of introducing your own argument as if it were not only a telling point on her side, but something you had been too dense to see. Arguing with her was like swinging at someone who abruptly disappeared and then sandbagged you from behind.

Roget was fuming, but he said nothing. The greenish surface below was approaching more and more slowly, and now he felt a slight but definite tightening of the couch straps that could only mean deceleration. They were being maneuvered in for a landing as carefully and efficiently as if they were doing it themselves.

A few seconds later, a green horizon line appeared in the direct-view ports, and they touched. Roget's and McMenamin's couches swung on their gimbals as the ship tilted slowly, bounced and came to rest.

Frances reached inside the wide collar of her pressure suit to smooth a ruffle that had got crumpled between the volcanic swell of her bosom and the front of the transparent suit. Watching her, Roget felt a sudden irrational flow of affection and—as usually happened—a simultaneous notification that his body disagreed with his mind's opinion of her. This trip, it had been tacitly agreed, was to be a kind of final trial period. At the end of it, either they would split up or decide to make it permanent, and up to now, Roget had been silently determined that it was going to be a split. Now he was just as sure that, providing they ever got to Mars or back to Earth, he was going to nail her for good.

He glanced at her face. She knew, all right, just as she'd known when he'd felt the other way. It should have irritated him, but he felt oddly pleased and comforted. He unstrapped himself, fastened down his helmet, and moved toward the airlock.

He stood on a pale-green, almost featureless surface that curved gently away in every direction. Where he stood, it was brilliantly lighted by the sun, and his

25

shadow was sharp and as black as space. About two thirds of the way to the horizon, looking across the short axis of the ship, the sunlight stopped with knife-edge sharpness, and he could make out the rest only as a ghostly reflection of starlight.

Their ship was lying on its side, with the pointed stern apparently sunk a few inches into the green surface of the alien ship. He took a cautious step in that direction, and nearly floated past it before he could catch himself. His boot magnets had failed to grip. The metal of this hull—if it *was* metal—must be something that contained no iron.

The green hull was shot through with other colors here, and it rose in a curious, almost rectangular mound. At the center, just at the tip of the earth vessel's jets, there was a pale area; around that was a dark ring which lapped up over the side of the ship. He bent to examine it. It was in shadow, and he used his helmet light.

The light shone through the mottled green susbtance; he could see the skin of his own ship. It was pitted, corroding. As he watched, another pinpoint of corruption appeared on the shiny surface, and slowly grew.

Roget straightened up with an exclamation. His helmet phones asked, "What is it, Leo?"

He said, "Acid or something eating the hull. Wait a minute." He looked again at the pale and dark mottlings under the green surface. The center area was not attacking the ship's metal; that might be the muzzle of whatever instrument had been used to pull them down out of their orbit and hold them there. But if it was turned off now . . . He had to get the ship away from the dark ring that was destroying it. He couldn't fire the jets because they were half buried; he'd blow the tubes if he tried.

He said, "You still strapped in?"

"Yes."

"All right, hold on." He stepped back to the center of the little ship, braced his corrugated boot soles against the hard green surface, and shoved.

The ship rolled. But it rolled like a top, around the

26

axis of its pointed end. The dark area gave way before it, as if it were jelly-soft. The jets still pointed to the middle of the pale area, and the dark ring still lapped over them. Roget moved farther down and tried again, with the same result. The ship would move freely in every direction but the right one. The attracting power, clearly enough, was still on.

He straightened dejectedly and looked around. A few hundred yards away, he saw something he had noticed before, without attaching any significance to it; a six-foot egg, of some lighter, more translucent substance than the one on which it lay. He leaped toward it. It moved sluggishly away, trailing a cloud of luminous gas. A few seconds later he had it between his gloved hands. It squirmed, then ejected a thin spurt of vapor from its forward end. It was alive.

McMenamin's head was silhouetted in one of the forward ports. He said, "See this?"

"Yes! What is it?"

"One of the crew, I think. I'm going to bring it in. You work the airlock—it won't hold both of us at once."

". . . All right."

The huge egg crowded the cabin uncomfortably. It was pressed up against the rear wall, where it had rolled as soon as Frances had pulled it into the ship. The two human beings stood at the other side of the room, against the control panel, and watched it.

"No features," said Roget, "unless you count those markings on the surface. This thing isn't from anywhere in the solar system, Frances—it isn't even any order of evolution we ever heard of."

"I know," she said abstractedly. "Leo, is he wearing any protection against space that you can see?"

"No," said Roget. "That's *him*, not a spacesuit. Look, you can see halfway into him. But—"

Frances turned to look at him. "That's it," she said. "It means this is his natural element—space!"

Roget looked thoughtfully at the egg. "It makes sense," he said. "He's adapted for it, anyhow—ovoid, for a high volume-to-surface ratio. Tough outer shell. Moves by jet propulsion. It's hard to believe, because we've never run into a creature like him before, but I don't see why not. On earth there are organisms, plants, that can live and reproduce in boiling water, and others that can stand near-zero temperatures."

"He's a plant, too, you know," Frances put in.

Roget stared at her, then back at the egg. "That color, you mean? Chlorophyll. It could be."

"Must be," she corrected firmly. "How else would he live in a vacuum?" And then, distressedly, "Oh, what a smell!"

They looked at each other. It *had* been something monumental in the way of smells, though it had only lasted a fraction of a second. There had been a series of separate odors, all unfamiliar and all overpoweringly strong. At least a dozen of them, Roget thought; they had gone past too quickly to count.

"He did it before, outside, and I saw the vapor." He closed his helmet abruptly and motioned McMenamin to do the same. She frowned and shook her head. He opened his helmet again. "It might be poisonous!"

"I don't think so," said McMenamin. "Anyway, we've got to try something." She walked toward the green egg. It rolled away from her, and she went past it into the bedroom.

In a minute she reappeared, carrying an armload of plastic boxes and bottles. She came back to Roget and knelt on the floor, lining up the containers with their nipples toward the egg.

"What's this for?" Roget demanded. "Listen, we've got to figure some way of getting out of here. The ship's being eaten up——"

"Wait," said McMenamin. She reached down and squeezed three of the nipples quickly, one after the other. There was a tiny spray of face powder, then one of cologne *(Nuit Jupitérienne)*, followed by a jet of good Scotch.

Then she waited. Roget was about to open his mouth when another blast of unfamiliar odors came from the egg. This time there were only three: two sweet ones and one sharp.

McMenamin smiled. "I'm going to name him Stinky,"

she said. She pressed the nipples again, in a different order. Scotch, face powder, *Nuit Jupitérienne*. The egg replied: sharp, sweet, sweet.

She gave him the remaining combination, and he echoed it; then she put a record cylinder on the floor and squirted the face powder. She added another cylinder and squeezed the cologne. She went along the line that way, releasing a smell for each cylinder until there were ten. The egg had responded, recognizably in some cases, to each one. Then she took away seven of the cylinders and looked expectantly at the egg.

The egg released a sharp odor.

"If we ever tell anybody," said Roget in an awed tone, "that you taught a six-foot Easter egg to count to ten by selective flatulence—"

"Hush, fool," she said. "This is a tough one."

She lined up three cylinders, waited for the sharp odor, then added six more to make three rows of three. The egg obliged with a penetrating smell which was a good imitation of citron extract, Frances' number nine. He followed it immediately with another of his own rapid, complicated series of smells.

"He gets it," said McMenamin. "I think he just told us that three times three are nine." She stood up. "You go out first, Leo. I'll put him out after you and then follow. There's something more we've got to show him before we let him go."

Roget followed orders. When the egg came out and kept on going, he stepped in its path and held it back. Then he moved away, hoping the thing would get the idea that they weren't trying to force it but wanted it to stay. The egg wobbled indecisively for a moment and then stayed where it was. Frances came out the next minute, carrying one of the plastic boxes and a flashlight.

"My nicest powder," she said regretfully, "but it was the only thing I could find enough of." She clapped her gloved hands together sharply, with the box between them. It burst, and a haze of particles spread around them, glowing faintly in the sunlight.

The egg was still waiting, somehow giving the impression that it was watching them alertly. McMenamin flicked on the flashlight and pointed it at Roget. It made a clear, narrow path in the haze of dispersed particles. Then she turned it on herself, on the ship, and finally upward, toward the tiny blue disk that was Earth. She did it twice more, then stepped back toward the airlock, and Roget followed her.

They stood watching as Tommy scurried off across the hull, squeezed himself into it and disappeared.

"That was impressive," Roget said. "But I wonder just how much good it's going to do us."

"He knows we're alive, intelligent, friendly, and that we come from Earth," said McMenamin thoughtfully. "Or, anyhow, we did our best to tell him. That's all we can do. Maybe he won't want to help us; maybe he can't. But it's up to him now."

III

The mental state of Tommy, as he dived through the hull of the ship and into the nearest radial corridor, would be difficult to describe fully to any human being. He was the equivalent of a very small boy—that approximation still holds good—and he had the obvious reactions to novelty and adventure. But there was a good deal more. He had seen living, intelligent beings of an unfamiliar shape and substance, who lived in metal and had some connection with one of those enormous, enigmatic ships called planets, which no captain of his own race dared approach.

And yet Tommy *knew,* with all the weight of knowledge accumulated, codified and transmitted over a span measured in billions of years, that there was no other intelligent race than his own in the entire universe, that metal, though life-giving, could not itself be alive, and that no living creature, having the ill luck to be spawned aboard a planet, could ever hope to escape so tremendous a gravitational field.

The final result of all this was that Tommy desperately wanted to go somewhere by himself and think. But he couldn't; he had to keep moving, in time with the scanning waves along the corridor, and he had to give all his mental energy to the problem of slipping past the search party.

The question was—how long had he been gone? If they had reached the hull while he was inside the metal thing, they might have looked for him outside and concluded that he had somehow slipped past them, back to the center of the ship. In that case, they would probably be working their way back, and he had only to follow them to the axis and hide in a chamber as soon as they left it. But if they were still working outward, his chances of escape were almost nil. And now it seemed more important to escape than it had before.

There was one possibility which Tommy, who, in most circumstances, would try anything, hated to think about. Fuel lines—tubes carrying the rushing, radiant ion vapor that powered the ship—adjoined many of these corridors, and it was certain that if he dared to enter one, he would be perfectly safe from detection as long as he remained in it. But, for one thing, these lines radiated from the ship's axis and none of them would take him where he wanted to go. For another, they were the most dangerous places aboard ship. Older crew members sometimes entered them to make emergency repairs, but they got out as quickly as they could. Tommy did not know how long he could survive there; he had an unpleasant conviction that it would not be long.

Only a few yards up the corridor was the sealed sphincter which gave entrance to such a tube. Tommy looked at it indecisively as the motion of the scanning waves brought him nearer. He had still not made up his mind when he caught a flicker reflected around the curve of the corridor behind him.

Tommy squeezed himself closer to the wall and watched the other end of the coridor approach with agonizing slowness. If he could only get around that corner . . .

The flicker of motion was repeated, and then he saw a thin rind of green poke into view. There was no more

31

time to consider entering the fuel line, no time to let the scanning waves' movement carry him around the corner. Tommy put on full speed, cutting across the next wave and down the cross-corridor ahead.

Instantly the Captain's voice shouted from the wall, "Ah! Was that him, the dirty scut? After him, lads!"

Tommy glanced behind as he turned another corner, and his heart sank. It was no cabin boy who was behind him, or even an Ordinary, but a Third Mate—so huge that he filled nearly half the width of the corridor, and so powerful that Tommy, in comparison, was like a boy on a bicycle racing an express train.

He turned another corner, realizing in that instant that he was as good as caught: the new corridor ahead of him stretched straight and without a break for three hundred yards. As he flashed down it, the hulk of the Mate appeared around the bend behind.

The Mate was coming up with terrifying speed, and Tommy had time for only one last desperate spurt. Then the other body slammed with stunning force against his, and he was held fast.

As they coasted to a halt, the Captain's voice rumbled from the wall, *"That's* it, Mister. Hold him where I can see him!"

The scanning areas were stationary now. The Mate moved Tommy forward until he was squarely in range of the nearest.

Tommy squirmed futilely. The Captain said, *"There's* our little jokester. It's a pure pleasure to see you again, Tommy. What—no witty remarks? Your humor all dried up?"

Tommy gasped, "Hope you enjoyed your nap, Captain."

"Very good," said the Captain with heavy sarcasm. "Oh, *very* entertaining, Tommy. Now would you have anything more to say, before I put the whips to you?"

Tommy was silent.

The Captain said to the Mate, "Nice work, Mister. You'll get extra rations for this."

The Mate spoke for the first time, and Tommy recognized his high, affected voice. It was George Adkins, who had recently spored and was so proud of the new life inside his body that there was no living with him. George said prissily, "Thank you, sir, I'm sure. Of course, I really shouldn't have exerted myself the way I just did, in my state."

"Well, you'll be compensated for it," the Captain said testily. "Now take the humorist down to Assembly Five. We'll have a little ceremony there."

"Yes, sir," said the Mate distantly. He moved off, shoving Tommy ahead of him, and dived into the first turning that led downward.

They moved along in silence for the better part of a mile, crossing from one lesser passage to another until they reached a main artery that led directly to the center of the ship. The scanning waves were still stationary, and they were moving so swiftly that there was no danger of being overheard. Tommy said politely, "You won't let them be too hard on me, will you, sir?"

The Mate did not reply for a moment. He had been baited by Tommy's mock courtesy before, and he was as wary as his limited intelligence allowed. Finally he said, "You'll get no more than what's coming to you, young Tom."

"Yes, sir. I know that, sir. I'm sorry I made you exert yourself, sir, in your condition and all."

"You should be," said the Mate stiffly, but his voice betrayed his pleasure. It was seldom enough that even a cabin boy showed a decent interest in the Mate's prospective parenthood. "They're moving about, you know," he added, unbending a little.

"Are they, sir? Oh, you must be careful of yourself, sir. How many are there, please, sir?"

"Twenty-eight," said the Mate, as he had on every possible occasion for the past two weeks. "Strong and healthy—so far."

"That's remarkable, sir!" cried Tommy. "Twenty-eight! If I might be so bold, sir, you ought to be careful of what you eat. Is the Captain going to give you your extra rations out of that mass he just brought in topside, sir?"

"I'm sure *I* don't know."

"Gosh!" exclaimed Tommy. "I wish I could be sure . . ."

He let the pause grow. Finally the Mate said querulously, "What do you mean? Is there anything wrong with the metal?"

"I don't really know, sir, but it isn't like any we ever had before. That is," Tommy added, "since I was spored, sir."

"Naturally," said the Mate. *"I've* eaten all kinds myself, you know."

"Yes, sir. But doesn't it usually come in ragged shapes, sir, and darkish?"

"Of course it does. Everybody knows that. Metal is nonliving, and only living things have regular shapes."

"Yes, sir. But I was topside, sir, while I was trying to get away, and I saw this metal. It's quite regular, except for some knobs at one end, sir, and it's as smooth as you are, sir, and shiny. If you'll forgive me, sir, it didn't look at all appetizing to me."

"Nonsense," said the Mate uncertainly. "Nonsense," he repeated, in a stronger tone. "You must have been mistaken. Metal can't be alive."

"That's just what I thought, sir," said Tommy excitedly. "But there are live things in this metal, sir. I saw them. And the metal wasn't just floating along the way it's supposed to, sir. I saw it when the Captain brought it down, and . . . But I'm afraid you'll think I'm lying, sir, if I tell you what it was doing."

"Well, what was it doing?"

"I swear I saw it, sir," Tommy went on. "The Captain will tell you the same thing, sir, if you ask him—he must have noticed."

"Sterilize it all, what *was* it doing?"

Tommy lowered his voice. "There was an ion trail shooting from it, sir. It was trying to get away!"

While the Mate was trying to absorb that, they reached the bottom of the corridor and entered the vast globular space of Assembly Five, lined with crewmen waiting to witness the punishment of Tommy Loy.

This was not going to be any fun at all, thought Tommy, but at least he had paid back the Third Mate in full measure. The Mate, for the moment, at any rate, was not taking any joy in his promised extra rations.

When it was over, Tommy huddled in a corner of the crew compartment where they had tossed him, bruised and smarting in every nerve, shaken by the beating he had undergone. The pain was still rolling through him in faint, uncontrollable waves, and he winced at each one, in spite of himself, as though it were the original blow.

In the back of his mind, the puzzle of the metal ship was still calling, but the other experience was too fresh, the remembered images too vivid.

The Captain had begun, as always, by reciting the Creed.

In the beginning was the Spore, and the Spore was alone.

(And the crew: *Praised be the Spore!*)

Next there was light, and the light was good. Yea, good for the Spore and the Spore's First Children.

(*Praised be they!*)

But the light grew evil in the days of the Spore's Second Children.

(*Woe unto them!*)

And the light cast them out. Yea, exiled were they, into the darkness and the Great Deep.

(*Pity for the outcasts in the Great Deep!*)

Tommy had mumbled his responses with the rest of them, thinking rebellious thoughts. There was nothing evil about light; they lived by it still. What must have happened—the Captain himself admitted as much when he taught history and natural science classes—was that the earliest ancestors of the race, spawned in the flaming heart of the Galaxy, had grown too efficient for their own good.

They had specialized, more and more, in extracting energy from starlight and the random metal and other elements they encountered in space; and at last they absorbed, willy-nilly, more than they could use. So they had moved, gradually and naturally, over many generations, out from that intensely radiating region into the "Great Deep"—the universe of thinly scattered stars.

35

And the process had continued, inevitably; as the level of available energy fell, their absorption of it grew more and more efficient.

Now, not only could they never return to their birth-place, but they could not even approach a single sun as closely as some planets did. Therefore the planets, and the stars themselves, were objects of fear. That was natural and sensible. But why did they have to continue this silly ritual, invented by some half-evolved, superstitious ancestor, of "outcasts" and "evil"?

The Captain finished:

Save us from the Death that lies in the Great Deep . . .

(The creeping Death that lies in the Great Deep!)

And keep our minds pure . . .

(As pure as the light in the days of the Spore, blessed be He!)

And our course straight . . .

(As straight as the light, brothers!)

That we may meet our lost brothers again in the Day of Reuniting.

(Speed that day!)

Then the pause, the silence that grew until it was like the silence of space. At last the Captain spoke again, pronouncing judgment against Tommy, ending, "Let him be whipped!"

Tommy tensed himself, thickening his skin, drawing his body into the smallest possible compass. Two husky Ordinaries seized him and tossed him at a third. As Tommy floated across the room, the crewman pressed himself tightly against the wall, drawing power from it until he could contain no more. And as Tommy neared him, he discharged it in a crackling arc that filled Tommy's body with the pure essence of pain, and sent him hurtling across the chamber to the next shock, and the next, and the next.

Until the Captain had boomed, "Enough!" and they had carried him out and left him here alone.

He heard the voices of crewmen as they drew their rations. One of them was grumbling about the taste, and another, sounding happily bloated, was telling him to shut up and eat, that metal was metal.

That would be the new metal, however much of it had been absorbed by now, mingled with the old in the reservoir. Tommy wondered briefly how much of it there was, and whether the alien ship—if it *was* a ship—could repair even a little damage to itself. But that assumed life in the metal, and in spite of what he had seen, Tommy couldn't believe in it. It seemed beyond question, though, that there were living things inside the metal; and when the metal was gone, how would they live?

Tommy imagined himself set adrift from the ship, alone in space, radiating more heat than his tiny volume could absorb. He shuddered.

He thought again of the problem that had obsessed him ever since he had seen the alien, five-pointed creatures in the metal ship. Intelligent life was supposed to be sacred. That was part of the Creed, and it was stated in a sloppy, poetic way like the rest of it, but it made a certain kind of sense. No crewman or captain had the right to destroy another for his benefit, because the same heredity was in them all. They were all potentially the same, none better than another.

And you ate metal, because metal was nonliving and certainly not intelligent. But if that stopped being true . . .

Tommy felt he was missing something. Then he had it: In the alien ship, trying to talk to the creatures that lived in metal, he had been scared almost scentless—but underneath the fright and the excitement, he had felt wonderful. It had been, he realized suddenly, like the mystic completion that was supposed to come when all the straight lines met, in the "Day of Reuniting"—when all the far-flung ships, parted for all the billions of years of their flight, came together at last. It was talking to someone different from yourself.

He wanted to talk again to the aliens, teach them to form their uncouth sounds into words, learn from them . . . Vague images swirled in his mind. They were products of an utterly different line of evolution. Who knew what they might be able to teach him?

And now the dilemma took shape. If his own ship absorbed the metal of theirs, they would die; therefore he would have to make the Captain let them go. But if he somehow managed to set them free, they would leave and he would never see them again.

A petty officer looked into the cubicle and said, "All right, Loy, out of it. You're on garbage detail. You eat after you work, if there's anything left. Lively, now!"

Tommy moved thoughtfully out into the corridor, his pain almost forgotten. The philosophical problems presented by the alien ship, too, having no apparent solution, were receding from his mind. A new thought was taking their place, one that made him glow inside with the pure rapture of the devoted practical jokester.

The whipping he was certainly going to get—and, so soon after the last offense, it would be a beauty—scarcely entered his mind.

IV

Roget climbed in, opening his helmet, and sat down wearily in the acceleration couch. He didn't look at the woman.

McMenamin said quietly, "Bad?"

"Not good. The outer skin's gone all across that area, and it's eating into the lead sheathing. The tubes are holding up pretty well, but they'll be next."

"We've done as much as we can, by rolling the ship around?"

"Just about. I'll keep at it, but I don't see how it can be more than a few hours before the tubes go. Then we're cooked, whatever your fragrant little friend does."

He stood up abruptly and climbed over the slanting wall which was now their floor, to peer out the direct-view port. He swore, slowly and bitterly. "You try the radio again while I was out?" he asked.

"Yes." She did not bother to add that there had been no response. Here, almost halfway between the orbits of Earth and Mars, they were hopelessly out of touch. A ship as small as theirs couldn't carry equipment enough to bridge the distance.

Roget turned around, said, "By God—" and then clenched his jaw and strode out of the room. McMenamin heard him walk through the bedroom and clatter around in the storage compartment behind.

In a few moments he was back with a welding torch in his hand. "Should have thought of this before," he said. "I don't know what'll happen if I cut into that hull— damn thing may explode, for all I know—but it's better than sitting doing nothing." He put his helmet down with a bang and his voice came tinnily in her helmet receiver. "Be back in a minute."

"Be careful," McMenamin said again.

Roget closed the outer lock door behind him and looked at the ravaged hull of the ship. The metal had been eaten away in a broad band all around the ship, just above the tail, as if a child had bitten around the small end of a pear. In places the clustered rocket tubes showed through. He felt a renewed surge of anger, with fear deep under it.

A hundred years ago, he reminded himself, the earliest space voyagers had encountered situations as bad as this one, maybe worse. But Roget was a city man, bred for city virtues. He didn't, he decided, know quite how to feel or act. What were you supposed to do when you were about to die, fifteen million miles from home? Try to calm McMenamin—who was dangerously calm already—or show your true nobility by making one of those deathbed speeches you read in the popular histories? What about suggesting a little suicide pact? There was nothing in the ship that would give them a cleaner death than the one ahead of them. About all he could do would be to stab Frances, then himself, with a screwdriver.

Her voice said in the earphones, "You all right?"

He said, "Sure. Just going to try it." He lowered himself to the green surface, careful not to let his knees touch the dark, corrosive area. The torch was a small, easily manageable tool. He pointed the snout at the dark area where it lapped up over the hull, turned the switch

39

on and pressed the button. Flame leaped out, washing over the dark surface. Roget felt the heat through his suit. He turned off the torch to see what effect it had had.

There was a deep, charred pit in the dark stuff, and it seemed to him that it had pulled back a little from the area it was attacking. It was more than he had expected. Encouraged, he tried again.

There was a sudden tremor under him and he leaped nervously to his feet, just in time to avoid the corrosive wave as it rolled under him. For a moment he was only conscious of the thick metal of his boot soles and the thinness of the fabric that covered his knees; then, as he was about to step back out of the way, he realized that it was not only the dark ring that had expanded, that was still expanding.

He moved jerkily—too late—as the pale center area swept toward and under him. Then he felt as if he had been struck by a mighty hammer.

His ears rang, and there was a mist in front of his eyes. He blinked, tried to raise an arm. It seemed to be stuck fast at the wrist and elbow. Panicked, he tried to push himself away, and couldn't. As his vision cleared, he saw that he was spread-eagled on the pale disk that had spread out under him. The metal collars of his wrist and elbow joints, all the metal parts of his suit, were held immovably. The torch lay a few inches away from his right hand.

For a few moments, incredulously, Roget still tried to move. Then he stopped and lay in the prison of his suit, looking at the greenish-cream surface under his helmet.

Frances' voice said abruptly, "Leo, is anything wrong?"

Roget felt an instant relief that left him shaken and weak. His forehead was cold. He said after a moment, "Pulled a damn fool trick, Frances. Come out and help me if you can."

He heard a click as her helmet went down. He added anxiously, "But don't come near the pale part, or you'll get caught too."

After a while she said, "Darling, I can't think of anything to do."

40

Roget was feeling calmer, somehow not much afraid any more. He wondered how much oxygen was left in his suit. Not more than an hour, he thought. He said, "I know. I can't, either."

Later he called, "Frances?"

"Yes?"

"Roll the ship once in a while, will you? Might get through to the wiring or something, otherwise."

". . . All right."

After that, they didn't talk. There was a great deal to be said, but it was too late to say it.

V

Tommy was on garbage detail with nine other unfortunates. It was a messy, hard, unpleasant business, fit only for a cabin boy—collecting waste from the compartment and corridor receptacles and pressing it into standard capsule shapes, then hauling it to the nearest polarizer. But Tommy, under the suspicious eye of the petty officer in charge, worked with an apparent total absorption until they had cleaned out their section of the six inmost levels and were well into the seventh.

This was the best strategic place for Tommy's departure, since it was about midway from axis to hull, and the field of operations of any pursuit was correspondingly broadened. Also, the volume in which they labored had expanded wedgewise as they climbed, and the petty officer, though still determined to watch Tommy, could no longer keep him constantly in view.

Tommy saw the officer disappear around the curve of the corridor, and kept on working busily. He was still at it, with every appearance of innocence and industry, when the officer abruptly popped into sight again about three seconds later.

The officer stared at him with baffled disapproval and said unreasonably, "Come on, come on, Loy. Don't slack."

"Right," said Tommy, and scurried faster.

A moment later Third Mate Adkins hove majestically

into view. The petty officer turned respectfully to face him.

"Keeping young Tom well occupied, I see," said the Mate.

"Yes, sir," said the officer. "Appears to be a reformed character, now, sir. Must have learned a lesson, one way or another."

"Ha!" said the Mate. "Very good. Oh, Loy, you might be interested in this—the Captain himself has told me that the new metal is perfectly all right. Unusually rich, in fact. I've had my first ration already—very good it was, too—and I'm going to get my extras in half an hour or so. Well, good appetite, all." And, while the lesser crewmen clustered against the walls to give him room, he moved haughtily off down the corridor.

Tommy kept on working as fast as he could. He was draining energy he might need later, but it was necessary to quiet the petty officer's suspicions entirely, in order to give himself a decent start. In addition, his artist's soul demanded it. Tommy, in his own way, was a perfectionist.

Third Mate Adkins was due to get his extras in about half an hour, and if Tommy knew the Captain's habits, the Captain would be taking his first meal from the newly replenished reservoir at about the same time. That set the deadline. Before the half hour was up, Tommy would have to cut off the flow of the new metal, so that stomachs which had been gurgling in anticipation would remain desolately void until the next windfall.

The Mate, in spite of his hypochondria, was a glutton. With any luck, this would make him bitter for a month. And the Old Man—but it was better not to dwell on that.

The petty officer hung around irresolutely for another ten minutes, then dashed off down the corridor to attend to the rest of his detail. Without wasting a moment, Tommy dropped the capsule he had just collected and shot away in the other direction.

The rest of the cabin boys, as fearful of Tommy as they were of constituted authority, would not dare to raise an outcry until they spotted the officer coming back. The officer, because of the time he had wasted in watching Tommy, would have to administer a thorough lecture on slackness to the rest of the detail before he returned.

Tommy had calculated his probable margin to a nicety, and it was enough, barring accidents, to get him safely away. Nevertheless, he turned and twisted from one system of corridors to another, carefully confusing his trail, before he set himself to put as much vertical distance behind him as he could.

This part of the game had to be accomplished in a fury of action, for he was free to move in the corridors only until the Captain was informed that he was loose again. After that, he had to play hare and hounds and hares with the moving strips through which the Captain could see him.

When the time he had estimated was three quarters gone, Tommy slowed and came to a halt. He inspected the corridor wall minutely, and found the almost imperceptible trace that showed where the scanning wave nearest him had stopped. He jockeyed his body clear of it, and then waited. He still had a good distance to cover before he dared play his trump, but it was not safe to move now; he had to wait for the Captain's move.

It came soon enough: the scanning waves erupted into simultaneous motion and anger. "Tommy!" they bellowed. "Tommy Loy! Come back, you unmentionable excrescence, or by Spore you'll regret it! Tommy!"

Moving between waves, Tommy waited patiently until their motion carried him from one corridor to another. The Captain's control over the waves was not complete: in some corridors they moved two steps upward for one down, in others the reverse. When he got into a downward corridor, Tommy scrambled out of it again as soon as he could and started over.

Gradually, with many false starts, he worked his way up to the thirteenth level, one level short of the hull.

Now came the hard part. This time he had to enter the fuel lines, not only for sure escape, but to gather the force he needed. And for the first time in his life, Tommy hesitated before something that he had set himself to do.

Death was a phenomenon that normally touched each member of Tommy's race only once—only captains died, and they died alone. For lesser members of the crew,

43

there was almost no mortal danger; the ship protected them. But Tommy knew what death was, and as the sealed entrance to the fuel line swung into view, he knew that he faced it.

He made himself small, as he had under the lash. He broke the seal. Quickly, before the following wave could catch him, he thrust himself through the sphincter.

The blast of ions gripped him, flung him forward, hurting him like a hundred whips. Desperately he held himself together, thickening his insulating shell against that deadly flux of energy; but still his body absorbed it, till he felt a horrid fullness.

The walls of the tube fled past him, barely perceptible in the rush of glowing haze. Tommy held in that growing tautness with his last strength, meanwhile looking for an exit. He neither knew nor cared whether he had reached his goal; he had to get out or die.

He saw a dim oval on the wall ahead, hurled himself at it, clung, and forced his body through.

He was in a horizontal corridor, just under the hull. He drank the blessed coolness of it for an instant, before moving to the nearest sphincter. Then he was out, under the velvet-black sky and the diamond blaze of stars.

He looked around. The pain was fading now; he felt only an atrocious bloatedness that tightened his skin and made all his movements halting. Forward of him, up the long shallow curve of the hull, he could see the alien ship, and the two five-pointed creatures beside it. Carefully, keeping a few feet between himself and the hull, he headed toward it.

One of the creatures was sprawled flat on the polarizer that had brought its ship down. The other, standing beside it, turned as Tommy came near, and two of its upper three points moved in an insane fashion that made Tommy feel ill. He looked away quickly and moved past them, till he was directly over the center of the polarizer and only a few inches away.

Then, with a sob of relief, he released the energy his body had stored. In one thick, white bolt, it sparked to the polarizer's center.

Shaken and spent, Tommy floated upward and surveyed what he had done. The muzzle of the polarizer was contracting, puckering at the center, the dark corrosive ring following it in. So much energy, applied in one jolt, must have shorted and paralyzed it all the way back to the ship's nerve center. The Captain, Tommy thought wryly, would be jumping now!

And he wasn't done yet. Tommy took one last look at the aliens and their ship. The sprawled one was up now, and the two of them had their upper points twined around each other in a nauseating fashion. Then they parted suddenly, and, facing Tommy, wiggled their free points. Tommy moved purposefully off across the width of the ship, heading for the other two heavy-duty polarizers.

He had to go in again through that hell not once more, but twice. Though his nerves shrank from the necessity, there was no way of avoiding it. For the ship could not alter its course, except by allowing itself to be attracted by a sun or other large body—which was unthinkable —but it could rotate at the Captain's will. The aliens were free now, but the Captain had only to spin ship in order to snare them again.

Four miles away, Tommy found the second polarizer. He backed away a carefully calculated distance before he re-entered the hull. At least he could know in advance how far he had to go—and he knew now, too, that the energy he had stored the first time had been adequate twice over. He rested a few moments; then, like a diver plunging into a torrent, he thrust himself into the fuel line.

He came out again, shuddering with pain, and pushed himself through the exit. He felt as bloated as he had before. The charge of energy was not as great, but Tommy knew that he was weakening. This time, when he discharged over the polarizer and watched it contract into a tiny, puckered mass, he felt as if he could never move again, let alone expose himself once more to that tunnel of flame.

The stars, he realized dully, were moving in slow, ponderous arcs over his head. The Captain was spinning ship.

45

Tommy sank to the hull and lay motionless, watching half attentively for a sight of the alien ship.

There it was, a bright dot haloed by the flame of its exhaust. It swung around slowly, gradually, with the rest of the firmament, growing smaller slowly.

"He'll get them before they're out of range," Tommy thought. He watched as the bright dot climbed overhead, began to fall on the other side.

The Captain had one polarizer left. It would be enough.

Wearily Tommy rose and followed the bright star. It was not a joke any longer. He would willingly have gone inside to the bright, warm, familiar corridors that led downward to safety and deserved punishment. But somehow he could not bear to think of those fascinating creatures—those wonderful playthings—going to fill the Captain's fat belly.

Tommy followed the ship until he could see the pale gleam of the functioning polarizer. Then he crawled through the hull once more, and again he found a sealed entrance to the fuel tube. He did not let himself think about it. His mind was numb already, and he pushed himself through uncaring.

This time it was worse than ever before; he had not dreamed that it could be so bad. His vision dimmed and he could barely see the exit, or feel its pressure, when he dragged himself out. Lurching drunkenly, he passed a scanning wave on his way to the hull sphincter, and heard the Captain's voice explode.

Outside, ragged black patches obscured his vision of the stars. The pressure inside him pressed painfully outward, again and again, and each time he held it back. Then he felt rather than saw that he was over the pale disk, and, as he let go the bolt, he lost consciousness.

When his vision cleared, the alien ship was still above him, alarmingly close. The Captain must have had it almost reeled in again, he thought, when he had let go that last charge.

Flaming, it receded into the Great Deep, and he watched it go until it disappeared.

He felt a great peace and a great weariness. The tiny

blue disk that was a planet had moved its apparent position a little nearer its star. The aliens were going back there, to their unimaginable home, and Tommy's ship was forging onward into new depths of darkness—toward the edge of the Galaxy and the greatest Deep.

He moved to the nearest sphincter as the cold bit at him. His spirits lifted suddenly as he thought of those three stabs of energy, equally spaced around the twelve-mile perimeter of the ship. The Captain would be utterly speechless with rage, he thought, like an aged martinet who had had his hands painfully slapped by a small boy.

For, as we warned you, the Captain was not precisely a captain, nor the ship precisely a ship. Ship and captain were one and the same, hive and queen bee, castle and lord.

In effect, Tommy had circumnavigated the skipper.

IN 1952 A GOOD FRIEND HAD A drinking problem and was making it partly mine. I began thinking about theoretical solutions to the problem of alcoholism, and came up with the idea of a phantom guardian who would stand between you and the jug. From this all the rest evolved. Later I used "The Analogues" as the first chapter of a novel, *Hell's Pavement*.

4

THE ANALOGUES

<<<<<<<<<<<<<<<<<<<<<<<<<<<<<<<<<<<<<<<<<<<<<<

THE CREATURE WAS LIKE AN EYE, A GLOBULAR
eye that could see in all directions, encysted in the gray,
cloudy mind that called itself Alfie Strunk. In that dimness thoughts squirmed, like dark fish darting; and the
eye followed them without pity.

It knew Alfie, knew the evil in Alfie; the tangled
skein of impotence and hatred and desire; the equation:
Love equals death. The roots of that evil were beyond
its reach; it was only an eye. But now it was changing.
Deep in its own center, little electric tingles came and
went. Energy found a new gradient, and flowed.

A thought shone in the gray cloud that was Alfie—
only half-formed, but unmistakable. And a channel
opened. Instantly, the eye thrust a filament of itself into
that passage.

Now it was free. Now it could act.

The man on the couch stirred and moaned. The doctor, who had been whispering into his ear, drew back
and watched his face. At the other end of the couch, the
technician glanced alertly at the patient, then turned
again to his meters.

The patient's head was covered to the ears by an ovoid
shell of metal. A broad strap of webbing, buckled under
his jaw, held it securely. The heads of screw-clamps protruded in three circles around the shell's girth, and a

thick bundle of insulated wires led from it to the control board at the foot of the couch.

The man's gross body was restrained by a rubber sheet, the back of his head resting in the trough of a rubber block.

"No!" he shouted suddenly. He mumbled, his loose features contorting. Then, "I wasn't gonna—No! Don't—" He muttered again, trying to move his body; the tendons in his neck were sharply outlined. *"Please,"* he said. Tears glittered in his eyes.

The doctor leaned forward and whispered. "You're going away from there. You're going away. It's five minutes later."

The patient relaxed and seemed to be asleep. A teardrop spilled over and ran slowly down his cheek.

The doctor stood up and nodded to the technician, who slowly moved his rheostat to zero before he cut the switches. "A good run," the doctor mouthed silently. The technician nodded and grinned. He scribbled on a pad, "Test him this aft.?" The doctor wrote, "Yes. Can't tell till then, but think we got him solid."

Alfie Strunk sat in the hard chair and chewed rhythmically, staring at nothing. His brother had told him to wait here while he went down the hall to see the doctor. It seemed to Alfie that he had been gone a long time.

Silence flowed around him. The room was almost bare—the chair he sat in, the naked walls and floor, a couple of little tables with books on them. There were two doors; one, open, led into the long bare hall outside. There were other doors in the hall, but they were all closed and their bumpy-glass windows were dark. At the end of the hall was a door, and that was closed, too. Alfie had heard his brother close it behind him, with a solid snick, when he left. He felt very safe and alone.

He heard something, a faint echo of movement, and turned his head swiftly. The noise came from beyond the second door in the room, the one that was just slightly ajar. He heard it again.

He stood up cautiously, not making a sound. He tiptoed to the door, looked through the crack. At first he saw nothing; then the footsteps came again and he saw a flash of color: a blue print skirt, a white sweater, a glimpse of coppery hair.

Alfie widened the crack, very carefully. His heart was pounding and his breath was coming faster. Now he could see the far end of the room. A couch, and the girl sitting on it, opening a book. She was about eleven, slender and dainty. A reading lamp by the couch gave the only light. She was alone.

Alfie's blunt fingers went into his trousers pocket and clutched futilely. They had taken his knife away.

Then he glanced at the little table beside the door, and his breath caught. There it was, his own switchblade knife, lying beside the books. His brother must have left it there and forgotten to tell him.

He reached for it—

"ALFIE!"

He whirled, cringing. His mother stood there, towering twice his height, with wrath in her staring gray eyes; every line of her so sharp and real that he couldn't doubt her, though he had seen her buried fifteen years ago.

She had a willow switch in her hand.

"No!" gasped Alfie, retreating to the wall. "Don't— I wasn't gonna do nothing."

She raised the switch. "You're no good, no good, no *good,*" she spat. "You've got the devil in you, and it's just got to be whipped out."

"Don't, *please*—" said Alfie. Tears leaked out of his eyes.

"Get away from that girl," she said, advancing, "Get clean away and don't ever come back. Go on—"

Alfie turned and ran, sobbing in his throat.

In the next room, the girl went on reading until a voice said, "Okay, Rita. That's all."

She looked up. "Is that *all?* Well, I didn't do much."

"You did enough," said the voice. "We'll explain to you what it's all about some day. Come on, let's go."

She smiled, stood up—and vanished as she moved out of range of the mirrors in the room below.

The two rooms where Alfie had been tested were

empty. Alfie's mother was already gone—gone with Alfie, inside his mind where he could never escape her again, as long as he lived.

Martyn's long, cool fingers gently pressed the highball glass. The glass accepted the pressure, a very little; the liquid rose almost imperceptibly in it. This glass would not break, he knew; it had no sharp edges and if thrown it would not hurt anybody much.

The music of the five-piece combo down at the end of the room was the same—muted, gentle, accommodating. And the alcohol content of the whisky in his drink was twenty-four point five per cent.

But men still got drunk, and men still reached for a weapon to kill.

And, incredibly, there were worse things that could happen. The cure was sometimes worse than the disease. We're witch doctors, he thought. We don't realize it yet, most of us, but that's what we are. The doctor who only heals is a servant; the doctor who controls life and death is a tyrant.

The dark little man across the table had to be made to understand that. Martyn thought he could do it. The man had power—the power of millions of readers, of friends in high places—but he was a genuine, not a professional, lover of democracy.

Now the little man raised his glass, tilted it in a quick, automatic gesture. Martyn saw his throat pulse, like the knotting of a fist. He set the glass down, and the soft rosy light from the bar made dragons' eyes of his spectacles.

"Well, Dr. Martyn?" His voice was sharp and rapid, but amiable. This man lived with tension; he was acclimated to it, like a swimmer in swift waters.

Martyn gestured with his glass, a slow, controlled movement. "I want you to see something before we talk. I had two reasons for asking you here. One is that it's an out-of-the-way place, and, as you'll understand, I have to be careful. If Dr. Kusko should learn I'm talking to you, and why—" Martyn moistened his lips. "I'm not ashamed to say I'm afraid of that man. He's a paranoid —capable of anything. But more about that later.

"The other reason has to do with a man who comes here every night. His name is Ernest Fox; he's a machinist, when he works. Over there at the bar. The big man in the checked jacket. See him?"

The other flicked a glance that way; he did not turn his head. "Yeah. The one with the snootful?"

"Yes. You're right, he's very drunk. I don't think it'll take much longer."

"How come they serve him?"

"You'll see in a minute," Martyn said.

Ernest Fox was swaying slightly on the bar stool. His choleric face was flushed, and his nostrils widened visibly with each breath he took. His eyes were narrowed, staring at the man to his left—a wizened little fellow in a big fedora.

Suddenly he straightened and slammed his glass down on the bar. Liquid spread over the surface in a glittering flood. The wizened man looked up at him nervously.

Fox drew his fist back.

Martyn's guest had half-turned in his seat. He was watching, relaxed and interested.

The big man's face turned abruptly, as if someone had spoken to him. He stared at an invisible something a yard away, and his raised arm slowly dropped. He appeared to be listening. Gradually his face lost its anger and became sullen. He muttered something, looking down at his hands. Then he turned to the wizened man and spoke, apparently in apology; the little man waved his hand as if to say, Forget it, and turned back to his drink.

The big man slumped again on the bar stool, shaking his head and muttering. Then he scooped up his change from the bar, got up and walked out. Someone else took his place almost immediately.

"That happens every night, like clockwork," said Martyn. "That's why they serve him. He never does any harm, and he never will. He's a good customer."

The dark little man was facing him alertly once more. "And?"

53

"A year and a half ago," Martyn said, "no place in the Loop would let him in the door, and he had a police record as long as your arm. He liked to get drunk, and when he got drunk he liked to start fights. Compulsive. No cure for it, even if there were facilities for such cases. He's still incurable. He's just the same as he was—just as manic, just as hostile. But—he doesn't cause any trouble now."

"All right, doctor, I check to you. Why not?"

"He's got an analogue," said Martyn. "In the classical sense, he is even less sane than he was before. He has auditory, visual and tactile hallucinations—a complete, integrated set. That's enough to get you entry to most institutions, crowded as they are. But, you see, these hallucinations are pro-societal. They were put there, deliberately. He's an acceptable member of society, because he has them."

The dark man looked half irritated, half interested. He said, "He sees things. What does he see, exactly, and what does it say to him?"

"Nobody knows that except himself. A policeman, maybe, or his mother as she looked when he was a child. Someone whom he fears, and whose authority he acknowledges. The subconscious has its own mechanism for creating these false images; all we do is stimulate it —it does the rest. Usually, we think, it just warns him, and in most cases that's enough. A word from the right person at the right moment is enough to prevent ninety-nine out of a hundred crimes. But in extreme cases, the analogue can actually oppose the patient physically—as far as he's concerned, that is. The hallucination is complete, as I told you."

"Sounds like a good notion."

"A very good notion—rightly handled. In ten years it will cut down the number of persons institutionalized for insanity to the point where we can actually hope to make some progress, both in study and treatment, with those that are left."

"Sort of a personal guardian angel, tailored to fit," said the dark man.

"That's exactly it. The analogue always fits the patient

54

because it *is* the patient—a part of his own mind, working against his conscious purposes when they cross the prohibition we lay down. Even an exceptionally intelligent man can't defeat his analogue, because the analogue is just as intelligent. Even knowing you've had the treatment doesn't help, although ordinarily the patient doesn't know. The analogue, to the patient, is absolutely indistinguishable from a real person—but it doesn't have any of a real person's weaknesses."

The other grinned. "Could I get one to keep me from drawing to inside straights?"

Martyn did not smile. "That isn't quite as funny as it sounds. There's a very real possibility that you could, about ten years from now . . . if Kusko has his way—and that's exactly what I want you to help prevent."

The tall, black-haired young man got out of the pickup and strolled jauntily into the hotel lobby. He wasn't thinking about what he was going to do; his mind was cheerfully occupied with the decoration of the enormous loft he had just rented on the lower East Side. It might be better, he thought, to put both couches along one wall, and arrange the bar opposite. Or put the Capehart there, with an easy chair on either side?

The small lobby was empty except for the clerk behind his minuscule counter and the elevator operator lounging beside the cage. The young man walked confidently forward.

"Yes, sir?" said the clerk.

"Listen," said the young man, "there's a man leaning out a window upstairs, shouting for help. He looks sick."

"What? Show me."

The clerk and the elevator operator followed him out to the sidewalk. The young man pointed to two open windows. "It was one of those, the ones in the middle on the top floor."

"Thanks, mister."

The young man said, "Sure," and watched the two hurry into the elevator. When the doors closed behind them, he strolled in again and watched the indicator rise. Then, for the first time, he looked down at the blue

55

rug. It was almost new, not fastened down, and just the right size. He bent and picked up the end of it.

"Drop it," said the voice.

The young man looked up in surprise. It was the man, the same man that had stopped him yesterday in the furniture store. Was he being followed?

He dropped the rug. "I thought I saw a coin under there."

"I know what you thought," the man said. "Beat it."

The young man walked out to his pickup and drove away. He felt chilly inside. Suppose this happened every time he wanted to take something—?

The dark man looked shrewdly at Martyn. "All right, doctor. Spill the rest of it. This Dr. Kusko you keep talking about—he's the head of the Institute, right? The guy who developed this process in the first place?"

"That's true," said Martyn, heavily.

"And you say he's a paranoid. Doesn't that mean he's crazy? Are you asking me to believe a crazy man could invent a thing like this?"

Martyn winced. "No, he isn't crazy. He's legally as sane as you or I, and even medically we would only call him disturbed. What we mean when we speak of a paranoid is simply that—well, here is a man who, if he did become insane, would be a paranoiac. He belongs to that type. Meanwhile, he has unreal attitudes about his own greatness and about the hostility of other people. He's a dangerous man. He believes that he is the one man who is right—standing on a pinnacle of rightness —and he'll do anything, *anything,* to stay there."

"For instance?" the dark man said.

"The Institute," Martyn told him, "has already arranged for a staff of lobbyists to start working for the first phase of its program when the world legislature returns to session this fall. Here's what they want for a beginning:

"One, analogue treatment for all persons convicted of crime 'while temporarily insane,' as a substitute for either institutionalization or punishment. They will ar-

56

gue that society's real purpose is to prevent the repetition of the crime, not to punish."

"They'll be right," said the dark man.

"Of course. Second, they want government support for a vast and rapid expansion of analogue services. The goal is to restore useful citizens to society, and to ease pressure on institutions, both corrective and punitive."

"Why not?"

"No reason why not—if it would stop there. But it won't." Martyn took a deep breath and clasped his long fingers together on the table. It was very clear to him, but he realized that it was a difficult thing for a layman to see—or even for a technically competent man in his own field. And yet it was inevitable, *it was going to happen,* unless he stopped it.

"It's just our bad luck," he said, "that this development came at this particular time in history. It was only thirty years ago, shortly after the war, that the problem of our wasted human resources really became so acute that it couldn't be evaded any longer. Since then we've seen a great deal of progess, and public sentiment is fully behind it. New building codes for big cities. New speed laws. Reduced alcoholic content in wine and liquor. Things like that. The analogue treatment is riding the wave.

"It's estimated that the wave will reach its maximum about ten years from now. And that's when the Institute will be ready to put through the second phase of its program. Here it is:

"One, analogue treatment against crimes of violence to be compulsory for all citizens above the age of seven."

The dark man stared at him. "Blue balls of fire. Will it work, on that scale?"

"Yes. It will completely eliminate any possibility of a future war, and it will halve our police problem."

The dark man whistled. "Then what?"

"Two," said Martyn, "analogue treatment against peculation, bribery, collusion and all the other forms of corruption to be compulsory for all candidates for public office. And that will make the democratic system foolproof, for all time."

The dark man laid his pencil down. "Dr. Martyn,

you're confusing me. I'm a libertarian, but there's got to be some method of preventing this race from killing itself off. If this treatment will do what you say it will do, I don't care if it does violate civil rights. I want to go on living, and I want my grandchildren—I have two, by the way—to go on living. Unless there's a catch you haven't told me about this thing, I'm for it."

Martyn said earnestly, "This treatment is a crutch. It is not a therapy, it does not cure the patient of anything. In fact, as I told you before, it makes him less nearly sane, not more. The causes of his irrational or antisocial behavior are still there, they're only repressed—temporarily. They can't ever come out in the same way, that's true; we've built a wall across that particular channel. But they will express themselves in some other way, sooner or later. When a dammed-up flood breaks through in a new place, what do you do?"

"Build another levee."

"Exactly,' said Martyn. "And after that? Another, and another, and another—"

Nicholas Dauth, cold sober, stared broodingly at the boulder that stood on trestles between the house and the orchard. It was a piece of New England granite, marked here and there with chalk lines.

It had stood there for eight months, and he had not touched a chisel to it.

The sun was warm on his back. The air was still; only the occasional hint of a breeze ruffled the treetops. Behind him he could hear the clatter of dishes in the kitchen, and beyond that the clear sounds of his wife's voice.

Once there had been a shape buried in the stone. Every stone had its latent form, and when you carved it, you felt as if you were only helping it to be born.

Dauth could remember the shape he had seen buried in this one: a woman and child—the woman kneeling, half bent over the child in her lap. The balancing of masses had given it grace and authority, and the free space had lent it movement.

He could remember it; but he couldn't see it any more. There was a quick, short spasm in his right arm and side, painful while it lasted. It was like the sketch of an action: turning, walking to where there was whisky—meeting the guard who wouldn't let him drink it, turning away again. All that had squeezed itself now into a spasm, a kind of tic. He didn't drink now, didn't try to drink. He dreamed about it, yes, thought of it, felt the burning ache in his throat and guts. But he didn't try. There simply wasn't any use.

He looked back at the unborn stone, and now, for an instant, he could not even remember what its shape was to have been. The tic came once more. Dauth had a feeling of pressure building intolerably inside him, of something restrained that demanded exit.

He stared at the stone, and saw it drift away slowly into grayness; then nothing.

He turned stiffly toward the house. "Martha!" he called.

The clatter of dishware answered him.

He stumbled forward, holding his arms out. "Martha!" he shouted. *"I'm blind!"*

"Correct me if I'm wrong," said the dark man. "It seems to me that you'd only run into that kind of trouble with the actual mental cases, the people who really have strong compulsions. And, according to you, those are the only ones who should get the treatment. Now, the average man doesn't have any compulsion to kill, or steal, or what have you. He may be tempted, once in his life. If somebody stops him, that one time, will it do him any harm?"

"For a minute or two, he will have been insane," said Martyn. "But I agree with you—if that were the end of it, there'd be no great harm. At the Institute, the majority believe with Kusko that that will be the end of it. They're tragically wrong. Because there's one provision that the Institute hasn't included in its program, but that would be the first thought of any lawmaker in the world. *Treatment against any attempt to overthrow the government.*"

The dark man sat silent.

"And from there," said Martyn, "it's only one short step to a tyranny that will last till the end of time." For an instant his own words were so real to him that he believed it would happen in spite of anything he could do: he saw the ghostly figure of Kusko—big, red-haired, grinning, spraddle-legged over the whole earth.

The other nodded. "You're right," he said. "You are so right. What do you want me to do?"

"Raise funds," said Martyn, feeling the beginning of a vast relief. "At present the Institute has barely enough to operate on a minimum scale, and expand very slowly, opening one new center a year. Offer us a charitable contribution—tax-deductible, remember—of two million, and we'll grab it. The catch is this: the donors, in return for such a large contribution, ask the privilege of appointing three members of the Institute's board of directors. There will be no objection to that, so long as my connection with the donation isn't known, because three members will not give the donors control. But they will give me a majority on this one issue—the second phase of the Institute's program.

"This thing is like an epidemic. Give it a few years, and nothing can stop it. But act now, and we can scotch it while it's still small enough to handle."

"Good enough. I won't promise to hand you two million tomorrow, but I know a few people who might reach into their pockets if I told them the score. I'll do what I can. Hell, I'll get you the money if I have to steal it. You can count on me."

Smiling, Martyn caught the waiter as he went by. "No, this is mine," he said, forestalling the dark man's gesture. "I wonder if you realize what a weight you've taken off my shoulders?"

He paid, and they strolled out into the warm summer night. "Incidentally," Martyn said, "there's an answer to a point you brought up in passing—the weakness of the treatment in the genuinely compulsive cases, where it's most needed. There are means of getting around that, though not of making the treatment into a therapy. It's a crutch, and that's all it will ever be. But for one example, we've recently worked out a technique in which the analogue appears, not as a guardian, but as the object of the attack—when there is an attack. In that way, the patient relieves himself instead of being further repressed, but he still doesn't harm anybody—just a phantom."

"It's going to be a great thing for humanity," said the dark man seriously, "instead of the terrible thing it might have been except for you, Dr. Martyn. Good night!"

"Good night," said Martyn gratefully. He watched the other disappear into the crowd, then walked toward the El. It was a wonderful night, and he was in no hurry.

A big, red-haired guy came in just as the waiter was straightening the table. The waiter stiffened his spine automatically: the big guy looked like Somebody.

"Which table was he sitting at—the tall man with the glasses who just went out?" The red-haired guy showed him a folded bill, and the waiter took it smoothly.

"This one right here," he said. "You a friend of his?"

"No. Just checking up."

"Well," said the waiter cheerfully, "they ought to keep him at home. See here?" He pointed to the two untouched drinks that stood at one side of the table, opposite where the tall man had been sitting. "Sits here for over half an hour—buys four drinks, leaves two of them setting there. And *talks,* like there was somebody with him. You know him? Is he crazy or what?"

"Not crazy," said Dr. Kusko gently. "Some would call him 'disturbed,' but he's harmless—now."

IGNORANT PERSONS PRONOUNCE THE title of this story "babble," but it is "baybel." I had so much fun with this one that I am almost ashamed to mention it. (Good stories ought to give you dyspepsia.) I drew the Hooligan first and described him afterwards. Then the rest was easy and pleasant. (In my youth I often daydreamed of turning civilization arsy-versy, and would have done it if I could.)

5

BABEL II

I

FROM THE FRONT HE LOOKED A LITTLE LIKE Happy Hooligan, if you remember that far back. From the side, where you got a better view of that silver-white crest, he looked more like a cross between George Arliss and a cockatoo.

He stood just under four feet tall, big head, crest and all. He had a wrinkled violet-gray skin, curious S-whorled ears, and a Tweedledum tummy; he was dressed in an electric-blue jacket and small-clothes of some crinkly material that glittered when he moved, with jackboots on his stubby legs and a white-metal disk, a quarter as big as he was, slung by a baldric from one narrow shoulder.

Lloyd Cavanaugh saw the apparition first, at eleven o'clock on a Wednesday morning in May, in the living room of his studio apartment on East 50th Street in Manhattan. It stepped into view, seemingly, from behind the drawing table at the far end of the room.

Which was nonsense. The drawing table, with its top horizontal and the breakfast dishes still on it, was shoved back against the closed drapes of the window. On the right, between the table and the record cabinet, there was about six inches clearance; on the left, between the table and the keg he kept his ink and brushes on, even less.

Cavanaugh, a bad-tempered young man with a long morose face casually connected to a knobby, loose-jointed body, scowled across the pool of brilliance on the model table and said, "What the hell?" He switched off the floods and turned on the room lights.

Suddenly illuminated, the Hooligan-thing blazed at him like a Christmas tree ornament. Its eyes blinked rapidly; then the long upper lip curled up in an astonishing crescent-shaped bucktoothed smile. It made a sound like *"Khakh-ptui!"* and nodded its head several times.

Cavanaugh's first thought was for the Hasselblad. He picked it up, tripod and all, carried it crabwise backward to safety behind the armchair, then crossed the room and took a poker out of the fireplace rack. Gripping this weapon, he advanced on the Hooligan.

The thing came to meet him, grinning and nodding. When they were two strides apart it stopped, bowed jerkily, and lifted the white disk at the end of the baldric, holding it at the top, with one of the flat sides toward Cavanaugh.

A picture formed in the disk.

In stereo and full color, it showed a ten-inch Cavanaugh bending over something on a tripod. The hands moved swiftly, fitting pieces together; then the figure stepped back and stared with evident approval at an oblong box shape at the top of the tripod, with a chromed cylinder projecting from the front of it. The Hasselblad.

Cavanaugh lowered the poker. Jaw unhinged, he stared at the disk, which was now blank, then at the Hooligan's violet face and the silvery growth above it, which was neither hair nor feathers, but something in between. . . . "How did you do that?" he demanded.

"Szu szat," said the Hooligan alertly. He jiggled the disk at Cavanaugh, pointed to his head, then to the disk, then to Cavanaugh's head, then to the disk again. Then he held the thing out at arm's length, cocking his head to one side.

Cavanaugh took the disk gingerly. Gooseflesh was prickling along his arms. "You want to know if I made the camera?" he said tentatively. "Is that it?"

"Szat it," said the Hooligan. He bowed again, nodded twice, and opened his eyes very wide.

Cavanaugh reflected. Staring at the disk, he imagined an enormous machine with a great many drive belts and moving parts, all whirling furiously. There it was, a little blurred, but not bad. He put a hopper on one side of it, made a man walk up and pour in a bucketful of scrap metal, and then showed a stream of cameras coming out the other side.

The Hooligan, who had been peering intently at the other side of the disk, straightened up and took the disk back with another bow. Then he whirled around rapidly three times, holding his nose with one hand and making violent gestures with the other.

Cavanaugh fell back a step, gripping his poker more firmly.

The Hooligan darted past him, moving so fast his legs twinkled, and fetched up with his chin on the edge of the model table, staring at the setup in the middle of the tabletop.

"Hey!" said Cavanaugh angrily, and followed him. The Hooligan turned and held out the disk again. Another picture formed: Cavanaugh bending over the table, this time putting tiny figures together and arranging them in front of a painted backdrop.

. . . Which was substantially what had happened. Cavanaugh was, by profession, a comic-book artist. He was indifferent to the work itself; it was automatic; it paid him well; but it had ruined him as a draftsman. He couldn't draw, paint or etch for fun any more. So he had taken up photography—specifically, tabletop photography.

He built his models out of clay and papier-mâché and wire and beads and bits of wood and a thousand other things; he painted or dyed them, composed them, lighted them—and then, with the Hasselblad and a special, very expensive shallow-focus lens, he photographed them.

The results, after the first year, had begun to be surprising.

The setup on the table now was a deceptively simple one. Background and middle distance were a tangle of fir and mountain laurel, scaled half an inch to a foot. In the foreground were three figures grouped around the remains of a campfire. They were not human; they were attenuated, gray, hairless creatures with big mild eyes, dressed in oddly cut hiking clothes.

Two, with their backs to a block of crumbling masonry half sunken in the ground, were leaning together over a sheet of paper unrolled from a metal cylinder. The third was seated on a stone, nearer the camera, with a shank of meat in its hand. The shape of the half-gnawed bones was disturbingly familiar; and when you looked more closely you would begin to wonder if those projections at the end could be fingers, all but concealed by the eater's hand. As a matter of fact, they were; but no matter how long you looked at the photograph you would never be quite sure.

The Hooligan was thrusting the disk at him again, grinning and winking and teetering on his heels. Cavanaugh, suppressing annoyance in favor of curiosity, accepted it and ran through the same sequence the Hooligan had shown him.

"That's right," he said. "I made it. So what?"

"Szo khvat!" The Hooligan's hand made a gesture, too swift to follow, and suddenly contained what looked like a large fruit, like a purple pear with warts. Seeing Cavanaugh's uncomprehending expression, he put it back wherever it had come from and produced a wadded mass of translucent pink threads. Cavanaugh scowled irritably. "Look—" he began.

The Hooligan tried again. This time he came up with a brilliant, faceted white stone about the size of a cherry.

Cavanaugh felt his eyes bulging. If that was a diamond . . .

"Khoi-ptoo!" said the Hooligan emphatically. He pointed to the stone and to Cavanaugh, then to himself and the model setup. His meaning was clear: he wanted to trade.

It was a diamond, all right; at least, it scribed a neat line in the glass of an empty beer bottle. It was also brilliant, pure white and, so far as Cavanaugh could tell, flawless. He put it on his postage scale; it weighed a little less than an ounce. Say twenty grams, and a carat was two hundred milligrams. . . . It worked out to a preposterous one hundred carats, a little less than the Hope diamond in its prime.

He stared at the thing suspiciously. There *had* to be a catch in it, but with the best will in the world he couldn't see any. The models were a means to an end; once he was finished with them, they simply took up room. So what could he lose?

The Hooligan was gazing at him, owl-eyed. Cavanaugh picked up the disk and gave him his answer: a series of pictures that showed Cavanaugh photographing the models, processing the film, and then ceremoniously accepting the diamond and handing the models over.

The Hooligan bowed repeatedly, capered, stood briefly on his hands, and patted Cavanaugh's sleeve, grinning. Taking this for consent, Cavanaugh put the Hasselblad back in place, turned on the floods, and began where he had left off. He took half a dozen color shots, then reloaded with black-and-white film and took half a dozen more.

The Hooligan watched everything with quivering attention. He followed Cavanaugh into the darkroom and goggled over the edge of the workbench while Cavanaugh developed the black-and-white film, fixed it, washed and dried it, cut it apart and printed it.

And as soon as the first print came out of the frame, the Hooligan made urgent gestures and held out another diamond, about half the size of the first. He wanted the prints, too!

Sweating, Cavanaugh dug into his files and brought up color prints and transparencies of his other work: the Hansel and Gretel series, Cavor and the Grand Lunar, *Walpurgisnacht,* Gulliver extinguishing the palace fire in Lilliput, the Head of the N.I.C.E. The Hooligan bought them all. As each bargain was struck, he picked up his purchase and put it away wherever it was that he got the diamonds. Cavanaugh watched him closely, but couldn't figure out where they went.

For that matter, where had the Hooligan come from?

Assured that Cavanaugh had no more pictures, the Hooligan was darting around the room, peering into corners, bending to look into bookshelves, standing on tiptoe to see what was on the mantelpiece. He pointed at a five-inch wooden figurine, a squatting, hatchet-faced man-shape with its arms crossed, elbows on knees—an Ifugao carving that Cavanaugh had brought home from the Philippines. In the disk, a copy of the Goldberg machine Cavanaugh had used to explain cameras appeared for an instant. The Hooligan cocked his head at him.

"No," said Cavanaugh. "Handmade." He took the disk and gave the Hooligan a view of a brown-skinned man gouging splinters out of a block of mahogany. Then, for kicks, he made the man shrink to a dot on an island on a globe that slowly turned, with Asia and Australia vanishing around one limb while the Americas rolled into sight from the other. He made a red dot for New York, and pointed at himself.

"Khrrrzt," said the Hooligan thoughtfully. He turned away from the Ifugao and pointed to a bright diamond-patterned rug that hung on the wall over the couch. "Khand-mate?"

Cavanaugh, who had just made up his mind to give up the Ifugao for another diamond, was nonplused. "Wait a minute," he said, and made another moving picture in the disk: himself handing over the Ifugao for the standard emolument.

The Hooligan leaped back, ears flapping, crest aquiver. Recovering somewhat, he advanced again and showed Cavanaugh a revised version: the Hooligan receiving a wood carving from, and handing a diamond to, the brown-skinned man Cavanaugh had pictured as its creator.

"Khand-mate?" he said again, pointing to the rug.

Somewhat sourly, Cavanaugh showed him the rug being woven by a straw-hatted Mexican. Still more sourly, he answered the Hooligan's pictographed "Where?" with a map of Mexico; and more sourly still, he identified and located the artists responsible for a Swedish silver pitcher, a Malay kris, an Indian brass hubble-bubble, and a pair of loafers hand-cobbled in Greenwich Village.

The Hooligan, it appeared, bought only at the source.

At any rate, if he wasn't going to get any more diamonds, he could get some information. Cavanaugh took the disk and projected a view of the Hooligan popping into sight and moving forward across the room. Then he ran it backward and looked inquiringly at the Hooligan.

For answer, he got a picture of a twilit depthless space where crested little creatures like the Hooligan walked among tall fungoid growths that looked like tiers of doughnuts on a stick. Another planet? Cavanaugh touched the disk and made the viewpoint tilt upward; the Hooligan obligingly filled in more of the featureless violet haze. No sun, no moon, no stars.

Cavanaugh tried again: a picture of himself, standing on the globe of the earth and peering at the night sky. Suddenly a tiny Hooligan-figure appeared, uncomfortably perched on a star.

The Hooligan countered with a picture that left Cavanaugh more confused than before. There were two globes, swinging in emptiness. One was solid-looking, and standing on it was a tiny man-shape; the other was violet mist, with the tubby, crested figure of a Hooligan inside it. The two spheres revolved very slowly around each other, coming a little nearer with each circuit, while the solid globe flickered light-dark, light-dark. Eventually they touched, clung, and the Hooligan-figure darted across. The solid globe flickered once more, the Hooligan shot back to the misty one, and the spheres separated, moving very gradually apart as they circled.

Cavanaugh gave up.

The Hooligan, after waiting a moment to be sure that Cavanaugh had no more questions, made his deepest bow to date and conjured up a final diamond: a beauty, larger than all but one or two that Cavanaugh already had.

Picture of Cavanaugh accepting the diamond and handing over something blurred: *What for?*

Picture of the Hooligan rejecting the blur: *For nothing.*

Picture of the Hooligan patting Cavanaugh's sleeve: *For friendship*.

Feeling ashamed of himself, Cavanaugh got a bottle of May wine and two glasses out of the bookshelf. He explained to the Hooligan, via the disk, what the stuff was and—sketchily—what it was supposed to do to you.

This was a mistake.

The Hooligan, beaming enormously between sips, drank the wine with every sign of enjoyment. Then, with an impressive flourish, he put a smallish green and white doodad on the table. It had a green crystalline base with a slender knob-tipped metal shaft sprouting upright from the center of it. That was all.

Feeling abnormally open-minded and expectant, Cavanaugh studied the Hooligan's pictograph explanation. The gadget, apparently, was the Hooligan equivalent of alcoholic beverages. (Picture of Cavanaugh and the Hooligan, with enormous smiles on their faces, while colored lights flashed on and off inside their transparent skulls.) He nodded when the little man glanced at him for permission. With one thick finger, the Hooligan carefully tapped the doodad's projecting knob. Knob and shaft vibrated rapidly.

Cavanaugh had the odd sensation that someone was stirring his brains with a swizzle stick. It tickled. It was invigorating. It was delightful. "Ha!" he said.

"Kho!" said the Hooligan, grinning happily. He picked up the doodad, put it away—Cavanaugh *almost* saw where it went—and stood up. Cavanaugh accompanied him to the door. He patted Cavanaugh's sleeve; Cavanaugh pumped his hand. Then, cheerfully bouncing three steps at a time, he disappeared down the stairwell.

From the window, a few minutes later, Cavanaugh saw him riding by—atop a Second Avenue bus.

II

The euphoric feeling diminished after a few minutes, leaving Cavanaugh in a relaxed but bewildered state of mind. To reassure himself, he emptied his bulging trousers pockets onto the table. Diamonds—solid, cool, sharp-edged, glowingly beautiful. He counted them; there were twenty-seven, ranging from over a hundred carats to about thirty; worth, altogether—how much?

Steady, he warned himself. There may be a catch in it yet. The thing to do was to get downtown to an appraiser's and find out. Conveniently, he knew where there was one—in the French Building, across the hall from Patriotic Comics. He picked out two of the stones, a big one and a little one, and zipped them into the inner compartment of his wallet. Jittering a little with excitement, he dumped the rest into a paper bag and hid them under the kitchen sink.

A yellow cab was cruising down the avenue. Cavanaugh hailed it and got in. "Forty-fifth and Fifth," he said.

"Boo?" said the driver, twisting to look at him.

Cavanaugh glowered. "Forty-fifth Street," he said distinctly, "and Fifth Avenue. Let's go."

"Zawss," said the driver, pushing his cap up, "owuh kelg trace wooj'l, fook. Bnog nood ig ye nolik?"

Cavanaugh got out of the cab. "Pokuth *chowig'w!*" said the driver, and zoomed away, grinding his gears.

Jaw unhinged, Cavanaugh stared after him. He felt his ears getting hot. "Why didn't I get his license number?" he said aloud. "Why didn't I stay upstairs where it was safe? Why do I live in this idiotic goddamn city?"

He stepped back onto the sidewalk. "Lowly, badny?" said a voice in his ear.

Cavanaugh whirled. It was an urchin with a newspaper in his hand, a stack of them under his arm. "Will you kindly mind your own business?" Cavanaugh said. He turned, took two steps toward the corner, then froze, faced around again, and marched back.

It was as he had thought: the headline of the paper in the boy's hand read, MOTN LNIUL IMAP QYFRAT.

The name of the paper, which otherwise looked like the *News,* was *Pionu Vajl.*

The newsboy was backing away from him, with a wary look in his eyes.

"Wait," said Cavanaugh hastily. He clutched in his pocket for change, found none, and got a bill out of his wallet with trembling fingers. He thrust it at the child. "I'll take a paper."

The boy took the bill, glanced at it, threw it on the pavement at Cavanaugh's feet, and ran like sixty.

Cavanaugh picked up the bill. In each corner of it was a large figure 4. Over the familiar engraving of G. Washington were the words FRA EVOFAP LFIFAL YK IQATOZI. Under it, the legend read YVA PYNNIT.

He clutched his collar, which was throttling him. That vibrating gadget— But that couldn't be it; it was the world that was scrambled, not Cavanaugh. And *that* was impossible, because . . .

A dirty little man in a derby rushed at him, grabbing for his lapels. "Poz'k," he gabbled, "fend gihekn, fend gihekn? Fwuz ebb l' mwukd sahtz'kn?"

Cavanaugh pushed him away and retreated.

The little man burst into tears. "FWUH!" he wailed. "Fwuh vekn r' NAHP shaoo?"

Cavanaugh stopped thinking. Out of the corner of his eye, he saw that a crosstown bus had just pulled up down at the end of the block. He ran for it.

The red-faced driver was half out of his seat, bellowing gibberish at a fat woman who was shrieking back at him, brandishing a dangerous parasol. Beyond them the narrow aisle was packed full of bewildered faces, annoyed faces, shouting faces. The air bristled with dislocated consonants.

Farther down, somebody shrieked and hammered on the rear door. Cursing, the driver turned around to open it. The fat woman seized this opportunity to clout him on the head, and when the resulting melee was over, Cavanaugh found himself halfway down the bus, well wedged in, without having paid his fare.

The bus moved. Hysterical passengers got off at every stop, but the ones that crowded on were in no better shape. Nobody, Cavanaugh realized numbly, could understand anybody; nobody could read anything written.

The din was increasing; Cavanaugh could hear the

driver's bellowing voice getting steadily hoarser and weaker. Up ahead, horns were blowing furiously. Concentrating with the greatest difficulty, he managed: *How far?* That was a crucial point—had whatever it was happened simultaneously all over New York . . . or all over the world? Or, horrid thought, was it a sort of infection that he was carrying with him?

He had to find out.

The traffic got thicker. At Sixth Avenue the bus, which had been moving by inches, stopped altogether and the doors slammed open. Peering forward, Cavanaugh saw the driver climb down, hurl his uniform cap to the street and disappear, shoulders hunched, into the crowd.

Cavanaugh got out and walked west into bedlam. Auto horns were howling, sirens shrieking; there was a fight every fifteen yards and a cop for every tenth fight. After a while it became obvious that he would never get to Broadway; he battled his way back to Sixth and turned south.

The loudspeaker over a record store was blaring a song Cavanaugh knew and detested; but instead of the all-too-familiar words, the raucous female voice was chanting:

"Kee-*ee* tho-*iv* i-*if* zeg*mlit podn mawgeth oo-ooguaatch* . . ."

It sounded just as good.

The street sign directly ahead of him read, 13FR. LF. Even the *numbers* were cockeyed.

Cavanaugh's head hurt. He went into a bar.

It was well patronized. Nobody in a white coat was in evidence, but about a third of the customers were behind the bar, serving the rest—a bottle at a time.

Cavanaugh elbowed his way into the first tier and hesitated between two bottles labeled respectively CIF 05 and ZITLFIOTL. Neither sounded particularly appetizing, but the amber liquid in each looked to be what he needed. He settled for the Zitlfiotl. After his second swallow, feeling more alert, he scanned the backbar and located a radio.

It was, he found when he reached it, already turned on, but nothing was coming out but a power hum. He twiddled with the knobs. At the right of the dial—which was eccentrically numbered from 77 to 408—he picked up an orchestra playing *Pictures at an Exhibition;* otherwise, nothing.

That, he decided, settled it. WQXR, with an all-music program, was on the air; the others were off. That meant that speech was coming out double-talk, not only in New York and New Jersey broadcasts, but in network programs from the West Coast. Or—wait a minute—even if a radio performer in Hollywood were able to speak straight English, wouldn't it be nonsense to an engineer in Manhattan?

This led him by easy stages to the next problem. Selecting an unfrequented table in the rear, and carrying his Zitlfiotl with him, he seated himself with circumspection and carefully laid out on the table the following important articles:

A partially used envelope.

A fountain pen.

A one-dollar bill.

His social-security card.

A salvaged newspaper.

Now, the question was, did any order remain in the patterns of human speech, or was all reduced to utter chaos? Scientific method, encouraged by Zitlfiotl, would discover the answer.

As a preliminary gambit, he wrote the letters of the alphabet, in a severely vertical line, on the unused surface of the envelope.

Next, after reflection, he copied down the text of the one-dollar bill. Thusly:

FRA EVOFAP LFIFAL YK IQATOZI YVA PYNNIT

Under each line, letter by letter, he added what *ought* to be the text of the one-dollar bill.

This gave him fifteen letters, which he wrote down in their proper places opposite the already established letters of the alphabet. Following the identical procedure with the *Pionu Vajl*, or *Daily News*, and, with his own signature, which appeared on the card as *Nnyup Ziciviemr,* gave him four letters more, with the result:

A E	H	O I	V N
B	I A	P D	W
C V	J W	Q M	X
D	K F	R H	Y O
E U	L S	S	Z C
F T	M G	T R	
G	N L	U Y	

Now came the supreme test. He copied down the *Vajl's* puzzling headline and transliterated it according to his findings:

MOTN LNIUL
GIRL SLAYS
IMAP QYFRAT
AGED MOTHER

A triumphant success. He could now communicate. The point is, he told himself lucidly, when I think I am saying "Listen to me," in actuality I am saying "Nolfav fy qa," and this is why nobody understands anyone else. And therefore, if I were to think I am saying "Nolfav fy qa," I would actually be saying "Listen to me." And in this way will we build the Revolution.

But it didn't work.

Some time later he found himself in a disused classroom with an unruly student body consisting of three men with spectacles and beards and a woman with hair in her eyes; he was attempting to teach them by means of blackboard exercises a new alphabet which began E, blank, V, blank, U, T, blank. The blanks, he explained, were most important.

At a later period he was standing on the first landing of the left-hand staircase in the lobby of the Forty-second Street Branch of the New York Public Library shouting to an assembled crowd, over and over, "Myp-piqvap opoyfl! Myp-piqvap opoyfl!"

And at a still later time he woke up, cold sober, leaning on an imitation-marble-topped table in a partially wrecked cafeteria. Sunlight was slanting through the plate glass onto the wall to his left; it must be either late afternoon or early morning.

Cavanaugh groaned. He had gone into that bar, he remembered, because his head hurt: about like taking a mickey finn for nausea.

And as for the rest of it—before *and* after . . . how much of that had he imagined?

He raised his head and stared hopefully at the lettering on the windows. Even back-to-front he could tell that it wasn't in English. The first letter was a Z.

He groaned again and propped his chin up with his hands, carefully, so as not to slosh. He tried to stay that way, not moving, not looking, not noticing, but eventually an insistent thought brought him upright again.

How long?

How long was this going to last? How long could it last before the whole world went to hell in a hand basket? Not very long.

Without language, how could you buy anything, sell anything, order anything? And if you could, what would you use for money—four-dollar bills marked YVA PYNNIT?

. . . Or, he amended bitterly, something equally outlandish. Because that was the point he had overlooked a few drunken hours ago—everybody's alphabet was different. To Cavanaugh, YVA PYNNIT. To somebody else, AGU MATTEK, or ENY ZEBBAL, or . . .

Twenty-six letters in the alphabet. Possible combinations 26 x 25 x 24 x 23 x 22 and so on down to x 1 . . . figure roughly one decimal place for each operation . . .

Something in the *septillions*.

Not as many if vowels were traded for vowels, consonants for consonants, as seemed to have happened in his case, but still plenty. More than the number of people alive in the world.

That was for the written word. For speech, he realized suddenly, it would be just about twenty-five decimal places worse. Not letters, phonemes—forty of them in ordinary spoken English.

A swizzle stick that stirred up your brains—that switched the reflex arcs around at random, connecting the receptor pattern for *K* with the response pattern for *H,* or *D* or anything. . . .

Cavanaugh traced a letter with his forefinger on the tabletop, frowning at it. Hadn't he always made an A like that—a vertical stroke and three horizontal ones?

But, damn it, that was the fiendish thing about it—memory didn't mean a thing, because all the memories were still there but they were scrambled. As if you had ripped out all the connections in a telephone switchboard and put them back differently.

Of course; it *had* to be that way—nobody had gone around repainting all the signs or reprinting all the newspapers or forging a phony signature on Cavanaugh's social-security card. That half-circle first letter of his name, even though it looked like a Z to him, was still a C.

Or was it? If a tree falls with nobody to hear it, is there a sound? And if beauty is in the eye of the beholder, then which way is up? Or, rather, thought Cavanaugh, repressing a tendency toward hysteria, *which way is out?*

First things first.

The Hooligan.

He came from some place that wasn't exactly a place, across a distance that wasn't exactly a distance. But it must be a difficult journey, because there was no record of any previous appearances of little cockatoo-crested art collectors. . . .

He bought the local handicrafts with stones that were priceless on this planet, and very likely dirt-common where he came from. Pretty beads for the natives. In politeness, you offered him a drink. And being polite right back at you, he gave you a shot of swizzle-sticks-in-the-head.

Firewater. A mild stimulant to the Hooligan, hell on wheels to the aborigines. Instead of getting two people mildly confused, it turned a whole planet pole over equator . . . and, communicating by pictures as he did, it was probable that the Hooligan *still* didn't know what damage he had done. He would finish his tour and go happily back home with his prizes, and then a few thousand years from now, maybe, when the human race had put itself together again into half-acre nations and two-for-a-nickel empires, another Hooligan would come along. . . .

Cavanaugh upset his chair.

Icicles were forming along his spine.

This wasn't the first time. It had happened at least once before, a few thousand years ago, in the valley of the Euphrates.

Not Bedlam—Babel.

III

The sun was quartering down toward the west, gilding a deserted Forty-second Street with the heartbreaking false promise of spring in New York. Leaning dizzily against the door frame, Cavanaugh saw broken display windows and dark interiors. He heard a confused roaring from somewhere uptown, but the few people who passed him were silent, bewildered.

There was a nasty wreck at the corner of Seventh Avenue, and another at Eighth; that accounted, he saw with relief, for the lack of traffic in this block. Holding the top of his head down with one hand, he scuttled across the street and dived into the black maw of the IRT subway.

The arcade and the station itself were empty, echoing. Nobody behind the newsstands, nobody playing the pinball machines, nobody in the change booth. Swallowing hard, Cavanaugh went through the open gate and clattered down the stairs to the downtown platform.

A train was standing in the express lane, doors open, lights burning, motor chuffing quietly. Cavanaugh ran down to the first car and went across the vestibule to the motorman's cubicle.

The control lever was missing.

Cursing, Cavanaugh climbed back to the street. He had to find the Hooligan; he had one chance in a million of doing it, and one wasted minute now might be the one minute that mattered.

The little man could be anywhere on the planet by now. But he'd expressed interest in objects in Cavanaugh's apartment that came variously from the Philippines, Mexico, Malaya, Sweden, India—and Greenwich Village. If, improbably, he hadn't got around to the Village yet, then Cavanaugh might be able to catch him there; it was the only hope he had.

On Eighth Avenue south of Forty-first, he came upon a yellow cab parked at the curb. The driver was leaning against the wall under a Zyzi-Zyni sign, talking to himself, with gestures.

Cavanaugh clutched him by the sleeve and made urgent motions southward. The driver looked at him vaguely, cleared his throat, moved two feet farther down the wall and resumed his interrupted discourse.

Fuming, Cavanaugh hesitated for a moment, then fumbled in his pockets for pen and paper. He found the envelope with his world-saving alphabet on it, tore it open to get a blank space, and sketched rapidly:

The driver looked at it boredly, then with a faint gleam of intelligence. Cavanaugh pointed to the first picture and looked at him interrogatively.

"Oweh?" said the driver.

"That's right," said Cavanaugh, nodding violently. "Now the next—"

The driver hesitated. "Mtshell?"

That couldn't be right, with a consonant at the end of it. Cavanaugh shook his head and pointed to the blacked-in circle.

"Vcode," said the driver.

Cavanaugh moved his finger to the white circle.

"Mah."

"Right!" said Cavanaugh. "Oweh mah—" He pointed to the third picture.

That was the tough one; the driver couldn't get it. "Vnakjaw?" he hazarded.

Not enough syllables. Cavanaugh shook his head and passed on to the fourth picture.

"Vbzyetch."

Cavanaugh nodded, and they started through the sequence again.

"Oweh—mah—vbzyetch." A look of enlightenment spread over the driver's face. "*Jick*agl! *Jick*agl Vbzyetch!"

"You've got it," Cavanaugh told him: "Sheridan Square. *Jick*agl Vbzyetch."

Halfway to the cab, the driver stopped short, with a remembering look on his face, and held out his hand insinuatingly.

Cavanaugh took the bills out of his wallet and fanned them at him. The driver shook his head. "Ngup-joke," he said sadly, and turned back toward his wall.

Twenty minutes later Cavanaugh was poorer by one thirty-carat diamond, and the cab driver, with a smile on his honest face, was opening the door for him at the western corner of Sheridan Square (which is triangular), a few yards from the bullet-colored statue of the General.

Cavanaugh made signs to him to wait, got a happy grin and a nod in reply, and ran down the block.

He passed Janigian's shop once without recognizing it, and for an excellent reason: there was not a shoe or a slipper visible anywhere in the big, bare work- and sales-room.

80

The door was ajar. Cavanaugh went in, stared suspiciously at the empty shelves and then at the door to the back room, which was closed by a hasp and the largest, heaviest padlock he had ever seen in his life. This was odd (a) because Janigian did not believe in locking his doors, and this one, in fact, had never even had a latch, and (b) because Janigian never went anywhere—having been permanently startled, some years ago, by E. B. White's commentary on the way the pavement comes up to meet your foot when you lift it.

Cavanaugh stepped forward, got his fingernails into the crack between the door and the jamb, and pulled.

The hasp, being attached to the jamb only by the sawed-off heads of two screws, came free; the door swung open.

Inside was Janigian.

He was sitting cross-legged on a small wooden chest, looking moderately wild-eyed. He had a rusty shotgun across his thighs, and two ten-inch butcher knives were stuck into the floor in front of him.

When he saw Cavanaugh he raised the gun, then lowered it a trifle. "Odeh!" he said. Cavanaugh translated this as "Aha!" which was Janigian's standard greeting.

"Odeh yourself," he said. He took out his wallet, removed his other diamond—the big one—and held it up.

Janigian nodded solemnly. He stood up, holding the shotgun carefully under one arm, and with the other, without looking down, opened the lid of the chest. He pulled aside a half-dozen dirty shirts, probed deeper, and scrabbled up a handful of something.

He showed it to Cavanaugh.

Diamonds.

He let them pour back into the chest, dropped the shirts back on top, closed the lid and sat down again. "Odeh!" he said.

This time it meant "Good-by." Cavanaugh went away.

His headache, which had left him imperceptibly somewhere on Forty-second Street, was making itself felt again. Cursing without inspiration, Cavanaugh walked back up to the corner.

Now what? Was he supposed to pursue the Hooligan to the Philippines, or Sweden, or Mexico?

Well, why not?

If I don't get him, Cavanaugh told himself, I'll be living in a cave a year from now. I'll make a lousy caveman. Grubs for dinner *again* . . .

The cabman was still waiting on the corner. Cavanaugh snarled at him and went into the cigar store across the street. From an ankle-deep layer of neckties, pocketbooks and mashed candy bars he picked out a five-borough map. He trudged back across the street and got into the cab.

The driver looked at him expectantly. "Your mother has hairy ears," Cavanaugh told him.

"Zee kwa?" said the driver.

"Three of them," Cavanaugh said. He opened the map to the Queens-Long Island section, managed to locate Flushing Bay, and drew an X—which, on second thought, he scribbled into a dot—where La Guardia Field ought to be.

The driver looked at it, nodded—and held out his meaty hand.

Cavanaugh controlled an impulse to spit. Indignantly, he drew a picture of the diamond he had already given the man, pointed to it, then to the cabman, then to the map.

The driver shrugged and gestured outside with his thumb.

Cavanaugh gritted his teeth, shut his eyes tight, and counted to twenty. Eventually, when he thought he could trust himself to hold anything with a sharp point, he picked up the pen, found the Manhattan section of the map, and made a dot at Fiftieth and Second Avenue. He drew another picture of a diamond, with an arrow pointing to the dot.

The driver studied it. He leaned farther over the seat and put a stubby finger on the dot. "Fa mack alaha gur'l hih?" he demanded suspiciously.

"Your father comes from a long line of orangutans with loathsome diseases," said Cavanaugh, crossing his heart.

Reassured by the polysyllables, the driver put his machine into motion.

At the apartment, while the driver lurked heavily in the living room, Cavanaugh picked out the very smallest diamond to pay his fare, and twelve others, from middling to big, for further emergencies. He also took two cans of hash, a can of tamales, an opener, a spoon, and a bottle of tomato juice in a paper bag; the thought of food revolted him at the moment, but he would have to eat sometime. Better than grubs, anyway. . . .

All the main arteries out of New York, Cavanaugh discovered, were choked—everybody who was on the island was apparently trying to get off, and vice versa. Nobody was paying much attention to traffic signals, and the battered results were visible at nearly every intersection.

It took them two hours to get to La Guardia.

Some sort of a struggle was going on around a car parked in front of the terminal building. As Cavanaugh's cab pulled up, the crowd broke and surged toward them; Cavanaugh had barely time to open the door and leap out. When he had bounced off the hood, tripped over somebody's feet, butted someone else in the stomach, and finally regained his balance a few seconds later, he saw the cab turning on two wheels, with one rear door hanging open, and a packed mass of passengers bulging out like a bee swarm. The cab's taillights wavered off down the road, a few stragglers running frantically after it.

Cavanaugh walked carefully around the diminished mob, still focused on the remaining car, and went into the building. He fought his way through the waiting room, losing his paper bag, several buttons from his shirt and nine tenths of his temper, and found an open gate onto the field.

The huge, floodlighted area was one inextricable confusion of people, dogs and airplanes—more planes than Cavanaugh had ever seen in one place before; forests of them—liners, transports, private planes of every size and shape.

The dogs were harder to account for. There seemed to be several dozen of them in his immediate vicinity, all large and vociferous. One especially active Dalmatian, about the size of a cougar, circled Cavanaugh twice and then reared up to put two tremendous forepaws on his chest. Cavanaugh fell like a tree. Man and dog stared at each other, eye to eye, for one poignant moment; then the beast whirled, thumping Cavanaugh soundly in the ribs, and was gone.

Raging, Cavanaugh arose and stalked forth onto the field. Somebody grabbed his sleeve and shouted in his ear; Cavanaugh swung at him, whirled completely around, and cannoned into somebody else, who hit him with a valise. Some time later, confused in mind and bruised of body, he found himself approaching a small, fragile-looking monoplane on whose wing sat an expressionless man in a leather jacket.

Cavanaugh climbed up beside him, panting. The other looked at him thoughtfully and raised his left hand, previously concealed by his body. There was a spanner in it.

Cavanaugh sighed. Raising one hand for attention, he opened his wallet and took out one of the larger gems.

The other man lowered the spanner a trifle.

Cavanaugh felt for his fountain pen; it was gone. Dipping one finger in the blood that was trickling from his nose, he drew a wobbly outline map of North America on the surface of the wing.

The other winced slightly, but watched with interest.

Cavanaugh drew the United States–Mexico border, and put a large dot, or blob, south of it. He pointed to the plane, to the dot, and held up the diamond.

The man shook his head.

Cavanaugh added a second.

The man shook his head again. He pointed to the plane, made motions as if putting earphones on his head, cocked his head in a listening attitude, and shook his head once more. *No radio.*

With one flattened hand, he made a zooming motion upward; with the other, he drew a swift line across his throat. *Suicide.*

Then he sketched an unmilitary salute. *Thanks just the same.*

Cavanaugh climbed down from the wing. The next pilot he found gave him the same answer; and the next; and the next. There wasn't any fifth, because, in taking a shortcut under a low wing, he tripped over two silently struggling gentlemen who promptly transferred their quarrel to him. When he recovered from a momentary inattention, they were gone, and so was the wallet with the diamonds.

Cavanaugh walked back to Manhattan.

Counting the time he spent asleep under a trestle somewhere in Queens, it took him twelve hours. Even an Oregonian can find his way around in Manhattan, but a Manhattanite gets lost anywhere away from his island. Cavanaugh missed the Queensborough Bridge somehow, wandered south into Brooklyn without realizing it (he would rather have died), and wound up some sixty blocks off his course at the Williamsburg Bridge; this led him via Delancey Street into the Lower East Side, which was not much improvement.

Following the line of least resistance, and yearning for civilization (i.e., midtown New York), Cavanaugh moved northwestward along that erstwhile cowpath variously named the Bowery, Fourth Avenue and Broadway. Pausing only to rummage in a Union Square fruit-drink stand for cold frankfurters, he reached Forty-second Street at half-past ten, twenty-three and one half hours after his introduction to the Hooligan.

Times Square, never a very inspiring sight in the morning, was very sad and strange. Traffic, a thin trickle, was moving spasmodically. Every car had its window closed tight, and Cavanaugh saw more than one passenger holding a rifle. The crowds on the littered sidewalks did not seem to be going anywhere, or even thinking about going anywhere. They were huddling.

Bookstores were empty and their contents scattered over the pavement; novelty shops, cafeterias, drugstores . . . the astonishing thing was that, here and there, trade was still going on. Money would still buy you a bottle of liquor, or a pack of cigarettes, or a can of food— the necessities. Pricing was a problem, but it was being solved in a forthright manner: above each counter, the main items of the store's stock in trade were displayed, each with one or two bills pasted to it. Cigarettes—George Washington. A fifth of whisky—Alexander Hamilton and Abraham Lincoln. A can of ersatzized meat—Andrew Jackson.

There was even one movie house open for business. It was showing a Charlie Chaplin Festival.

Cavanaugh was feeling extremely lightheaded and unsubstantial. Babylon, that great city! he thought; and Somewhere, parently, in the ginnandgo gap between antediluvious and annadominant the copyist must have fled with his scroll. . . .

The human race had now, in effect, Had It. New York was no longer a city; it was simply the raw material for an archaeologist's puzzle—a midden heap. And thinking of *Finnegan* again, he remembered, What a mnice old mness it all mnakes!

He looked at the faces around him, blank with a new misery, the misery of silence. That's what hits them the hardest, he thought. The speechlessness. They don't care about not being able to read—it's a minor annoyance. But they like to talk.

And yet, the human race could have survived if only the spoken word had been bollixed up, not the written word. It would have been easy enough to work out universal sound symbols for the few situations where speech was really vital. Nothing could replace the textbooks, the records, the libraries, the business letters.

By now, Cavanaugh thought bitterly, the Hooligan was trading shiny beads for grass skirts in Honolulu, or carved walrus tusks in Alaska, or . . .

Or was he? Cavanaugh stopped short. He had, he realized, been thinking of the Hooligan popping into view all over the globe the way he had appeared in his apartment—and, when he was through, popping back to where he belonged from wherever he happened to be.

But, if he could travel that way, *why had he left Cavanaugh's place on a Second Avenue bus?*

Cavanaugh scrabbled frantically through his memory. His knees sagged.

The Hooligan had showed him, in the disk, that the two—universes, call them—came together rarely, and when they did, touched at one point only. Last time, the plain of Shinar. This time, Cavanaugh's living room.

And that one flicker, light-dark-light, before the pictured Hooligan moved back to its own sphere . . .

Twenty-four hours.

Cavanaugh looked at his watch. It was 10:37.

He ran.

Lead-footed, three quarters dead, and cursing himself, the Hooligan, the human race, God the Creator and the entire imaginable cosmos with the last breath in his body, Cavanaugh reached the corner of Forty-ninth and Second just in time to see the Hooligan pedaling briskly up the avenue on a bicycle.

He shouted, or tried to; nothing but a wheeze came out.

Whistling with agony, he lurched around the corner and ran to keep from falling on his face. He almost caught up with the Hooligan at the entrance to the building, but he couldn't stop to get the breath to make a noise. The Hooligan darted inside and up the stairs; Cavanaugh followed.

He can't open the door, he thought, halfway up. But when he reached the third-floor landing, the door was open.

Cavanaugh made one last effort, leaped like a salmon, tripped over the doorsill, and spread-eagled himself on the floor in the middle of the room.

The Hooligan, one step away from the drawing table, turned with a startled "Chaya-dnih?"

Seeing Cavanaugh, he came forward with an expression of pop-eyed concern. Cavanaugh couldn't move.

Muttering excitedly to himself, the Hooligan produced the green-and-white doodad from somewhere—much, presumably, as a human being might have gone for the medicinal brandy—and set it on the floor near Cavanaugh's head.

"Urgh!" said Cavanaugh. With one hand, he clutched the Hooligan's disk.

The pictures formed without any conscious planning: the doodad, the lights flashing off and on in a skull—dozens, hundreds of skulls—then buildings falling, trains crashing, volcanoes erupting. . . .

The Hooligan's eyes bulged half out of their sockets. "Hakdaz!" he said, clapping his hands to his ears. He seized the disk and made conciliatory pictures—the doodad and a glass of wine melting into each other.

"I know that," said Cavanaugh hoarsely, struggling up to one elbow. "But *can you fix it?*" He made a picture of the Hooligan gesturing at the flashing lights, which promptly vanished.

"Deech, deech," said the Hooligan, nodding violently. He picked up the doodad and somehow broke the green base of it into dozens of tiny cubes, which he began to reassemble, apparently in a different order, with great care.

Cavanaugh hauled himself up into an armchair and let himself go limp as a glove. He watched the Hooligan, telling himself drowsily that if he wasn't careful, he'd be asleep in another minute. There was something odd about the room, something extraordinarily soothing. . . . After a moment he realized what it was.

The silence.

The two fishwives who infested the floor below were not screaming pleasantries across the courtyard at each other. Nobody was playing moron music on a radio tuned six times too loud for normal hearing.

The landlady was not shouting instructions from the top floor to the janitor in the basement.

Silence. Peace.

For some reason, Cavanaugh's mind turned to the subject of silent films: Chaplin, the Keystone Cops, Douglas Fairbanks, Garbo . . . they would have to bring them out of the cans again, he thought, for everybody, not just the patrons of the Museum of Modern Art Film Library. . . .

Congress would have to rig up some sort of Telautograph system, with a screen above the Speaker's desk, perhaps.

Television. Television, thought Cavanaugh dreamily, would have to shut up and put up.

No more campaign oratory.

No more banquet speeches.

No more singing commercials.

Cavanaugh sat up. "Listen," he said tensely. "Could you fix just the writing—not the speech?"

The Hooligan goggled at him and held out the disk.

Cavanaugh took it and slowly began putting the idea into careful pictures. . . .

The Hooligan was gone—vanished like a burst soap bubble at the end of a headfirst dive across Cavanaugh's drawing table.

Cavanaugh sat where he was, listening. From outside, after a moment, came a confused, distance-muted roar. All over the city—all over the world, Cavanaugh supposed—people were discovering that they could read again; that the signs meant what they said; that each man's sudden island had been rejoined to the main.

It lasted twenty minutes and then faded slowly. In his mind's eye, Cavanaugh saw the orgy of scribbling that must be beginning now. He sat, and listened to the blessed silence.

In a little while a growing twinge forced itself upon his attention, like a forgotten toothache. After a moment, Cavanaugh identified it as his conscience. Just who are you, conscience was saying, to take away the gift of speech—the thing that once was all that distinguished man from the apes?

Cavanaugh dutifully tried to feel repentant, but it didn't work. Who said it was a gift? he asked his conscience. What did we use it for?

I'll tell you, he said. In the cigar store: Hey, waddaya think of them Yankees? Yeah, that was som'n, wasn' it? Sure was! I tell you . . .

At home: So, how was the office t'day? Aa. Same goddamn madhouse. How'd it go with you? Awright. I can't complain. Kids okay? Yaa. Uh-huh. What's f-dinner?

At a party: Hello, Harry! Whattaya say, boy! How

are ya? That's good. How's the . . . so I said to him, you can't tell me what I'm gonna . . . like to, but it don't agree with me. It's my stummick; th' doctor says . . . organdy, with little gold buttons . . . Oh, yeah? Well, how would you like a poke in the snoot?

On the street corners: Lebensraum . . . Nordische Blut . . .

I, said Cavanaugh, rest my case.

Conscience did not reply.

In the silence, Cavanaugh walked across the room to the record cabinet and pulled out an album. He could read the lettering on its spine: MAHLER, *The Song of the Earth*.

He picked out one of the disks and put it on the machine—the "Drunkard's Song" in the fifth movement.

Cavanaugh smiled beatifically, listening. It was an artificial remedy, he was thinking; from the Hooligan's point of view, the human race was now permanently a little tipsy. And so what?

The words the tenor was singing were gibberish to Cavanaugh—but then they always had been; Cavanaugh spoke no German. He knew what the words meant.

> *Was geht mich denn der Frühling an!?*
> *Lasst mich betrunken sein!*
> "What then is the spring to me?
> . . . Let me be drunk!"

IN 1954, WHEN WE WERE LIVING IN Pennsylvania on no money, my second wife was about to give birth to our first child. Talking about the delivery before it happened, she uttered the five words that I used as the last line of this story.

"Special Delivery" is about an unborn superman; I had to give his father some profession, and I made him a schoolteacher because there were things I wanted to say about that line of work. My sympathy in this story is divided, but goes mainly to the child —I'm sorry that the plot required him to be choked off.

6

SPECIAL DELIVERY

◄◄◄◄◄◄◄◄◄◄◄◄◄◄◄◄◄◄◄◄◄◄◄◄◄◄◄◄◄◄◄◄◄◄◄

LEN AND MOIRA CONNINGTON LIVED IN A rented cottage with a small yard, a smaller garden and too many fir trees. The lawn, which Len seldom had time to mow, was full of weeds, and the garden was overgrown with blackberry brambles. The house itself was clean and smelled better than most city apartments, and Moira kept geraniums in the windows; however, it was dark on account of the firs and on the wrong side of town. Approaching the door one late spring afternoon, Len tripped on a flagstone and scattered examination papers all the way to the porch.

When he picked himself up, Moira was giggling in the doorway. "That was funny."

"The hell it was," said Len. "I banged my nose." He picked up his Chemistry B papers in a stiff silence; a red drop fell on the last one. "God *damn* it!"

Moira held the screen door for him, looking contrite and faintly surprised. She followed him into the bathroom. "Len, I didn't mean to laugh. Does it hurt much?"

"No," said Len, staring fiercely at his scraped nose in the mirror, although in point of fact it was throbbing like a gong.

"That's good. It was the funniest thing—I mean, funny-peculiar," she said hastily.

Len stared at her; the whites of her eyes were showing. "Is there anything the matter with you?" he demanded.

"I don't know," she said on a rising note. "Nothing like that ever happened to me before. I didn't think it was funny at all, I was worried about you, and I didn't know I was going to laugh—" She laughed again, a trifle nervously. "Maybe I'm cracking up?"

Moira was a dark-haired young woman with a placid, friendly disposition; Len had met her in his senior year at Columbia, with—looking at it impartially, which Len seldom did—regrettable results. At present, in her seventh month, she was shaped like a rather bosomy kewpie doll.

Emotional upsets, he remembered, may occur frequently during this period. He leaned to get past her belly and kissed her forgivingly. "You're probably tired. Go sit down and I'll get you some coffee."

. . . Except that Moira had never had any hysterics till now, or morning sickness, either—she burped instead—and anyhow, was there anything in the literature about fits of giggling?

After supper he marked seventeen sets of papers desultorily in red pencil, then got up to look for the baby book. There were four dog-eared paperbound volumes with smiling infants' faces on the covers, but the one he wanted wasn't there. He looked behind the bookcase and on the wicker table beside it. "Moira!"

"Hm?"

"Where the bloody hell is the other baby book?"

"I've got it."

Len went and looked over her shoulder. She was staring at a mildly obscene drawing of a fetus lying in a sort of upside-down Yoga position inside a cutaway woman's body.

"That's what he looks like," she said. "Mama."

The diagram was of a fetus at term. "What was that about your mother?" Len asked, puzzled.

"Don't be silly," she said abstractedly.

He waited, but she didn't look up or turn the page. After a while he went back to his work.

He watched her. Eventually she leafed through to the back of the book, read a few pages, and put it down.

She lighted a cigarette and immediately put it out again. She fetched up a resounding belch.

"That was a good one," said Len admiringly. Moira's belches surpassed anything ever heard in the men's locker rooms at Columbia; they shook doors and rattled windows.

Moira sighed.

Feeling tense, Len picked up his coffee cup and started toward the kitchen. He halted beside Moira's chair. On the side table was her after-dinner cup, still full of coffee: black, scummed with oil droplets, stone-cold.

"Didn't you want your coffee?"

She looked at the cup. "I did, but . . ." She paused and shook her head, looking perplexed. "I don't know."

"Well, do you want another cup now?"

"Yes, please. No."

Len, who had begun a step, rocked back on his heels. "Which, damn it?"

Her face got all swollen. "Oh, Len, I'm so mixed up," she said, and began to tremble.

Len felt part of his irritation spilling over into protectiveness. "What you need," he said firmly, "is a drink."

He climbed a stepladder to get at the top cabinet shelf which housed their liquor when they had any; small upstate towns and their school boards being what they were, this was one of many necessary precautions.

Inspecting the doleful three fingers of whisky in the bottle, Len swore under his breath. The couldn't afford a decent supply of booze, or new clothes for Moira, or— The original idea had been for Len to teach for a year while they saved enough money so that he could go back for his master's; more lately, this proving unlikely, they had merely been trying to put aside enough for summer school, and even that was beginning to look like the wildest optimism.

High-school teachers without seniority weren't supposed to be married. Or graduate physics students, for that matter.

He mixed two stiff highballs and carried them back into the living room. "Here you are. Skoal."

"Ah," she said appreciatively. "That tastes—Ugh."
She set the glass down and stared at it with her mouth
half open.

"What's the matter now?"

She turned her head carefully, as if she were afraid it
would come off. "Len, *I don't know*. Mama."

"That's the second time you've said that. What is this
all—"

"Said what?"

"Mama. Look, kid, if you're—"

"I didn't." She looked a little feverish.

"Sure you did," said Len reasonably. "Once when you
were looking at the baby book, and then again just now,
after you said ugh to the highball. Speaking of which—"

"Mama drink milk," said Moira, speaking with exag-
gerated clarity.

Moira hated milk. Len swallowed half his highball,
turned and went silently into the kitchen.

When he came back with the milk, Moira looked at it
as if it contained a snake. "Len, I didn't say that."

"Okay."

"I didn't. I didn't say mama and I didn't say that
about the milk." Her voice quavered. "And I didn't laugh
at you when you fell down."

"It was somebody else."

"It *was*." She looked down at her gingham-covered
bulge. "You won't believe me. Put your hand there. A
little lower."

Under the cloth her flesh was warm and solid against
his palm. "Kicks?" he inquired.

"Not yet. Now," she said in a strained voice. "You in
there. If you want your milk, kick three times."

Len opened his mouth and shut it again. Under his
hand there were three squirming thrusts, one after the
other.

Moira closed her eyes, held her breath and drank the
milk down in one long horrid gulp.

"Once in a great while," Moira read, "cell cleavage will
not have followed the orderly pattern that produces a

95

normal baby. In these rare cases some parts of the body will develop excessively, while others do not develop at all. This disorderly cell growth, which is strikingly similar to the wild cell growth that we know as cancer—" Her shoulders moved convulsively. "Bluh."

"Why do you keep reading that stuff if it makes you feel that way?"

"I have to," she said absently. She picked up another book from the stack. "There's a page missing."

Len attacked the last of his egg in a noncommittal manner. "Wonder it's held together this long," he said. This was perfectly just; the book had had something spilled on it, partially dissolving the glue, and was in an advanced state of anarchy; however, the fact was that Len had torn out the page in question four nights ago, after reading it carefully: the topic was "Psychoses in Pregnancy."

Moira had now decided that the baby was male, that his name was Leonardo (not referring to Len but to da Vinci), that he had informed her of these things along with a good many others, that he was keeping her from her favorite foods and making her eat things she detested, like liver and tripe, and that she had to read books of his choice all day long in order to keep him from kicking her in the bladder.

It was miserably hot; Commencement was only two weeks away, Len's students were fish-eyed and galvanic by turns. Then there was the matter of his contract for next year, and the possible opening at Oster High, which would mean more money, and the Parent-Teachers' thing tonight at which Superintendent Greer and his wife would be regally present. . . .

Moira was knee-deep in Volume I of *Der Untergang des Abendlandes,* moving her lips; an occasional guttural escaped her.

Len cleared his throat. "Moy?"

". . . *und also des tragischen*—what in God's name he means by that— What, Len?"

He made an irritated noise. "Why not try the English edition?"

"Leo wants to learn German. What were you going to say?"

Len closed his eyes for a moment. "About this PTA business—you sure you want to go?"

"Well, of *course*. It's pretty important, isn't it? Unless you think I look too sloppy—"

"No. No, damn it. But are you feeling up to it?"

There were faint violet crescents under Moira's eyes; she had been sleeping badly. "Sure," she said.

"All right. And you'll go see the sawbones tomorrow."

"I said I would."

"And you won't say anything about Leo to Mrs. Greer or anybody—"

She looked slightly embarrassed. "No. Not till he's born, I think, don't you? It would be an awful hard thing to prove—you wouldn't even have believed me if you hadn't felt him kick."

This experiment had not been repeated, though Len had asked often enough; all little Leo had wanted, Moira said, was to establish communication with his mother—he didn't seem to be really interested in Len at all. "Too young," she explained.

And still . . . Len recalled the frogs his biology class had dissected last semester. One of them had had two hearts. This disorderly cell growth . . . like a cancer. Unpredictable: extra fingers or toes—or a double helping of cortex?

"And I'll burp like a lady, if at all," Moira said cheerfully.

When the Conningtons arrived, the room was empty except for the ladies of the committee, two nervously smiling male teachers and the impressive bulk of Superintendent Greer. Card-table legs *skreeked* on the bare floor; the air was heavy with wood polish and musk.

Greer advanced, beaming fixedly. "Well, isn't this nice. How are you young folks this warm evening?"

"Oh, we thought we'd be *earlier*, Mr. Greer," said Moira with pretty vexation. She looked surprisingly schoolgirlish and chic; the lump that was Leo was hardly noticeable unless you caught her in profile. "I'll go right now and help the ladies. There must be *something* I can still do."

"No, now, we won't hear of it. But I'll tell you what you can do—you can go right over there and say hello to Mrs. Greer. I know she's dying to sit down and have a good chat with you. Go ahead now—don't worry about this husband of yours; I'll take care of him."

Moira receded into a scattering of small shrieks of pleasure, at least half of them arcing across a gap of mutual dislike.

Greer, exhibiting perfect dentures, exhaled Listerine. His pink skin looked not only scrubbed but disinfected; his gold-rimmed glasses belonged in an optometrist's window, and his tropical suit had obviously come straight from the cleaner's. It was impossible to think of Greer unshaven, Greer smoking a cigar, Greer with a smudge of axle grease on his forehead, or Greer making love to his wife.

"Well, sir, this weather . . ."

"When I think of what this valley was like twenty years ago . . ."

"At today's prices . . ."

Len listened with growing admiration, putting in comments where required; he had never realized before that there were so many absolutely neutral topics of conversation.

A few more people straggled in, raising the room temperature about half a degree per capita. Greer did not perspire, he merely glowed.

Across the room Moira was now seated chummily with Mrs. Greer, a large-bosomed woman in an outrageously unfashionable hat. Moira appeared to be telling a joke; Len knew perfectly well that it was a clean one, but he listened tensely, all the same, until he heard Mrs. Greer yelp with laughter. Her voice carried well. "Oh, that's *priceless!* Oh, dear, I *only* hope I can remember it!"

Len, who had resolutely not been thinking of ways to turn the conversation toward the Oster vacancy, stiffened again when he realized that Greer had abruptly begun to talk shop. His heart began pounding absurdly; Greer was asking highly pertinent questions in a good-humored but businesslike way—drawing Len out, and not even bothering to be Machiavellian about it.

Len answered candidly, except when he was certain he knew what the superintendent wanted to hear; then he lied like a Trojan.

Mrs. Greer had conjured up a premature pot of tea; and oblivious to the stares of the thirstier teachers present, she and Moira were hogging it, heads together, as if they were plotting the overthrow of the Republic or exchanging recipes.

Greer listened attentively to Len's final reply, which was delivered with as pious an air as if Len had been a Boy Scout swearing on the *Manual;* but since the question had been "Do you plan to make teaching your career?" there was not a word of truth in it.

He then inspected his paunch and assumed a mild theatrical frown. Len, with that social sixth sense which is unmistakable when it operates, knew that his next words were going to be: "You may have heard that Oster High will be needing a new science teacher next fall. . . ."

At this point Moira barked like a seal.

The ensuing silence was broken a moment later by a hearty scream, followed instantly by a clatter and a bone-shaking thud.

Mrs. Greer was sitting on the floor; legs sprawled, hat over her eye, she appeared to be attempting to perform some sort of orgiastic dance.

"It was Leo," Moira said incoherently. "You know she's English—she said of course a cup of tea wouldn't hurt me, and she kept telling me to go ahead and drink it while it was hot, and I couldn't—".

"No. No. Wait," said Len in a controlled fury. "What—"

"So I *drank* some. And Leo kicked up and made me burp the burp I was saving. And—"

"Oh, Christ."

"Then he kicked the tea cup out of my hand into her lap, and I wish I was *dead*."

On the following day, Len took Moira to the doctor's office where they read dog-eared copies of *The Rotarian* and *Field and Stream* for an hour.

Dr. Berry was a round little man with soulful eyes and a twenty-four-hour bedside manner. On the walls of his office, where it is customary for doctors to hang at least seventeen diplomas and certificates of membership, Berry had three; the rest of the space was filled with enlarged, colored photographs of beautiful, beautiful children.

When Len followed Moira determinedly into the consulting room, Berry looked mildly shocked for a moment, then apparently decided to carry on as if nothing *outré* had happened. You could not say that he spoke, or even whispered; he rustled.

"Now, Mrs. Connington, we're looking just fine today. How have we been feeling?"

"Just fine. My husband think's I'm insane."

"That's g— Well, that's a funny thing for him to think, isn't it?" Berry glanced at the wall midway between himself and Len, then shuffled some file cards rather nervously. "Now. Have we had any burning sensations in our urine?"

"No. Not as far as I'm— No."

"Any soreness in our stomach?"

"Yes. He's been kicking me black and blue."

Berry misinterpreted Moira's brooding glance at Len, and his eyebrows twitched involuntarily.

"The baby," said Len. "The baby kicks her."

Berry coughed. "Any headaches? Dizziness? Vomiting? Swelling in our legs or ankles?"

"No."

"All rightie. Now let's just find out how much we've gained, and then we'll get up on the examining table."

Berry drew the sheet down over Moira's abdomen as if it were an exceptionally fragile egg. He probed delicately with his fat fingertips, then used the stethoscope.

"Those X-rays," said Len. "Have they come back yet?"

"Mm-hm," said Berry. "Yes, they have." He moved the stethoscope and listened again.

"Did they show anything unusual?"

Berry's eyebrows twitched a polite question.

"We've been having a little argument," Moira said in a strained voice, "about whether this is an ordinary baby or not."

Berry took the stethoscope tubes out of his ears. He gazed at Moira like an anxious spaniel. "Now let's not worry about *that*. We're going to have a perfectly healthy, wonderful baby, and if anybody tells us differently, why, we'll just tell them to go jump in the lake, won't we?"

"The baby is absolutely normal?" Len said in a marked manner.

"Absolutely." Berry applied the stethoscope again. His face blanched.

"What's the matter?" Len asked after a moment. The doctor's gaze was fixed and glassy.

"*Vagitus uterinus,*" Berry muttered. He pulled the stethoscope off abruptly and stared at it. "No, of course it couldn't be. Now isn't that a nuisance: we seem to be picking up a radio broadcast with our little stethoscope here. I'll just go and get another instrument."

Moira and Len exchanged glances. Moira's was almost excessively bland.

Berry came confidently in with a new stethoscope, put the diaphragm against Moira's belly, listened for an instant and twitched once all over, as if his mainspring had broken. Visibly jangling, he stepped away from the table. His jaw worked several times before any sound came out.

"Excuse me," he said, and walked out in an uneven line.

Len snatched up the instrument he had dropped.

Like a bell ringing under water, muffled but clear, a tiny voice was shouting: "*You bladder-headed pill-pusher! You bedside vacuum! You fifth-rate tree surgeon! You inflated enema bag!*" A pause. "*Is that you,*"

101

Connington? Get off the line; I haven't finished with Dr. Bedpan yet."

Moira smiled, like a Buddha-shaped bomb. "Well?" she said.

"We've got to think," Len kept saying over and over.

"You've got to think." Moira was combing her hair, snapping the comb smartly at the end of each stroke. "I've had plenty of time to think, ever since it happened. When you catch up—"

Len flung his tie at the carved wooden pineapple on the corner of the footboard. "Moy, be *reasonable.* The chances against the kid kicking three times in any one-minute period are only about one in a hundred. The chances against anything like—"

Moira grunted and stiffened for a moment. Then she cocked her head to one side with a listening expression, a new mannerism of hers that was beginning to send intangible snakes crawling up Len's spine.

"What?" he asked sharply.

"He says to keep our voices down, he's thinking."

Len's fingers clenched convulsively, and a button flew off his shirt. Shaking, he pulled his arms out of the sleeves and dropped the shirt on the floor. "Look. I just want to get this straight. When he talks to you, you don't hear him shouting all the way up past your liver and lights. What—"

"You know perfectly well. He reads my mind."

"That isn't the same as—" Len took a deep breath. "Let's not get off on that. What I want to know is what is it like, do you seem to hear a real voice, or do you just know what he's telling you, without knowing how you know, or—"

Moira put the comb down in order to think better. "It isn't like hearing a voice. You'd never confuse one with the other. It's more— The nearest I can come to it, it's like remembering a voice. Except that you don't know what's coming."

"My God." Len picked his tie off the floor and abstractedly began knotting it on his bare chest. "And he sees what you see, he knows what you're thinking, he can hear when people talk to you?"

"Of course."

"But damn it, this is tremendous!" Len began to blunder around the bedroom, not looking where he was going. "They thought Macaulay was a genius. This kid isn't even *born*. Quints, schmints. I *heard* him. He was cussing Berry out like Monty Woolley."

"He had me reading *The Man Who Came to Dinner* two days ago."

Len made his way around a small bedside table by trial and error. "That's another thing. How much could you say about his . . . his personality? I mean, does he seem to know what he's doing, or is he just striking out wildly in all directions?" He paused. "Are you sure he's really conscious at all?"

Moira began, "That's silly——" and stopped. "Define consciousness," she said doubtfully.

"All right, what I really mean is—— Why am I wearing this necktie?" He ripped it off and threw it over a lampshade. "What I mean——"

"Are you sure you're really conscious?"

"Okay. You make joke, I laugh, ha. What I'm trying to ask you is, have you seen any evidence of creative thought, organized thought, or is he just . . . integrating, along the lines of, of instinctive responses. Do you——"

"I know what you mean. Shut up a minute. . . . I don't know."

"I mean, is he awake, or asleep and dreaming about us, like the Red King?"

"I don't *know*."

"And if that's it, what'll happen when he wakes up?"

Moira took off her robe, folded it neatly, and maneuvered herself between the sheets. "Come to bed."

Len got one sock off before another thought struck him. "He reads your mind. Can he read other people's?" He looked appalled. "Can he read mine?"

"He doesn't. Whether it's because he can't, I don't know. I think he just doesn't care."

Len pulled the other sock halfway down and left it

there. In another tone he said, "One of the things he doesn't care about is whether I have a job."

"No . . . He thought it was funny. I wanted to sink through the floor, but I had all I could do to keep from laughing when she fell down. . . . Len, what are we going to do?"

He swiveled around and looked at her. "Look," he said, "I didn't mean to sound that gloomy. We'll do something. We'll fix it. Really."

"All right."

Careful of his elbows and knees, Len climbed into the bed beside her. "Okay now?"

"Mm . . . Ugh." Moira tried to sit up suddenly and almost made it. She wound up propped on one elbow and said indignantly, "Oh, no."

Len stared at her in the dimness. "What?"

She grunted again. "Len, get up. All *right*. Len, *hurry!*"

Len fought his way convulsively past a treacherous sheet and staggered up, goose-pimpled and tense. "Now what?"

"You'll have to sleep on the couch. The sheets are in the bottom—"

"On that couch? Are you crazy?"

"I can't help it," she said in a thin voice. "Please don't let's argue, you'll just have to—"

"Why?"

"We can't sleep in the same bed," she wailed. "He says it's—oh!—unhygienic!"

Len's contract was not renewed. He got a job waiting on tables in a resort hotel, an occupation which pays more money than teaching future citizens the rudiments of three basic sciences, but for which Len had no aptitude. He lasted three days at it; he was then idle for a week and a half, until his four years of college physics earned him employment as a clerk in an electrical shop. His employer was a cheerfully aggressive man who assured Len that there were great opportunities in radio-TV, and firmly believed that atom-bomb tests were causing all the bad weather.

Moira, in her eighth month, walked to the country library every day and trundled a load of books home in the perambulator. Little Leo, it appeared, was working his way simultaneously through biology, astrophysics, phrenology, chemical engineering, architecture, Christian Science, psychosomatic medicine, marine law, business management, Yoga, crystallography, metaphysics and modern literature.

His domination of Moira's life remained absolute, and his experiments with her regimen continued. One week, she ate nothing but nuts and fruit washed down with distilled water; the next, she was on a diet of porterhouse steak, dandelion greens and Hadacol.

With the coming of full summer, fortunately, few of the high-school staff were in evidence. Len met Dr. Berry once on the street. Berry started, twitched, and walked off rapidly in an entirely new direction.

The diabolical event was due on or about July 29. Len crossed off each day on their wall calendar with an emphatic black grease pencil. It would, he supposed, be an uncomfortable thing at best to be the parent of a super-prodigy—Leo would no doubt be dictator of the world by the time he was fifteen, unless he was assassinated first—but almost anything would be a fair price for getting Leo out of his maternal fortress.

Then there was the day when Len came home to find Moira weeping over the typewriter, with a half-inch stack of manuscript beside her.

"It isn't anything, I'm just tired. He started this after lunch. Look."

Len turned the face-down sheaf the right way up.

> Droning. Abrasing
> the demiurge
> Hier begrimms the tale:
> Eyes undotted, grewling
> and looking, turns off
> a larm, seizes cloes.
> Stewed! Bierly a wretch!
> Pence, therefore jews we. Pons!
> Let the pants take air of themsulves.

Searches in the bottom of a hole
for soap; hawks up a good gob.
Flayed on fable, a
round cut of cat's meat . . .

The first three sheets were all like that. The fourth was a perfectly good Petrarchan sonnet reviling the current administration and the party of which Len was an assenting member.

The fifth was hand-lettered in the Cyrillic alphabet and illustrated with geometric diagrams. Len put it down and stared shakily at Moira.

"No, go on," she said. "Read the rest."

The sixth and seventh were dirty limericks, and the eighth, ninth and so on to the end of the stack were what looked like the first chapters of a rattling good historical adventure novel.

Its chief characters were Cyrus the Great, his gallon-bosomed daughter Lygea, of whom Len had never previously heard, and a one-armed Graeco-Mede adventurer named Xanthes; there were also courtesans, spies, apparitions, scullery slaves, oracles, cutthroats, lepers, priests, whoremasters and men-at-arms in magnificent profusion.

"He's decided," said Moira, "what he wants to be when he's born."

Leo refused to be bothered with mundane details. When there were eighty pages of the manuscript, Moira invented a title and by-line for it—*The Virgin of Perse-polis*, by Leon Lenn—and mailed it off to a literary agent in New York. His response, a week later, was cautiously enthusiastic and a trifle plaintive. He asked for an outline of the remainder of the novel.

Moira replied that this was impossible, trying to sound as unworldly and impenetrably artistic as she could. She enclosed the thirty-odd pages Leo had turned out in the meantime.

Nothing was heard from the agent for two weeks. At the end of this time Moira received an astonishing document, exquisitely printed and bound in imitation leather, thirty-two pages including the index, containing three times as many clauses as a lease.

This turned out to be a book contract. With it came the agent's check for nine hundred dollars.

Len tilted his mop handle against the wall and straightened carefully, conscious of every individual gritty muscle in his back. How did women do housework every day, seven days a week, fifty-two bloody weeks a year? It was a little cooler now that the sun was down, and he was working stripped to shorts and bath slippers, but he might as well have been wearing an overcoat in a Turkish bath.

The clatter of Moira's monstrous new typewriter stopped, leaving a faint hum. Len went into the living room and sagged on the arm of a chair. Moira, gleaming sweatily in a flowered housecoat, was lighting a cigarette.

"How's it going?"

She switched off the machine wearily. "Page two-eighty-nine. Xanthes killed Anaxander."

"Thought he would. How about Ganesh and Zeuxias?"

"I don't know." She frowned. "I can't figure it out. You know who it was that raped Mariamne in the garden?"

"No, who?"

"*Ganesh*."

"You're kidding."

"Nope." She pointed to the stack of typescript. "See for yourself."

Len didn't move. "But Ganesh was in Lydia, buying back the sapphire. He didn't get back till—"

"I know, I know. But he *wasn't*. That was Zeuxias in a putty nose and his beard dyed. It's all perfectly logical, the way he explains it. Zeuxias overheard Ganesh talking to the three Mongols—you remember, Ganesh thought there was somebody behind the curtain, only that was when they heard Lygea scream, and while their backs were turned—"

"All right, but for God's sake this fouls everything up. If Ganesh never went to Lydia, then he *couldn't* have had anything to do with distempering Cyrus's armor. And Zeuxias couldn't, either, because——"

"I *know*. It's exasperating. I know he's going to pull another rabbit out of the hat and clear everything up, but I don't see how."

Len brooded. "It beats me. It had to be either Ganesh or Zeuxias. Or Philomenes. But look, damn it, if Zeuxias knew about the sapphire all the time, that rules out Philomenes once and for all. Unless . . . No. I forgot about that business in the temple. Whuff. Do you think he really knows what he's doing?"

"I'm certain. Lately I've been able to tell what he's thinking even when he isn't talking to me—I mean just generally, like when he's puzzling over something, or when he's feeling mean. It's going to be something brilliant, and he knows what it is, but he won't tell me. We'll just have to wait."

"I guess." Len stood up, grunting. "You want me to see if there's anything in the pot?"

"Please."

Len wandered into the kitchen, turned the flame on under the Silex, stared briefly at the dishes waiting in the sink, and wandered out again. Since the onslaught of The Novel, Leo had relinquished his interest in Moira's diet, and she had been living on coffee. Small blessings . . .

Moira was leaning back with her eyes closed, looking very tired. "How's the money?" she asked without moving.

"Lousy. We're down to twenty-one bucks."

She raised her head and opened her eyes wide. "We couldn't be. Len, how could anybody go through nine hundred dollars that fast?"

"Typewriter. And the dictaphone that Leo thought he wanted, till about half an hour after it was paid for. We spent about fifty on ourselves, I guess. Rent. Groceries. It goes, when there isn't any coming in."

She sighed. "I thought it would last longer."

"So did I. . . . If he doesn't finish this thing in a few days, I'll have to go look for work again."

"Oh. That isn't so good."

"I know it, but——"

"All right, if it works out, fine, if it doesn't . . . He must be near the end by now." She stubbed out her cigarette abruptly and sat up, hands poised over the keyboard. "He's getting ready again. See about that coffee, will you?"

Len poured two cups and carried them in. Moira was still sitting in front of the typewriter, with a curious half-formed expression on her face.

Abruptly the carriage whipped over, muttered to itself briefly and thumped the paper up twice. Then it stopped. Moira's eyes got bigger and rounder.

"What's the matter?" said Len. He went and looked over her shoulder.

The last line on the page read:

(TO BE CONTINUED IN OUR NEXT)

Moira's hands curled into small, helpless fists. After a moment she turned off the machine.

"What?" said Len incredulously. "To be continued— What kind of talk is that?"

"He says he's bored with the novel," Moira replied dully. "He says he knows the ending, so it's artistically complete; it doesn't matter whether anybody else thinks so or not." She paused. "But he says that isn't the real reason."

"Well?"

"He's got two. One is that he doesn't want to finish the book till he's certain he'll have complete control of the money it earns."

"Well," said Len, swallowing a lump of anger, "that makes a certain amount of sense. It's his book. If he wants guarantees . . ."

"You haven't heard the other one."

"All right, let's have it."

"He wants to teach us, so we'll never forget, who the boss is in this family."

"Len, I'm awfully tired."

"Let's just go over it once more; there has to be some way— He still isn't talking to you?"

"I haven't felt anything from him for the last twenty minutes. I think he's asleep."

"All right, let's suppose he *isn't* going to listen to reason—"

"We might as well."

Len made an incoherent noise. "Okay. I still don't see why we can't write the last chapter ourselves—a few pages—"

"Who can?"

"Well, not me, but you've done a little writing— damned good, too. And if you're so sure all the clues are there— Look, if you say you can't do it, okay, we'll hire somebody. A professional writer. It happens all the time. Thorne Smith's last novel—"

"Ugh."

"Well, it *sold*. What one writer starts, another can finish."

"Nobody ever finished *The Mystery of Edwin Drood*."

"Oh, hell."

"Len, it's impossible. It *is*. Let me finish. If you're thinking we could have somebody rewrite the last part Leo did—"

"Yeah, I just thought of that."

"Even that wouldn't do any good, you'd have to go all the way back, almost to page one, it would be another story when you got through. Let's go to bed."

"Moy, do you remember when we used to worry about the law of opposites?"

"Mm?"

"The law of *opposites*. When we used to be afraid the kid would turn out to be a pick-and-shovel man with a pointy head."

"Uh. Mm."

He turned. Moira was standing with one hand on her belly and the other behind her back. She looked as if she were about to start practicing a low bow but doubted she could make it.

"What's the matter now?" he asked.

"Pain in the small of my back."

"Bad one?"

"No . . ."

"Belly hurt, too?"

She frowned. "Don't be foolish. I'm feeling for the contraction. There it comes."

"The . . . but you just said the small of your back."

"Where do you think labor pains usually start?"

The pains were coming at twenty-minute intervals, and the taxi had not arrived. Moira was packed and ready. Len was trying to set her a good example by remaining calm. He strolled over to the wall calendar, gazed at it in an offhand manner, and turned away.

"Len, I know it's only the fifteenth of July."

"Huh? I didn't say that aloud."

"You said it seven times. Sit down; you're making me nervous."

Len perched on the corner of the table, folded his arms, and immediately got up to look out the window. On the way back he circled the table in an aimless way, picked up a bottle of ink and shook it to see if the cap was on tight, stumbled over a wastebasket, carefully upended it and sat down with an air of *J'y suis, j'y reste.* "Nothing to worry about," he said firmly. "Women do this all the time."

"True."

"What for?" he demanded violently.

Moira grinned at him, then winced slightly and looked at the clock. "Eighteen minutes. This is a good one."

When she relaxed, Len put a cigarette in his mouth and lighted it in only two tries. "How's Leo taking it?"

"Isn't saying. He feels—" She concentrated. "Apprehensive. He's feeling strange and he doesn't like it. . . . I don't think he's entirely awake. Funny."

"I'm glad this is happening now," Len announced.

"So am I, but . . ."

"Look," said Len, moving energetically to the arm of her chair, "we've always had it pretty good, haven't we? Not that it hasn't been tough at times, but—you know."

"I know."

"Well, that's the way it'll be again, once this is over. I don't care how much of a superbrain he is, once he's born—you know what I mean? The only reason he's had

111

the bulge on us all this time is he could get at us and we couldn't get at him. He's got the mind of an adult, he can learn to act like one. It's that simple."

Moira hesitated. "You can't take him out to the woodshed. He's going to be a helpless baby, physically, like anybody else's. He has to be taken care of. You can't—"

"No, all right, but there are plenty of other ways. If he behaves, he gets read to. Like that."

"That's right, but—there's one other thing I thought of. You remember when you said suppose he's asleep and dreaming . . . and what happens if he wakes up?"

"Yeah."

"Well, that reminded me of something else, or maybe it's the same thing. Did you know that a fetus in the womb gets only about half the amount of oxygen in his blood that he'll have when he starts to breathe?"

Len looked thoughtful. "Forgot. Well, that's just one more thing Leo does that babies aren't supposed to do."

"Use as much energy as he does, you mean. All right, but what I'm getting at is, it can't be because he's getting more than the normal amount of oxygen, can it? I mean, he's the prodigy, not me. He must be using it more efficiently. . . . And if that's it, what happens when he's getting twice as much?"

They had soaped and shaved and disinfected her, along with other indignities, and now she could see herself in the reflector of the big delivery-table light—the image clear and bright, like everything else, but very haloed and swimmy, and looking like a statue of Sita. She had no idea how long she had been here—that was the scopolamine, probably—but she was getting pretty tired.

"Bear down," said the staff doctor kindly, and before she could answer, the pain came up like violins and she had to gulp at the tingly coldness of laughing gas. When the mask lifted she said, "I *am* bearing down," but the doctor had gone back to the other end of her and wasn't listening.

Anyhow, she had Leo. *How are you feeling?*

His answer was muddled—because of the anesthetic?

—but she didn't really need it; her perception of him was clear: darkness and pressure, impatience, a slow Satanic anger . . . and something else. Uncertainty? Apprehension?

"Two or three more ought to do it. Bear down."

Fear. Unmistakable now. And a desperate determination.

"Doctor, he doesn't want to be born!"

"Seems that way sometimes, doesn't it? Now bear down good and hard."

Tell him stop blurrrrrr too dangerrrrrrr stop I feel wowrrrr stop I tellrrrr stop.

"What, Leo, what?"

"Bear down."

Faintly, like a voice far under water: *Hurry I hate you tell him . . . sealed incubator . . . tenth oxygen, nine tenths inert gases . . . Hurry.*

The pressure abruptly relaxed.

Leo was born.

The doctor was holding him up by the heels, red, bloody, wrinkled, trailing a lumpy soft snake. The voice was still there, very small, very far away: *Too late. The same as death.* Then a hint of the old cold arrogance: *Now you'll never know . . . who killed Cyrus.*

The doctor slapped him smartly on the minuscule buttocks. The wizened, malevolent face writhed open; but it was only the angry squall of an ordinary infant that came out. Leo was gone, like a light turned off under the measureless ocean.

Moira raised her head weakly. "Give him one for me," she said.

"THING OF BEAUTY" WAS A JOY TO write because I knew all the people in it and loved them. Gordon Fish is modeled after an old fraud who undertook to cure my myopia in the forties—Chester Cohen and I journeyed out to Queens once a week to peer into the eyepieces of his exercise machines. Santa Monica is where my second wife and I lived after we decided that a professional writer didn't have to stay in New York; and she actually worked for a while in a rib joint like the one in the story. The story is satirical, but I'm serious about the drawing machine.

7

THING OF BEAUTY

≪≪≪≪≪≪≪≪≪≪≪≪≪≪≪≪≪≪≪≪≪≪≪≪≪≪≪≪

THERE WAS A TIME SLIP IN SOUTHERN CALI-
fornia at about one in the afternoon. Mr. Gordon Fish
thought it was an earthquake. He woke up confused and
sullen from his midday nap, blinking fiercely, as pink as
a spanked baby's behind, with his sandy-yellow beard
and eyebrows bristling. He got off the sofa and listened.
No screams, no rumble of falling buildings, so probably
it was all right.

He heard a knock.

Squinting uneasily, Fish went to the door. He had left
his glasses on the table, but never mind; it might be a
client, or even an investigator from the city. In which
case . . . He opened the door.

A slender man in purple was standing there. He was
small, hardly an inch taller than Gordon Fish. He said,
"Three twenty-two and a half Platt Terrace?" His face
was an oval blur; he seemed to be wearing some kind
of tight uniform, like a bellboy's—but purple?

"That's right, three twenty-two and a half, this is it,"
said Fish, straining to make out the fellow's salmon-
colored face. He caught sight of some other people standing behind him, and a shadowy bulk, like a big box of
some kind. "I don't know if you——"

"All right, fezh, bring it in," said the man, turning to
speak over his shoulder. "Bung, did we have a time finding you," he said to Fish, and pushed his way into the

115

living room. Behind him, other men in tight purple clothing came staggering under the weight of boxes, first a big one, then two smaller ones, then a *really* big one, then a clutter of smaller boxes.

"Listen, wait, there must be some mistake," said Fish, dancing out of the way. "I didn't order—"

The first man in purple looked at some papers in his hand. "Three twenty-two and a *half* Platt *Terrace?*" he said. His voice sounded slurred and angry, as if he were half drunk or had just waked up, like Fish himself.

Fish was unreasonably irritated. "I tell you I didn't order anything! I don't care if— You walk in here, into a man's home, just like— Listen! You get that out of there!" Infuriated, he rushed at two of the men who were setting down one of the smaller boxes on the sofa.

"This is the address," said the first man in a bored voice. He shoved some papers into Fish's hand. "You don't want 'em, send 'em back. We just deliver 'em." The purple men began to move toward the door.

The spokesman went out last. "Bung, are *you* a dvich!" he said, and closed the door.

Raging, Fish fumbled for his glasses. They ought to be right *there,* but the movers had upset everything. He went to the door anyway, twitching with anger. Dammit, if he could just find his glasses he'd *report* them, but . . . He opened the door. The purple-uniformed men, a little knot of them, were standing in the courtyard looking bewildered. One of them turned a salmon-colored dot of a face. "Hey, which way is . . ." Something. It sounded like "enchmire."

There was a tremor, and Fish lurched against the door frame. It felt like an earth shock, a heavy one, but when he looked up the palm trees in the street were not swaying, and the buildings were solid and firm. But the purple men were gone.

Swearing frantically to himself, Fish went back into the living room and slammed the door behind him. The biggest box was in his way. He kicked it, and a slat fell out. He kicked it again, grunting with angry satisfaction. The whole side fell down with a clatter, revealing a black-enameled panel. Fish kicked that, and bruised his toe.

"Hm," said Fish, looking at the sleek black finish of whatever it was. "Hah." It looked like money. Peering, he ran his finger along the metal. Cool and smooth. Why, it might be almost anything. Industrial machinery, worth thousands of dollars to the right party. With rising excitement, Fish ran to the table, found his glasses pushed into some magazines, and ran back, fitting the glasses over his mean little eyes.

He pulled some more slats aside. The box fell away, disclosing an oddly shaped hunk of metal with knobs, dials and switches in the top. An engraved white plate read: "TECKNING MASKIN," and then some numbers. It sounded ominous and important. Heart beating, Fish rubbed his fingers over the knurled knobs and the gleaming switch handles. There was a faint click. He had accidentally moved one switch, he saw, from "Av" to "På." The dials were lighting up, and a set of long hooked arms, like claws, were slowly drifting out over the flat empty space in the middle.

Hastily, Fish turned the switch back to "Av." The lights went out; the arms, looking disappointed, he thought, drifted back into their enclosures.

Well, it *worked,* whatever it was, which was funny, because come to think of it he hadn't plugged it in anywhere. Fish stared at the machine uneasily, rubbing his pudgy hands together. Batteries? In a machine that size? And those funny dials, the peculiar *expression* the whole thing had, and "Teckning Maskin"—not even English. There it sat, all eight or nine pieces of it, filling up his living room—one crate, he saw with a pang, blocked off his view of the TV. Suppose it was all some kind of *joke?*

The instant he thought of it, he saw the whole thing in a flash. The crates sitting here, and then in a few days the bill would come in the mail—maybe they wouldn't even take the things away until he'd paid the shipping —and all the time, the joker would be laughing himself sick. Laughing, whoever it was that had ordered the machines in Fish's name—some old enemy, or it could even be someone he thought of as a *friend.*

With tears of rage in his eyes, he rushed to the door again, flung it open and stood panting, staring around the courtyard. But there was nobody there. He slammed the door and stood looking helplessly at the crates. If they would fight *fair!* How was he going to watch *Dragnet,* and, good heavens, where was he going to talk to clients—in the *kitchen?*

"Oh!" said Fish, and he kicked another crate hard. Slats gave, and something fell out, a little yellow booklet. Fish glimpsed more black-enameled machinery inside. He bent wildly to pick up the booklet and tried to tear it across, but it hurt his hands. He threw it across the room, shouting, "Well, then!" He danced from one crate to another, kicking. Slats littered the floor. Gleaming machines stood up from the mess, some with dials, some without. Fish stopped, out of breath, and stared at them with a new bewilderment.

A trick—no, it couldn't be. Big industrial machines like that—it wasn't like ordering something from a department store. But then what? A mistake. Fish sat down on the arm of a chair and frowned, scrubbing his beard with his fingers. In the first place, now, he hadn't *signed* anything. Even if they came back tomorrow, if he could manage to get rid of say one piece, he could always claim there had been *eight* instead of *nine.* Or suppose he even got rid of all of it, discreetly of course, then when they came back he could simply deny the whole thing. Say he never heard of any machinery. Fish's nerves began to twitch. He jumped up, looked around, sat down again. Speed, speed, that was the thing. Get it over with. But what kind of machinery *was* it?

Fish frowned, squirmed, got up and sat down. Finally he went to the phone, looked up a number and dialed. He smoothed down his vest, cleared his throat musically. "Ben? This is Gordon Fish, Ben. . . . Just fine. Now, Ben—" his voice dropped confidentially—"I happen to have a client who wants to dispose of a Teckning Maskin. Eight— What? Teckning Maskin. It's machinery, Ben. T-E-C-K-N-I-N-G— No? Well, that's the name they gave me. I have it written down right here. You never— Well, that's funny. Probably some mistake. I tell you, Ben, I'll check back and see. Yes, thanks a lot. Thanks, Ben, bye-bye."

He hung up, chewing his whiskers in vexation. If Ben Abrams had never *heard* of it, then there couldn't be any market for it, not in *this* part of the country anyhow. . . . Something funny. He was beginning to have a hunch about this thing now. Something . . . He prowled around the machines, looking at them this way and that. Here was another engraved white plate; it said "TECKNING MASKIN," and under that "BANK 1," and then two columns of numbers and words: "3 Folk, 4 Djur, 5 Byggnader," and so on, a lot more. Crazy words; it didn't even look like any language he'd ever *heard* of. And then those maniacs in the purple uniforms . . . Wait a minute! Fish snapped his fingers, stopped, and stood in a pose of thought. Now what was it that fellow had said just as he was leaving? It had made him mad, Fish remembered— something like, "Boy, are you a dvich." Made him mad as a hornet; it *sounded* insulting, but what did it *mean?*

And then that kind of earthquake just before they got here—woke him up out of a sound sleep, left him feeling all funny. And then another one after they left—only *not* an earthquake, because he remembered distinctly that the palm trees didn't even tremble.

Fish ran his finger delicately over the shining curved edge of the nearest machine. His heart was thumping; his tongue came out to lick his lips. He had a feeling— no, he really *knew*—nobody would be coming back for the machines.

They were his. Yes, and there was money in them, somewhere; he could smell it. But how? What did they *do?*

He opened all the crates carefully. In one of them, instead of a machine, there was a metal box full of creamy-thick sheets of paper. They were big rectangular sheets, and they looked as if one would just about fit onto the flat center space on the biggest machine. Fish tried one, and it did.

Well, what could go wrong? Fish rubbed his fingers nervously, then turned the switch on. The dials lighted and the hooked arms drifted out, as before, but nothing else happened. Fish leaned nearer again and looked at the other controls. There was a pointer and a series of

119

marks labeled "Av," "Bank 1," "Bank 2," and so on down to "Bank 9." He moved the pointer cautiously to "Bank 1." The arms moved a little, slowly, and stopped.

What else? Three red buttons marked "Utplåna," "Torka" and "Avslå." He pressed one down, but nothing happened. Then a series of white ones, like on an adding machine, all numbered. He pressed one down at random, then another, and was about to press a third when he leaped back in alarm. The hooked arms were moving, rapidly and purposefully. Where they passed over the paper, thin dark-gray lines were growing.

Fish leaned closer, his mouth open and his eyes bulging. The little points under the ends of the arms were riding smoothly over the paper, leaving graceful lines behind them. The arms moved, contracted on their little pivots and springs, swept this way and that, lifted slightly, dropped again and moved on. Why, the machine was drawing—drawing a picture while he watched! There was a face forming under the arm over on the right, then a neck and shoulder—kind of a sappy-looking man, it was, like a Greek statue. Then over here on the left, at the same time, another arm was drawing a bull's head, with some kind of flowers between the horns. Now the man's body—he was wearing one of those Greek togas or whatever you call them—and the back of the bull curving around up on top. And now the man's arm, and the bull's tail, and now the other arm, and the bull's hind legs.

There it was. A picture of a man throwing flowers at this bull, who was kind of leaping and looking at the man over his shoulder. The arms of the machine stopped moving, and then pulled back out of sight. The lights went out, and the switch clicked by itself back to "Av."

Fish took the paper and looked it over, excited but a little disappointed. He didn't know anything about *art,* of course, but he knew this was no good—all flat looking and kind of simple, like a kid would draw. And that bull —whoever saw a bull dancing like that? With flowers between its horns? Still, if the machine would draw this, maybe it would draw something better; he couldn't quite see the angle. Where would you sell drawings, even good ones? But it was there, somewhere. Exhibit the machine, like in a fair of science and industry? No, his mind hurriedly buried the thought—too exposed, too many questions. Heavens, if Vera found out he was still alive, or if the police in Scranton . . .

Drawings. A machine that made drawings. Fish looked at it, all eight lumpy black-enameled massive pieces of it scattered around his living room. It seemed like a lot of machinery just to make *drawings*. He admitted it: he was disappointed. He had expected, well, metal stampings or something like that, something real. Crash, bang, the big metal jaw comes down, and tink, the bright shaped piece falls out into the basket. There was machinery for you; but this . . .

Fish sat back and pondered, twitching the paper disapprovingly between his fingers. Things were always letting him down like this. Really, his best line was marriage. He had been married five times, and always made a little profit out of it. He smoothed the vest down over his suety front. Between times, he turned to whatever was handy—marital counseling some years, or gave life readings if he could get enough clients, or naturopathy. It all depended. But somehow every time it looked as if he had a real gold mine, it slipped out from under his hand. He reddened with discomfort as he thought of the one winter he had been forced to go to work in a *shoe store*. . . . Having this house had softened him up, too, he had been getting lazy—just a client or two a week for life readings. He ought to be getting busy, working up new contacts before his money ran out.

The thought of poverty made him ravenously hungry, as it always did. He kneaded his stomach. Time for lunch. He got his jacket hurriedly, and, as an afterthought, rolled up the drawing—it would not fold—and tucked it under his arm.

He drove to the barbecue place three blocks down the boulevard where he had been eating a lot of his meals lately, to save funds. The counterman was a young fellow named Dave, lean and pale, with a lock of straight dark hair falling over his forehead. Fish had got into friendly conversation with him and knew he was going to art

121

school nights, over in Pasadena. Fish had tried to get him over for a life reading, but the youngster had said frankly that he "didn't believe in it" in such an honest and friendly way that Fish bore him no ill-will.

"Bowl o' chile, Dave," he said cheerfully, hoisting himself up on a stool with the rolled drawing precariously on his lap. His feet dangled; the paper was squeezed tight between his vest and the counter.

"Hello, Doc. Coming up."

Fish hunched forward over the bowl, loosening his collar. The one other customer paid and left.

"Say, Dave," said Fish indistinctly, munching, "like to get your opinion of something. Unh." He managed to get the rolled paper free and opened it on the counter. "What do you think—is it any good?"

"Say," said Dave, coming nearer. "Where'd you get *that?*"

"Mm. Nephew of mine," Fish answered readily. "He wants me to advise him, you know, if he should go on with it, because——"

"Go on with it! Well, say. Where's he been studying, anyhow?"

"Oh, just by himself, you know—back home." Fish took another mouthful. "Ver' bright boy, you understand, but——"

"Well, if he learned to draw like that all by himself, why he must be a world-beater."

Fish forgot to chew. "You really mean it?"

"Why, sure. Listen, are you sure he drew this himself, Doc?"

"Oh, certainly." Fish waved the imputation of dishonesty away. "Ver' honest boy, I know'm well. No, 'f he tells me he drew it, why——" he swallowed—"he drew it. But now don't fool me, is it—do you really think it's as *good*——"

"Well, I tell you the truth, when I first saw it, *I* thought Picasso. You know, his classical period. Of course I see now it's different, but, my gosh, it's good. I mean, if you want *my* opinion, why——"

Fish was nodding to indicate that this only confirmed his own diagnosis. "M-hm. M-hm. Well, I'm glad to hear you say it, son. You know, being a relative of the boy, I thought— Of course, I'm very impressed. Very impressed. I thought of Pricasso, too, same as you. Of course, now from the money end of it—" he wagged his head dolefully—"you know and I know . . ."

Dave scratched his head under the white cap. "Oh, well, he ought to be able to get commissions, all right. I mean, if I had a line like that—" He traced in air the outline of the man's lifted arm.

"Now, when you say *commissions,*" Fish said, squirming with eagerness.

"Oh, well, you know, for portraits, or industrial designs or, you know, whatever he wants to go in for." Dave shook his head in admiration, staring at the drawing. "If this was only in color."

"How's that, Dave?"

"Why, I was just thinking—see, there's a competition up in San Gabriel for a civic center mural. Ten-thousand-dollar prize. Now I don't know, it might not win, but why don't you have him render this in color and send it in?"

"Color," said Fish blankly. The machine wouldn't color anything, he was sure. He could get a box of water color paints, but . . . "Well, now, the fact is," he said, hastily revolving ideas, "you know, the boy is laid up. Hurt his hand—oh, not serious," he said reassuringly (Dave's mouth had fallen into an *O* of sympathy), "but won't be able to draw any more pictures for a while. It's a shame, he could use the money, you know, for doctor bills." He chewed and swallowed. "Tell you, this is just a wild idea, now, but why couldn't you color it up and send it in, Dave? Course if it doesn't win, I couldn't pay you, but—"

"Well, gee, I don't know how he'd like that, Doc. I mean, suppose he'd have something else in mind, like some other color scheme altogether. You know, I wouldn't like to—"

"I'll take full responsibility," said Fish firmly. "Don't you worry about that, and if we win, why I'll see that you're paid handsomely for your work, Dave. Now there, how's that?"

"Well, sure, then, Doc. I mean, sure," said Dave, nodding and blushing. "I'll do it tonight and tomorrow, and get it right off in the mail. Okay? Then—oh, uh, one thing, what's your nephew's name?"

"George Wilmington," said Fish at random. He pushed the cleaned chile bowl away. "And, uh, Dave, I believe I'll have an order of ribs, with French fries on the side."

Fish went home with a vastly increased respect for the machine. The civic center competition, he was positive, was in the bag. Ten thousand dollars! For one drawing! Why, there was millions in it! He closed and locked the front door carefully behind him, and pulled down the Venetian blinds to darken the gloomy little living room still further. He turned on the lights. There the machine still was, all eight gleaming pieces of it, scattered around on the floor, the furniture, everywhere. He moved excitedly from one piece to another, caressing the slick black surfaces with his palm. All that expensive machinery—all his!

Might as well put it through its paces again, just to see. Fish got another sheet of creamy paper from the stack, put it in position, and turned the switch to "Pä." He watched with pleasure as the dials lighted, the hooked arms drifted out and began to move. Lines grew on the paper: first some wavy ones at the top—could be anything. And farther down, a pair of long, up-curved lines, kind of like handlebars. It was like a puzzle, trying to figure out what it was going to be.

Under the wavy lines, which Fish now perceived to be hair, the pointer drew eyes and a nose. Meanwhile the other one was gliding around the outline of what, it became clear in a moment, was a bull's head. Now here came the rest of the girl's face, and her arm and one leg—not bad, but kind of beefy—and now the bull's legs, sticking out all different ways, and then, whoops, it wasn't a bull: there was the whatyoumaycallum with the teats swinging; it was a cow. So, a girl riding on a cow, with flowers between its horns like before.

Fish looked at the drawing in disappointment. People and cows—was that all the thing could *do?*

124

He scrubbed his beard in vexation. Why, for heaven's sake, suppose somebody wanted a picture of something *besides* bulls and people? It was ridiculous—eight big pieces of machinery . . .

Wait a minute. "Don't go off half cocked, Gordon," he told himself aloud. That was what Florence, his second, always used to say, except she always called him "Fishy." He winced with discomfort at the memory. Well, anyway, he noticed now that the same buttons he had pressed down before were still down. That must have something to do with it. Struck by another thought, he trotted over and looked at the machine marked "Bank 1." Now this list here, number 3 was "Folk," and number 4 was "Djur." Those were the numbers he had pressed on the big machine, so . . . maybe "folk" meant *people,* and "djur," why, that might be some crazy word for *bulls.* Then if he pressed a different set of buttons, why, the machine would have to draw something else.

In fifteen minutes he verified that this was the case. Pressing down the first two buttons, "Land" and "Planta," gave him drawings of outdoor scenes, just hills and trees. "Folk" was people, and "Djur" seemed to be animals; now he got goats or dogs instead of bulls. "Byggnader" was buildings. Then it got more complicated.

A button marked "Arbete" gave him pictures of people at work; one labeled "Kärlek" produced scenes of couples kissing—all in the kind of Greek-looking clothes —and the landscapes and buildings were sort of vague and dreamy. Then there was a whole row of buttons under the heading "Plats," and another headed "Tid," that seemed to control the time and place of the pictures. For instance, when he pressed "Egyptisk" and "Gammal," along with "Folk," "Byggnader" and, on a hunch, "Religion," he got a picture of some priests in Egyptian headdresses bowing in front of a big statue of Horus. Now *there* was something!

The next day he nailed up the crates again, leaving the tops loose so that he could remove them whenever he wanted to use the machines. In the process, he came across the little yellow booklet he had thrown away. There were diagrams in it, some of which made sense and some didn't, but the printing was all in the same unfamiliar language. Fish put the booklet away in a bureau drawer, under an untidy heap of clothes, and forgot about it. Grunting and sweating, he managed to push the smaller crates into corners and rearranged the furniture so there was room to put the big one against the wall. It still looked terrible, but at least he could get around, and have clients in, and he could see the TV again.

Every day he ate lunch at the barbecue place, or at least stopped in, and every day, when Dave saw him come in, he shook his head. Then all afternoon he would sit with a glass of beer, or maybe a plate of nuts or fudge, watching the machine draw. He used up all the paper in the stack and started turning them over to use the other sides.

But where was the money coming from? After some thought, Fish built a simple magic-writing box, and used it with his Egyptian drawings—he had a dozen, all of different gods, but after the first one the machine didn't draw any priests—to show clients what they had been up to in previous incarnations. He began to get a little more business, and once or twice his instinct told him he could raise the fee on account of the drawings, but that was only pocket money. He knew there was *millions* in it, he could almost taste it, but where?

Once it occurred to him that maybe he could take out a patent on the machine and sell it. Trouble with that was, he didn't have any idea how the thing worked. It seemed like the little machines must have pictures inside, or pieces of pictures, and the big machine put them together—how? Fuming with impatience, Fish took the big crate apart again, moved furniture out of the way, and fumbled at the smooth black side of the machine to see if there was any way of opening it up.

After a moment his fingers found two shallow depressions in the metal; he pushed experimentally, then pressed upward, and the side plate of the machine came off in his hands.

It weighed almost nothing. Fish put it aside, staring doubtfully into the interior of the machine. It was all dark in there, nothing but a few very tiny specks of light, like mica dust hanging motionless. No wires, no nothing. Fish got a sheet of paper and put it in position, and turned the machine on. Then he squatted down. The tiny specks of light seemed to be moving, circling slowly around one another in time to the motion of the drawing arms. It was darker in there, and looked farther away, somehow, than it had any right to.

Holding the front of the machine, Fish touched another shallow depression and, without really meaning to, he pushed upward. The whole front of the machine fell off, and the other side with it.

He sprawled backward frantically to get out of the way, but the top of the machine didn't fall. It stayed there, rock-steady, although there was nothing holding it up but the back panel.

And underneath, nothing. No framework, just the thick darkness, with the little stars going slowly around as the machine drew.

Fish hastily picked up the front and side panels and put them back. They slid easily and perfectly into place, and fitted so closely that he couldn't see any line between them.

After that, he put the crate back together and never tried to look inside the machine again.

Dave hurried around the end of the counter to him. "Doc! Where you been?" He was drying his hands on his apron and grinning nervously, with a sort of poleaxed expression around his eyes. A customer around the other side of the counter looked up, then went on chewing with his mouth open.

"Well, I had quite a lot of things to do," Fish began automatically. Then he began to feel excited. "Say! You don't mean—"

Dave fished a long white envelope out of his back pocket. "Came yesterday! Look here!" The envelope crackled in his nervous fingers. He pulled out a folded letter, and Fish seized it. Dave looked over his shoulder, breathing heavily, as he read.

DEAR MR. WILMINGTON:

It is my very great pleasure to inform you that your design has been awarded the First Prize in the San Gabriel Civic Center Mural Competition. In the opinion of the judges, the classic simplicity of your entry, together with its technical mastery, made it far superior to anything else submitted.

Enclosed please find our check for three thousand dollars ($3,000.00). . . .

"Where?" cried Fish, looking up.

"Right here," said Dave, with a grin that looked painful. He held up a salmon-colored strip of paper. The red-printed lettering read: "EXACTLY 3,000.00 DOLLARS*****."

Fish hugged Dave, who hugged him back, and then looked at the letter again.

. . . the remainder to be paid when the design is executed to the satisfaction of the Committee. . . .

"Executed?" said Fish, with a sinking feeling. "What's that mean? Dave, what's he mean here, where he says—"

"When he paints the mural on the wall. Gee, Doc, I just can't tell you—"

"Who?"

"Your nephew. George Wilmington. See, when he paints the mural—"

"Oh," said Fish. "Oh. Well, you see, Dave, the fact *is*—"

Dave's long face grew solemn. "Oh, gosh, I never thought. You mean he's not well enough to draw yet?"

Fish shook his head mournfully. "No, sir. It's a terrible shame, Dave, but—" He folded the check absently and slipped it into his pocket.

"I thought you said, I mean, it wasn't serious or anything. . . ."

Fish continued to shake his head. "Turned out, there was more to it than they thought. It looks like now, they just don't know when he'll ever be able to draw again."

"Oh, Doc," said Dave, stricken.

"That's the way it is. These things—the doctors don't know as much about 'em as they'd like you to think, Dave." Fish went on staring fiercely at the letter, barely listening to the sound of his own voice. *To be paid when the design is executed* . . .

"Look here," he said, interrupting Dave's murmurs of commiseration. "It don't say *who* has to execute it, now does it? Notice right there? Says 'when the design is executed.' "

"How about a glassa water over here?" called the customer.

"Coming right up, sir. Look, Doc, I think you got an idea." He retired sidewise toward the counter, still talking. "You know, anybody could scale that up and do the actual painting—any competent artist, I mean. Gee, I'd do it myself, I mean if George didn't care. And if it was all right with the committee, why, you know, it would be an opportunity for me." He gave the customer his water, mopped the counter blindly and came back.

Fish leaned over the counter, beard in hand, frowning. "Wilmington" was just a name. Dave could take the part, just as well as not, and it would be a lot better in one way, because then Fish himself could stay out of sight. But, whoops, if they did that, then Dave would *be* Wilmington, and he might want to take off on his own. . . .

"Well, Dave," he said, "are you a *good* artist?"

Dave looked embarrassed. "Gee, Doc, you put me on the spot, but, well, anyway, they liked how I rendered the design, didn't they? See, I used a color scheme of deep aqua and a kind of buff, with accents of rose, you know, to make it cheerful? And, gee, if I did it on the paper, I could do it on a wall."

"Sold!" said Fish heartily, and clapped Dave on the shoulder. "George don't know it yet, but he just got himself an assistant!"

129

A slim female figure popped up at him suddenly from beside a potted palm. "Mr. Wilmington? If I could just have a moment . . ."

Fish paused, one hand going to his chin in the old gesture, although he had shaved off the beard over a year ago. He felt exposed without it, and his features tended to twitch when he was startled like this. "Why, yes, uh, miss . . ."

"My name is Norma Johnson. You don't know me, but I have some drawings here . . ."

She was carrying a big black portfolio fastened with tapes. Fish sat down beside her and looked at the drawings. They looked all right to him, but skimpy, like the kind of thing he turned out mostly himself. What he *liked* was pictures with some meat to them, like Norman Rockwell, but the one time he had set the machine to draw something like that, his agent—the first one, Connolly, that crook!—had told him there was no market for "genre stuff."

The girl's fingers were trembling. She was very neat and pale, with black hair and big expressive eyes. She turned over the last drawing. "Are they any good?" she asked.

"Well, now, there's a good deal of spirit there," said Fish comfortably. "And a very fine sense of design."

"Could I ever be successful at it?"

"Well . . ."

"See, the thing is," she said rapidly, "my Aunt Marie wants me to stay here in San Francisco and come out next season. But I don't want to. So she agreed, if you said I had real talent, that she would send me abroad to study. But if you didn't, I'd give up."

Fish looked at her intently. Her fingernails were short but looked cared for. She was wearing a simple white blouse and a little blue jacket and skirt; there was a whiff of woodsy perfume. Fish smelled money.

He said, "Well, my dear, let me put it this way. Now you could go to Europe and spend a lot of money—ten thousand, twenty thousand dollars." She watched him without blinking. "Fifty thousand," said Fish delicately.

130

"But what would be the point of it? Those fellows ove
there don't know as much as they'd like you to think."

She fumbled blindly for her purse and gloves. "I see.
She started to get up.

Fish put a pudgy hand on her arm. "Now what
would suggest," he said, "why don't you come and stud
with me for a year instead?"

Her pale face lengthened. "Oh, Mr. Wilmington
would you?"

"Well, anybody with as much talent as these draw
ings—" Fish patted the portfolio on her knee—"why, w
have to do something, because—"

She stood up excitedly. "Will you come tell that to
Aunt Marie?"

Fish smoothed down the front of his pink shirt. "Why
gladly, my dear, gladly."

"She's right here in the lounge."

Fish followed her and met Aunt Marie, who was a
handsome woman of about fifty, plump but beautifully
tailored in brown linen. They agreed that Norma would
take a studio near Mr. Wilmington's home in Santa
Monica, and that Mr. Wilmington would look in several
times a week and give her the full benefit of his great
experience, in return for ten thousand dollars per an-
num. It was, as Fish pointed out to them, less than half
the amount he usually got now for major commissions;
but, never mind, every little bit helped. Murals, institu-
tional advertising, textile designs, private sales to collectors—my God, how it was rolling in!

The only thing that really worried him was the machine itself. He kept it now in a locked inner room of
the house he was renting—twenty rooms, furnished, ter-
rific view of the Pacific Ocean, lots of room for parties
—and up to a point he could work it like a kiddy car.
One time or another, he had figured out and memorized
every one of the dozens of labeled buttons on the "Bank"
machines, and just by combining the right ones, he could
get any kind of a drawing he wanted. For instance, that
commission for stained glass for a church—"Religion,"
"People," "Palestine," "Ancient," and there you were.

The trouble was, the machine wouldn't draw the same

131

hing twice in a row. On that church window job, he got
ne picture of Christ and then couldn't get another, no
matter how long he tried, so he had to fill out with saints
nd martyrs. The church put up a beef, too. Then some-
mes at night, for his own amusement, he used to put
he machine through its paces—for instance, set it for
Historical figures" and "Romantisk," which seemed to
·e the machine's name for the present era, and then push
he button marked "Överdriva," and watch the famous
aces come out with big cartoony noses, and teeth like
icket fences.

Or he would set it for "Love," and then various inter-
·sting times and places—ancient Rome gave him some
·picy ones, and Samoa was even better.

But every time he did this, the machine turned out
ewer drawings; and finally it wouldn't do any more like
hat at all.

Was there some kind of a censor built into the thing?
Did it *disapprove* of him?

He kept thinking of the funny way those men in pur-
·le uniforms had delivered the thing. They had the right
address, but the wrong . . . time? Whatever it was, he
knew the machine wasn't intended for him. But who was
t meant for? What was a "dvich"?

There were eight pieces—six banks, the master machine, and one which he had discovered would enlarge
any detail of a drawing to almost full size. He could
handle all that. He could manage the controls that gov-
erned the complexity or simplicity of a drawing, gave it
more or less depth, changed its style and mood. The only
buttons he wasn't sure of were the three red ones marked
"Utplåna," "Torka," and "Avslå." None of them seemed
to *do* anything. He had tried all three both ways, and
they didn't seem to make any difference. In the end he
left them the way they had been: "Torka" down, the
other two up, for lack of any better idea. But big and
red like that, they must be important.

He found them mentioned in the booklet, too:
"*Utplåna en teckning, press knappen 'Utplåna.' Av-
*ägsna ett mönster från en bank efter anvädning, press

knappen 'Torka.' Avslå en teckning innan slutsatsen, press knappen 'Avslå.' "

Press knappen, press knappen, that must be "push button." But *when?* And that business about "mönster," that made him a little nervous. He had been pretty lucky so far, figuring out how to work the whole machine without any accidents. Suppose there was still something that could go wrong—suppose the booklet was a *warning?*

He prowled restlessly around the empty house—empty, and untidy, because he wouldn't have any servants in the place. You never knew who was going to spy on you. A woman came in two days a week to clean the place up—all but the locked room—and once in a while he'd bring a couple of girls up for a party, but he always threw them out the next morning. He was busy, all right, seeing a lot of people, traveling around, but he'd had to drop all his old friends when he decided to become Wilmington, and he didn't dare make any new ones for fear of giving himself away. Besides, everybody was out for something. The fact was, dammit, he wasn't *happy.* What the hell good was all the money he was making, all the things he'd bought, if they didn't make him happy? Anyhow, pretty soon now that oil stock would start paying off—the salesman had assured him that the drillers were down within a few hundred feet of oil right now—and then he'd be a millionaire; he could retire—move to Florida or someplace.

He paused in front of his desk in the library. The booklet was still there, lying open. The thing was, even suppose that was some language anybody had ever heard of, who would he dare show it to? Who could he trust?

An idea occurred to him, and he leaned over, staring at the yellow pages with their incomprehensible text. After all, he could already figure out some of the words; he didn't have to show anybody the whole book, or even a whole sentence. . . . Then there was that information business that came with his deluxe set of the Encyclopaedia Britannica—he ought to have it right here somewhere. Fish hunted in the file drawers and finally came up with a folder and a sheet of gummed yellow stamps.

Grunting, he sat down at the desk, and after much

cigar-chewing, scribbling and crossing out, he typed the following:

DEAR SIRS:
Kindly inform me as to what language the enclosed words are, and also what they mean. Kindly give this matter your best attention, as I am in a hurry.

On a separate sheet he wrote all the doubtful words from the paragraph about the red buttons, cannily mixing them up so no one could guess what order they came in. Feeling a little foolish, he carefully drew in all the tiny circles and dots. Then he addressed an envelope, stuck one of the yellow stamps to his letter, and mailed the thing off before he could regret it.

"My rhetorical question is," said Fish craftily to the young physicist, shouting over the hum of cocktail-party conversation, "purely in interest of science, could you make a machine that would draw?" He beamed over his glasses at the horn-rimmed blur of the young man's face. He had had three martinis, and whew! he was floating. But fully in command of his senses, of course.

"Well, draw what? If you mean charts and graphs, sure, or something like a pantograph, to enlarge—"

"No, no. Draw *beau'ful* pictures." The last word sprayed a little. Fish rocked forward and back again. "Purely rhetorical question." He put his glass down with precision on a passing tray and took another one, which spilled icy liquid down his wrist. He gulped to save it.

"Oh. Well, in that case, no. I would say not. I assume you mean it would originate the drawings, not just put out what was programmed into it. Well, that would mean, in the first place, you'd have to have an incredibly big memory bank. Say if you wanted the machine to draw a horse, it would have to know what a horse looks like from every angle and in every position. Then it would have to select the best one out of say ten or twenty billion—and then draw it in proportion with whatever else is in the drawing, and so on. Then, for God's sake,

134

if you wanted *beauty,* too, I suppose it would have to consider the relation of every part to every other part, on some kind of esthetic principle. *I* wouldn't know how to go about it."

Fish, thick-fingered, probed for his olive. "Say it's impossible, hey?" he asked.

"Well, with present techniques, anyhow. I guess we'll be staying out of the art business for another century or two." The blur smiled and lifted its highball glass.

"Ah," said Fish, putting a hand on the young man's lapel to support himself and keep the other from moving out of the corner. "Now, suppose you had machine like that. Now, suppose that machine kept forgetting things. What would be the reason for that?"

"Forgetting things?"

"What I said." With a disastrous sense that he was talking too much, Fish was about to go on, but a sudden hand on his arm forestalled him. It was one of the bright young men—beautiful suit, beautiful teeth, beautiful handkerchief in pocket. "Mr. Wilmington, I just wanted to say, what an absolutely marvelous piece of work that new mural is. One enormous foot. I don't know what the significance is, but the draftsmanship is marvelous. We must get you on *File Seven* some afternoon and have you explain it."

"Never go on television," said Fish, frowning. He had been fending off invitations like this one for almost a year.

"Oh, too bad. Nice to have met you. Oh, by the way, somebody asked me to tell you there's a phone call for you over there." He waved his arm and drifted away.

Fish excused himself and set an adventurous course across the room. The phone was lying on one of the side tables giving him a black look. He picked it up jauntily. "Hello-o."

"Dr. Fish?"

Fish's heart began to knock. He put the martini glass down. "Who's that?" he demanded blankly.

"This is Dave Kinney, Doc."

Fish felt a wave of relief. "Oh, Dave. I thought you

135

were in Boston. Or, I suppose you *are,* but the connection—"

"I'm right here in Santa Monica. Look, Doc, something's come up that—"

"What? what're you doing here? Now I hope you haven't quit school, because—"

"This is summer vacation, Doc. Look, the fact is, I'm here in Norma Johnson's studio."

Fish stood with the sweaty black phone in his hand and said nothing. Silence hummed in the wires.

"Doc? Mrs. Prentice is here too. We've been kind of talking things over, and we think you ought to come over and explain a few things."

Fish swallowed, with difficulty.

"Doc, you hear me? I think you ought to come over. *They're* talking about calling the police, but I wanted to give you a chance first, so—"

"I'll be right over," said Fish hoarsely. He hung up the phone and stood bemused, with his hand to his flushed forehead. Oh, Lord, three—no, four—martinis and this had to happen! He felt dizzy. Everybody seemed to be standing at a slight angle on the Kelly-green carpet, all the bright young men in glossy summer jackets and the pastel women in cocktail dresses with bright, phony smiles on their faces. What did they care if all he could get out of the machine any more was parts of bodies? His last one a big clenched fist, and now a foot, and don't you think the committee didn't beef. They beefed plenty but they had to take it, because they had already announced the commission. Now this morning his agent had called up. Some church group in Indiana, they wanted sample sketches. So it was all going down the drain while he watched, and now this. Dave, good God, you'd think at least he would stay stuck off in Boston, and how the *hell* did he ever run into Norma?

One of the newspaper reporters turned away from the free lunch and planted himself in Fish's path as he lurched toward the door. "Oh, Mr. Wilmington, what would you say was the real significance of that foot?"

"Gow my way," said Fish, staggering around him.

He took a cab home, told the driver to wait, ducked

in for a quick shower and a cup of black coffee, and came out again, shaky but not as drunk as before. Those God-damn cocktails . . . He never used to get like this when he just drank beer. Things were better back on Platt Terrace; how did he ever get mixed up in this crazy art game anyway?

His stomach felt hollow. He hadn't eaten any lunch, he remembered. Well, too late now. He braced himself and rang the bell.

Dave opened the door. Fish greeted him with cries of pleasure, shaking his limp hand. "Dave, boy! Good to see you! How long has it been, anyway?" Without waiting for a reply, he bustled on into the room. It was a gray, windowless place that always made him nervous; instead of a roof there was one big slanting skylight, high overhead; the light filtered down cool and colorless through the translucent panes. There was an easel in one corner and some drawings pinned up on the otherwise bare walls. Down at the far end, Norma and her aunt were sitting on the red-padded bench. "Norma, how are you, honey? And Mrs. Prentice—now this is a real pleasure!"

That wasn't hard to say—she really did look good in that new dark-blue suit. He could tell he was projecting the old charm, and he thought he saw her eyes glint with pleasure. But it was only for an instant, and then her expression hardened. "What's this I hear about your not even coming to see Norma?" she demanded.

Fish registered deep surprise. "Why . . . why, Norma, didn't you explain to your aunt? Excuse me a minute." He darted over to the drawings on the wall. "Well. Now these are really excellent, Norma; there's a good deal of improvement here. The symmetry, you see, and the dynamic *flow*—"

Norma said, "Those are three months old." She was wearing a man's shirt and dungarees, and looked as if she might have been crying recently, but her face was carefully made up.

"Well, honey, I wanted to come back, even after what you said. I did come around, twice, you know, but you didn't answer your bell."

137

"That's not so."

"Well, I s'pose you might have been out," said Fish cheerfully. He turned to Mrs. Prentice. "Norma was upset, you know." His voice dropped. "About a month after we started, she told me to get out and not come back."

Dave had drifted back across the room. He sat down beside Norma without comment.

"The idea of taking the poor child's money for *nothing*," said Mrs. Prentice vehemently. "Why didn't you give it back?"

Fish pulled up a folding chair and sat down close to her. "Mrs. Prentice," he said quietly, "I didn't want Norma to make a mistake. I told her, now, if you'll live up to your agreement and study with me for a year, I said, and then if you're not satisfied, why, I'll gladly refund ev-ry cent."

"You weren't doing me any *good*," said Norma, with a hysterical note in her voice.

Fish gave her a look of sorrowful patience.

"He'd just come in, and look at my work, and say something like, 'This has a good feeling,' or 'The symmetry is good,' or some *meaningless* thing like that. I was getting so nervous I couldn't even *draw*. That's when I wrote you, Aunt Marie, but you were in Europe. My golly, I had to do something, didn't I?" Her hands were clenched white in her lap. "There, dear," Mrs. Prentice murmured, and gave her arm a little squeeze.

"I've been going to day classes at the Art Center," Norma said between her teeth. "It was all I could *afford*."

Mrs. Prentice's eyes sparkled with indignation. "Mr. Wilmington, I don't think we have to discuss this much longer. I want you to return the money I paid you. I think it's disgraceful, a well-known artist like you, *stooping—*"

"Mrs. Prentice," said Fish, pitching his voice lower again, "if it wasn't for my faith in Norma's great future as an artist, why I would hand you over ev-ry cent. But as it is she would be making a great mistake, so I suggest again—"

"Doc," said Dave rudely, "you give her back that money pretty damn quick." He leaned forward to speak to the older woman. "You want to know what his real name is, it's Fish. Anyhow, it was when I met him. This whole thing is just a joke. Why, he's no artist. The real George Wilmington is his nephew; he's an invalid out in Wisconsin. Doc here has just been fronting for him, because he's too sick to stand the publicity and all. Now, that's the truth. Or as much of it as I know."

Fish said sorrowfully, "Dave, is this the thanks I get for putting you through art school?"

"You got me the scholarship, but it didn't cost you anything. I found that out from the director. I guess you just wanted to put me out of the way so I wouldn't talk too much. Hell, Doc, that was all right. But when I met Norma here, over at your place yesterday——"

"What? When was that?"

"About ten o'clock." Fish winced; he had been in bed with a bad head and hadn't answered the bell; if he'd only known! "You weren't home, so we got to talking, and—well, pretending to be your nephew, that's one thing, but when you promise to teach somebody when you can't even draw a line yourself!"

Fish raised a hand. "Now, Dave, there's a thing or two you don't know. You say my real name is Fish. Now did you ever see my birth certificate, or did you know anybody that knew me as a child? How do you know my name is Fish?"

"Well, you *told* me."

"That's right, Dave, I did. And you say the real George Wilmington is an invalid out in Wisconsin. You ever see him, Dave? You ever been in Wisconsin?"

"Well, no, but——"

"Neither have I. No, Dave——" he lowered his voice solemnly—"every single thing I told you about that was just a lie. And I admit it." Now here was the place for a tear. Fish turned his mind to the creditors, the trouble with the machine, the oil stock salesman who had gone south with his money, the lawyers who were robbing him blind trying to get it back, the ungratefulness of everybody. A warm trickle crept out onto his cheek and, lowering his head, he knuckled it away.

"Well, what?" said Dave, bewildered.

Fish said with an effort, "I had reasons. Certain reasons. You know, it's . . . it's hard for me to talk about 'em. Mrs. Prentice, I wonder if I could just see you alone for a minute."

She was leaning forward a little, looking at him with concern. It never failed—a woman like that couldn't stand to see a man cry.

"Well, it's certainly all right with *me,*" said Norma, getting up. She walked away, and Dave followed her. After a moment the door closed behind them.

Fish blew his nose, dabbed unobtrusively at his eyes, straightened up bravely and put his handkerchief away. "Mrs. Prentice, I don't s'pose you know that I'm a widower." Her eyes widened a little. "It's true, I lost my dear wife. I don't usually talk about it, as a matter of fact, but somehow—I don't know if you've been bereaved yourself, Mrs. Prentice."

She said nervously, "Didn't Norma tell you? I'm a widow, Mr. Wilmington."

"No!" said Fish. "Isn't that strange? I felt something —you know, a *vibration.* Well, Mrs. Prentice—can I call you Marie?—you know, after my loss—" time for another tear now; once started, they came easily—"I just went to pieces. I don't excuse myself, I didn't want to live. I couldn't touch a pencil for a year. And even to this day I can't draw a line if there's anybody watching me. Now—there's the reason for this whole mixup. That business about my nephew and all, that was just a story I made up to make things a little easier. That's what I *thought.* I don't know, I'm so clumsy where it takes a little tact. I'm just like a bull in a china closet, Marie. And that's the whole story." He sat back, blew his nose vigorously again.

Mrs. Prentice's eyes were moist, but her handsome face had a wary expression. "I honestly don't know what to think, Mr. Wilmington. You say you can't draw in public—"

"Call me George. You see, it's what the psychologists call a truma."

"Well, how would this be? I'll step outside for a few

minutes, and you draw a picture. Now, I think that would be—"

Fish was shaking his head sadly. "It's worse than I told you. I can't draw *anywhere* except in one room in my house—I've got it fixed up with her picture, and some mementos." He gulped hard, but decided against a third tear. "I'm sorry, I'd do it for you if I could, but . . ."

She sat quietly in thought for a moment. "Then let's say this. You go home, Mr. Wilmington, and draw something—a sketch of me, my face, from memory. I believe any competent artist could do that?"

Fish hesitated, not liking to say no.

"Now, you see, that will settle it. You couldn't get a snapshot of me and send it off to Wisconsin—there wouldn't be time. I'll give you, oh, half an hour."

"Half an—"

"That should be enough, shouldn't it? So that when I come to call on you, in half an hour from now, if you have a sketch of me—a likeness—why then I'll know that you're telling the truth. If not . . ."

Boxed in, Fish made the best of it. He got to his feet with a confident smile. "Well, now, that's fair enough. One thing, I know I could never forget *your* face. And I want to tell you how relieved I am that we had this little talk, incidentally, and—well, I better go and get that drawing started. I'll expect you in half an hour, Marie!" He paused at the door.

"I'll be there . . . George," she said.

Grunting and twitching, Fish stormed into the house banging doors behind him. Place was a mess—sofa cushions and newspapers all over the living room—but, never mind, she might marry him to clean up his house. Thing was—he unlocked the private room, feverishly swept the cover off the big machine, and began pushing buttons on one of the banks—thing was, get that sketch made. One chance in a hundred. But better than no chance at all. He switched on the machine, watched in helpless impatience while the arms drifted out and hung motionless.

A face—and a likeness! Only hope he had was to put it together from bits and pieces. Nothing left now that

141

would work in the whole machine but some useless items, mechanical drawings and architecture, and a few scraps of anatomy. Let there be enough for one more face! And let it be something like Marie's face!

The machine clicked suddenly and began to trace a line. Fish stood over it in hand-wringing anxiety, watching how the combined motion of the two revolving pivots translated the straight push of the arm into a subtle line. Pretty thing to watch, even if he never could like what it made. Now here it came curving around; now the arm was lifting, going back. A nose! It was drawing a nose!

It was a kind of Greek nose, shapely but thick, not much like Marie's fine curved nose, but, never mind, he could talk her into it—give him the raw material, he could always sell. Let there be *any* kind of a female face, so long as it wasn't ugly. Come on, now, an eye!

But the arms stopped and hung motionless again. The machine hummed quietly, the dials were lighted; nothing happened.

Eaten by impatience, Fish looked at his watch, clapped his palm over it, peeked, swore, and wandered rapidly out of the room. Sometimes lately the machine would just sit like that for minutes at a time, as if it were trying and trying to work, but somehow not succeeding, and then, *click,* off it would go again. He hurried back, looked —still nothing—and went back, pacing the empty rooms, looking for something to do.

For the first time he noticed there was some mail in the basket under the letter drop. Mostly bills. He threw them behind the living-room sofa, but one was a long, bulky brown envelope with "Encyclopaedia Britannica Library Research Service" in the corner.

It had been so long ago, it took him a moment to remember. A couple of weeks after he sent in his letter, there had been a polite printed postcard acknowledging it, then nothing for months. Somewhere along the line he had decided he wasn't going to get an answer. There wasn't any such language. . . . Well, let's see. He picked the end of the envelope open.

His restless eye was caught by the dining-room clock. Look at the time! Clutching the envelope forgetfully, he rushed into the private room again. The machine was still sitting motionless, humming, lighted. There was nothing on the paper but a noble nose.

Fish pounded on the side of the big machine, with no result except to his fist, and then on the bank that was in use. Nothing. He turned away, noticed he was still holding the envelope, and irritably plucked out the papers inside.

There was a stiff orange folder, stapled at the top. When he lifted the cover, there was a single sheet of paper inside. At the top, the Britannica letterhead, and "V. A. Sternback, Director." Then, in the middle, "SWEDISH WORDS."

His eye ran down the list, startled. There were all the words he had copied off, and opposite each one a word in English. *Teckning* . . . drawing. *Mönster* . . . pattern. *Utplåna* . . . to erase. *Använding* . . . application, use.

Fish looked up. Then that was why nothing had happened when he pressed the *Utplåna* button—he'd always tried it before the machine made a drawing, never while there was a finished one on the board. Now why hadn't he thought of that? Yes, and here was *Avslå* . . . to reject. And *slutsatsen* . . . completion. "To reject a drawing before completion, press . . ." He'd never done that, either.

What about the middle button? *Torka* . . . to wipe. To wipe? Let's see, there was another word—*Avlägsna,* that was it. Sometimes the phrase *"Avlägsna ett mönster"* would be running through his head when he was half awake, like a whispered warning. . . . Here it was. *Avlägsna* . . . to remove.

His hands were shaking. "To remove a pattern from bank after use, press button 'Wipe.' " He let the folder fall. All this time, not knowing, he'd been systematically using up the precious patterns in the machine, throwing them away one by one, until now there was nothing left —just eight big hunks of useless machinery, made for somebody somewhere who spoke Swedish. . . .

The machine clicked softly and the other arm began to move. It traced a graceful upright line, some distance

143

in front of the nose. It looped over and came back down again, then up. . . .

Somewhere distant, the doorbell rang imperiously.

Fish stared, mesmerized, at the paper. The moving point traced another graceful open loop, then another, like a squeezed-together roller coaster. Then another one, moving inexorably and without hurry: now there were four. Without pausing, it extended the last line downward and then brought it across. The line met the tip of the nose and curved back.

The four open loops were fingers. The fifth one was a thumb.

The machine, humming quietly, withdrew its arms into their recesses. After a moment the lights went dark and the hum stopped. Outside, the doorbell rang again, and went on ringing.

THIS IS THE FIRST OF A SERIES OF stories that God sent me as a punishment for having said that the time-travel story was dead. Each of these stories, of which there are four or five, disposes of time paradoxes in a new and different way. In "Anachron" I flirt with heresy.

8

ANACHRON

<<<<<<<<<<<<<<<<<<<<<<<<<<<<<<<<<<<<<<<<<<<<<<

THE BODY WAS NEVER FOUND. AND FOR THAT
reason alone, there was no body to find.

It sounds like inverted logic—which, in a sense, it is
—but there's no paradox involved. It was a perfectly orderly and explicable event, even though it could only
have happened to a Castellare.

Odd fish, the Castellare brothers. Sons of a Scots-
Englishwoman and an expatriate Italian, born in England, educated on the Continent, they were at ease
anywhere in the world and at home nowhere.

Nevertheless, in their middle years, they had become
settled men. Expatriates like their father, they lived on
the island of Ischia, off the Neapolitan coast, in a palace
—*quattrocento,* very fine, with peeling cupids on the
walls, a multitude of rats, no central heating and no
neighbors.

They went nowhere; no one except their agents and
their lawyers came to them. Neither had ever married.
Each, at about the age of thirty, had given up the
world of people for an inner world of more precise and
more enduring pleasures. Each was an amateur—a fa-
natical, compulsive amateur.

They had been born out of their time.

Peter's passion was virtu. He collected relentlessly, it
would not be too much to say savagely; he collected as
some men hunt big game. His taste was catholic, and his

146

acquisitions filled the huge rooms of the palace and half the vaults under them—paintings, statuary, enamels, porcelain, glass, crystal, metalwork. At fifty, he was a round little man with small, sardonic eyes and a careless patch of pinkish goatee.

Harold Castellare, Peter's talented brother, was a scientist. An amateur scientist. He belonged in the nineteenth century, as Peter was a throwback to a still earlier epoch. Modern science is largely a matter of teamwork and drudgery, both impossible concepts to a Castellare. But Harold's intelligence was in its own way as penetrating and original as a Newton's or a Franklin's. He had done respectable work in physics and electronics, and had even, at his lawyer's insistence, taken out a few patents. The income from these, when his own purchases of instruments and equipment did not consume it, he gave to his brother, who accepted it without gratitude or rancor.

Harold, at fifty-three, was spare and shrunken, sallow and spotted, with a bloodless, melancholy countenance; on his upper lip grew a neat hedge of pink-and-salt mustache, the companion piece and antithesis of his brother's goatee.

On a certain May morning, Harold had an accident.

Goodyear dropped rubber on a hot stove; Archimedes took a bath; Becquerel left a piece of uranium ore in a drawer with a photographic plate. Harold Castellare, working patiently with an apparatus which had so far consumed a great deal of current without producing anything more spectacular than some rather unusual corona effects, sneezed convulsively and dropped an ordinary bar magnet across two charged terminals.

Above the apparatus a huge, cloudy bubble sprang into being.

Harold, getting up from his instinctive crouch, blinked at it in profound astonishment. As he watched, the cloudiness abruptly disappeared and he was looking *through* the bubble at a section of tessellated flooring that seemed to be about three feet above the real floor. He could also see the corner of a carved wooden bench, and on the bench a small, oddly shaped stringed instrument.

147

Harold swore fervently to himself, made agitated notes, and then began to experiment. He tested the sphere cautiously with an electroscope, with a magnet, with a Geiger counter. Negative. He tore a tiny bit of paper from his notepad and dropped it toward the sphere. The paper disappeared; he couldn't see where it went.

Speechless, Harold picked up a meter stick and thrust it delicately forward. There was no feeling of contact; the rule went into and through the bubble as if the latter did not exist. Then it touched the stringed instrument, with a solid click. Harold pushed. The instrument slid over the edge of the bench and struck the floor with a hollow thump and jangle.

Staring at it, Harold suddenly recognized its tantalizingly familiar shape.

Recklessly he let go the meter stick, reached in and picked the fragile thing out of the bubble. It was solid and cool in his fingers. The varnish was clear, the color of the wood glowing through it. It looked as if it might have been made yesterday.

Peter owned one almost exactly like it, except for preservation—a viola d'amore of the seventeenth century.

Harold stooped to look through the bubble horizontally. Gold and rust tapestries hid the wall, fifty feet away, except for an ornate door in the center. The door began to open; Harold saw a flicker of umber.

Then the sphere went cloudy again. His hands were empty; the viola d'amore was gone. And the meter stick, which he had dropped inside the sphere, lay on the floor at his feet.

"Look at that," said Harold simply.

Peter's eyebrows went up slightly. "What is it, a new kind of television?"

"No, no. Look here." The viola d'amore lay on the bench, precisely where it had been before. Harold reached into the sphere and drew it out.

Peter started. "Give me that." He took it in his hands, rubbed the smoothly finished wood. He stared at his brother. "By God and all the saints," he said. "Time travel."

Harold snorted impatiently. "My dear Peter, 'time' is a meaningless word taken by itself, just as 'space' is."

"But, barring that, time travel."

"If you like, yes."

"You'll be quite famous."

"I expect so."

Peter looked down at the instrument in his hands. "I'd like to keep this, if I may."

"I'd be very happy to let you, but you can't."

As he spoke the bubble went cloudy; the viola d'amore was gone like smoke.

"There, you see?"

"What sort of devil's trick is that?"

"It goes back. . . . Later you'll see. I had that thing out once before, and this happened. When the sphere became transparent again, the viol was where I had found it."

"And your explanation for this?"

Harold hesitated. "None. Until I can work out the appropriate mathematics—"

"Which may take you some time. Meanwhile, in layman's language—"

Harold's face creased with the effort and interest of translation. "Very roughly, then—I should say it means that events are conserved. Two or three centuries ago—"

"Three. Notice the sound holes."

"Three centuries ago, then, at this particular time of day, someone was in that room. If the viola were gone, he or she would have noticed the fact. That would constitute an alteration of events already fixed; therefore it doesn't happen. For the same reason, I conjecture, we can't see into the sphere, or—" he probed at it with a fountain pen—"I thought not—or reach into it to touch anything; that would also constitute an alteration. And anything we put into the sphere while it is transparent comes out again when it becomes opaque. To put it very crudely, we cannot alter the past."

"But it seems to me that we did alter it. Just now,

when you took the viol out, even if no one of that time saw it happen."

"This," said Harold, "is the difficulty of using language as a means of exact communication. If you had not forgotten all your calculus . . . However. It may be postulated (remembering of course that everything I say is a lie, because I say it in English) that an event which doesn't influence other events is not an event. In other words—"

"That, since no one saw you take it, it doesn't matter whether you took it or not. A rather dangerous precept, Harold; you would have been burned at the stake for that at one time."

"Very likely. But it can be stated in another way or, indeed, in an infinity of ways which only seem to be different. If someone, let us say God, were to remove the moon as I am talking to you, using zero duration, and substitute an exact replica made of concrete and plaster of Paris, with the same mass, albedo and so on as the genuine moon, it would make no measurable difference in the universe as we perceive it—and therefore we cannot certainly say that it hasn't happened. Nor, I may add, does it make any difference whether it has or not."

" 'When there's no one about on the quad,' " said Peter.

"Yes. A basic and, as a natural consequence, a meaningless problem of philosophy. Except," he added, "in this one particular manifestation."

He stared at the cloudy sphere. "You'll excuse me, won't you, Peter? I've got to work on this."

"When will you publish, do you suppose?"

"Immediately. That's to say, in a week or two."

"Don't do it till you've talked it over with me, will you? I have a notion about it."

Harold looked at him sharply. "Commercial?"

"In a way."

"No," said Harold. "This is not the sort of thing one patents or keeps secret, Peter."

"Of course. I'll see you at dinner, I hope?"

"I think so. If I forget, knock on the door, will you?"

"Yes. Until then."

"Until then."

At dinner, Peter asked only two questions.

"Have you found any possibility of changing the time your thing reaches—from the seventeenth century to the eighteenth, for example, or from Monday to Tuesday?"

"Yes, as a matter of fact. Amazing. It's lucky that I had a rheostat already in the circuit; I wouldn't dare turn the current off. Varying the amperage varies the time set. I've had it up to what I think was Wednesday of last week—at any rate, my smock was lying over the workbench where I left it, I remember, Wednesday afternoon. I pulled it out. A curious sensation, Peter— I was wearing the same smock at the time. And then the sphere went opaque and of course the smock vanished. That must have been myself, coming into the room."

"And the future?"

"Yes. Another funny thing. I've had it forward to various times in the near future, and the machine itself is still there, but nothing's been done to it—none of the things I'm thinking I might do. That might be because of the conservation of events, again, but I rather think not. Still farther forward there are cloudy areas, blanks; I can't see anything that isn't in existence now, apparently, but here, in the next few days, there's nothing of that.

"It's as if I were going away. Where do you suppose I'm going?"

Harold's abrupt departure took place between midnight and morning. He packed his own grip, it would seem, left unattended, and was seen no more. It was extraordinary, of course, that he should have left at all, but the details were in no way odd. Harold had always detested what he called "the tyranny of the valet." He was, as everyone knew, a most independent man.

On the following day Peter made some trifling experiments with the time-sphere. From the sixteenth century he picked up a scent bottle of Venetian glass; from the eighteenth, a crucifix of carved rosewood; from the

151

nineteenth, when the palace had been the residence of an Austrian count and his Italian mistress, a hand-illuminated copy of De Sade's *La Nouvelle Justine*, very curiously bound in human skin.

They all vanished, naturally, within minutes or hours —all but the scent bottle. This gave Peter matter for reflection. There had been half a dozen flickers of cloudiness in the sphere just futureward of the bottle; it ought to have vanished, but it hadn't. But then, he had found it on the floor near a wall with quite a large rat hole in it.

When objects disappeared unaccountably, he asked himself, was it because they had rolled into rat holes, or because some time fisher had picked them up when they were in a position to do so?

He did not make any attempt to explore the future. That afternoon he telephoned his lawyers in Naples and gave them instructions for a new will. His estate, including his half of the jointly owned Ischia property, was to go to the Italian government on two conditions: (1) that Harold Castellare should make a similar bequest of the remaining half of the property and (2) that the Italian government should turn the palace into a national museum to house Peter's collection, using the income from his estate for its administration and for further acquisitions. His surviving relatives—two cousins in Scotland—he cut off with a shilling each.

He did nothing more until after the document had been brought out to him, signed and witnessed. Only then did he venture to look into his own future.

Events were conserved, Harold had said—meaning, Peter very well understood, events of the present and future as well as of the past. But was there only one pattern in which the future could be fixed? Could a result exist before its cause had occurred?

The Castellare motto was *Audentes fortuna juvat*—into which Peter, at the age of fourteen, had interpolated the word *"prudentesque"*: "Fortune favors the bold—and the prudent."

Tomorrow: no change; the room he was looking at was so exactly like this one that the time sphere seemed to vanish. The next day: a cloudy blur. And the next, and the next . . .

Opacity, straight through to what Peter judged, by the distance he had moved the rheostat handle, to be ten years ahead. Then, suddenly, the room was a long marble hall filled with display cases.

Peter smiled wryly. If you were Harold, obviously you could not look ahead and see Peter working in your laboratory. And if you were Peter, equally obviously, you could not look ahead and know whether the room you saw was an improvement you yourself were going to make, or part of a museum established after your death, eight or nine years from now, or . . .

No. Eight years was little enough, but he could not even be sure of that. It would, after all, be seven years before Harold could be declared legally dead. . . .

Peter turned the vernier knob slowly forward. A flicker, another, a long series. Forward faster. Now the flickering melted into a grayness; objects winked out of existence and were replaced by others in the showcases; the marble darkened and lightened again, darkened and lightened, darkened and remained dark. He was, Peter judged, looking at the hall as it would be some five hundred years in the future. There was a thick film of dust on every exposed surface; rubbish and the carcass of some small animal had been swept carelessly into a corner.

The sphere clouded.

When it cleared, there was an intricate trail of footprints in the dust, and two of the showcases were empty.

The footprints were splayed, trifurcate, and thirty inches long.

After a moment's deliberation Peter walked around the workbench and leaned down to look through the sphere from the opposite direction. Framed in the nearest of the four tall windows was a scene of picture-postcard banality: the sun-silvered bay and the foreshortened arc of the city, with Vesuvio faintly fuming in the background. But there was something wrong about the colors, even grayed as they were by distance.

Peter went and got his binoculars.

153

The trouble was, of course, that Naples was green. Where the city ought to have been, a rankness had sprouted. Between the clumps of foliage he could catch occasional glimpses of gray-white that might equally well have been boulders or the wreckage of buildings. There was no movement. There was no shipping in the harbor.

But something rather odd was crawling up the side of the volcano. A rust-orange pipe, it appeared to be, supported on hairline struts like the legs of a centipede, and ending without rhyme or reason just short of the top.

While Peter watched, it turned slowly blue.

One day further forward: now all the display cases had been looted; the museum, it would seem, was empty.

Given, that in five centuries the world, or at any rate the department of Campania, has been overrun by a race of Somethings, the human population being killed or driven out in the process; and that the conquerors take an interest in the museum's contents, which they have accordingly removed.

Removed where, and why?

This question, Peter conceded, might have a thousand answers, nine hundred and ninety-nine of which would mean that he had lost his gamble. The remaining answer was: to the vaults, for safety.

With his own hands Peter built a hood to cover the apparatus on the workbench and the sphere above it. It was unaccustomed labor; it took him the better part of two days. Then he called in workmen to break a hole in the stone flooring next to the interior wall, rig a hoist, and cut the power cable that supplied the time-sphere loose from its supports all the way back to the fuse box, leaving him a single flexible length of cable more than a hundred feet long. They unbolted the workbench from the floor, attached casters to its legs, lowered it into the empty vault below, and went away.

Peter unfastened and removed the hood. He looked into the sphere.

Treasure.

Crates, large and small, racked in rows into dimness.

With pudgy fingers that did not tremble, he advanced the rheostat. A cloudy flicker, another, a leaping blur of them as he moved the vernier faster—and then there were no more, to the limit of the time-sphere's range.

Two hundred years, Peter guessed—A.D. 2700 to 2900 or thereabout—in which no one would enter the vault. Two hundred years of "unliquidated time."

He put the rheostat back to the beginning of that un-interrupted period. He drew out a small crate and prized it open.

Chessmen, ivory with gold inlay, Florentine, four-teenth century. Superb.

Another, from the opposite rack.

T'ang figurines, horses and men, ten to fourteen inches high. Priceless.

The crates would not burn, Tomaso told him. He went down to the kitchen to see, and it was true. The pieces lay in the roaring stove untouched. He fished one out with a poker; even the feathery splinters of the unplaned wood had not ignited.

It made a certain extraordinary kind of sense. When the moment came for the crates to go back, any physical scrambling that had occurred in the meantime would have no effect; they would simply put themselves to-gether as they had been before, like Thor's goats. But burning was another matter; burning would have re-leased energy which could not be replaced.

That settled one paradox, at any rate. There was an-other that nagged at Peter's orderly mind. If the things he took out of that vault, seven hundred-odd years in the future, were to become part of the collection bequeathed by him to the museum, preserved by it, and eventually stored in the vault for him to find—then precisely where had they come from in the first place?

It worried him. Peter had learned in life, as his brother had in physics, that one never gets anything for nothing.

Moreover, this riddle was only one of his perplexities, and that not among the greatest. For another example,

155

there was the obstinate opacity of the time-sphere whenever he attempted to examine the immediate future. However often he tried it, the result was always the same: a cloudy blank, all the way forward to the sudden unveiling of the marble gallery.

It was reasonable to expect the sphere to show nothing at times when he himself was going to be in the vault, but this accounted for only five or six hours out of every twenty-four. Again, presumably, it would show him no changes to be made by himself, since foreknowledge would make it possible for him to alter his actions. But he laboriously cleared one end of the vault, put up a screen to hide the rest and made a vow—which he kept —not to alter the clear space or move the screen for a week. Then he tried again—with the same result.

The only remaining explanation was that sometime during the next ten years something was going to happen which he would prevent if he could; and the clue to it was there, buried in that frustrating, unbroken blankness.

As a corollary, it was going to be something which he *could* prevent if only he knew what it was . . . or even when it was supposed to happen.

The event in question, in all probability, was his own death. Peter therefore hired nine men to guard him, three to a shift—because one man alone could not be trusted, two might conspire against him, whereas three, with the very minimum of effort, could be kept in a state of mutual suspicion. He also underwent a thorough medical examination, had new locks installed on every door and window, and took every other precaution ingenuity could suggest. When he had done all these things, the next ten years were as blank as before.

Peter had more than half expected it. He checked through his list of safeguards once more, found it good, and thereafter let the matter rest. He had done all he could; either he would survive the crisis or he would not. In either case, events were conserved; the time-sphere could give him no forewarning.

Another man might have found his pleasure blunted by guilt and fear; Peter's was whetted to a keener edge.

If he had been a recluse before, now he was an eremite; he grudged every hour that was not given to his work. Mornings he spent in the vault, unpacking his acquisitions; afternoons and evenings, sorting, cataloguing, examining and—the word is not too strong—gloating. When three weeks had passed in this way, the shelves were bare as far as the power cable would allow him to reach in every direction, except for crates whose contents were undoubtedly too large to pass through the sphere. These, with heroic self-control, Peter had left untouched.

And still he had looted only a hundredth part of that incredible treasure house. With grappling hooks he could have extended his reach by perhaps three or four yards, but at the risk of damaging his prizes; and in any case this would have been no solution but only a postponement of the problem. There was nothing for it but to go through the sphere himself and unpack the crates while on the other "side" of it.

Peter thought about it in a fury of concentration for the rest of the day. So far as he was concerned, there was no question that the gain would be worth any calculated risk; the problem was how to measure the risk and if possible reduce it.

Item: He felt a definite uneasiness at the thought of venturing through that insubstantial bubble. Intuition was supported, if not by logic, at least by a sense of the dramatically appropriate. Now, if ever, would be the time for his crisis.

Item: Common sense did not concur. The uneasiness had two symbols. One was the white face of his brother Harold just before the water closed over it; the other was a phantasm born of those gigantic, splayed footprints in the dust of the gallery. In spite of himself, Peter had often found himself trying to imagine what the creatures that made them must look like, until his visualization was so clear that he could almost swear he had seen them.

Towering monsters they were, with crested ophidian heads and great unwinking eyes; and they moved in a strutting glide, nodding their heads, like fantastic barnyard fowl.

But, taking these premonitory images in turn: first, it was impossible that he should ever be seriously inconvenienced by Harold's death. There were no witnesses, he was sure; he had struck the blow with a stone; stones also were the weights that had dragged the body down, and the rope was an odd length Peter had picked up on the shore. Second, the three-toed Somethings might be as fearful as all the world's bogies put together; it made no difference, he could never meet them.

Nevertheless, the uneasiness persisted. Peter was not satisfied; he wanted a lifeline. When he found it, he wondered that he had not thought of it before.

He would set the time-sphere for a period just before one of the intervals of blankness. That would take care of accidents, sudden illnesses, and other unforeseeable contingencies. It would also insure him against one very real and not at all irrational dread: the fear that the mechanism which generated the time-sphere might fail while he was on the other side. For the conservation of events was not a condition created by the sphere but one which limited its operation. No matter what happened, it was impossible for him to occupy the same place-time as any future or past observer; therefore, when the monster entered that vault, Peter would not be there any more.

There was, of course, the scent bottle to remember. Every rule has its exception; but in this case, Peter thought, the example did not apply. A scent bottle could roll into a rat hole; a man could not.

He turned the rheostat carefully back to the last flicker of grayness; past that to the next, still more carefully. The interval between the two, he judged, was something under an hour: excellent.

His pulse seemed a trifle rapid, but his brain was clear and cool. He thrust his head into the sphere and sniffed cautiously. The air was stale and had a faint, unpleasant odor, but it was breathable.

Using a crate as a stepping stool, he climbed to the top of the workbench. He arranged another crate close to the sphere to make a platform level with its equator. And

158

seven and a half centuries in the future, a third crate stood on the floor directly under the sphere.

Peter stepped into the sphere, dropped, and landed easily, legs bending to take the shock. When he straightened, he was standing in what to all appearances was a large circular hole in the workbench; his chin was just above the top of the sphere.

He lowered himself, half squatting, until he had drawn his head through and stepped down from the crate.

He was in the future vault. The sphere was a brightly luminous thing that hung unsupported in the air behind him, its midpoint just higher than his head. The shadows it cast spread black and wedge-shaped in every direction, melting into obscurity.

Peter's heart was pounding miserably. He had an illusory stifling sensation, coupled with the idiotic notion that he ought to be wearing a diver's helmet. The silence was like the pause before a shout.

But down the aisles marched the crated treasures in their hundreds.

Peter set to work. It was difficult, exacting labor, opening the crates where they lay, removing the contents and nailing the crates up again, all without disturbing the positions of the crates themselves, but it was the price he had to pay for his lifeline. Each crate was in a sense a microcosm, like the vault itself—a capsule of unliquidated time. But the vault's term would end some fifty minutes from now, when crested heads nodded down these aisles; those of the crates' interiors, for all that Peter knew to the contrary, went on forever.

The first crate contained lacework porcelain; the second, shakudō sword hilts; the third, an exquisite fourth-century Greek ornament in *repoussé* bronze, the equal in every way of the Siris bronzes.

Peter found it almost physically difficult to set the thing down, but he did so; standing on his platform crate in the future with his head projecting above the sphere in the present—like (again the absurd thought!) a diver rising from the ocean—he laid it carefully beside the others on the workbench.

Then down again, into the fragile silence and the

159

gloom. The next crates were too large, and those just beyond were doubtful. Peter followed his shadow down the aisle. He had almost twenty minutes left: enough for one more crate, chosen with care, and an ample margin.

Glancing to his right at the end of the row, he saw a door. It was a heavy door, rivet-studded, with a single iron step below it. There had been no door there in Peter's time; the whole plan of the building must have been altered. *Of course!* he realized suddenly. If it had not, if so much as a single tile or lintel had remained of the palace as he knew it, then the sphere could never have let him see or enter this particular here-and-now, this—what would Harold have called it?—this nexus in space-time.

For if you saw any now-existing thing as it was going to appear in the future, you could alter it in the present —carve your initials in it, break it apart, chop it down— which was manifestly impossible, and therefore . . .

And therefore the first ten years were necessarily blank when he looked into the sphere, not because anything unpleasant was going to happen to him, but because in that time the last traces of the old palace had not yet been eradicated.

There was no crisis.

Wait a moment, though! Harold had been able to look into the near future. . . . But—of course—Harold had been about to die.

In the dimness between himself and the door he saw a rack of crates that looked promising. The way was uneven; one of the untidy accumulations of refuse that seemed to be characteristic of the Somethings lay in windrows across the floor. Peter stepped forward carefully— but not carefully enough.

Harold Castellare had had another accident—and again, if you choose to look at it in that way, a lucky one. The blow stunned him; the old rope slipped from the stones; flaccid, he floated where a struggling man might have drowned. A fishing boat nearly ran him down, and picked him up instead. He was suffering from a concussion, shock, exposure, asphyxiation and was more than three quarters dead. But he was still alive when he was delivered, an hour later, to a hospital in Naples.

There were, of course, no identifying papers, labels or monograms in his clothing—Peter had seen to that—and for the first week after his rescue Harold was quite genuinely unable to give any account of himself. During the second week he was mending but uncommunicative, and at the end of the third, finding that there was some difficulty about gaining his release in spite of his physical recovery, he affected to regain his memory, gave a circumstantial but entirely fictitious identification and was discharged.

To understand this as well as all his subsequent actions, it is only necessary to remember that Harold was a Castellare. In Naples, not wishing to give Peter any unnecessary anxiety, he did not approach his bank for funds but cashed a check with an incurious acquaintance, and predated it by four weeks. With part of the money so acquired he paid his hospital bill and rewarded his rescuers. Another part went for new clothing and for four days' residence in an inconspicuous hotel, while he grew used to walking and dressing himself again. The rest, on his last day, he spent in the purchase of a discreetly small revolver and a box of cartridges.

He took the last boat to Ischia and arrived at his own front door a few minutes before eleven. It was a cool evening, and a most cheerful fire was burning in the central hall.

"Signor Peter is well, I suppose," said Harold, removing his coat.

"Yes, Signor Harold. He is very well, very busy with his collection."

"Where is he? I should like to speak to him."

"He is in the vaults, Signor Harold. But . . ."

"Yes?"

"Signor Peter sees no one when he is in the vaults. He has given strict orders that no one is to bother him, Signor Harold, when he is in the vaults."

"Oh, well," said Harold. "I daresay he'll see me."

It was a thing something like a bear trap, apparently, except that instead of two semicircular jaws it had four segments that snapped together in the middle, each with a shallow, sharp tooth. The pain was quite unendurable.

Each segment moved at the end of a thin arm, cunningly hinged so that the ghastly thing would close over whichever of the four triggers you stepped on. Each arm had a spring too powerful for Peter's muscles. The whole affair was connected by a chain to a staple solidly embedded in the concrete floor; it left Peter free to move some ten inches in any direction. Short of gnawing off his own leg, he thought sickly, there was very little he could do about it.

The riddle was, what could the thing possibly be doing here? There were rats in the vaults, no doubt, now as in his own time, but surely nothing larger. Was it conceivable that even the three-toed Somethings would set an engine like this to catch a rat?

Lost inventions, Peter thought irrelevantly, had a way of being rediscovered. Even if he suppressed the time-sphere during his lifetime and it did not happen to survive him, still there might be other time-fishers in the remote future—not here, perhaps, but in other treasure houses of the world. And that might account for the existence of this metal-jawed horror. Indeed, it might account for the vault itself—a better man-trap—except that it was all nonsense; the trap could only be full until the trapper came to look at it. Events, and the lives of prudent time-travelers, were conserved.

And he had been in the vault for almost forty minutes. Twenty minutes to go, twenty-five, thirty at the most, then the Somethings would enter and their entrance would free him. He had his lifeline; the knowledge was the only thing that made it possible to live with the pain that was the center of his universe just now. It was like going to the dentist, in the bad old days before procaine; it was very bad, sometimes, but you knew that it would end.

He cocked his head toward the door, holding his breath. A distant thud, another, then a curiously unpleasant squeaking, then silence.

But he had heard them. He knew they were there. It couldn't be much longer now.

Three men, two stocky, one lean, were playing cards in the passageway in front of the closed door that led to the vault staircase. They got up slowly.

"Who is he?" demanded the shortest one.

Tomaso clattered at him in furious Sicilian; the man's face darkened, but he looked at Harold with respect.

"I am now," stated Harold, "going down to see my brother."

"No, Signor," said the shortest one positively.

"You are impertinent," Harold told him.

"Yes, Signor."

Harold frowned. "You will not let me pass?"

"No, Signor."

"Then go and tell my brother I am here."

The shortest one said apologetically but firmly that there were strict orders against this also; it would have astonished Harold very much if he had said anything else.

"Well, at least I suppose you can tell me how long it will be before he comes out?"

"Not long, Signor. One hour, no more."

"Oh, very well, then," said Harold pettishly, turning half away. He paused. "One thing more," he said, taking the gun out of his pocket as he turned, "put your hands up and stand against the wall there, will you?"

The first two complied slowly. The third, the lean one, fired through his coat pocket, just like the gangsters in the American movies.

It was not a sharp sensation at all, Harold was surprised to find; it was more as if someone had hit him in the side with a cricket bat. The racket seemed to bounce interminably from the walls. He felt the gun jolt in his hand as he fired back, but couldn't tell if he had hit anybody. Everything seemed to be happening very slowly, and yet it was astonishingly hard to keep his balance. As he swung around he saw the two stocky ones with their hands half inside their jackets, and the lean one with his mouth open, and Tomaso with bulging eyes.

Then the wall came at him and he began to swim along it, paying particular attention to the problem of not dropping one's gun.

As he weathered the first turn in the passageway the roar broke out afresh. A fountain of plaster stung his eyes; then he was running clumsily, and there was a bedlam of shouting behind him.

Without thinking about it he seemed to have selected the laboratory as his destination; it was an instinctive choice, without much to recommend it logically. In any case, he realized halfway across the central hall, he was not going to get there.

He turned and squinted at the passageway entrance; saw a blur move and fired at it. It disappeared. He turned again awkwardly, and had taken two steps nearer an armchair which offered the nearest shelter, when something clubbed him between the shoulderblades. One step more, knees buckling, and the wall struck him a second, softer blow. He toppled, clutching at the tapestry that hung near the fireplace.

When the three guards, whose names were Enrico, Alberto and Luca, emerged cautiously from the passage and approached Harold's body, it was already flaming like a Viking's in its impromptu shroud; the dim horses and men and falcons of the tapestry were writhing and crisping into brilliance. A moment later an uncertain ring of fire wavered toward them across the carpet.

Although the servants came with fire extinguishers and with buckets of water from the kitchen, and although the fire department was called, it was all quite useless. In five minutes the whole room was ablaze; in ten, as windows burst and walls buckled, the fire engulfed the second story. In twenty a mass of flaming timbers dropped into the vault through the hole Peter had made in the floor of the laboratory, utterly destroying the time-sphere apparatus and reaching shortly thereafter, as the authorities concerned were later to agree, an intensity of heat entirely sufficient to consume a human body without leaving any identifiable trace. For that reason alone, there was no trace of Peter's body to be found.

The sounds had just begun again when Peter saw the light from the time-sphere turn ruddy and then wink out like a snuffed candle.

In the darkness, he heard the door open.

Here IS ANOTHER OF MY TIME stories, put together out of bits and pieces of Far Rockaway, Milne, Einstein, etc. (I didn't see why the speculations of modern physicists shouldn't be used as incantations.) I don't think "Extempore" is terribly probable, but see for yourself.

9

EXTEMPORE

EVERYBODY KNEW; EVERYBODY WANTED TO help Rossi the time-traveler. They came running up the scarlet beach, naked and golden as children, laughing happily.

"Legend is true," they shouted. "He is here, just like great-grandfathers say!"

"What year is this?" Rossi asked, standing incongruously shirt-sleeved and alone in the sunlight—no great machines bulking around him, no devices, nothing but his own spindling body.

"Thairty-five twainty-seex, Mista Rossi!" they chorused.

"Thank you. Good-bye."

"Good-byee!"

Flick. Flick. Flick. Those were days. *Flicketaflicketaflick*—weeks, months, years. WHIRRR . . . Centuries, millennia streaming past like sleet in a gale!

Now the beach was cold, and the people were buttoned up to their throats in stiff black cloth. Moving stiffly, like jointed stick people, they unfurled a huge banner: "SORI WI DO NOT SPIC YOUR SPICH. THIS IS YIR 5199 OF YOUR CALINDAR. HELO MR ROSI."

They all bowed, like marionettes, and Mr. Rossi bowed back. *Flick. Flick. Flicketaflicketa*WHIRRR . . .

The beach was gone. He was inside an enormous building, a sky-high vault, like the Empire State turned into one room. Two floating eggs swooped at him and hovered alertly, staring with poached eyes. Behind them reared a tilted neon slab blazing with diagrams and symbols, none of which he could recognize before *flicketa*WHIRRRR . . .

This time it was a wet stony plain, with salt marshes beyond it. Rossi was not interested and spent the time looking at the figures he had scrawled in his notebook. 1956, 1958, 1965 and so on, the intervals getting longer and longer, the curve rising until it was going almost straight up. If only he'd paid more attention to mathematics in school . . . *flick*RRR . . .

Now a white desert at night, bitter cold, where the towers of Manhattan should have been. Something mournfully thin flapped by over *flk*RRRR . . .

Blackness and fog was all he could *fk*RRRR . . .

Now the light and dark blinks in the grayness melted and ran together, flickering faster and faster until Rossi was looking at a bare leaping landscape as if through soap-smeared glasses—continents expanding and contracting, icecaps slithering down and back again, the planet charging toward its cold death while only Rossi stood there to watch, gaunt and stiff, with a disapproving, wistful glint in his eye.

His name was Albert Eustace Rossi. He was from Seattle, a wild bony young man with a poetic forelock and the stare-you-down eyes of an animal. He had learned nothing in twelve years of school except how to get passing marks, and he had a large wistfulness but no talents at all.

He had come to New York because he thought something wonderful might happen.

He averaged two months on a job. He worked as a short-order cook (his eggs were greasy and his hamburgers burned), a platemaker's helper in an offset shop, a shill in an auction gallery. He spent three weeks as a literary agent's critic, writing letters over his employer's signature to tell hapless reading-fee clients that their stories stank. He wrote bad verse for a while and sent it hopefully to all the best magazines, but concluded he was being held down by a clique.

He made no friends. The people he met seemed to be interested in nothing but baseball, or their incredibly boring jobs, or in making money. He tried hanging around the Village, wearing dungarees and a flowered shirt, but discovered that nobody noticed him.

It was the wrong century. What he wanted was a villa in Athens; or an island where the natives were childlike and friendly, and no masts ever lifted above the blue horizon; or a vast hygienic apartment in some future underground Utopia.

He bought certain science-fiction magazines and read them defiantly with the covers showing in cafeterias. Afterward, he took them home and marked them up with large exclamatory blue and red and green pencil and filed them away under his bed.

The idea of building a time machine had been growing a long while in his mind. Sometimes in the morning on his way to work, looking up at the blue cloud-dotted endlessness of the sky, or staring at the tracery of lines and whorls on his unique fingertips, or trying to see into the cavernous unexplored depths of a brick in a wall, or lying on his narrow bed at night, conscious of all the bewildering sights and sounds and odors that had swirled past him in twenty-odd years, he would say to himself, Why not?

Why not? He found a secondhand copy of J. W. Dunne's *An Experiment with Time* and lost sleep for a week. He copied off the charts from it, Scotch-taped them to his wall; he wrote down his startling dreams every morning as soon as he awoke. There was a time outside time, Dunne said, in which to measure time; and a time outside that, in which to measure the time that measured time, and a time outside that. . . . Why not?

An article in a barbershop about Einstein excited him, and he went to the library and read the encyclopedia articles on relativity and spacetime, frowning fiercely, going back again and again over the paragraphs he never did understand, but filling up all the same with a threshold feeling, an expectancy.

What looked like time to him might look like space to somebody else, said Einstein. A clock ran slower the faster it went. Good, fine. Why not? But it wasn't Einstein, or Minkowski or Wehl who gave him the clue; it was an astronomer named Milne.

There were two ways of looking at time, Milne said. If you measured it by things that moved, like clock hands and the earth turning and going around the sun, that was one kind; Milne called it dynamical time and his symbol for it was τ. But if you measured it by things happening in the atom, like radioactivity and light being emitted, that was another kind; Milne called it kinematic time, or t. And the formula that connected the two showed that it depended on which you used whether the universe had ever had a beginning or would ever have an end—yes in τ time, no in t.

Then it all added together: Dunne saying you didn't really have to travel along the timetrack like a train, you just thought you did, but when you were asleep you forgot, and that was why you could have prophetic dreams. And Eddington: that all the great laws of physics we had been able to discover were just a sort of spidery framework, and that there was room between the strands for an unimaginable complexity of things.

He believed it instantly; he had known it all his life but had never had any words to think it in—that this reality wasn't all there was. Pay checks, grimy window sills, rancid grease, nails in the shoe—how could it be?

It was all in the way you looked at it. That was what the *scientists* were saying—Einstein, Eddington, Milne, Dunne, all in a chorus. So it was a thing anybody could do, if he wanted it badly enough and was lucky. Rossi had always felt obscurely resentful that the day was past when you could discover something by looking at a teakettle or dropping gunk on a hot stove; but here, incredibly, was one more easy road to fame that everybody had missed.

Between the tip of his finger and the edge of the soiled plastic cover that hideously draped the hideous table, the shortest distance was a straight line containing an infinite number of points. His own body, he knew, was mostly empty space. Down there in the shadowy regions of the atom, in t time, you could describe how fast an electron was moving or where it was, but never both; you could never decide whether it was a wave or a particle; you couldn't even prove it existed at all, except as the ghost of its reflection appeared to you.

Why not?

It was summer, and the whole city was gasping for breath. Rossi had two weeks off and nowhere to go; the streets were empty of the Colorado vacationers, the renters of cabins in the mountains, the tailored flyers to Ireland, the Canadian Rockies, Denmark, Nova Scotia. All day long the sweaty subways had inched their loads of suffering out to Coney Island and Far Rockaway and back again, well salted, flayed with heat, shocked into a fishy torpor.

Now the island was still; flat and steaming, like a flounder on a griddle; every window open for an unimagined breath of air; silent as if the city were under glass. In dark rooms the bodies lay sprawled like a cannibal feast, all wakeful, all moveless, waiting for Time's tick.

Rossi had fasted all day, having in mind the impressive results claimed by Yogis, early Christian saints and Amerinds; he had drunk nothing but a glass of water in the morning and another at blazing noon. Standing now in the close darkness of his room, he felt that ocean of Time, heavy and stagnant, stretching away forever. The galaxies hung in it like seaweed, and down at the bottom it was silted unfathomably deep with dead men. (Seashell murmur: I am.)

There it all was, temporal and eternal, t and tau, everything that was and would be. The electron dancing in its imaginary orbit, the May fly's moment, the long drowse of the sequoias, the stretching of continents, the lonely drifting of stars; it canceled them all against each other, and the result was stillness.

The sequoia's truth did not make the May fly false. If a man could only see some other aspect of that totality, feel it, believe it—another relation of tau time to t . . .

He had chalked a diagram on the floor—not a pentacle but the nearest thing he could find, the quadrisected circle of the Michelson apparatus. Around it he had

171

scrawled, "$e = mc^2$," "Z^2/n^2," "$M = M_0 + 3K + 2V$."
Pinned up shielding the single bulb was a scrap of paper
with some doggerel on it:

$$\frac{t, \tau, t, \tau, t \ \tau \ t}{c}$$
$$R \sqrt{3}$$
Cartesian co-ordinates x, y, z
$- c^2t^2 = me$

It was in his head, hypnotically repeating: *t, tau, t, tau,
t tau t . . .*

As he stood there, the outlines of the paper swelled
and blurred, rhythmically. He felt as if the whole universe were breathing, slowly and gigantically, all one,
the smallest atom and the farthest star.

c over R times the square root of three . . .

He had a curious drunken sense that he was standing
outside, that he could reach in and give himself a push,
or a twist—no, that wasn't the word, either. . . . But
something was happening; he felt it, half in terror and
half in delight.

less c squared, t squared, equals . . .

An intolerable tension squeezed Rossi tight. Across
the room the paper, too near the bulb, crisped and
burned. And (as the tension twisted him somehow, finding a new direction for release) that was the last thing
Rossi saw before *flick,* it was daylight, and the room was
clotted with moist char, *flick,* someone was moving across
it, too swift to *flick. Flick. Flick. Flick, flick, flicketaflicketa . . .*

And here he was. Most incredibly, what had seemed
so true *was* true: by that effort of tranced will, he had
transferred himself to another time rate, another relationship to *t* to *τ* —a variable relationship, like a huge
merry-go-round that whirled, and paused, and whirled
again.

He had got on; how was he going to get off?

And—most terrifying question—where was the merry-go-round going? Whirling headlong to extinction and cold death, where the universe ended—or around the wheel again, to give him a second chance?

The blur exploded into white light. Stunned but safe inside his portable anomaly, Rossi watched the flaming earth cool, saw the emerging continents furred over with green, saw a kaleidoscope whirl of rainstorm and volcanic fury, pelting ice, earthquake, tsunami, fire!

Then he was in a forest, watching the branches sway as some great shape passed.

He was in a clearing, watching as a man in leather breeches killed a copper-skinned man with an ax.

He was in a log-walled room, watching a man in a wide collar stand up, toppling table and crockery, his eyes like onions.

He was in a church, and an old man behind the pulpit flung a book at him.

The church again, at evening, and two lonely women saw him and screamed.

He was in a bare, narrow room reeking of pitch. Somewhere outside, a dog set up a frenzied barking. A door opened and a wild, whiskery face popped in; a hand flung a blazing stick and flame leaped up. . . .

He was on a broad green lawn, alone with a small boy and a frantic white duck. "Good morrow, sir. Will you help me catch this pesky . . ."

He was in a little pavilion. A gray-bearded man at a desk turned, snatching up a silver cross, whispering fiercely to the young man at his side, *"Didn't I tell you!"* He pointed the cross, quivering. "Quick, then! Will New York continue to grow?"

Rossi was off guard. "Sure. This is going to be the biggest city . . ."

The pavilion was gone; he was in a little perfumed nook, facing a long room across a railing. A red-haired youth, dozing in front of the fire, sat up with a guilty start. He gulped. "Who . . . who's going to win the election?"

"What election?" said Rossi. "I don't—"

173

"Who's going to win?" The youth came forward, pale-faced. "Hoover or Roosevelt? Who?"

"Oh, that election. Roosevelt."

"Uh, will the country . . ."

The same room. A bell was ringing; white lights dazzled his eyes. The bell stopped. An amplified voice said, "When will Germany surrender?"

"Uh, 1945," said Rossi, squinting. "May, 1945. Look—whoever you are—"

"When will Japan surrender?"

"Same year. September. Look, whoever you are . . ."

A tousle-headed man emerged from the glare, blinking, wrapping a robe around his bulging middle. He stared at Rossi while the mechanical voice spoke behind him.

"Please name the largest new industry in the next ten years."

"Uh, television, I guess. Listen, you right there, can't you . . ."

The same room, the same bell ringing. This was all wrong, Rossi realized irritably. Nineteen thirty-two, 1944 (?) —the next ought to be at least close to where he had started. There was supposed to be a row of cheap rooming houses—his room, *here*.

". . . election, Stevenson or Eisenhower?"

"Stevenson. I mean, Eisenhower. Now look, doesn't *anybody*—"

"When will there be an armistice in Korea?"

"Last year. *Next* year. You're mixing me up. Will you turn off that—"

"When and where will atomic bombs next be used in—"

"Listen!" Rossi shouted. "I'm getting mad! If you want me to answer questions, let me ask some! Get me some help! Get me—"

"What place in the United States will be safest when—"

"*Einstein!*" shouted Rossi.

But the little gray man with the bloodhound eyes couldn't help him, nor the bald mustachioed one who was there the next time. The walls were inlaid now with intricate tracings of white metal. The voice began asking him questions he couldn't answer.

The second time it happened, there was a *puff* and a massive rotten stench rolled into his nostrils. Rossi choked. "Stop that!"

"Answer!" blared the voice. "What's the meaning of those signals from space?"

"I don't know!" *Puff*. Furiously: "But there isn't any New York past here! It's all gone—nothing left but . . ."
Puff!

Then he was standing on the lake of glassy obsidian, just like the first time.

And then the jungle, and he said automatically, "My name is Rossi. What year . . ." But it wasn't the jungle, really. It had been cleared back, and there were neat rows of concrete houses, like an enormous tank trap, instead of grass-topped verandas showing through the trees.

Then came the savanna, and that was all different, too—there was a looming piled ugliness of a city rising half a mile away. Where were the nomads, the horsemen?

And next . . .

The beach: but it was dirty gray, not scarlet. One lone dark figure was hunched against the sun glare, staring out to sea; the golden people were gone.

Rossi felt lost. Whatever had happened to New York, back there—to the whole world, probably—something he had said or done had made it come out differently. Somehow they had saved out some of the old grimy, rushing civilization, and it had lasted just long enough to blight all the fresh new things that ought to have come after it.

The stick men were not waiting on their cold beach.

He caught his breath. He was in the enormous building again, the same tilted slab blazing with light, the same floating eggs bulging their eyes at him. That hadn't changed, and perhaps nothing he could do would ever change it; for he knew well enough that that wasn't a human building.

But then came the white desert, and after it the fog, and his glimpses of the night began to blur together, faster and faster. . . .

That was all. There was nothing left now but the swift vertiginous spin to the end-and-beginning, and then the wheel slowing as he came around again.

Rossi began to seethe. This was worse than dishwashing—his nightmare, the worst job he knew. Standing here, like a second hand ticking around the face of Time, while men who flickered and vanished threaded him with questions: a thing, a tool, a gyrating information booth!

Stop, he thought, and pushed—a costive pressure inside his brain—but nothing happened. He was a small boy forgotten on a carousel, a bug trapped between window and screen, a moth circling a lamp. . . .

It came to him what the trouble was. There had to be the yearning, that single candle-cone focus of the spirit: that was the moving force, and all the rest—the fasting, the quiet, the rhymes—was only to channel and guide.

He would have to get off at the one place in the whole endless sweep of time where he wanted to be. And that place, he knew now without surprise, was the scarlet beach.

Which no longer existed, anywhere in the universe.

While he hung suspended on that thought, the flickering stopped at the prehistoric jungle; and the clearing with its copper dead man; and the log room, empty; the church, empty, too.

And the fiery room, now so fiercely ablaze that the hair of his forearms puffed and curled.

And his cool lawn, where the small boy stood agape.

And the pavilion: the graybeard and the young man leaning together like blasted trees, livid-lipped.

There was the trouble: they had believed him, the first time around, and acting on what he told them, they had changed the world.

Only one thing to be done—destroy that belief,

fuddle them, talk nonsense, like a ghost called up at a séance!

"Then you tell me to put all I have in land," says graybeard, clutching the crucifix, "and wait for the increase!"

"Of course!" replied Rossi with instant cunning. "New York's to be the biggest city—in the whole state of Maine!"

The pavilion vanished. Rossi saw with pleasure that the room that took its place was high-ceilinged and shabby, the obvious forerunner of his own roach-haunted cubbyhole in 1955. The long paneled room with its fireplace and the youth dozing before it were gone, snuffed out, a might-have-been.

When a motherly looking woman lurched up out of a rocker, staring, he knew what to do.

He put his finger to his lips. "The lost candlestick is under the cellar stairs!" he hissed, and vanished.

The room was a little older, a little shabbier. A new partition had been added, bringing its dimensions down to those of the room Rossi knew, and there was a bed, and an old tin washbasin in the corner. A young woman was sprawled open-mouthed, fleshy and snoring, in the bed; Rossi looked away with faint prim disgust and waited.

The same room: *his* room, almost: a beefy stubbled man smoking in the armchair with his feet in a pan of water. The pipe dropped from his sprung jaw.

"I'm the family banshee," Rossi remarked. "Beware, for a short man with a long knife is dogging your footsteps." He squinted and bared his fangs; the man, standing up hurriedly, tipped the basin and stumbled half across the room before he recovered and whirled to the door, bellowing, leaving fat wet tracks and silence.

Now; *now* . . . It was night, and the sweaty unstirred heat of the city poured in around him. He was standing in the midst of the chalk marks he had scrawled a hundred billion years ago. The bare bulb was still lighted; around it flames were licking tentatively at the edges of the table, cooking the plastic cover up into lumpy hissing puffs.

Rossi the shipping clerk; Rossi the elevator man; Rossi the *dishwasher!*

He let it pass. The room kaleidoscope-flicked from brown to green; a young man at the washbasin was pouring something amber into a glass, gurgling and clinking.

"Boo!" said Rossi, flapping his arms.

The young man whirled in a spasm of limbs, a long arc of brown droplets hanging. The door banged him out, and Rossi was alone, watching the drinking glass roll, counting the seconds until . . .

The walls were brown again; a calendar across the room said 1965 MAY 1965. An old man, spidery on the edge of the bed, was fumbling spectacles over the rank crests of his ears. "You're real," he said.

"I'm not," said Rossi indignantly. He added, "Radishes. Lemons. Grapes. Blahhh!"

"Don't put me off," said the old man. He was ragged and hollow-templed, like a birdskull, colored like earth and milkweed floss, and his mouth was a drum over porcelain, but his oystery eyes were burning bright. "I knew the minute I saw you—you're Rossi, the one that disappeared. If you can do that—" his teeth clacked— "you must know, you've got to tell me. Those ships that have landed on the moon—what are they building there? What do they want?"

"I don't know. Nothing."

"Please," said the old man humbly. "You can't be so cruel. I tried to warn people, but they've forgotten who I am. If you know: if you could just tell me . . ."

Rossi had a qualm, thinking of heat flashing down in that one intolerable blow that would leave the city squashed, glistening, as flat as the thin film of a bug. But remembering that, after all, the old man was not real, he said, "There isn't anything. You made it up. You're dreaming."

And then, while the pure tension gathered and strained inside him, came the lake to obsidian.

And the jungle, just as it ought to be—the brown people caroling, "Hello, Mister Rossi, hello again, hello!"

And the savanna, the tall black-haired people reining in, breeze-blown, flash of teeth: "Hillo, Misser Rossi!"

And the *beach*.

The scarlet beach with its golden, laughing people: "Mista Rossi, Mista Rossi!" Heraldic glory under the clear sky, and out past the breakers the clear heart-stirring glint of sun on the sea: and the tension of the longing breaking free (stop), no need for symbols now (stop), a lifetime's distillation of *I wish* . . . spurting, channeled, done.

There he stands where he longed to be, wearing the same pleased expression, forever caught at the beginning of a hello—Rossi, the first man to travel in Time, and Rossi, the first man to Stop.

He's not to be mocked or mourned. Rossi was born a stranger; there are thousands of him, unconsidered gritty particles in the gears of history: the ne'er-do-wells, the superfluous people, shaped for some world that has never yet been invented. The air-conditioned utopias have no place for them; they would have been bad slaves and worse masters in Athens. As for the tropic isles—the Marquesas of 1800, or the Manhattan of 3526—could Rossi swim a mile, dive six fathoms, climb a fifty-foot palm? If he had stepped alive onto that scarlet shore, would the young men have had him in their canoes, or the maidens in their bowers? But see him now, stonily immortal, the symbol of a wonderful thing that happened. The childlike golden people visit him every day, except when they forget. They drape his rock-hard flesh with garlands and lay little offerings at his feet; and when he lets it rain, they thump him.

I**T WAS WHILE I WAS WRITING "BACK-ward, O Time"**—in Milford, Pennsylvania, in 1956—that I made an important discovery. Working my way through the scenes of the story in order, I came to one that would not write. I decided to skip it and come back to it later, and wrote the rest of the scenes in any order that occurred to me, leaving out anything that I didn't feel like writing. Then I cut the pages apart and rearranged them on the cot in my office, meaning to see what was missing and supply it. Lo, the story was all there.

10

BACKWARD, O TIME

‹‹‹‹‹‹‹‹‹‹‹‹‹‹‹‹‹‹‹‹‹‹‹‹‹‹‹‹‹‹‹‹‹‹‹‹‹

HE REMEMBERED THE RAIN, AND THE WHITE glare of auto headlights all around him. He could see nothing more, but he knew Emily was lying nearby, covered by someone's overcoat, not moving. It was painful, being born like this—a white knife, piercing him with each breath. All that drifted out of reach. When he woke again, they were both in the car, whirling violently back from the grinding clash of a collision. The other car receded; its headlamps finally turned to a dim glow on the far side of the hill, and vanished. The road reeled back, silently, smoothly.

Sullivan watched the stars wheel through the night as he drove. He was tired and at peace, wanting nothing, accepting everything with a quiet wonder.

How strange and wonderful it all was, entering his home for the first time—five beautifully furnished rooms, just right for Emily and himself. The books with their leather and cloth bindings. The pictures, the boxes of cigars, the wardrobes and dressers full of rich, dark clothing cut to his measure. Life, thought Laurence Wallace Sullivan, was good.

That morning before the fire, his hand took a comfortably worn leather volume from the shelves, and opened it to a thumb-marked page.

Time's graven footsteps in the sands
Behind us, if we but approach,
Sublime our own lives we can make.
Remind us, lives of all great men!

Wonderful words . . . He glanced at his watch. The sky outside his study window was lightening, from deep azure to robin's egg, faintly green over the skeletal forest of antennas. He felt stuffed; it was time for dinner. He replaced the book on its shelf, and strolled into the dining room, sighing and stretching.

The firm of Sullivan and Gaynor, he found, operated an unprinting plant that filled a three-story building on Vesey Street. The enormous machines devoured every kind of printed matter and turned it into neat rolls of paper, cans of ink, metal ingots. Their operation was far too complex for Sullivan to understand fully, and he did not try, contenting himself with the correspondence and the financial reports that flowed across his desk. Gaynor, his partner, spent more time in the plant: a red-faced, dyspeptic man with a raucous voice.

Nevertheless, Sullivan flattered himself that he understood the romance of his business: words, words from all over the world streamed into this building in nature's senseless profusion—words endlessly repeated, words plucked from dead fires and from trashcans, to be carefully unprinted and reduced to one copy only of each sermon, pamphlet, book, advertising leaflet . . . Like arrow-shapes, fan-shapes of floating paper, each found its way unerringly to the one man for whom it was intended. Sullivan (in his humble way, of course) was a public servant, a guardian of regress.

The swift years went by. Summers, on Cape Cod, Sullivan began to feel a strange discontent, listening to the curlews piping on the sands, or watching a sudden evening squall carry water streaking up from the sea. In his lips the pale Havana cigars prolonged themselves behind their smooth inch-long ash, until at last they rounded themselves off, and he drew the flame, capped them with his silver knife, and put them carefully away in the humidor. Emily's hair was darkening; they talked more now, and quarreled more. Sometimes she looked strangely at him. Where was it all heading? What was life for?

He was ten years old when he discovered sex, with Emily—a brief and unsatisfactory experience, not soon repeated. Two years later, he met Peggy.

It was in an apartment house in the fifties, where he had never been before. The door opened as he turned to it one afternoon, and she slapped his face, hard. Then they were inside, glaring at each other, breathing heavily. Sullivan felt a fury for her that was all mingled with disgust and desire. After a few minutes, sullenly, they began to take off their clothes . . .

After Peggy came Alice, and after Alice, Connie. That was in 1942; Sullivan was fifteen, in the prime of his vigor. In that year the stranger who was his son came home from Italy. Robert had just been discharged from the army; he called himself R. Gaynor Sullivan at first, was gawky and insolent, but after he enrolled in college things went better. Then in a surprisingly short time he was home again, and the apartment was not big enough. They moved to a house in Long Island City: more confusion, and Sullivan's relations with his wife were strained. He was working too hard; the firm's business was booming, due partly to a heavy lump-sum repayment to Emily's father.

Each month, the check stubs. Money poured into the account, from grocer, dentist, doctors . . . he was always hard pressed to withdraw enough to keep it balanced.

In the evenings his familiar face stared back at him from the mirror, haggard and gray. His fingers rubbed the smooth cheek; the razor came riding diagonally up with a crisp sound, trailing lather and making the bristles sprout behind it. Then the warm brush to remove the lather, and the same face, with its beard restored. What if he should leave it smooth some day? But shaving was customary.

The firm had moved several times, finally settling in a loft on Bleecker Street. Their operations had simplified; more and more employees had been let go, until Sullivan, Gaynor and three printers could run the place themselves. Sullivan often took a hand at the job press; once you had learned the trick of it, there was a soothing, almost hypnotic quality in the rhythm that flickered a blank page from the platen and slapped a printed one in to be erased, all in the acrobatic moment of safety when the metal jaws gaped. Gaynor was a much more likable fellow these days; Sullivan's days at work were filled with pleasure, as his nights at home. The boy had grown incredibly dear to him, and he was in love with Emily: he had never, Sullivan thought, been so happy.

The last vouchers had been filled; the final entries had been erased from the ledgers. The workmen were unbolting the presses and dismantling them to be carried away. There was nothing more to do but to shake hands on it, and go their separate ways. He and Gaynor ceremonially locked the door together and adjourned to the bar downstairs, feeling a premonitory glow.

"Here's to success!"

"Maybe now this fella Roosevelt is going out, we'll see some changes."

They clinked their glasses solemnly, set them down on the waitress' tray. Sobered, they left. Gaynor was going back to Minneapolis where he had a job as foreman of an unprinting plant; Sullivan himself was going to have to hunt for a while before he found a job as assistant to a paper broker. But not for long; the Boom was coming up in a few years.

Sullivan uncrumpled the *Sun,* relishing the heavy feel of the gray pages. "That woman is out of office in Texas," he announced, adding, "Good riddance!" Yes, that was what the headline said. Women governors—what was the world coming to?

Emily, folding diapers, did not seem to hear. She was losing her figure again; she seemed pale, tired and listless. Little Robert was grunting in his cradle; he had shrunk to a fat handful, more animal than baby. He slept nearly all the time, when he was not howling, or further distending Emily's swollen breasts. Life was a queer business. In another month it would be time to take them

184

both to the hospital, and only Emily would be coming back. That was funny; he had loved the child, and took an affectionate interest in it even now, but it would be almost a relief to get rid of it. Afterward, it would be a good six months before Emily got her figure back . . .

She glanced at him sidelong. She was still a lovely woman, Emily: but what did she secretly think of him? What was it really all about?

The minister's voice droned in his ears. Emily, looking more beautiful than he had ever seen her, gently moved out of his embrace. He took the ring from her finger, and handed it to Bob. "I divorce thee with this ring," he said.

Afterward they went out together, many times, but never to bed except once, hastily, in the back room one night when her parents were away. At a party one morning they chatted inconsequentially; then a polite stranger said, "Emily, I want you to say goodbye to Larry Sullivan," and led him away. He knew he would never see her again.

From that day on, there was an emptiness in his life. He tried to fill it with amusements—too much liquor, too much music. He met girls, and kissed them, took them on dates, but he missed his wife. It was hard to get used to, living alone after all these years.

Still, life had its compensations. There was an endless interest in watching the changes the years brought—seeing it all work out.

Automobiles lost all trace of their former streamlines, became elegantly spare or even boxy, hinting at victorias and broughams to come. There were fewer machines on the streets, and fewer people; the air was purer. Garbo replaced Grable on the silver screen. Abruptly, then, the movies ceased to talk. The incomparable Chaplin came into his own; the Keystone cops were born. Sullivan watched it all with fascinated eyes. Technological regress was certainly a wonderful thing! And yet sometimes Sullivan found himself thinking nostalgically of the old blaring, bustling days.

Luckily there was still the War to come. Europe was

rousing from her long sleep; and to the East, Holy Russia was being born.

Sullivan nervously fingered the scar on his shin. He was due to go to field hospital with it, he judged—it was tight and raw-feeling, and itched. It was the worst scar he had, puckered and stretching halfway up his shinbone; he would be glad to get rid of it, and go on to the front. War was not much like the movies, so far.

He walked out of the barracks tent into the sunlight, helping himself along with his slender cane. There were a lot of other casualties; he supposed this must be the prelude of the big battle of the Argonne that he had read about in the prophecies. That would be where his number came up. What would it be, a mortar shell, or hand-to-hand—or even something anticlimactic, like falling over a tent-rope in the dark? He wished the time would come, and get it over.

He met his father, briefly, when he came home from France. The old man was very gray and shaky, and they did not seem to have much in common; it was a relief on both sides, Sullivan thought, when he went off to Cornell.

He was enrolled as a senior, which meant he had to go the full four years. Sullivan did not mind that; after all, the years you spent in college were the most important ones of your life. Here everything you had thought and read, all you knew, all you had been, poured out of you and funneled down to the instructee of that particular class. Then the instructee would sum it all up in one of his lectures, dry or brilliant according to who it was; and eventually the essence of it would get into the ultimate copy of a textbook, to be absorbed by the author and so returned to nature, used up, got rid of.

In the spring he went out for football. He was registered in the athletic prediction books as playing two full seasons on the varsity. The books did not say so, but probably that was where he was going to get rid of the crook in his nose.

Professor Toohey was an old duck who took a fancy to Sullivan before he had been in college a year. They used to spout beer, down in Toohey's dark cellar where he kept a keg for it, and talk philosophy. "There's something to think about," Toohey might begin, circling up to a subject they had discussed before. "How can we tell? The reverse sequence of causation may be just as valid as the one we are experiencing. Cause-and-effect are arbitrary, after all."

"But it sounds pretty fantastic," Sullivan would say cautiously.

"It's hard for us to imagine, just because we're not used to it. It's only a matter of viewpoint. Water would run downhill, and so on. Energy would flow the other way—from total concentration to total dispersion. Why not?"

Sullivan tried hard to visualize that peculiar world; it gave him a half-pleasant shudder. Imagine never knowing the date of your death . . . "Everything would be backwards. If you meant 'catch,' you'd have to say 'throw.' All the words would have to mean different things—all the verbs that express duration, anyway. There are difficulties to it."

"It all makes perfectly good sense in its own terms. Friction would be a factor to be subtracted from energy calculations, not added. And so on. The universe would be expanding; we'd heat our houses with furnaces instead of cooling them. Grass would grow out of seeds. And you would take food into your body and expel waste matter, instead of increting and exgesting as we do. That's right!"

Sullivan grinned. "You mean, we'd come out of the bodies of women and be buried in the ground when we died?"

"Think about it for a minute. It would seem perfectly natural. We might live backward, death to birth, and never know the difference. Which came first, the chicken or the egg? Do wars cause armies, or armies wars? What do we mean by causation, anyway? Think about it."

"Hmmm."

And the formal end-question: "Sullivan, what do you think about the principle of causation?"

He wished he knew.

The world was growing larger and brighter, now that he was fifty-two. Sullivan had a furious energy that drove him out of doors all day in good weather; even in winter he stood about, watching the freezing ground water rush up the drainspout, or letting the snow form on his head and shoulders, drifting up into the white sky as it did from the ground on which he stood. Whatever came, he took without question; if his fingers and nose were bright pink with cold when he went out, the snow would warm them; if he awoke with a black eye, a friend would heal it with his fist. Sullivan climbed his friends' backs and leaped off, and they his, with peals of cracked idiot laughter. They fidgeted in class, made comical faces at one another from behind books, swarmed yelling up hill and down again. For repletion there was mealtime, and time was the cure for hunger. The hardest thing was that Mrs. Hastings would not let him out of bed when he awoke early in the morning, though any fool could see he was not going to sleep anymore; after that his day was one long gallop.

There came a day when Sullivan and his father were seized with a nervous anticipation; it took the form of tears on Sullivan's part, scowls and throat-clearings on his father's. All day they were good for nothing, and could not look at each other. At last, in the late afternoon, they dressed to go out.

His father drove, following the roads automatically. When they got out, Sullivan saw that they were in a cemetery.

Something clutched tight at his heart. His father's arm came unwelcome around him, the strong fingers hard on his arm as he stumbled. Others were moving nearby: at last they all grouped, and turned, and were standing beside a half-open grave. Two men were uncovering the box already, expertly catching each shovel-load of dirt as it leaped, thrusting it sharply into the pile and waiting for the next.

Afterward, they raised the box with broad straps until it rested on boards laid across the hole in the ground. The minister, standing on the far side of the grave, unfolded his hands and spoke.

" . . . From dust thou comest, and dust thou art . . ." When he was finished, he coughed apologetically and was silent. The crowd began to flow away. The workmen stood beside the grave and the box, bareheaded in the sunlight, hands at their sides.

Sullivan was trying to get used to an unaccustomed pain that had come to live in his chest. It was like being sick, but he was not sick. It was not even an honest pain, caused by medicine; it was just a kind of persistent crying ache that would not go away.

He saw now, with the eye of disillusionment, that all his past gaiety had been foolish. Here he was in the last decade of his life, fifty-two years behind him, and what could he show for it? Nothing but this ache of loss. His hand worked reflexively at the contents of his pocket, and brought up a spiny handful: jackknife, pencil stub, assorted nails, a wad of grimy string, two marbles and an aggie, three pennies, a gray chip of rock with shiny specks in it, cracker crumbs, and over everything, pocket lint. Dust and ashes.

A hot tear crawled up his cheek.

The old man came into the room wearily, setting a broom down in the corner. He had been taking care of the house himself, these last few days; Mrs. Hastings had disappeared, and Sullivan did not think she was coming back.

"Put your coat on, Larry," said his father with a sigh.

Sullivan did as he was told. In silence they went out to the corner and waited for the street car. Gradually Sullivan began to recognize the route they took. It was the same way they had gone that time when he had his tonsils put in. A touch of fear came to him, but he endured it and said nothing.

It was the hospital they were going to, all right. In the dark lobby, they did not look at each other. Sullivan's father stood with his bowler in both hands, talking to a doctor, while Sullivan walked mechanically past him down the hall.

Where was he going in this unpleasant dark place with its sharp smells of ether and formaldehyde, and its clicking sharp-heeled nurses with sour faces over their trays? The closed doors moved past on either side.

Sullivan stopped, and turned, with an unaccountable tightness in his throat, and found himself facing a door like the others. But this one was going to open.

The knob turned; Sullivan could not bear it. He wanted to run, but felt rooted to the spot. What, oh what was it? The door was opening, and inside, on the bed—

A gray woman. Her tired eyes opened, and she tried to smile at him.

A painful rapture swelled inside his chest. Now at last he understood; he understood everything.

"Mother," he said.

"THE LAST WORD" IS ONE OF THREE stories I have written using orthodox Christian materials—God, the devil, etc.—which proves that my childhood training had some use after all.

11

THE LAST WORD

THE FIRST WORD, I LIKE TO THINK, WAS "Ouch." Some caveman, trying to knock a stone into better shape with another stone, slipped, hit his thumb —and there you are. Language.

I have an affection for these useless and unverifiable facts. Take the first dog. He, I feel sure, was an unusually clever but cowardly wolf, who managed to terrorize early man into throwing him a scrap. Early man himself was a terrible coward. Man and wolf discovered that they could hunt together, in their cowardly fashion, and there you are again. "Domesticated animals."

I admit that I was lax during the first few thousand years. By the time I realized that Man needed closer supervision, many of the crucial events had already taken place. I was then a young—well, let us say a young fallen angel. Had I been older and more experienced, history would have turned out very differently.

There was that time when I happened across a young Egyptian and his wife sitting on a stone near the bank of the Nile. They looked glum; the water was rising. A hungry jackal was not far away, and it crossed my mind that if I distracted the young people's attention for a few minutes, the jackal might surprise them.

"High enough for you?" I asked agreeably, pointing to the water.

They looked at me rather sharply. I had put on the appearance of a human being, as nearly as possible, but the illusion was no good without a large cloak, which was odd for the time of year.

The man said, "If it never got any higher, it would suit me."

"Why, I'm surprised to hear you say that," I replied. "If the river didn't rise, your fields wouldn't be so fertile—isn't that right?"

"True," said the man, "but also if it didn't rise, my fields would still be my fields." He showed me where the water was carrying away his fences. "Every year we argue over the boundaries, after the flood, and this year my neighbor has a cousin living with him. The cousin is a big, unneccessarily muscular man." Broodingly, he began to draw lines in the dirt with a long stick.

These lines made me a little nervous. The Sumerians, up north, had recently discovered the art of writing, and I was still suffering from the shock.

"Well, life is a struggle," I told the man soothingly. "Eat or be eaten. Let the strong win, and the weak go to the wall."

The man did not seem to be listening. "If there was some way," he said, staring at his marks, "that we could keep tally of the fences, and put them back exactly the way they were before—"

"Nonsense," I interrupted. "You're a wicked boy to suggest such a thing. What would your old dad say? Whatever was good enough for him . . ."

All this time, the woman had not spoken. Now she took the long stick out of the man's hand and examined it curiously. "But why not?" she said, pointing to the lines in the dirt. The man had drawn an outline roughly like that of his fields, with the stone marking one corner.

It was at that moment that the jackal charged. He was gaunt and desperate, and his jaws were full of sharp yellow teeth.

With the stick she was holding, the woman hit him over the snout. The jackal ran away, howling piteously.

"Tut," I said, taken aback. "Life is struggle. . . ."

The woman said a rude word, and the man came at

me with a certain light in his eye, so I went away. And do you know, when I came back after the next flood, they were measuring off the fields with ropes and poles?

Cowardice again—that man did not want to argue about the boundaries with his neighbor's muscular cousin. Another lucky accident, and there you are. Geometry.

If only I had had the foresight to send a cave bear after the first man who showed that original, lamentable spark of curiosity . . . Well, it was no use wishing. Not even I could turn the clock back.

Oh, I gained a few points as time went on. Instead of trying to suppress the inventive habit, I learned to direct it along useful lines. I was instrumental in teaching the Chinese how to make gunpowder. (Seventy-five parts saltpeter, thirteen parts brimstone, twelve parts charcoal, if you're interested. But the grinding and mixing are terribly difficult; they never would have worked it out by themselves.) When they used it only for fireworks, I didn't give up; I introduced it again in Europe. Patience was my long suit. I never took offense. When Luther threw an inkwell at me, I was not discouraged. I persevered.

I did not worry about my occasional setbacks; it was my successes that threatened to overthrow me. After each of my wars, there was an impulse that drew men closer together. Little groups fought each other until they formed bigger groups; then the big groups fought each other until there was only one left.

I had played this game out over and over, with the Egyptians, the Persians, the Greeks, and, in the end, I had destroyed every one. But I knew the danger. When the last two groups spanned the world between them, the last war might end in universal peace, because there would be no one left to fight.

My final war would have to be fought with weapons so devastating, so unprecedentedly awful, that man would never recover from it.

It was.

On the fifth day, riding the gale, I could look down on a planet stripped of its forests, its fields, even its topsoil: there was nothing left but the bare, riven rock, cratered like the moon. The sky shed a sickly purple light, full of lightnings that flickered like serpents' tongues. Well, I had paid a heavy price, but Man was gone.

Not quite. There were two left, a man and a woman. I found them alive and healthy, for the time being, on a crag that overhung the radioactive ocean. They were inside a transparent dome, or field of force, that kept out the contaminated air.

You see how near I had come to final defeat? If they had managed to distribute that machine widely before my war started . . . But this was the only one they had made. And there they were inside it, like two white mice in a cage.

They recognized me immediately. The woman was young and comely, as they go.

"This is quite an ingenious device," I told them courteously. In actuality, it was an ugly thing, all wires and tubes and so on, packed layers deep under the floor, with a big semicircular control board and a lot of flashing lights. "It's a pity I didn't know about it earlier; we might have put it to some use."

"Not this one," said the man grimly. "This is a machine for peace. Just incidentally, it generates a field that will keep out an atomic explosion."

"Why do you say, 'just incidentally'?" I asked him.

"It's only the way he talks," the woman said. "If you had held off another six months, we might have beaten you. But now I suppose you think you've won."

"Oh, indeed," I said. "That is, I will have, before long. Meanwhile, we might as well make ourselves comfortable."

They were standing in tense, aggressive attitudes in front of the control board, and took no notice of my suggestion. "Why do you say I 'think' I've won?" I asked.

"It's just the way I talk. Well, at least we gave you a long fight of it."

The man put in, "And now you're brave enough to show yourself." He had a truculent jaw. There had been a good many like him in the assault planes, on the first day of the war.

"Oh," I said, "I've been here all the time."

"From the very beginning?" the woman asked.

I bowed to her. "Almost," I said, to be strictly fair.

There was a little silence, one of those uncomfortable pauses that interrupt the best of talks. A tendril of glowing spray sprang up just outside. After a moment, the floor settled slightly.

The man and woman looked anxiously at their control board. The colored lights were flashing. "Is that the accumulators?" I heard the woman ask in a strained, low voice.

"No," the man answered. "They're all right—still charging. Give them another minute."

The woman turned to me. I was glad of it, because there was something about their talk together that disturbed me. She said, "Why couldn't you let things alone? Heaven knows we weren't perfect, but we weren't that bad. You didn't have to make us do that to each other."

I smiled. The man said slowly, "Peace would have poisoned him. He would have shriveled up like a dried apple." It was the truth, or near enough, and I did not contradict him. The floor lurched again.

"You're waiting to watch us suffer," the woman said. "Aren't you?"

I smiled.

"But that may take a long time. Even if we fall into the ocean, this globe will keep us alive. We might be in here for months before our food gives out."

"I can wait," I said pleasantly.

She turned to her husband. "Then we *must* be the last," she said. "Don't you see? If we weren't, would he be here?"

"That's right," said the man, with a note in his voice that I did not like. He bent over the control board. "There's nothing more to keep us here. Ava, will you . . ." He stepped back, indicating a large red-handled switch.

The woman stepped over and put her hand on it. "One moment," I said uneasily. "What are you doing? What is that thing?"

She smiled at me. "This isn't just a machine to generate a force field," she said.

"No?" I asked. "What else?"

"It's a time machine," the man said.

"We're going back," the woman whispered, "to the beginning."

Back, to the beginning, to start all over.

Without me.

The woman said, "You've won Armageddon, but you've lost Earth."

I knew the answer to that, of course, but she was a woman and had the last word.

I gestured toward the purple darkness outside. "Lost Earth? What do you call this?"

She poised her hand on the switch.

"Hell," she said.

And I have remembered her voice, through ten thousand lonely years.

THIS IS A STORY THAT OFFENDED
Harlan Ellison and Robert Silverberg—Ellison has never ceased to criticize me for it to this day—because it seemed to them that I had broken a cardinal rule by saying to the reader ´that which was not true. If they had read the story with more care, they would have noticed that it is one of the characters—drunken and dishonest, an obviously unreliable witness—who says the thing that is untrue, and furthermore that what he says is paired with another assertion that is also disproved in the course of the action. "Man in the Jar" is really nothing more than a sheckleyized version of the joke about the man who thought he was dead. A psychiatrist tried to reason with him, pointing out that dead men don't breathe, don't talk, etc., but the madman refused to grant any of this. Finally the psychiatrist got him to admit that dead men don't bleed. The doctor got out his scalpel and used it; the madman stared at the blood welling from his thumb and said, "What do you know, doc—dead men *do* bleed!"

12

MAN IN THE JAR

‹‹‹‹‹‹‹‹‹‹‹‹‹‹‹‹‹‹‹‹‹‹‹‹‹‹‹‹‹‹‹‹‹‹

THE HOTEL ROOM ON THE PLANET MENG WAS small and crowded. Blue-tinged sunlight from the window fell on a soiled gray carpet, a massive sandbox dotted with cigarette butts, a clutter of bottles. One corner of the room was piled high with baggage and curios. The occupant, a Mr. R. C. Vane of Earth, was sitting near the door: a man about fifty, clean shaven, with bristling iron-gray hair. He was quietly, murderously drunk.

There was a tap on the door and the bellhop slipped in—a native, tall and brown, with greenish black hair cut too long in the back. He looked about nineteen. He had one green eye and one blue.

"Set it there," said Vane.

The bellhop put his tray down. "Yes, sir." He took the unopened bottle of Ten Star off the tray, and the ice bucket, and the seltzer bottle, crowding them in carefully among the things already on the table. Then he put the empty bottles and ice bucket back on the tray. His hands were big and knob-jointed; he seemed too long and wide-shouldered for his tight green uniform.

"So this is Meng City," said Vane, watching the bellhop. Vane was sitting erect and unrumpled in his chair, with his striped moth-wing jacket on and his string tie tied. He might have been sober, except for the deliberate way he spoke, and the redness of his eyes.

"Yes, sir," said the bellhop, straightening up with the tray in his hands. "This your first time here, sir?"

"I came through two weeks ago," Vane told him. "I did not like it then, and I do not like it now. Also, I do not like this room."

"Management is sorry if you don't like the room, sir. Very good view from this room."

"It's dirty and small," said Vane, "but it doesn't matter. I'm checking out this afternoon. Leaving on the afternoon rocket. I wasted two weeks upcountry, investigating Marack stories. Nothing to it—just native talk. Miserable little planet." He smiled, eyeing the bellhop. "What's your name, boy?"

"Jimmy Rocksha, sir."

"Well, Jimmy Rocks in the Head, look at that pile of stuff." Tourist goods, scarves and tapestries, rugs, blankets and other things were mounded over the piled suitcases. It looked like an explosion in a curio shop. "There's about forty pounds of it I have no room for, not counting that knocked-down jar. Any suggestions?"

The bellhop thought about it slowly. "Sir, if I might suggest, you might put the scarves and things inside the jar."

Vane said grudgingly, "That might work. You know how to put those things together?"

"I don't know, sir."

"Well, let us see you try. Go on, don't stand there."

The bellhop set his tray down again and crossed the room. A big bundle of gray pottery pieces, tied together with twine, had been stowed on top of Vane's wardrobe trunk, a little above the bellhop's head. Rocksha carefully removed his shoes and climbed on a chair. His brown feet were bare and clean. He lifted the bundle without effort, got down, set the bundle on the floor, and put his shoes back on.

Vane took a long swallow of his lukewarm highball, finishing it. He closed his eyes while he drank, and nodded over the glass for a moment afterward, as if listening to something inside him. "All right," he said, getting up, "let us see."

The bellhop loosened the twine. There were six long,

thick, curving pieces, shaped a little like giant shoehorns. Then there were two round ones. One was bigger; that was the bottom. The other had a handle; that was the lid. The bellhop began to separate the pieces carefully, laying them out on the carpet.

"Watch out how you touch those together," Vane grunted, coming up behind him. "I wouldn't know how to get them apart again."

"Yes, sir."

"That's an antique which I got upcountry. They used to be used for storing grain and oil. The natives claim the Maracks had the secret of making them stick the way they do. Ever heard that?"

"Upcountry boys tell a lot of fine stories, sir," said the bellhop. He had the six long pieces arranged, well separated, in a kind of petal pattern around the big flat piece. They took up most of the free space; the jar would be chest-high when it was assembled.

Standing up, the bellhop took two of the long curved pieces and carefully brought the sides closer together. They seemed to jump the last fraction of an inch, like magnets, and merged into one smooth piece. Peering, Vane could barely make out the join.

In the same way, the bellhop added another piece to the first two. Now he had half the jar assembled. Carefully he lowered this half jar toward the edge of the big flat piece. The pieces clicked together. The bellhop stooped for another side piece.

"Hold on a minute," said Vane suddenly. "Got an idea. Instead of putting that thing all together, then trying to stuff things into it, use your brain. Put the things in, *then* put the rest of the side on."

"Yes, sir," said the bellhop. He laid the piece of crockery down again and picked up some light blankets, which he dropped on the bottom of the jar.

"Not that way, dummy," said Vane impatiently. "Get *in* there—pack them down tight."

The bellhop hesitated. "Yes, sir." He stepped delicately over the remaining unassembled pieces and knelt on the bottom of the jar, rolling the blankets and pressing them snugly in.

Behind him, Vane moved on tiptoe like a dancer, putting two long pieces quietly together—*tic!*—then a third—*tic!*—and then as he lifted them, *tic, clack!* the sides merged into the bottom and the top. The jar was complete.

The bellhop was inside.

Vane breathed hard through flared nostrils. He took a cigar out of a green-lizard pocket case, cut it with a lapel knife, and lit it. Breathing smoke, he leaned over and looked down into the jar.

Except for a moan of surprise when the jar closed, the bellhop had not made a sound. Looking down, Vane saw his brown face looking up. "Let me out of this jar, please, sir," said the bellhop.

"Can't do that," said Vane. "They didn't tell me how, upcountry."

The bellhop moistened his lips. "Upcountry, they use a kind of tree grease," he said. "It creeps between the pieces, and they fall apart."

"They didn't give me anything like that," said Vane indifferently.

"Then please, sir, you break this jar and let me come out."

Vane picked a bit of tobacco off his tongue. He looked at it curiously and then flicked it away. "I spotted you," he said, "in the lobby the minute I came in this morning. Tall and thin. Too strong for a native. One green eye, one blue. Two weeks I spent, upcountry, looking; and there you were in the lobby."

"Sir—?"

"You're a Marack," said Vane flatly.

The bellhop did not answer for a moment. "But sir," he said incredulously, "Maracks are *legends,* sir. Nobody believes that anymore. There are no Maracks."

"You lifted that jar down like nothing," said Vane. "Two boys put it up there. You've got the hollow temples. You've got the long jaw and the hunched shoulders." Frowning, he took a billfold out of his pocket and took out a yellowed card. He showed it to the bellhop. "Look at that."

It was a faded photograph of a skeleton in a glass case. There was something disturbing about the skeleton. It was too long and thin; the shoulders seemed hunched, the skull was narrow and hollow-templed. Under it, the printing said, ABORIGINE OF NEW CLEVELAND, MENG (SIGMA LYRAE II) and in smaller letters, *Newbold Anthropological Museum, Ten Eyck, Queensland, N. T.*

"Found it between the pages of a book two hundred years old," said Vane, carefully putting it back. "It was mailed as a postcard to an ancestor of mine. A year later, I happened to be on Nova Terra. Now get this. The museum is still there, but that skeleton is not. They deny it ever was there. Curator seemed to think it was a fake. None of the native races on Meng have skeletons like that, he said."

"Must be a fake, sir," the bellhop agreed.

"I will tell you what I did next," Vane went on. "I read all the contemporary accounts I could find of frontier days on this planet. A couple of centuries ago, nobody on Meng thought the Maracks were legends. They looked enough like the natives to pass, but they had certain special powers. They could turn one thing into another. They could influence your mind by telepathy, if you weren't on your guard against them. I found this interesting. I next read all the export records back to a couple of centuries ago. Also, the geological charts in *Planetary Survey*. I discovered something. It just happens, there is no known source of natural diamonds anywhere on Meng."

"No, sir?" said the bellhop nervously.

"Not one. No diamonds, and no place where they ever could have been mined. But until two hundred years ago, Meng exported one billion stellors' worth of flawless diamonds every year. I ask, where did they come from? And why did they stop?"

"I don't know, sir."

"The Maracks made them," said Vane. "For a trader named Soong and his family. They died. After that, no more diamonds from Meng." He opened a suitcase, rummaged inside it a moment, and took out two objects. One was a narrow oval bundle of something wrapped in stiff yellow plant fibers; the other was a shiny gray-black lump half the size of his fist.

"Do you know what this is?" Vane asked, holding up the oval bundle.

"No, sir."

"Airweed, they call it upcountry. One of the old men had this one buried under his hut, along with the jar. *And* this." He held up the black lump. "Nothing special about it, would you say? Just a piece of graphite, probably from the old mine at Badlong. But graphite is pure carbon. And so is a diamond."

He put both objects carefully down on the nearby table, and wiped his hands. The graphite had left black smudges on them. "Think about it," he said. "You've got exactly one hour, till three o'clock." Delicately he tapped his cigar over the mouth of the jar. A few flakes of powdery ash floated down on the bellhop's upturned face.

Vane went back to his chair. He moved deliberately and a little stiffly, but did not stagger. He peeled the foil off the bottle of Ten Star. He poured himself a substantial drink, added ice, splashed a little seltzer in. He took a long, slow swallow.

"Sir," said the bellhop finally, "you know I can't make any diamonds out of black rock. What's going to happen, when it comes three o'clock, and that rock is still just a piece of rock?"

"I think," said Vane, "I will just take the wrappings off that airweed and drop it in the jar with you. Airweed, I am told, will expand to hundreds of times its volume in air. When it fills the jar to the brim, I will put the lid on. And when we're crossing that causeway to the spaceport, I think you may get tipped off the packrat into the bay. The bottom is deep silt, they tell me." He took another long, unhurried swallow.

"Think about it," he said, staring at the jar with red eyes.

Inside the jar, it was cool and dim. The bellhop had enough room to sit fairly comfortably with his legs crossed, or else he could kneel, but then his face came right up to the mouth of the jar. The opening was too

204

small for his head. He could not straighten up any farther, or put his legs out. The bellhop was sweating in his tight uniform. He was afraid. He was only nineteen, and nothing like this had ever happened to him before.

The clink of ice came from across the room. The bellhop said, "Sir?"

The chair springs whined, and after a moment the Earthman's face appeared over the mouth of the jar. His chin was dimpled. There were gray hairs in his nostrils, and a few gray and black bristles in the creases of loose skin around his jaw. His red eyes were hooded and small. He looked down into the bellhop's face without speaking.

"Sir," the bellhop said earnestly, "do you know how much they pay me here at this hotel?"

"No."

"Twelve stellors a week, sir, and my meals. If I could make diamonds, sir, why would I be working here?"

Vane's expression did not change. "I will tell you that," he said. "Soong must have been sweating you Maracks to get a billion stellors a year. There used to be thousands of you on this continent alone, but now there are so few that you can disappear among the natives. I would guess the diamonds took too much out of you. You're close to extinction now. And you're all scared. You've gone underground. You've still got your powers, but you don't dare use them—unless there's no other way to keep your secret. You were lords of this planet once, but you'd rather stay alive. Of course, all this is merely guesswork."

"Yes, sir," said the bellhop despairingly.

The house phone rang. Vane crossed the room and thumbed the key down, watching the bellhop from the corner of his eye. "Yes?"

"Mr. Vane," said the voice of the desk clerk, "if I may ask, did the refreshments you ordered arrive?"

"The bottle came," Vane answered. "Why?"

The bellhop was listening, balling his fists on his knees. Sweat stood out on his brown forehead.

"Oh nothing really, Mr. Vane," said the clerk's voice, "only the boy did not come back. He is usually very reliable, Mr. Vane. But excuse me for troubling you."

"All right," said Vane stonily, and turned the phone off. He came back to the jar. He swayed a little, rocking back and forth from heels to toes. In one hand he had the highball glass; with the other he was playing with the little osmiridium knife that hung by an expanding chain from his lapel. After a while he said, "Why didn't you call for help?"

The bellhop did not answer. Vane went on softly, "Those hotel phones will pick up a voice across the room, I know. So why were you so quiet?"

The bellhop said unhappily, "If I did yell, sir, they would find me in this jar."

"And so?"

The bellhop grimaced. "There's some other people that still believe in Maracks, sir. I have to be careful, with my eyes. They would know there could only be the one reason why you would treat me like this."

Vane studied him for a moment. "And you'd take a chance on the airweed, and the bay, just to keep anyone from finding out?"

"It's a long time since we had any Marack hunts on this planet, sir."

Vane snorted softly. He glanced up at the wall clock. "Forty minutes," he said, and went back to his chair by the door.

The bellhop said nothing. The room was silent except for the faint whir of the clock. After a while Vane moved to the writing desk. He put a printed customs declaration form in the machine and began tapping keys slowly, muttering over the complicated Interstellar symbols.

"Sir," said the bellhop quietly, "you know you can't kill a biped person and just get away. This is not like the bad old times."

Vane grunted, tapping keys. "Think not?" He took a sip from his highball and set it down again with a clink of ice.

"Even if they find out you have mistreated the headman upcountry, sir, they will be very severe."

"They won't find out," Vane said. "Not from him."

"Sir, even if I could make you your diamond, it

206

would only be worth a few thousand stellors. That is nothing to a man like you."

Vane paused and half turned. "Flawless, that weight, it would be worth a hundred thousand. But I'm not going to sell it." He turned back to the machine, finished a line, and started another.

"No, sir?"

"No. I'm going to keep it." Vane's eyes half closed; his fingers poised motionless on the keys. He seemed to come to himself with a start, hit another key, and rolled the paper out of the machine. He picked up an envelope and rose, looking over the paper in his hand.

"Just to keep it, sir, and look at it now and then?" the bellhop asked softly. Sweat was running down into his eyes, but he kept his fists motionless on his knees.

"That's it," said Vane with the same faraway look. He folded the paper slowly and put it into the envelope as he walked toward the message chute near the door. At the last moment he checked himself, snapped the paper open again and stared at it. A slow flush came to his cheeks. Crumpling the paper slowly in his hands, he said, "That almost worked." He tore the paper across deliberately, and then again, and again, before he threw the pieces away.

"Just one symbol in the wrong box," he said, "but it was the right wrong symbol. I'll tell you where you made your mistake though, boy." He came closer.

"I don't understand," said the bellhop.

it and smoothed it out. "Right here, in the box where the loyalty oath to the Archon is supposed to go, I wrote the symbol for 'pig.' If I sent that down, the thought police would be up here in fifteen minutes." He balled up the paper again, into an even smaller wad, and dropped it on the carpet. "Think you can make me forget to pick that up again and burn it, before I leave?" he said amiably. "Try."

The bellhop swallowed hard. "Sir, you did that *yourself*. You made a slip of the finger."

Vane smiled at him for the first time, and walked away.

The bellhop put his back against the wall of the jar and pushed with all his strength against the opposite side. He pushed until the muscles of his back stood out in knotted ropes. The pottery walls were as solid as rock.

He was sweating more than ever. He relaxed, breathing hard; he rested his head on his knees and tried to think. The bellhop had heard of bad Earthmen before, but he had never seen one like this.

He straightened up. "Sir, are you still there?"

The chair creaked and Vane came over, glass in hand.

"Sir," said the bellhop earnestly, "if I can prove to you that I'm really not a Marack, will you let me go? I mean, you'll have to let me go then, won't you?"

"Why, certainly," said Vane agreeably. "Go ahead

"You thought if you could get me to thinking about that diamond, my mind would wander. It did—but I knew what was happening. Here's where you made your mistake. I don't give a damn about that diamond."

"Sir?" said the bellhop in bewilderment.

"A stellor to you is a new pair of pants. A stellor to me, or a thousand stellors, is just a poker chip. It's the game that counts. The excitement."

"Sir, I don't know what you mean."

Vane snorted. "You know, all right. You're getting a little dangerous now, aren't you? You're cornered, and the time's running out. So you took a little risk." He stooped, picked up one of the scraps of paper, unfolded

"Well, sir, haven't you heard other things about the Marack—some other test?"

Vane looked thoughtful; he put his chin down on his chest and his eyes filmed over.

"About what they can or can't do?" the bellhop suggested. "If I tell you, sir, you might think I made it up."

"Wait a minute," said Vane. He was swaying slightly, back and forth, his eyes half closed. His string tie was still perfectly tied, his striped moth-wing jacket immaculate. He said, "I remember something. The Marack hunters used this a good deal, I understand. Maracks can't stand liquor. It makes them sick."

"You're positive about that, sir?" the bellhop said eagerly.

"Of course I'm positive. It's like poison to a Marack."

"All right then, sir!"

Vane nodded, and went to the table to get the bottle of Ten Star. It was still two-thirds full. He came back with it and said, "Open your mouth."

The bellhop opened his mouth wide and shut his eyes. He did not like Earth liquor, especially brandy, but he thought he could drink it if it would get him out of this jar.

The liquor hit his teeth and the back of his mouth in one solid splash; it poured down both cheeks and some of it ran up his nose. The bellhop choked and strangled. The liquor burned all the way down his throat and windpipe; tears blinded him; he couldn't breathe. When the paroxysm was over, he gasped, "Sir—sir—that wasn't a fair test. You shouldn't have poured it on me like that. Give me a little bit in a glass."

"Now, I want to be fair," said Vane. "We'll try it again." He found an empty glass, poured two fingers of brandy into it, and came back. "Easy does it," he said, and trickled a little into the bellhop's mouth.

The bellhop swallowed, his head swimming in brandy fumes. "Once more," said Vane, and poured again. The bellhop swallowed. The liquor was gathering in a ball of heat inside him. "Again." He swallowed.

Vane stood back. The bellhop opened his eyes and looked blissfully up at him. "You see, sir? No sickness. I drank it, and I'm not sick!"

"Hmm," said Vane with an interested expression. "Well, imagine that. Maracks *can* drink liquor."

The bellhop's victorious smile slowly faded. He looked incredulous. "Sir, don't joke with me," he said.

Vane sniffed. "If you think it's a joke—" he said with heavy humor.

"Sir, you *promised*."

"Oh, no. By no means," said Vane. "I said if you could prove to me that you are not a Marack. Go ahead, prove it. Here's another little test for you, incidentally. An anatomist I know looked at that skeleton and told me it was constricted at the shoulders. A Marack can't lift his hand higher than his head. So begin by telling me why you stood on a chair to get my bundle down —or better yet, just put your arm out the neck of that jar."

There was a silence. Vane took another cigar out of the green-lizard case, cut it with the little osmiridium knife, and lit it without taking his eyes off the bellhop. "Now you're getting dangerous again," he said. "You're thinking it over, down there. This begins to get interesting. You're wondering how you can kill me from inside that jar, without using your Marack powers. Go ahead. Think about it."

He breathed smoke, leaning toward the jar. "You've got fifteen minutes."

Working without haste, Vane rolled up all the blankets and other souvenirs and strapped them into bundles. He removed some toilet articles from the dresser and packed them away in his grip. He took a last look around the room, saw the paper scraps on the floor and picked up the tiny pellet he had made of one of them. He showed it to the bellhop with a grin, then dropped it into the ash-receiver and burned it. He sat down comfortably in the chair near the door. "Five minutes," he said.

"Four minutes," he said.

"Three minutes."

"Two minutes."

"All right," said the bellhop.

"Yes?" Vane got up and stood over the jar.

"I'll do it—I'll make the diamond."

"Ahh?" said Vane, half questioningly. He picked up the lump of graphite and held it out.

"I don't need to touch it," the bellhop said listlessly. "Just put it down on the table. This will take about a minute."

"Umm," said Vane, watching him keenly. The bellhop was crouched in the jar, eyes closed; all Vane could see of him was the glossy green-black top of his head.

His voice was muffled. "If you just hadn't had that airweed," he said sullenly.

Vane snorted. "I didn't need the airweed. I could have taken care of you in a dozen ways. This knife"—he held it up—"has a molar steel blade. Cut through anything, like cheese. I could have minced you up and floated you down the drain."

The bellhop's face turned up, pale and wide-eyed.

"No time for that now, though," Vane said. "It would have to be the airweed."

"Is that how you're going to get me loose, afterward?" the bellhop asked. "Cut the jar, with that knife?"

"Mm? Oh, certainly," said Vane, watching the graphite lump. Was there a change in its appearance, or not?

"I'm disappointed, in a way," he said. "I thought you'd give me a fight. You Maracks are overrated, I suppose."

"It's all done," said the bellhop. "Take it, please, and let me out."

Vane's eyes narrowed. "It doesn't look done to me," he said.

"It just looks black on the outside, sir. Just rub it off."

Vane did not move.

"Go ahead, sir," said the bellhop urgently. "Pick it up and see."

"You're a little too eager," Vane said. He took a fountain pen out of his pocket and used it to prod the graphite gingerly. Nothing happened; the lump moved freely across the tabletop. Vane touched it briefly with one finger, then picked it up in his hand. "No tricks?" he said quizzically. He felt the lump, weighed it, put it down again. There were black graphite smears in his palm.

Vane opened his lapel knife and cut the graphite lump down the middle. It fell into two shiny black pieces. "Graphite," said Vane, and with an angry gesture he stuck the knife blade into the table.

He turned to the bellhop, dusting off his hands. "I don't get you," he said, prodding the oval bundle of the airweed experimentally. He picked it up. "All you did was stall. You won't fight like a Marack, you won't give in like a Marack. All you'll do is die like a Meng-boy, right?" He shook his head. "Disappointing." The

211

dry wrappings came apart in his hands. Between the fibers a dirty-white bulge began to show.

Vane lifted the package to drop it into the jar, and saw that the bellhop's scared face filled the opening. While he hesitated briefly, the gray-white floss of the airweed foamed slowly out over the back of his hand. Vane felt a constriction, and instinctively tried to drop the bundle. He couldn't. The growing, billowing floss was sticky—it stuck to his hand. Then his sleeve. It grew, slowly but with a horrifying steadiness.

Gray-faced, Vane whipped his arm around, trying to shake off the weed. Like thick lather, the floss spattered downward but did not separate. A glob of it hit his trouser leg and clung. Another, swelling, dripped down to the carpet. His whole right arm and side were covered deep under a mound of white. The floss had now stopped growing and seemed to be stiffening.

The bellhop began to rock himself back and forth inside the jar. The jar tipped, then fell back. The bellhop rocked harder. The jar was inching its way across the carpet.

After a few moments the bellhop paused to put his face up and see which way he was going. Vane, held fast by the weed, was leaning toward the table, straining hard, reaching with his one free hand toward the knife he had put there. The carpet bulged after him in a low mound, but too much furniture was holding it.

The bellhop lowered his head and rocked the jar again, harder. When he looked up, Vane's eyes were closed tight, his face red with effort. He was extended as far as he could reach across the table, but his fingers were still clawing air an inch short of the knife. The bellhop rocked hard. The jar inched forward, came to rest solidly against the table, pinning Vane's arm against it by the flaring sleeve.

The bellhop relaxed and looked up. Feeling himself caught, the Earthman had stopped struggling and was looking down. He tugged, but could not pull the sleeve free.

Neither spoke for a moment.

"Stalemate," said Vane heavily. He showed his teeth

to the bellhop. "Close, but no prize. I can't get at you, and you can't hurt me."

The bellhop's head bowed as if in assent. After a moment his long arm came snaking up out of the jar. His fingers closed around the deadly little knife.

"A Marack *can* lift his arm higher than his head, sir," he said.

"THE ENEMY" IS ONE OF TWO STORIES that I wrote when I was having some eye trouble and thought I might go blind and was dictating into a tape recorder. The sound of one's own voice makes one solemn, not to mention the idea of going blind. These two stories—the other one is "Mary"—seem to me distinct from everything else I have written. Just think, if I had been born blind, I might have written a lot more like this.

13

THE ENEMY

≪≪≪≪≪≪≪≪≪≪≪≪≪≪≪≪≪≪≪≪≪≪≪≪≪≪≪≪≪≪≪≪≪≪≪

THE SPACESHIP LAY ON A ROCKBALL IN THE middle of the sky. There was a brilliance in Draco; it was the sun, four billion miles away. In the silence, the stars did not blink or waver: they burned, cold and afar. Polaris blazed overhead. The Milky Way hung like a frozen rainbow above the horizon.

In the yellow circle of the airlock, two figures appeared, both women, with pale, harsh faces behind the visors of their helmets. They carried a folding metal disk a hundred yards away and set it up on three tall insulators. They went back to the ship, moving lightly on tiptoe, like dancers, and came out again with a bulky collection of objects wrapped in a transparent membrane.

They sealed the membrane to the disk and inflated it by means of a hose from the ship. The objects inside were household articles: a hammock on a metal frame, a lamp, a radio transceiver. They entered the membrane through its flexible valve and set the furniture in order. Then, carefully, they brought in three last items—three tanks of growing green things, each in its protective bubble.

They unloaded a spidery vehicle with six enormous puffed wheels and left it standing on three insulators of its own.

The work was done. The two women stood facing each

other beside the bubble house. The elder said, "If your finds are good, stay here till I return in ten months. If not, leave the equipment and return in the escape shell."

They both glanced upward, where a faint spark was moving against the field of stars. The parent ship had left it in orbit before landing. If needed, it could be called down to land automatically by radio; otherwise, there was no need to waste the fuel.

"Understood," said the younger one. Her name was Zael; she was fifteen, and this was her first time away from the space city alone. Isar, her mother, went to the ship and entered it without another glance. The lock door closed; the spark overhead was drifting down toward the horizon. A short burst of flame raised the parent ship; it drifted, rising and turning as it went. Then the torch blazed out again, and in a few moments the ship was only a brighter star.

Zael turned off her suit light and stood in the darkness under the enormous half-globe of the sky. It was the only sky she knew; like her mother's mother before her, she was space-born. Centuries ago, driven out of the fat green worlds, her people had grown austere, like the arid fields of stars they roamed among. In the five great space cities, and on Pluto, Titan, Mimas, Eros and a thousand lesser worlds, they struggled for existence. They were few; life was hard and short; it was no novelty for a fifteen-year-old child to be left alone to mine a planetoid.

The ship was a dim spark, climbing up the long slant toward the ecliptic. Up there, Isar and her daughters had deliveries to make and cargoes to take on at Pluto. Gron, their city, had sent them down this long detour to make a survey. The planetoid was now approaching the sun, on its eccentric cometary orbit, for the first time in twenty thousand years. Once here, it would be folly not to surface-mine the planetoid for whatever it might be worth. One child could do that, and survey the planetoid as well.

Alone, Zael turned impassively to the six-wheeled crawler. She might have rested awhile in the bubble house, but she had some hours of suit time left, and there was no need to waste it. She lifted herself easily against the slight gravity into the cab, turned on the lights and started the motor.

The spidery vehicle crawled ahead on its six individually sprung wheels. The terrain was astonishingly broken; giant spires and craters alternated with ravines and with fissures, some of them forty feet wide and thousands of feet deep. The planetoid's orbit passed near the sun, according to the astronomers, perhaps nearer than the orbit of Venus. Even now, the temperature of the rocks was a few degrees above absolute zero. This was a cold beyond anything Zael had ever experienced. She could feel it drawing at her feet through the long insulator spikes of her boot soles. The molecules of every stone were slowed to stillness; the whole world was one frozen yawn of hunger.

But once it had been a hot world. The record was here. At every perihelion passage, the rocks must have split, again and again, to make this nightmare of tumbled stone.

The surface gravitation was only one tenth *g*, almost like free-fall; the light, puffy-wheeled vehicle crawled easily up slopes within a few degrees of the vertical. Where it could not climb, it went around. Narrow fissures were bridged by the crawler's extensible legs; when she came to larger ones, Zael fired a harpoon which soared across the gap and embedded itself on the other side. The crawler edged forward, toppled and swung at the end of its cable; but while the slight gravity drew it toward the far side of the fissure, the crawler's winch motor was reeling in the cable. It arrived with a faint jar at the opposite side and, without pausing, inched up and over.

Sitting erect behind her instruments, Zael was charting the mineral deposits she passed over. It was a satisfaction to her to find they were rich enough to repay surface mining. The cities could make almost anything out of anything, but they needed a primary source: they had to have metals.

Methodically, she spiraled outward from the bubble house, charting a region no more than thirty miles in diameter. In the unpressurized crawler, it was not feasible to take in a larger area.

Laboring alone, hour after hour under the unchanging sky, she identified the richest lodes, marked them and established routes. Between times, she ate and slept in the bubble house, tended her necessary plants, serviced her equipment. Out of her armor, she was slender and spare, quick in her movements, with the harsh, thin-lipped comeliness of her people.

When her chart was made, she rode out again. At each marked spot, she dropped two widely separated poles. Self-embedding, each pair generated a current which ionized the metals or metallic salts and would slowly deposit pure metal around the cathode. Eventually the concentration would be such that the metal could be sawed out in blocks for convenient loading.

Only then did she turn her attention to the traces of shaped metal that clung here and there to the rocks. They were fragments, for the most part, such as were commonly found on cold satellites like Mimas and Titan, and occasionally on stony asteroids. It was not a matter of any importance; it simply meant that the planetoid had been inhabited or colonized at one time by the same pre-human civilization that had left its traces throughout the solar system.

But she had been sent to see whatever was to be seen. Her real work was almost done; she conscientiously examined the traces, photographed some, took others for specimens. She beamed regular radio reports to Gron; sometimes, five days later, there would be a curt acknowledgment waiting for her in the printer; sometimes not. Regularly she made the rounds of the poles, testing the concentration of metal. She was ready to replace any faulty poles she might find, but the occasion did not arise; Gron equipment seldom failed.

The planetoid hung in its millennial arc. The sky imperceptibly turned around it. The moving spark that was the escape shell traced its path, again and again. Zael grew restless and took the crawler on wider explorations. Deep in the cold crannies of the mountains, she found some metal constructions that were not mere fragments but complete works—dwellings or machines. The dwellings, if they were that, were made for some creature smaller than man; the doorways were ovals not more than a foot across. She dutifully radioed this information back to Gron and received the usual acknowledgment.

Then one day the printer came to life out of season. The message read: I AM COMING. ISAR.

The ship would be three months slower than the message. Zael kept her calendar, rode her rounds, her starlit face impassive. Above her the escape shell, unneeded now, made its monotonous passage over and over. Zael was tracing the remnants of a complex of surface structures that had miraculously survived, some half buried, others naked to the stars. She found where they led, in a crater only forty miles from her base, a week before the ship was due.

In the crater was a heavily reinforced globe of metal, dented and scarred, but not broken. As Zael's light shone steadily on it, a sudden puff of vapor went out; the globe seemed to haze over briefly. Zael peered, interested: the minute warmth of the light beam must have thawed some film of frozen gas.

Then it happened again, and this time she could see distinctly: the jet escaped from a thin, dark seam that had not been there before.

The seam widened as she watched. The globe was splitting. In the narrow gap between the two halves, something moved. Startled, Zael threw the crawler into reverse. The cab lights dipped as the crawler retreated up-slope. In the dimness outside the light beams, she saw the globe expanding still more. There was an ambiguous motion between the barely visible halves of the globe, and she wished she had not taken the light away.

The crawler was tilting sidewise up a steep, broken slab of rock. Zael turned downward, still backing at a sharp angle. The light swung away from the globe altogether, then came back to it as she leveled out.

The two halves of the globe had separated completely. In the middle, something jerked as the light struck it. She could see nothing but a thick, gleaming coil of metal. While she hesitated, there was new motion between the halves of the globe. Something gleamed briefly; there was a short ground shock, and then something struck the cab a hard, resonant blow. The lights whirled bewilderingly and went out.

In the darkness, the cab was tipping. Zael clutched at the controls, but she was too slow. The crawler went over on its back.

Zael felt herself being flung out of the cab. As she rolled over, ears ringing, her first and sharpest impression was of the cold that struck through her armor at gauntlet and knee. She scrambled up quickly to a squatting position, supporting herself on the brushlike spiked soles of her boots.

Even the brief contact had made her fingers smart with cold. She searched automatically for the crawler, which meant safety and warmth. She saw it smashed on the mountainside. Even so, her instinct drew her toward it, but she had hardly taken a first step before the wrecked machine leaped again and rolled another dozen yards down the slope.

She turned now, for the first time fully realizing that something down there was shooting at the crawler. Then she saw a glimmering shape that writhed up toward the wrecked machine. Her helmet light was not turned on; she crouched still and felt two grinding, metallic shocks transmitted through the rock.

The moving thing appeared again on the other side of the crawler, vanished inside, and after a long time came out again. Zael caught a glimpse of a narrow head upraised, and two red eyes gleaming. The head dropped; the sinuous form glided down into a ravine, coming toward her. Her only thought was to get away. She scrambled up in the dark, circled a spire. She saw the gleaming head upraised farther down, among a tangle of boulders, and went at a headlong, dangerous run across the slope to the wrecked crawler.

The control board was ruined, levers bent off or flattened down, dials smashed. She straightened to look at the engine and transmission, but saw at once that it was no use; the heavy drive shaft was bent out of true. The crawler would never run again without shop repairs.

Down in the bowl, she caught sight of the silvery shape casting along the edge of a fissure. Keeping it in view, she examined her suit and instruments all over. As far as she could tell, the suit was tight, her oxygen tanks and recirculation system undamaged.

She was thinking coldly and clearly as she looked at the split globe, gaping empty under the stars. The thing must have been coiled in there, inert, for thousands of years. Perhaps there had been a light-sensitive device in the globe, designed to open it when the planetoid approached the sun again. But her light had broken the globe prematurely; the thing inside was awake before its time. What was it, and what would it do, now that it was alive again?

Whatever happened, her first duty was to warn the ship. She turned on the broadcast transmitter in her suit; its range was small, but now that the ship was so near, there was a chance.

She waited long minutes, but no answer came. From where she stood, the sun was not visible; one of the high crags must be blocking her transmission.

The loss of the crawler had been a disaster. She was alone and afoot, forty miles across an impassable terrain from the bubble house. Her chances of survival now, she knew, were very small.

Still, to save herself now, without finding out more about the thing, would be less than her duty. Zael looked doubtfully down at the empty globe in the starlight. The way between was broken and dangerous; she would have to go slowly, for fear of attracting the thing if she used a light.

She started down nevertheless, picking her way carefully among the tumbled stones. Several times she leaped fissures too long to bypass. When she was halfway down the slope, she saw movement, and froze. The thing writhed into view over a broken ridge—she saw the triangular head again, and a waving ruff of tentacles—and then disappeared inside the open globe.

Zael moved cautiously nearer, circling to get a view directly into the gap. After a few moments the thing emerged again, curiously stiff and thick-looking. On a

221

level place outside the globe, it separated into two parts, and she saw now that one was the thing itself, the other a rigid metal framework, narrow and perhaps ten feet long. The thing retreated inside the globe again. When it came out, it was burdened with a bulbous mechanism which it fitted on somehow to one end of the framework. It continued working for some time, using the tentaclelike jointed members that sprouted from just behind its head. Then it returned to the globe, and this time came out with two large cubical objects. These it began to attach to the opposite end of the framework, connecting them by a series of tubes to the bulbous mechanism.

For the first time, the suspicion entered her mind that the thing was building a spacecraft. Nothing could look less like a conventional ship, to be sure: there was no hull, nothing but a narrow shaft on which the thing could lie, the bulbous object which might be an engine, and the two big containers for reaction mass. Abruptly, she was certain. She had no Geiger with her—it was back in the crawler—but she felt sure there must be radioactives in the bulbous mechanism—a micropile, unshielded, for a spaceship without a hull! It would kill any living creature that rode on it—but what creature of flesh and blood could survive for twenty thousand years on this airless planetoid, at close to absolute zero?

She stood gravely still. Like all her people, she had seen the evidences of an eons-old war among the cold planetoids. Some thought the war had ended with the deliberate destruction of the fifth planet, the one which had formerly occupied the place of the asteroids. A bitter war, that one must have been; and now Zael thought she could understand why. If one side had been human-like, and the other like this thing, then neither could rest until it had wiped out the other. And if this thing were now to escape, and perhaps breed more of its kind . . .

Zael inched forward, making her way from stone to stone, moving only when the thing was out of sight. The alien had finished attaching several small ambiguous objects to the front of the frame. It went back inside the globe. To Zael, the structure looked almost complete. It did not seem possible to encumber it any more and still leave space for the rider.

Her heart was thudding. She left her concealment and went forward in a clumsy tiptoe pace that was faster than leaping. When she was almost in reach of the framework, the thing came out of the open globe. It glided toward her, enormous in the starlight, with its metal head rearing high.

Out of pure instinct she hit the light switch. The helmet beams flared: she had an instant's glimpse of skeletal metal ribs and gleaming jaws. Then the thing was thrashing away from her into the darkness. For a moment more she was stunned. She thought, it can't stand light! And she scrambled forward desperately into the globe.

The thing was coiled there, hiding. When the light struck it, it hurled itself out the other side. Zael pursued again, and caught it once more on the far side of the low ridge. It dived into a ravine and was gone.

She turned back. The framework lay on the rock where it had been left. Zael picked it up tentatively. It had more mass than she had expected, but she was able to swing it at arm's length until it gained a respectable speed. She dashed it against the nearest stone; the impact numbed her fingers. The framework leaped free, slid to rest on the stone. The two containers were detached: the bulbous mechanism was bent away from the frame. She picked it up again, and again swung it hard against the rock. The frame bent and buckled; small pieces came loose. She swung it again, and again, until the frame broke and the bulbous part came free.

The alien thing was not in sight. Zael carried the pieces of the framework to the nearest fissure and dropped them in. In her helmet beams, they drifted silently down and were gone.

She returned to the globe. The creature was still nowhere to be seen. She examined the interior: it was full of oddly shaped partitions and of machines, most too large to be moved, some that were detached and portable. She could not with certainty identify any of them as weapons. To be safe, she took all the movable objects and dropped them after the framework.

She had done all she could, and perhaps more than was prudent. Her task now was to survive—to get back to the bubble house, call the escape shell down, and get away.

She turned back up the slope, past the wrecked crawler, retracing her route until she came to the crater wall.

The crags loomed over her, hundreds of feet above her head, and so sheer that when she tried to climb them, even her momentum would not keep her upright; she began to topple back and had to dance her way slowly down again to firmer footing.

She made the full circuit of the crater before she was convinced: there was no way out.

She was sweating under the armor: a bad beginning. The ragged tops of the mountains seemed to bend forward, peering down at her mockingly. She stood still to calm herself, took a salt pill and a sip of water from the dispenser in her helmet. The indicators showed that she had less than five hours of air left. It was little enough. She had to get out.

She chose what seemed to be the easiest slope within reach. She went up it with a rush. When her momentum began to fail, she used her hands. The cold bit through her gauntlets like needles of fire. The slightest contact was painful; to grasp firmly became an agony. She was within yards of the top when her fingers began to grow numb. She clawed upward furiously, but her fingers refused to grip; her hands slid uselessly away from the rock.

She was falling. She toppled slowly down the slope she had climbed with so much pain; caught herself with an effort and came to rest, shaken and trembling, at the bottom.

Cold despair settled at her heart. She was young; she had no taste for death, even for a quick and clean one. To die slowly, gasping for air in a foul suit, or bleeding out her warmth against the stone, would be horrible.

Out across the crater floor, she saw a dim movement in the starlight. It was the alien thing; what could it be doing, now that she had destroyed its means of escape? The thought came to her slowly that perhaps it could not get out of the crater either. After a moment, hesitantly, she went down the slope toward it.

Halfway down, she remembered to turn off her suit lights so as not to drive it away. The crater floor was crisscrossed with innumerable fissures. As she came nearer, she saw that the split sphere was surrounded by them on all sides. Down at one end of this long, irregular island of rock, the alien was throwing itself back and forth.

It turned to face her as she leaped the last gap. She could see its red eyes gleaming in the darkness, and the circle of thin, jointed arms that formed a collar behind its head. As she approached, the head reared higher, and the jaws gaped.

The sight of the thing, so near, filled her with a cold loathing she had never experienced before. It was not only that the creature was metal, and alive; it was some radiance of evil that seemed to reach her directly from the thing, as if to say, I am the death of all you love.

The blind, red eyes stared with implacable hatred. How could she make it understand?

The body of the thing was sinuous and strong; its jointed arms could grasp and hold. It was made for climbing, but not for jumping.

Abruptly, her loathing for the alien was more than she could master. She turned and jumped the chasm again. On the far side, she looked back. The alien was swaying high, with more than half its length raised from the rock. She saw now that there was another cluster of gripping members at its tail. The thing glided forward to the very edge of the fissure and swayed upright again, jaws agape, eyes glaring.

They had nothing in common but hatred—and fear. Staring across at the alien, Zael realized that it must be as afraid as she. Metal though it was, it could not live forever without warmth. She had broken its machines, and now, like her, it was trapped. But how could she make it understand?

She moved a few yards away along the edge of the

225

fissure, and then jumped again, back to the alien's side. It watched her alertly. The thing was intelligent; it must be. It must know that she was not native to the planetoid, and therefore that she must have a ship, or some means of escape.

She spread her arms. The alien's circle of limbs widened in response: but was that a gesture of invitation or of menace? Suppressing her fear and repugnance, she walked nearer. The tall shape swayed above her in the starlight. She saw now that the segments of the alien's body were metal rings that slid smoothly upon one another. Each ring was slightly open at the bottom, and inside she could glimpse some mechanism.

Such a thing could never have evolved on any world; it must have been made, for some unguessable purpose. The long, supple body was built for pursuit and capture; the jaws were for killing. Only a depth of hatred beyond her comprehension could have conceived this horror and let it loose in the world of the living.

She forced herself to move a step nearer. She pointed to herself, then back to the crater wall. She turned and leaped across the fissure, recovered herself and leaped back.

It seemed to her that the alien's attitude, as it stared at her, was an almost human parody of wariness and doubt. She pointed to herself, and to the alien; again, she turned and leaped across the chasm, then leaped back. She pointed to herself and to the alien, and then gestured across the fissure, a wide, slow motion of one arm. She waited.

After a long time the alien moved slowly forward. She retreated, as slowly, until she was at the edge of the fissure. Trembling, she held out her arm. Slowly the great head dipped; the circle of grasping members waved forward to wrap itself around her sleeve. The red eyes stared blindly into hers from a few inches away.

She turned and kicked off strongly. She tried to allow for the alien's mass, but the unaccustomed drag on her arm tipped her backward in midflight. They landed together with a grating jar. Awkwardly, Zael scrambled up, away from the cold that serached through her armor. The alien was swaying erect, near—too near.

By instinct again, she hit the light switch. The thing writhed away in silvery coils.

Zael was trembling with reaction. Her heart pounded at her throat. With an effort, she turned off the light again. The thing rose into view, waiting for her, a dozen yards away.

When she moved, it moved, keeping its distance. When they reached the next fissure, she stood still until it again approached and laid its grasping members on her arm.

On the far side, they separated once more. In this way, they traversed four of the islands of rock before they came to the crater wall.

The alien thrust its body slowly up along the steep incline. At full stretch, the gripping arms found a hold; the tail swung free. The long body looped gracefully up; the tail members found another hold above the alien's head.

It paused there, looking down at her. Zael spread her arms; she pantomimed climbing, then stepped back, shaking her head. She held out her arms again.

The alien hesitated. After a long moment, the head members gripped again; the tail swung down. Zael braced herself as the alien slid nearer. The smooth, shining head loomed over her. In that frozen moment, Zael found herself thinking that to the alien, the universe might be like a photographic negative: all the evil things good, the good things evil. It gave her a queer sense of exhilaration to realize when they met, the alien too might be embracing darkness.

Then the head glided past her shoulder; the heavy coils looped around her body with a faint scraping sound. The thing was cold, but not with the numbing super-cold of the rocks. As the coils tightened, she felt the chill, constrictive strength of the great body. Then she was being lifted off her feet. The steep wall tilted and swung at a crazy angle.

A faintness sapped her strength as she lay in the metal coils. The stars swung around her head; they steadied and burned still. The alien had set her down at the top of the crater wall.

The cold coils slowly slipped away. Shaken and stunned, Zael followed the alien down the broken, tilted land. The touch still burned in her flesh. It was like a meaning that lay so heavily and coldly inside her that she had to puzzle to make it out. It was like a ring that, having been worn so long, still seems to be there after it has been removed.

Down in the tumbled vastness of the valley, the alien's head was upraised, waiting for her. Humbly she went down to it, where it lay at the edge of a fissure. This time, instead of clutching her arm, the heavy mass coiled itself around her.

She leaped. At the other side, slowly, almost reluctantly, the supple body slid down and away from her. When they came to a high place, again the alien took her in its cold embrace and swung her up, weightlessly, like a woman in a dream.

The sun was in the sky, low over the horizon. Zael put her hand to the radio switch, hesitated, and let her hand fall away. What could she tell them? How could she make them understand?

Time slipped away. When they passed one of her mining areas, where the cold purple light flickered from the rocks, she knew they were on the right path. She steered by that, and by the sun. At each fissure, the alien coiled itself around her shoulders; at each steep ascent, it cradled her about the waist and lifted her in long, free arcs to the top.

When, standing on a height, she saw the bubble house, she realized with a shock that she had lost account of time. She looked at the indicators. There was half an hour of air left.

The knowledge brought to wakefulness some part of her mind which had been submerged and asleep. She knew that the other had seen the bubble house too; there was a new tension in its manner, a new fixity in the way it stared ahead. She tried to recall the topography that lay between this spot and the house. She had been over it dozens of times, but always in the crawler. It was very different now. The high ridges that had been only momentary obstacles before were now impassable. The whole aspect of the country was changed; she could not be certain even of her landmarks any longer.

They were passing the last of the mining areas. The cold purple light rolled across the rocks. Just beyond this point, Zael recalled, there should be a wide fissure; the alien, a few yards distant, was not looking her way. Bending forward, she broke into a stiff-toed run. The fissure was there; she reached the edge and jumped.

On the far side, she turned to look. The alien was writhing back and forth at the edge of the fissure, its collar of limbs extended in fury, its red eyes blazing. After a moment, its motion slowed and stopped. They stared at each other across the gap of silence; then Zael turned away.

The indicators gave her fifteen minutes more. She set off at a brisk pace and soon found herself descending into a deep ravine she recognized. All around her were the landmarks of the route she was accustomed to take in the crawler. Ahead and to the right, where stars gleamed in a gap, must be the place where a broken fall of rock formed a natural stairway to the top of the ravine. But as she neared the place, something made her uneasy. The far wall of the ravine was too sheer and too tall.

She stood beneath the gap at last, and there was no stairway.

She must have mistaken the spot. There was nothing for it but to cast along the ravine until she came to the right place. After a moment's indecision, she set off hurriedly to the left.

At every step, the ravine promised to become familiar. Surely, she could not have gone so far wrong in so short a time! The dots of light from her helmet beams danced ahead of her, mockingly elusive. Abruptly, she realized that she was lost.

There were seven minutes of air left.

The thought came to her that the alien must still be where she had left it, trapped on one of the islands of rock. If she went straight back to it, now, without hesitating a second, there might still be time.

With an involuntary groan of protest, she turned back. Her movements were hurried and unsure; once she stumbled, and caught herself barely in time to prevent a bad fall. Yet she dared not slow down or stop for a moment. Inside the helmet, her breath was labored; the familiar reek of the recirculated air seemed to have grown stuffier and more foul.

She looked at the indicators: five minutes.

Topping a rise, she saw a liquid glint of metal moving down among the purple fires. She leaped the last fissure and came to a wary halt. The alien was approaching her slowly. The great metal head was expressionless, the jaws closed; the ruff of grasping members was almost still; only, now and then, one of the jointed limbs twitched abruptly. There was a grim, waiting stillness about it that she found disquieting, but she had no time for caution.

Hurriedly, with abrupt gestures, she tried to pantomime her need. She held out her arms. The alien glided forward slowly, and slowly wrapped its coils around her.

She scarcely felt the leap, or the landing. The alien glided beside her; close, this time, near enough to touch. Down into the starlit half-darkness of the ravine they went, Zael treading uncertainly because she could not use her helmet lights. They paused at the foot of the precipice. The alien turned to look at her for a moment.

Zael's ears were ringing. The great head swayed toward her and passed by. The metal arms gripped the rock; the great body swung up, over her head. She looked up to see it looping diagonally across the face of the rock; it glimmered briefly against the stars and then was gone.

Zael stared after it in incredulous horror. It had happened too quickly; she did not understand how she could have been so stupid. She had not even tried to grasp the coils as they passed!

The indicators were blurred; the needles hung near zero. Staggering a little, she set off down the ravine to the right. She had perhaps a minute or two of air left, and then five or six minutes of slow asphyxiation. She might still find the stair; she was not dead yet.

The ravine wall, instead of sinking to an easier level, rose in spires and pinnacles. Zael stopped, cold and sodden with weariness. The silent peaks rose high against the stars. There was no help there, nor in all the dead, vampirish world around her.

Something leaped out of the stone at her feet. Startled, she drew back. The thing was spinning away under the stars. As she watched, another fragment of rock burst into view, and then another. This time she saw it fall, strike the stone and rebound.

She jerked her head back. Halfway down the rock face, swinging easily from hold to hold, came the alien. A cloud of rock fragments, dislodged by its passage, floated slowly down and rebounded about her head. The alien slid the last few yards and came to rest beside her.

Her head was swimming. She felt the heavy coils wind themselves around her; felt herself lifted and carried. The coils were too tight; she could not get her breath. When she was released, the pressure did not relax.

Reeling, she went forward toward the bubble house, where it winked and beckoned from the low horizon. Her throat was afire. Beside her, the alien went like quicksilver among the rocks.

Once she fell—an appalling, slow, helpless fall into the bruising cold—and the alien's heavy coils helped her up.

They came to a fissure. Zael stood tottering on the lip of it, dimly understanding now why the alien had come back for her. It was tit for tat; and now she was too bemused to play that game again. The alien's grasping members were on her sleeve.

Up there, somewhere in Draco, Isar's ship was on the way. Zael fumbled for the radio switch. Her voice came hoarse and strange: "Mother . . ."

The heavy body was winding itself around her shoulders. Breathing hurt her chest, and her vision was dim. Gathering her strength, she jumped.

On the far side, she moved with a blurred slowness.

231

She could see the bubble-house light winking prismatically at the end of an avenue of mist, and she knew that she had to get to it. She was not sure why; perhaps it had something to do with the silvery being that glided beside her.

The hum of a carrier wave suddenly filled her earphones. "Zael, is that you?"

She heard the words, but their meaning slipped away. The bubble house was near now; she could see the flexible valve of its doorway. She had the idea that the silver thing must not be allowed to go inside, or it might breed there, and then there would be a plague of metal creatures running everywhere.

She turned clumsily to prevent it, but lost her balance and fell against the side of the bubble. The great silvery head was looming over her. She saw the jaws open and a pair of gleaming fangs slide into view. The head dipped delicately, the jaws seized her thigh, and the fangs went in, once. Without haste, the thing coiled itself away, out of her range of vision.

A coldness was spreading outward from her thigh. She saw two thin jets of vapor escaping from the armor where it was pierced. She turned her head; the alien creature was just disappearing through the flexible valve into the bubble. Inside, she could see it coursing back and forth, avoiding the one tiny light. It nosed at the hammock, the lamp, then the radio transceiver. Remembering, Zael said plaintively, "Mother?"

As if in answer, the carrier hum came again, and the voice said, "Zael, what is it?"

She tried to respond, but her thick tongue could not find the words. She felt weak and cold, but not at all afraid. Fumbling in her kit, she found the adhesive paste and smeared it over the punctures. The paste bubbled for a moment, then hardened. Something slow and languorous was spreading from the icy hurt in her thigh. As she turned again, she saw that the alien was still curved over the radio transceiver. Even from here, she could see the bright red knob of the escape shell signaler. As she watched, one of the alien's limbs grasped it and pushed it down.

She glanced up. After a moment the crawling orange spark in the sky seemed to pause and then grow slowly larger. The light burned to a bright star, then to a golden flare.

The escape shell came down on the rocky plain a hundred yards away. The torch winked out. Dazzled, she saw the dark shape of the alien come gliding down out of the bubble house.

It stopped, and for a moment the cruel head was poised, looking down at her. Then it flowed on.

The airlock door was a circle of yellow light. The alien seemed to hesitate before it; then it moved on and disappeared inside. The door closed. After a few moments the torch blazed again, and the shell rose on a pillar of fire.

Zael lay cradled against the bubble's resilient curve. Dimly the thought was in her mind that inside the bubble, a few feet away, were air and warmth. Whatever venom the alien had deposited in her flesh, perhaps it would not kill her for a long time. Her mother's ship was coming. She had a chance to live.

But the escape shell was still rising on its long golden plume; and she had eyes for nothing but that terrible beauty ascending into the night.

ANTHONY BOUCHER, AN OTHERWISE level-headed man, published a long series of punning short-short stories about the adventures of Ferdinand Feghoot from 1956 well into the sixties. I am one of those who hate other people's puns, and I couldn't bear these stories, but I couldn't keep from reading them either. Finally I had to write one myself or explode. Boucher not only bought "Eripmav," he paid me more than he paid the author of the Feghoots.

14

ERIPMAV

<<<<<<<<<<<<<<<<<<<<<<<<<<<<<<<<<<<<<<<

ON THE PLANET VEEGL, IN THE FOMALHAUT
system, we found a curious race of cellulose vampirês.
The Veeglians, like all higher life on their world,
are plants; the Veeglian vampire, needless to say, is a
sapsucker.

One of the native clerks in our trade mission, a plant-
girl named Xixl, had been complaining of lassitude and
showing an unhealthy pink color for some weeks. The
girl's parent stock suspected vampirism; we were skepti-
cal, but had to admit that the two green-tinged punctures
at the base of her axis were evidence of something wrong.

Accordingly, we kept watch over her sleep-box for
three nights running. (The Veeglians sleep in boxes of
soil, built of heavy slabs of the hardmeat tree, or *woogl;*
they look rather like coffins.) On the third night, sure
enough, a translator named Ffengl, a hefty, blue-haired
fellow, crept into her room and bent over the sleep-box.

We rushed out at the blackguard, but he turned quick
as a wink and fairly flew up the whitemeat stairs. (The
flesh of Veegl's only animal life, the "meat-trees," or
oogl, petrifies rapidly in air and is much used for construction.) We found him in an unsuspected vault at
the very top of the old building, trying to hide under the
covers of an antique bed. It was an eerie business. We
sizzled him with blasts from our proton guns, and yet

to the end, with un-Veeglian vitality, he was struggling to reach us with his tendrils.

Afterward he seemed dead enough, but the local wise-heads advised us to take certain precautions.

So we buried him with a steak through his heart.

MANY YEARS AGO ALFRED BESTER wrote a story called "The Unseen Blushers" in which various s-f writers appeared under transparent pseudonyms. Ever since then I had wanted to do the same, and in 1956 I did it. Some of the names of the characters in "A Likely Story" are anagrams, some are not.

15

A LIKELY STORY

<<<<<<<<<<<<<<<<<<<<<<<<<<<<<<<<<<<<<<<

THAT WAS THE DAMNEDEST DECEMBER I ever saw in New York. Whatever the weather is, Manhattan *always* gets the worst of it—frying hot in summer, snow or slush up to your ankles in winter—and all along the seaboard, it was a mean season. Coming in from Pennsylvania the day before, we'd been held up twice while the tracks were cleared. But when I stepped out of the hotel that night, the Saturday after Christmas, it was like a mild October; the air was just cool, with a fresh hint of snow in it. There was a little slush in the gutters, not much; the pavements were dry.

I was late, or I would have gone back and ditched the rubbers; I hate the foolish things to begin with, one reason I moved to the country—out there, I wear house slippers half the year, galoshes the rest; there's no in-between. I took off my gloves, opened my scarf, and breathed deep lungfuls while I walked to the corner for a cab. I began to wonder if it had been smart to move ninety miles out of town just because I didn't like rubbers.

The streets didn't seem overcrowded. I got a cab without any trouble. Nobody was hurrying; it was as if the whole population was sitting peacefully at home or in some bar, in no rush to be anywhere else.

"Listen," I said to the cabbie, "this is still New York, isn't it?"

He jerked his chin at me. "Hah?"

"Where's the crowds? I said. "Where's the rotten weather? What happened?"

He nodded. "I know whatcha mean. Sure is funny. Crazy weather."

"Well, when did this happen?"

"Hah?"

"I said, how long has this been going on?"

"Cleared up about three o'clock. I looked out the winda, and the sun was shinin'. Jeez! You know what I think?"

"You think it's them atom bombs," I told him.

"That's right. You know what I think, I think it's them *atom* bombs." He pulled up opposite a canopy and folded down his flag.

In the lobby, I found an arrow-shaped sign that said MEDUSA CLUB.

The Medusa Club is, loosely speaking, an association of professional science fiction writers. No two of them will agree on what science fiction is—or on anything else —but they all write it, or have written it, or pretend they can write it, or something. They have three kinds of meetings, or two and a half. One is for club politics, one is for drinking, and the third is also for drinking, only more so. As a rule, they meet in people's apartments, usually Preacher Flatt's or Ray Alvarez's, but every year at this time they rent a hotel ballroom and throw a whingding. I'm a member in bad standing; the last time I paid my dues was in 1950.

Rod Pfehl (the P is silent, as in Psmith) was standing in the doorway, drunk, with a wad of dollar bills in his hand. "I'm the treasurer," he said happily. "Gimme." Either he was the treasurer, or he had conned a lot of people into thinking so. I paid him and started zigzagging slowly across the floor, trading hellos, looking for liquor.

Tom Q. Jones went by in a hurry, carrying a big camera. That was unusual; Tom Q. is head components designer for a leading radio-TV manufacturer, and has sold, I guess, about two million words of science fiction, but this was the first time I had ever seen him in motion, or with anything but a highball in his hand. I spotted Punchy Carrol, nut-brown in a red dress; and Duchamp biting his pipe; and Leigh MacKean with her pale proto-Nordic face, as wistful and fey as the White Knight's; and there was a fan named Harry Somebody, nervously adjusting his hornrims as he peered across the room; and, this being the Christmas Party, there were a lot of the strangest faces on earth.

Most of them were probably friends of friends, but you never knew; one time there had been a quiet banker-type man at a Medusa meeting, sitting in a corner and not saying much, who turned out to be Dorrance Canning, an old idol of mine; he wrote the "Woman Who Slept" series and other gorgeous stuff before I was out of knee pants.

There were two blue-jacketed bartenders, and the drinks were eighty-five cents. Another reason I moved to the country is that the amusements are cheaper. Nursing my collins, I steered around two broad rumps in flounced satin and ran into Tom Q. He snapped a flash-bulb in my face, chortled something, and went away while I was still dazzled. Somebody else with a lemon-colored spot for a head shook my left hand and muttered at me, but I wasn't listening; I had just figured out that what Tom had said was, "There's no *film* in it!"

Somebody fell down on the waxed floor; there was a little flurry of screams and laughter. I found myself being joggled, and managed to put away an inch of the collins to save it. Then I thought I saw Art Greymbergen, my favorite publisher, but before I could get 'anywhere near him Carrol's clear Sunday-school voice began calling, "The program is about to begin—please take your seats!" and a moment later people were moving sluggishly through the bar archway.

I looked at my watch, then hauled out my copy of the little mimeographed sheet, full of earnest jocularity, that the club sent out every year to announce the Party. It said that the program would begin somewhere around ten, and it was that now.

This was impossible. The program always pivoted on Bill Plass, and Bill never got there, or anywhere, until the party was due to break up.

But I looked when I got down near the bandstand, and by God there he was, half as large as life, gesturing, flashing his Charlie Chaplin grin, teetering like a nervous firewalker. He saw me and waved hello, and then went on talking to Asa Akimisov, Ph.D. (A-K-I-M-I-S-O-V, please, and never mind the Akimesian, or Akimsiov.)

Maybe it *was* them atom bombs. I found a vacant folding chair with a good view of the platform, and a better one of a striking brunette in blue. Akimisov got up on the platform, with his neck sticking out of his collar like a potted palm (he had lost forty pounds, again), and began telling jokes. Ace is the second funniest man in Medusa, the first being Plass; the peculiar thing is that Plass writes humor professionally, and delivers his annual set-pieces the same way—the rest of the time he is merely a perfectly fascinating morbid wit—but Akimisov, who writes nothing but the most heavily thoughtful fiction in the business, bubbles with humor all the time, a poor man's Sam Levenson. I was going to write an article once proving that a writer's personality on paper was his real one turned inside out, but I fell afoul of some exceptions. Like Tom Q., who was still flashing his bulbs over at the side of the platform, and being noisily suppressed—you could paper him all over with his published stories, and never know the difference.

The program was good, even for Medusa. Ned Burgeon, wearing a sky-blue dinner jacket and a pepper-and-salt goatee, played his famous twenty-one-string guitar; a dark-haired girl, a new one to me, sang in a sweet, strong contralto; there was a skit involving Punchy Carrol as a dream-beast, L. Vague Duchamp as a bewildered spaceman, and B. U. Jadrys, the All-Lithuanian Boy, as a ticket agent for the Long Island Railroad. Then came Plass's annual monologue, and there is just nothing like those. I'm not exaggerating out of parochial pride (once a year is enough Medusa for me): the simple truth is that Plass is a comic genius.

He had his audience laid out flat, gasping and clutching its sides. Why should a man like that waste his time writing fiction?

Toward the end he paused, looked up from his notes, and ad-libbed a biting but not very funny wisecrack about—well, I'd better not say about what. A certain member in the audience stiffened and half got up, and there was a little embarrassed murmur under the laughter, but it was over in a minute. Bill looked flustered. He went back to his prepared speech, finished, and got a roar of applause.

I did my share, but I was worried. Bill can charm the rattles off a snake; if he wanted to go in for quack-doctoring, nut cultism or Canadian mining stock, let alone night-club comedy, he could be a millionaire. That *gaffe* simply hadn't been like him, at all. Still, it was Bill's Dostoevskian soul that made him the funny man he was, and God only knew what had been happening to him in the year since I'd been in town . . .

Akimisov, as m.c., delivered the final words. He bowed, straightened, and his pants fell down.

In the dressing room, when I got back there, Bill was busy apologizing to the member on whose toes he had trodden—that apology would have soothed a tiger with a toothache—and Akimisov, with a bewildered expression, was holding up his pants. That was what I was curious about; it was another false note—I didn't think Ace would stoop that low for a laugh. The pants were too big for him, of course, but Ace had always struck me as the kind of guy who wears a belt *and* suspenders.

He did; but the tongue had come out of the belt-buckle, and all the suspenders buttons had popped, all at once. Scouts were being sent out to look for a belt that would fit.

I wandered out into the hall again. I was beginning to get a peculiar feeling on one drink. Too many fresh vegetables; I can't take it like I used to. So I went to the bar and got another.

When I came out, the brunette in the blue evening gown was standing near the doorway listening to Larry Bagsby. Next thing I knew, she let out a whoop, grabbed her bosom, and fetched Larry a good one on the ear. This was unfair. I was a witness, and Larry hadn't done a thing except look; her overworked shoulder straps had simply given way, like Akimisov's suspenders.

Curiouser and curiouser . . . The noises around me were picking up in volume and tempo, for all the world like a dance-hall scene in a Western movie, just before somebody throws the first table. There was a thud and a screech off to my right; I gathered that somebody else had fallen down. Then a tinkle of bursting glass, and another little chorus of shouts, and then another thud. It went on like that. The crowd was on the move, in no particular direction; everybody was asking everybody else what was going on.

I felt the same way, so I went looking for Ray Alvarez; you can always count on him to tell you the answer, or make one up.

Tom Q. went by, flashing that camera, and it wasn't till the mob had swallowed him that I realized he wasn't replacing the bulb between shots—the same one was blazing over and over.

Well, a few years ago it was silly putty; the year before that, Diarrhetics. This year, everlasting flash bulbs—and no film in the camera.

Ned Burgeon passed me, his grin tilting his whiskers dangerously near the lighted stub in his cigarette holder; he was carrying the guitar case as if he were wading ashore with it. I saw Duchamp off to one side, talking to somebody, gesturing emphatically with his pipe.

It isn't so, but occasionally you get the impression that science fiction writers are either very tall or very short. I watched H. Drene Pfeiffer stilt by, Ray Bolgerish in an astonishing skin-tight suit of horseblanket plaid, followed by Will Kubatius and the *heldentenor* bulk of Don W. Gamble, Jr. I lowered my sights. Sandwiched between the giants there ought to have been half a dozen people I'd have been glad to see—if not Alvarez, then Bill Plass or his brother Horty; or Jerry Thaw; Bagsby; Preacher Flatt, who looks too much like a marmoset to be true . . . But no: down on those lower levels there was nobody but an eleven-year-old boy who had got in by mistake, and the ubiquitous fan, Harry *You*-Know, the one with the glasses and all that hair. I tacked, veering slightly, and beat across the room the other way.

There was another crash of glass, a *big* one, and a louder chorus of yells. It wasn't all automatic female shrieks, this time; I caught a couple of male voices, raised in unmistakable anger.

The crowd was thinning out a little; droves of friends

of friends appeared to be heading for the coat room. Across one of the clear spaces came a pretty blonde, looking apprehensive. In a minute I saw why. Her skirt billowed out around her suddenly and she yelled, crouched, holding the cloth down with both hands, then sunfished away into the crowd. A moment later the same thing happened to a tall brown-haired girl over to my left.

That was too much. Glancing up, I happened to see the big cut-glass chandelier begin swaying gently from side to side, jingling faintly, working up momentum. I moved faster, buttonholing everyone I knew: "Have you seen Ray? Have you seen Ray?"

I heard my name, and there he was, standing like stout Cortez atop the piano, where he could see the whole room like an anthill. I climbed up beside him. Alvarez, to quote Duchamp's description, is a small rumpled man with an air of sleepy good-nature. This is apt until you get close to him, when you discover he is about as sleepy as a hungry catamount. "Hi," he said, with a sidewise glance.

"Hi. What do you think's doing it?"

"It could be," said Ray, speaking firmly and rapidly, "a local discontinuity in the four-dimensional plenum that we're passing through. Or it could be poltergeists—that's perfectly possible, you know." He gave me a look, daring me to deny it.

"You think so?"

"It *could* be."

"By golly, I believe you're right," I said. This is the only way to handle Alvarez when he talks nonsense. If you give him the slightest degree of resistance, he will argue along the same line till doomsday, just to prove he can.

"Mmm," he said thoughtfully, screwing up his face. "No, I don't—think—so."

"No?"

"No," he said positively. "You notice how the thing seems to travel around the room?" He nodded to a fist fight that was breaking out a few yards from us, and then to a goosed girl leaping over by the bar entrance.

244

"There's a kind of irregular rhythm to it." He moved his hand, illustrating. "One thing happens—then another thing—now here it comes around this way again—"

A fat friend of a friend and her husband backed up against the platform just below us, quivering. There was something wrong with my fingers; they felt warm. The collins glass was turning warm. Warm, *hell*—I yelped and dropped it, sucking my fingers. The glass looped and fell neatly on the flowered hat of the friend of a friend, and liquid splattered. The woman hooted like a peanut whistle. She whirled, slipped in the puddle and lurched off into the arms of a hairy authors' agent. Her husband dithered after her a couple of steps, then came back with blood in his eye. He got up as far as the piano stool when, as far as I could make out, his pants split up the back and he climbed down again, glaring and clutching himself.

"Now it's over in the middle," said Ray imperturbably. "It *might* be poltergeists, I won't say it isn't. But I've got a hunch there's another answer, actually."

I said something dubious. A hotel-manager-looking kind of man had just come in and was looking wildly around. Punchy Carrol went up to him, staring him respectfully right in the eye, talking a quiet six to his dozen. After a moment he gave up and listened. I've known Punchy ever since she was a puppy-eyed greenhorn from Philadelphia, and I don't underestimate her anymore. I knew the manager-type would go away and not call any cops—at least for a while.

I glanced down at the floor, and then looked again. There were little flat chips of ice scattered in the wetness. That could have been from the ice cubes; but there was *frost* on some of the pieces of glass.

Hot on the bottom, cold on top!

"Ray," I said, "something's buzzing around in my mind. Maxwell's demon." I pointed to the frosted bits of glass. "That might— No, I'm wrong, that couldn't account for all these—"

He took it all in in one look. "Yes, it could!" he snapped. His cat-eyes gleamed at me. "Maxwell had the theory of the perfect heat pump—it would work if

245

you could only find a so-called demon, about the size of a molecule, that would bat all the hot molecules one way, and all the cold ones the other."

"I know," I said. "But—"

"Okay, I'm just explaining it to you."

What he told me was what I was thinking: Our unidentified friend had some way of changing probability levels. I mean, all the molecules of air under a woman's skirt *could* suddenly decide to move in the same direction—or all the molecules in a patch of flooring *could* lose their surface friction—it just wasn't likely. If you could *make* it likely—there wasn't any limit. You could make honest dice turn up a thousand sevens in a row. You could run a car without an engine; make rain or fair weather; reduce the crime index to zero; keep a demagogue from getting re-elected . . .

Well, if all that was true, I wanted in. And I didn't have the ghost of a chance—I was out of touch; I didn't know anybody. Ray knew everybody.

"Spread out, folks!" said a bullhorn voice. It was Samwitz, of course, standing on a bench at the far wall. Kosmo Samwitz, the Flushing Nightingale; not one of the Medusa crowd, usually—a nice enough guy, and a hardworking committeeman, but the ordinary Manhattan meeting hall isn't big enough to hold his voice. "Spread out—make an equal distance between you. That way we can't get into any fights." People started following his orders, partly because they made sense, partly because, otherwise, he'd go on bellowing.

"That's good—that's good," said Samwitz. "All right, this meeting is hereby called to order. The chair will entertain suggestions about what the nature of these here phenomenon are . . ."

Ray showed signs of wanting to get down and join the caucus; he loves parliamentary procedure better than life itself; so I said hastily, "Let's get down with the crowd, Ray. We can't see much better up here, anyway."

He stiffened. "You go if you want to," he said quietly. "I'm staying here, where I can keep an eye on things."

The chandelier was now describing stately circles, causing a good deal of ducking and confusion, but the meeting was getting on with its business, namely, arguing about whether to confirm Kosmo by acclamation or nominate and elect a chairman in the usual way. That subject, I figured, was good for at least twenty minutes. I said, "Ray, will you tell me the truth if I ask you something?"

"Maybe." He grinned.

"Are you doing this?"

He threw his head back and chuckled. "No-o, I'm not doing it." He looked at me shrewdly, still grinning. "Is that why you were looking for me?"

I admitted it humbly. "It was just a foolish idea," I said. "Nobody we know could possibly——"

"*I* don't know about that," he said, squinting thoughtfully.

"Ah, come on, Ray."

He was affronted. "Why not? We've got some pretty good scientific brains in Medusa, you know. There's Gamble—he's an atomic physicist. There's Don Bierce; there's Duchamp; there's——"

"I know," I said, "I know, but where would any of them have got hold of a thing like *this?*"

"They could have invented it," he said stoutly.

"You mean like Balmer and Phog Relapse running the Michelson experiment in their cellar, and making it come out that there *is* an ether drift, only it's *down?*"

He bristled. "No, I do not——"

"Or like Lobbard discovering Scatiology?"

"Ptah! No! Like Watt, like Edison, Galileo"—he thumbed down three fingers emphatically—"Goodyear, Morse, Whitney——"

Down below, the meeting had taken less than five minutes to confirm Samwitz as chairman. I think the chandelier helped; they ought to install one of those in every parliamentary chamber.

The chair recognized Punchy, who said sweetly that the first order of business ought to be to get opinions from the people who knew something, beginning with Werner Kley.

Werner accordingly made a very charming speech, full of Teutonic rumbles, the essence of which was that he didn't know any more about this than a rabbit. He suggested, however, that pictures should be taken. There was a chorus of "Tom!" and Jones staggered forward with his war-cry: "There isn't any *film* in it!"

Somebody was dispatched to get film; somebody else trotted out to telephone for reporters and cameramen, and three or four other people headed in a businesslike way for the men's room.

Ray was simultaneously trying to get the chair's attention and explaining to me, in staccato asides, how many epochal inventions had been made by amateurs in attic workshops. I said—and this was really bothering me—"But look: do you see anybody with any kind of a gadget? How's he going to hide it? How's he going to focus it, or whatever?"

Ray snorted. "It might be hidden in almost anything. Burgeon's guitar—Gamble's briefcase—Mr. Chairman!"

Duchamp was talking, but I could feel it in my bones that Samwitz was going to get around to Ray next. I leaned closer. "Ray, listen—a thing like this—they wouldn't keep it to themselves, would they?"

"Why not? Wouldn't you—for a while, anyway?" He gave me his bobcat grin. "I can think of quite—a—few things I could do, if I had it."

So could I; that was the whole point. I said, "Yeah. I was hoping we could spot him before the crowd does." I sighed. "Fat chance, I suppose."

He gave me another sidelong look. "That shouldn't be so hard," he drawled.

"You *know* who it is?"

He put on his most infuriating grin, peering to see how I took it. "I've, got, a few, ideas."

"Who?"

Wrong question. He shook his head with a that-would-be-telling look.

Somebody across the room went down with a crash; then somebody else. "Sit on the floor!" Ray shouted, and they all did, squatting cautiously like old ladies at a picnic. The meeting gathered speed again.

I looked apprehensively at the narrow piano top we

were standing on, and sat down with my legs hanging over. Ray stayed where he was, defying the elements.

"You know, all right," I said, looking up at him, "but you're keeping it to yourself." I shrugged. "Well, why shouldn't you?"

"O-kay," he said good-naturedly. "Let's figure it out. Where were you when it started?"

"In the bar."

"Who else was there? Try to remember exact-ly."

I thought. "Art Greymbergen. Fred Balester. Gamble was there—"

"Okay, that eliminates him—and you, incidentally—because it started in here. Right, so far?"

"Right!"

"Hmmm. Something happened *to* Akimisov."

"And Plass—that booboo he made?"

Ray dismissed Plass with a gesture. He was looking a little restive; another debate was under way down below, with Punchy and Leigh MacKean vociferously presenting the case for psychokinesis, and being expertly heckled by owlish little M. C. (Hotfoot) Burncloth's echo-chamber voice. "It's too much," I said quickly. "There's too many of them left. We'll never—"

"It's perfectly simple!" Ray said incisively. He counted on his fingers again. "Burgeon—Kley—Duchamp—Bierce—Burncloth—MacKean—Jibless. Eight people."

"One of the visitors?" I objected.

He shook his head. "I know who all these people are, generally," he said. "It's got to be one of those eight. I'll take Kley, Bierce, Jibless and MacKean—you watch the other four. Sooner or later they'll give themselves away."

I had *been* watching. I did it some more.

A wave of neck-clutching passed over the crowd. Cold breezes, I expect. Or hot ones, in some cases. Tom Jones leaped up with a cry and sat down again abruptly.

"Did you see anything?" Ray asked.

I shook my head. Where, I wondered, was the good old science-fiction camaraderie? If I'd been the lucky one, I would have let the crowd in—well, a few of them, anyway—given them jobs and palaces and things. Not that they would have been grateful, probably, the treacherous, undependable, neurotic bums . . .

They were looking nervous now. There had been that little burst of activity after a long pause (even the chandelier seemed to be swinging slowly to rest), and now the—call it the stillness—was more than they could stand. I felt it too: that building up of tension. Whoever it was, was getting tired of little things.

A horrible jangling welled out of Burgeon's guitar case; it sounded like a bull banjo with the heaves. Ned jumped, dropped his cigarette holder, got the case open and I guess put his hand on the strings; the noise stopped. That eliminated him . . . or did it?

Take it another way. What would the guy have to be like who would waste a marvel like this on schoolboy pranks at a Medusa Christmas party? Not Jibless, I thought—he abominates practical jokers. Bierce didn't seem to be the type either, although you could never tell; the damnedest wry stories get hatched occasionally in that lean ecclesiastic skull. Duchamp was too staid (but was I sure?); MacKean was an enigma. Gamble? Just maybe. Burgeon? Jones? It could be either, I thought, but I wasn't satisfied.

I glanced at Ray again, and mentally crossed him off for the second or third time. Ray's an honorable man, within his own complicated set of rules; he might mislead me, with pleasure, but he wouldn't lie outright.

But I had the feeling that the answer was square in front of me, and I was blind to it.

The meeting was just now getting around to the idea that somebody present was responsible for all the nonsense. This shows you the trouble with committees.

A shocking idea hit me abruptly; I grabbed Ray by the coat-sleeve. "Ray, this cockeyed weather—I just remembered. *Suppose it's local.*"

His eyes widened; he nodded reluctantly. Then he stiffened and snapped his fingers at somebody squatting just below us—the invisible fan, Harry Somebody. I hadn't even noticed him there, but it's Ray's business to know everything and keep track of everybody—that's why he's up on his hill.

The fan came over. Ray handed him something.

"Here's some change, Harry—run out and call up the weather bureau. Find out whether this freak weather is local or not, and if it is, just where the boundaries are. Got that?"

Harry nodded and went out. He was back only a couple of minutes later. "I got the weather bureau all right. They say it's local—just Manhattan and Queens!"

Something snapped. I did a fast jig on the piano top, slipped and came crashing down over the keys, but I hardly noticed it. I got a death-grip on Ray's trouser leg. "Listen! If he can do that—he doesn't have to be in the same room. Doesn't Gamble live out in—"

There were cries of alarm over by the open courtyard window. The room was suddenly full of cats—brindle ones, black ones, tabbies, white ones with pink ribbons around their necks, lunatic Siamese.

After them came dogs: one indistinguishable wave of liquid leaping torsos, flying ears, gullets. In half a second the room was an incident written by Dante for the Mutascope.

I caught a glimpse of a terrier bounding after two cats who were climbing Samwitz' back; I saw Duchamp asprawl, pipe still in his mouth, partially submerged under a tidal eddy of black and white. I saw Tom Q. rise up like a lighthouse, only to be bowled over by a frantically scrambling Leigh MacKean.

Ray touched my arm and pointed. Over by the far wall, his back against it, Gamble stood like a slightly potbound Viking. He was swinging that massive briefcase of his, knocking a flying cat or dog aside at every swipe. Two women had crawled into his lee for shelter; he seemed to be enjoying himself.

Then the briefcase burst. It didn't just come open; it flew apart like a comedy suitcase, scattering a whirlwind of manuscript paper, shirts, socks—and nothing else.

The tide rushed toward the window again: the last screech and the last howl funneled out. In the ringing silence, somebody giggled. I couldn't place it, and neither could Ray, I think—then. Stunned, I counted scratched noses.

Samwitz was nowhere in sight; the crowd had thinned a good deal, but all of the eight, thank heaven, were still there—MacKean sitting groggily in a stranger's lap, Werner Kley nursing a bloody nose, Tom Q., camera still dangling from his neck, crawling carefully on hands and knees toward the door . . .

He reached it and disappeared. An instant later, we heard a full chorus of feminine screams from the lobby, and then the sound of an enormous J. Arthur Rank-type gong.

Ray and I looked at each other with a wild surmise. "*Tom* lives in Queens!" he said.

I scrambled down off the piano and the platform, but Ray was quicker. He darted into the crowd, using his elbows in short, efficient jabs. By the time I got to the door he was nowhere in sight.

The lobby was full of large powdery women in flowered dresses, one of them still shrieking. They slowed me down, and so did tripping over one of those big cylindrical jardinieres full of sand and snipes. I reached the street just in time to see Ray closing the door of a cab.

I hadn't the wind to shout. I saw his cheerful face and Tom's in the small yellow glow of the cab light; I saw Tom Q. raise the camera, and Ray put out his hand to it. Then the cab pulled away into traffic, and I watched its beady red taillights down the avenue until they winked out of sight.

Some time later, walking down the cold morning street, I discovered there was somebody with me, keeping step, not saying anything. It was Harry Er-Ah.

He saw I had noticed him. "Some party," he remarked.

I said yeah.

"That was pretty funny, what happened in the lobby."

"I didn't see it."

"He came tearing through there on all fours. Right into the middle of all those women. They probably thought he was a mad dog or something."

I took two more steps, and stopped, and looked at him. "That was *all* he did?" I said.

"Sure."

"Well, then," I said with mounting exasperation, "in the name of— Oh. Wait a minute. You're wrong," I told him, calming down again. "There was the gong. He made that gong noise."

"Did he?" said Harry. One nervous hand went up and adjusted the hornrims.

I felt a little tugging at my shirt front, and looked down to see my necktie slithering out. I swatted at it instinctively, but it ducked away and hovered, swaying like a cobra.

Then it dropped. He showed me his open hand, and there was a wire running up out of his sleeve, with a clip on the end of it. For the first time, I noticed two rings of metal wired behind the lens frames of his eyeglasses.

He pulled his other hand out of his pocket, and there was a little haywire rig in it—batteries and a couple of tubes and three tuning knobs.

Fans, I was thinking frozenly—sixteen or eighteen, maybe, with pimples and dandruff and black fingernails, and that wonderful, terrible eagerness boiling up inside them . . . slaving away at backyard rocketry experiments, wiring up crazy gadgets that never worked, printing bad fiction and worse poetry in mimeographed magazines . . . How could I have forgotten?

"I wasn't going to tell anybody," he said. "No matter what happened. If they'd *looked* at me, just once, they would have seen. But as long as you're worrying so much about it—" He blinked, and said humbly, "It scares me. What do you think I ought to do?"

My fingers twitched. I said, "Well, this will take some thinking about, Harry. Uh, can I—"

He backed off absentmindedly as I stepped toward him. "I've been thinking about it," he said. "As a matter of fact, I haven't been to bed since yesterday morning. I worked on it straight through from four o'clock yesterday. Twenty hours. I took caffeine tablets. But go ahead, tell me. What would you do if you"—he said it apologetically—"were me?"

I swallowed. "I'd go at it slowly," I said. "You can make a lot of mistakes by—"

He interrupted me, with a sudden fiendish glint in his eye. "The man that has this is pretty important, don't

253

you think?" And he grinned. "How would you like to see my face on all the stamps?"

I shuddered in spite of myself. "Well—"

"I wouldn't *bother,*" he said. "I've got something better to do first."

"Harry," I said, leaning, "if I've said anything . . ."

"You didn't say anything." He gave me such a look as I hope I never get from a human again. "Big shot!"

I grabbed for him, but he was too quick. He leaped back, jamming the gadget into his pocket, fumbling at the spectacles with his other hand. I saw his feet lift clear of the pavement. He was hanging there like a mirage, drifting backward and upward just a little faster than I could run.

His voice came down, thin and clear: "I'll send you a postcard from . . ."

I lost the last part; anyhow, it couldn't have been what it sounded like.

Just over a month later came Palomar's reports of unaccountable lights observed on the dark limb of Mars. Every science fiction reader in the world, I suppose, had the same thought—of a wanderer's footprints fresh in the ancient dust, his handprints on controls not shaped for hands, the old wild light wakened. But only a few of us pictured hornrims gleaming there in the Martian night . . .

I drove over to Milford and had a look through Ham Jibless' homemade telescope. I couldn't see the lights, of course, but I could see that damned infuriating planet, shining away ruddy there across thirty-six million miles of space, with its eternal *Yah, yah, you can't catch me!*

Medusa meetings have been badly attended since then, I'm told; for some reason, it gives the members the green heaves to look at each other.

DURING AN UNPRODUCTIVE SESSION
at the typewriter in 1959, I said the hell with
it and decided to go and lie down. While
horizontal, with the dorsal muscles relaxed,
I got the idea for "Time Enough," thus
establishing a principle that I have followed
successfully ever since: when you're not
writing, get away from the typewriter. I
don't get ideas at my desk; I get them in the
bathroom ("Not With a Bang"), in super-
markets ("The Handler"), and in bed
("Time Enough").

16

TIME ENOUGH

<<<<<<<<<<<<<<<<<<<<<<<<<<<<<<<<<<<<<<

THE WALLS AND THE CONTROL PANEL WERE
gray, but in the viewscreen it was green summer noon.

"That's the place," said the boy's voice in Vogel's ear.

The old man gently touched the controls, and the
viewpoint steadied, twenty feet or so above the ground.
In the screen, maple leaves swayed in a light breeze.
There was just a glimpse of the path below, deep in
shadow.

The display, on the tiny screen, was as real as if one
could somehow squeeze through the frame and drop
into those sunlit leaves. A warm breath of air came into
the room.

"Guess I could go there blindfold, I remember it so
well," he heard Jimmy say. The boy seemed unable to
stop talking; his hands tightened and relaxed on his
knees. "I remember, we were all standing around in
front of the drugstore in the village, and one of the kids
said let's go swimming. So we all started off across town,
and first thing I knew, we weren't going down to the
beach; we were going out to the old quarry."

The leaves danced suddenly in a stronger breeze.
"Guess we'll see them in about a minute," Jimmy said.
"If you got the right time, that is." His weight shifted,
and Vogel knew he was staring up at the dials on the
control board, even before his high voice read aloud:

"May twenty-eight, nineteen sixty. Eleven-nine-thirty-two A.M."

His voice grew higher. "Here they come."

In the screen, a flicker of running bodies passed under the trees. Vogel saw bare brown backs, sports shirts, tee shirts, dark heads and blond. There were eight or nine boys in the pack, all aged about twelve; the last, lagging behind, was a slender brown-haired boy who seemed a little younger. He paused, clearly visible for a moment through the leaves, and looked up with a white face. Then he turned and was gone into the dark flickering green.

"There I go," said Jimmy's raw voice. "Now we're climbing up the slope to the quarry. Dark and kind of clammy up there, so many old spruces you can't even see the sky. That moss was just like cold mud when you stepped on it barefoot."

"Try to relax," said Vogel carefully. "Would you like to do it later?"

"No, now," said Jimmy convulsively. His voice steadied. "I'm a little tensed up, I guess, but I can do it. I wasn't really *scared;* it was the way it happened, so sudden. They never gave me time to get ready."

"Well, that's what the machine is for," said Vogel soothingly. "More time—time enough for everything."

"I know it," said Jimmy in an inattentive voice.

Vogel sighed. These afternoons tired him; he was not a young man any more and he no longer believed in his work. Things did not turn out as you expected. The work had to be done, of course; there was always the chance of helping someone, but it was not the easy, automatic thing that youth in its terrible confidence believed.

There was a rustle in the screen, and Vogel saw Jimmy's hands clench into desperate fists on his knees.

A boy flashed into view, the same boy, running clumsily with one hand over his face. His head rocked back and forth. He blundered past, whipped by undergrowth, and the swaying branches closed behind him.

Jimmy's hands relaxed slowly. "There I go," his voice

said, low and bitter. "Running away. Crying like a baby."

After a moment Vogel's spidery fingers reached out to the controls. The viewpoint drifted slowly closer to the ground. Galaxies of green leaves passed through it like bright smoke, and then the viewpoint stopped and tilted, and they were looking up the leaf-shadowed path, as if from a point five feet or so above the ground.

Vogel asked carefully, "Ready now?"

"Sure," said Jimmy, his voice thin again.

The shock of the passage left him stumbling for balance, and he fetched up against a small tree. The reeling world steadied around him; he laughed. The tree trunk was cool and papery under his hand; the leaves were a dancing green glory all around. He was back in Kellogg's Woods again, on that May day when everything had gone wrong, and here it was, just the same as before. The same leaves were on the trees; the air he breathed was the same air.

He started walking up the trail. After a few moments he discovered that his heart was thumping in his chest. He *hated* them, all the big kids with their superior, grinning faces. They were up there right now, waiting for him. But this time he would show them, and then afterward, slowly, it would be possible to stop hating. He knew that. But oh, Christ, how he hated them now!

It was dark under the spruces as he climbed, and the moss was squashy underfoot. For a passing moment he was sorry he had come. But it was costing his family over a thousand dollars to have him sent back. They were giving him this golden chance, and he wouldn't waste it.

Now he could hear the boys' voices, calling hollow, and the cold splash as one of them dived.

Hating and bitter, he climbed to where he could look down across the deep shadowed chasm of the old quarry. The kids were all tiny figures on the other side, where the rock slide was, the only place where you could climb out of the black water. Some of them were sitting on the rocks, wet and shivering. Their voices came up to him small with distance.

Nearer, he saw the dead spruce that lay slanting downward across the edge of the quarry, with its tangled roots in the air. The trunk was silvery gray, perhaps a foot thick at the base. It had fallen straight down along the quarry wall, an old tree with all the stubs of limbs broken off short, and its tip was jammed into a crevice. Below that, there was a series of ledges you could follow all the way down.

But first you had to walk the dead tree.

He climbed up on the thick, twisting roots, trying not to be aware just yet how they overhung the emptiness below. Down across the shadowed quarry, he could see pale blurs of faces turning up one by one to look at him.

Now he vividly remembered the way it had been before, the line of boys tightrope-walking down the tree, arms waving for balance, bare or tennis-shoed feet treading carefully. If only they hadn't left him till last!

He took one step out onto the trunk. Without intending to, he glanced down and saw the yawning space under him—the black water, and the rocks.

The tree swayed under him. He tried to take the next step and found he couldn't. It was just the same as before, and he realized now that it was *impossible* to walk the tree—you would slip and fall, down, down that cliff to the rocks and the cold water. Standing there fixed between the sky and the quarry, he could tell himself that the others had done it, but it didn't help. What good was that, when he could *see,* when anybody could see, it was impossible?

Down there, the boys were waiting, in their cold and silent comradeship.

Jimmy stepped slowly back. Tears of self-hatred burned his lids, but he climbed over the arching roots and left the quarry edge behind him, hearing the clear, distant shouts begin again as he stumbled down the path.

"Don't blame yourself too much," said Vogel in his gray voice. "Maybe you just weren't ready, this time."

Jimmy wiped his eyes angrily with the heel of his

hand. "I wasn't ready," he muttered. "I thought I was, but . . . Must have been too nervous, that's all."

"Or, maybe . . ." Vogel hesitated. "Some people think it's better to forget the past and solve our problems in the present."

Jimmy's eyes widened with shock. "I couldn't give up *now!*" he said. He stood up, agitated. "Why, my whole life would be ruined—I mean, I never thought I'd hear a thing like that from you, Mr. Vogel. I mean, the whole *point* of this machine, and everything . . ."

"I know," said Vogel. "The past can be altered. The scholar can take his exam over again, the lover can propose once more, the words that were thought of too late can be spoken. So I always believed." He forced a smile. "It's like a game of cards. If you don't like the hand that is dealt to you, you can take another, and after that, another. . . ."

"That's right," said Jimmy, sounding appeased. "So if you look at it that way, how can I lose?"

Vogel did not reply but stood up courteously to see him to the door.

"So, then, I'll see you tomorrow, Mr. Vogel," Jimmy said.

Vogel glanced at the wall calendar; it read, *April 21, 1978.* "Yes, all right," he answered.

In the doorway, Jimmy looked back at him with pathetic hopefulness—a pale, slender, thirty-year-old man, from whose weak eyes a lost boy seemed to be staring, pleading. . . . "There's always tomorrow, isn't there, Mr. Vogel?" he asked.

"Yes," said Vogel wearily. "There's always tomorrow."

THIS IS THE OTHER STORY I WROTE (in part) when I thought I might be going blind, and I don't feel quite so flippant about it as I do about some others. For one thing, my third wife (whom I married just about then) got into the story somehow, and I still see her there. For another, in the course of revision, she talked me into putting myself into it too. There we are, and whenever I read "Mary" I hear our voices.

17

MARY

≪≪≪≪≪≪≪≪≪≪≪≪≪≪≪≪≪≪≪≪≪≪≪≪≪≪≪≪≪≪

THIRTY SISTERS, ALIKE AS PEAS, WERE SITting at their looms in the court above the Gallery of Weavers. In the cool shadow, their white dresses rustled like the stirrings of doves, and their voices now murmured, now shrilled. Over the courtyard was a canopy of green glass, through which the sun appeared to swim like a golden-green fish: but over the roofs could be seen the strong blue of the sky, and even, at one or two places, the piercing white sparkle of the sea.

The sisters were ivory-skinned, strong-armed and straight of back, with eyebrows arched black over bright eyes. Some had grown fat, some were lean, but the same smiles dimpled their cheeks, the same gestures threw back their sleek heads when they laughed, and each saw herself mirrored in the others.

Only the youngest, Mary, was different. Hers was the clan face, but so slender and grave that it seemed a stranger's. She had been brought to birth to replace old Anna-one, who had fallen from the lookout and broken her neck sixteen springs ago; and some said it had been done too quick, that Mary was from a bad egg and should never have been let grow. Now the truth was that Mary had in her genes a long-recessive trait of melancholy and unwordliness, turned up by accident in the last cross; but the Elders, who after all knew best, had decided to give her the same chance as anyone.

For in the floating island of Iliria, everyone knew that the purpose of life was happiness; and therefore to deprive anyone of life was a great shame.

At the far side of the court, Vivana called from her loom, "They say a new Fisher came from the mainland yesterday!" She was the eldest of the thirty, a coarse, good-natured woman with a booming laugh. "If he's handsome, I may take him, and give you others a chance at my Tino. Rose, how would you like that? Tino would be a good man for you." Her loom whirled, and rich, dark folds of liase rippled out. It was an artificial fiber, formed, spun, woven and dyed in the loom, hardening as it reached the air. A canister of the stuff, like tinted gelatin, stood at the top of every loom. It came from the Chemist clan, who concocted it by mysterious workings out of the sea water that tumbled through their vats.

"What, is he tiring of you already?" Rose called back. She was short and moon-faced, with strong, clever fingers that danced on the keyboard of her loom. "Probably you belched in his face once too often." She raised her shrill voice over the laughter. "Now let me tell you, Vivana, if the new Fisher is as handsome as that, I may take him myself, and let you have Mitri." Mounds of apple-green stuff tumbled into the basket at her feet.

Between them, Mary worked on, eyes cast down, without smiling.

"Gogo and Vivana!" someone shouted.

"Yes, that's right—never mind about the Fisher! Gogo and Vivana!" All the sisters were shouting and laughing. But Mary still sat quietly busy at her loom.

"All right, all right," shouted Vivana, wheezing with laughter. "I will try him, but then who's to have Gunner?"

"Me!"

"No, me!"

Gunner was the darling of the Weavers, a pink man with thick blond lashes and a roguish grin.

"No, let the youngsters have a chance," Vivana called reprovingly. "Joking aside, Gunner is too good for you old scows." Ignoring the shrieks of outrage, she went on, "I say let Viola have him. Better yet, wait, I have an idea—how about Mary?"

The chatter stilled; all eyes turned toward the silent girl where she sat, weaving slow cascades of creamy white liase. She flushed quickly, and bowed her head, unable to speak. She was sixteen, and had never taken a lover.

The women looked at her, and the pleasure faded out of their faces. Then they turned away, and the shouting began again:

"Rudi!"

"Ernestine!"

"Hugo!"

"Areta!"

Mary's slim hands faltered, and the intricate diapered pattern of her weaving was spoiled. Now the bolt would have to be cut off, unfinished. She stopped the loom, and drooped over it, pressing her forehead against the smooth metal. Tears burned her eyelids. But she held herself still, hoping Mia, at the next loom, would not see.

Below in the street, a sudden tumult went up. Heads turned to listen: there was the wailing of flutes, the thundering of drums, and the sound of men's rich voices, all singing and laughing.

A gate banged open, and a clatter of feet came tumbling up the stair. The white dresses rustled as the sisters turned expectantly toward the arch.

A knot of laughing, struggling men burst through, full into the midst of the women, toppling looms, while the sisters shrieked in protest and pleasure.

The men were Mechanics, dark-haired, gaunt, leavened by a few blond Chemists. They were wrestling, Mechanic against Chemist, arms locked about each other's necks, legs straining for leverage. One struggling pair toppled suddenly, overturning two more. The men scrambled up, laughing, red with exertion.

Behind them was a solitary figure whose stillness drew Mary's eyes. He was tall, slender and grave, with russet hair and a quiet mouth. While the others shouted and pranced, he stood looking around the courtyard. For an instant his calm gray eyes met hers, and Mary felt a sudden pain at the heart.

"Dear, what is it?" asked Mia, leaning closer.

"I think I am ill," said Mary faintly.

"Oh, not now!" Mia protested.

Two of the men were wrestling again. A heave, and the dark Mechanic went spinning over the other's hip.

A shout of applause went up. Through the uproar, Vivana's big voice came booming, "You fishheads, get out! Look at this, half a morning's work ruined! Are you all drunk? Get out!"

"We're all free for the day!" one of the Mechanics shouted. "You too—the whole district! It's in the Fisher's honor! So come on, what are you waiting for?"

The women were up, in a sudden flutter of voices and white skirts, the men beginning to spread out among them. The tall man still stood where he was. Now he was looking frankly at Mary, and she turned away in confusion, picking up the botched fabric with hands that did not feel it.

She was aware that two Mechanics had turned back, were leading the tall man across the courtyard, calling, "Violet—Clara!" She did not move; her breath stopped.

Then they were pausing before her loom. There was an awful moment when she thought she could not move or breathe. She looked up fearfully. He was standing there, hands in his pockets, slumped a little as he looked down at her.

He said, "What is your name?" His voice was low and gentle.

"Mary," she said.

"Will you go with me today, Mary?"

Around her, the women's heads were turning. A silence spread; she could sense the waiting, the delight held in check.

She could not! Her whole soul yearned for it, but she was too afraid, there were too many eyes watching. Miserably, she said, "No," and stopped, astonished, listening to the echo of her voice saying gladly, "Yes!"

Suddenly her heart grew light as air. She stood, letting the loom fall, and when he held out his hand, hers went into it as if it knew how.

"So you have a rendezvous with a Mainland Fisher?" the Doctor inquired jovially. He was pale-eyed and merry in his broad brown hat and yellow tunic; he popped open his little bag, took out a pill, handed it to Mary. "Swallow this, dear."

"What is it for, Doctor?" she asked, flushing.

"Only a precaution. You wouldn't want a baby to grow right in your belly, would you? Ha, ha, ha! That shocks you, does it? Well, you see, the Mainlanders don't sterilize the males, their clan customs forbid it, so they sterilize the females instead. We have to be watchful, ah, yes, we Doctors! Swallow it down, there's a good girl."

She took the pill, drank a sip of water from the flask he handed her.

"Good, good—now you can go to your little meeting and be perfectly safe. Enjoy yourself!" Beaming, he closed his bag and went away.

On the high Plaza of Fountains, overlooking the quayside and the sea, feasts of shrimp and wine, seaweed salad, caviar, pasta, iced sweets had been laid out under canopies of green glass. Orchestrinos were playing. Couples were dancing on the old ceramic cobbles, white skirts swinging, hair afloat in the brilliant air. Farther up, Mary and her Fisher had found a place to be alone.

Under the bower in the cool shade, they lay clasped heart to heart, their bodies still joined so that in her ecstasy she could not tell where hers ended or his began.

"Oh, I love you, I love you!" she murmured.

His body moved, his head drew back a little to look at her. There was something troubled in his gray eyes. "I didn't know this was going to be your first time," he said. "How is it that you waited so long?"

"I was waiting for you," she said faintly, and it seemed to her that it was so, and that she had always known it. Her arms tightened around him, wishing to draw him closer to her body again.

But he held himself away, looking down at her with the same vague uneasiness in his eyes. "I don't understand," he said. "How could you have known I was coming?"

"I knew," she said. Timidly her hands began to stroke the long, smooth muscles of his back, the man's flesh, so different from her own. It seemed to her that her fingertips knew him without being told; they found the tiny spots that gave him pleasure, and lingered there, without her direction.

His body stiffened; his gray eyes half closed. "Oh, Mary," he said, and then he was close against her again, his mouth busy on hers: and the pleasure began, more piercing and sweet than she had ever dreamed it could be. Now she was out of herself again, half aware that her body was moving, writhing; that her voice was making sounds and speaking words that astonished her to hear . . .

Near the end she began to weep, and lay in his arms afterward with the luxurious tears wetting her cheeks, while his voice asked anxiously, "Are you all right? Darling, are you all right?" and she could not explain, but only held him tighter, and wept.

Later, hand in hand, they wandered down the bone-white stairs to the quayside strewn with drying nets, the glass floats sparkling sharp in the sun, spars, tackle and canvas piled everywhere. Only two boats were moored at the floating jetty below; the rest were out fishing, black specks on the glittering sea, almost at the horizon.

Over to eastward they saw the desolate smudge of the mainland and the huddle of stones that was Porto. "That's where you live," she said wonderingly.

"Yes."

"What do you do there?"

He paused, looked down at her with that startled unease in his glance. After a moment he shrugged. "Work. Drink a little in the evenings, make love. What else would I do?"

A dull pain descended suddenly on her heart and would not lift its wings. "You've made love to many women?" she asked with difficulty.

"Of course. Mary, what's the matter?"

"You're going back to Porto. You're going to leave me."

Now the unnamed thing in his eyes had turned to

open incredulity. He held her arms, staring down at her. "What else?"

She put her head down obstinately, burying it against his chest. "I want to stay with you," she said in a muffled voice.

"But you *can't*. You're an Islander—I'm a Mainlander."

"I know."

"Then why this foolishness?"

"I don't know."

He turned her without speaking, and they stepped down from the promenade, went into the shadow of some storehouses that abutted on the quayside. The doors were open, breathing scents of spices and tar, new cordage, drying fish. Beyond them was a pleasant courtyard with boats piled upside down on one side, on the other a table, an umbrella, chairs, all cool in the afternoon shadow. From there they took a shallow staircase up into a maze of little streets full of the dim, mysterious blue light that fell from canopies of tinted glass between roofs. Passing a house with open shutters, they heard the drone of childish voices. They peered in: it was the nursery school—forty young Bakers, Chemists, Mechanics, fair skins and dark, each in a doll-like miniature of his clan costume, all earnestly reciting together while the shovel-hatted Teacher stood listening at the greenboard. Cool, neutral light came from the louvered skylights; the small faces were clear and innocent, here a tiny Cook in his apron, there two Carters sitting together, identical in their blue smocks, there a pale Doctor, and beside him, Mary saw with a pang, a little Weaver in white. The familiar features were childishly blunted and small, the ivory skin impossibly pure, the bright eyes wide. "Look —that one," she whispered, pointing.

He peered in. "She looks like you. More like you than the others. You're different from all the rest, Mary—that's why I like you." He looked down at her with a puzzled expression; his arms tightened around her. "I've never felt quite this way about a girl before; what are you doing to me?" he said.

She turned to him, embracing him, letting her body

268

go soft and compliant against his. "Loving you, darling," she said, smiling up, her eyes half-closed.

He kissed her fiercely, then pushed her away, looking almost frightened. "See here, Mary," he said abruptly, "we've got to understand something."

"Yes?" she said faintly, clinging to him.

"I'm going to be back in Porto tomorrow morning," he said.

"Tomorrow!" she said. "I thought—"

"My work was done this morning. It was a simple adjustment of the sonics. You'll catch plenty of fish from now on . . . There's nothing more for me to do here."

She was stunned; she could not believe it. Surely there would be at least another night . . . that was little enough to ask.

"Can't you stay?" she said.

"You know I can't." His voice was rough and strained. "I go where they tell me, come when they say come."

She tried to hold back the time, but it slipped away, ran through her fingers. The sky darkened slowly from cerulean to Prussian blue, the stars came out and the cool night wind stirred over the jetty.

Below her, in a cluster of lights, they were making the boat ready. Orchestrinos were playing up the hillside, and there was a little crowd of men and women gathering to say good-bye. There was laughter, joking, voices raised good-naturedly in the evening stillness.

Klef, pale in the lights, came up the stairs to where she stood, his head tilted as he came, his grave eyes holding hers.

"I'm not going to cry," she said.

His hands took her arms, gripping her half in tenderness, half impatiently. "Mary, you know this is wrong. Get over it. Find yourself other men—be happy."

"Yes, I'll be happy," she said.

He stared down at her in uncertainty, then bent his head and kissed her. She held herself passive in his arms, not responding or resisting. After a moment he let her go and stepped back. "Good-bye, Mary."

"Good-bye, Klef."

He turned, went quickly down the steps. The laughing voices surrounded him as he went toward the boat; after a moment she heard his voice, too, lifted in cheerful farewells.

In the morning she awoke knowing that he was gone. A frightening knowledge of loss seized her, and she sat up with her heart leaping.

Down the high dormitory, smelling faintly of cinnamon oil and fresh linens, the sisters were beginning to rustle sleepily out of their cubicles, murmuring and yawning. The familiar hiss of the showers began at the far end of the room. The white-curtained windows were open, and from her bed Mary could see the cream and terra-cotta roofs spread out in a lazy descent. The air was cool and still and mysteriously pure: it was the best moment of the day.

She rose, washed herself and dressed mechanically. "What is it, dear?" asked Mia, bending toward her anxiously.

"Nothing. Klef is gone."

"Well, there'll be others." Mia smiled and patted her hand, and went away. There was a closeness between them, they were almost of an age, and yet even Mia could not be comfortable long in Mary's company.

Mary sat with the others at table, silent in the steaming fragrances of coffee and new bread, the waves of cheerful talk that flowed around her. Carrying her loom, she went down with the rest into the court and sat in her usual place. The work began.

Time stretched away wearily into the future. How many mornings in her life would she sit here, where she sat now, beginning to weave as she did now? How could she endure it? How had she ever endured it? She put her fingers on the controls of the loom, but the effort to move them appalled her. A tear dropped bright on the keyboard.

Mia leaned over toward her. "Is there anything the matter? Don't you feel well?"

Her fists clenched uselessly. "I can't—I can't—" was

all she could utter. Hot tears were running down her face; her jaw was shaking. She bowed her head over the loom.

Iliria was neither wearisomely flat, nor cone-shaped nor pyramidal in its construction, like some of the northern islands, but was charmingly hollowed, like a cradle. The old cobblestoned streets rose and fell; there were stairways, balconies, arcades; never a vista, always a new prospect. The buildings were pleasingly various, some domed and spired, others sprawling. Cream was the dominant color, with accents of cool light blue, yellow, and rose. For more than three hundred years the island had been afloat, just as it now was: the same plazas with their fountains, the same shuttered windows, the same rooftops.

During the last century, some colonies had been creeping back onto the land as the contamination diminished; but every Ilirian knew that only island life was perfect. Above, the unchanging streets and buildings served each generation as the last; down below, the storage chambers, engine rooms, seines, preserving rooms, conveniently out of sight and hearing, went on functioning as they always had. Unsinkable, sheathed in ceramic above and below, the island would go on floating just as it now was, forever.

It was strange to Mary to see the familiar streets so empty. The morning light lay softly along the walls; in corners, blue shadow gathered. Behind every door and window there was a subdued hum of activity; the clans were at their work. All the way to the church circle, she passed no one but a Messenger and two Carters with their loads: all three looked at her curiously until she was out of sight.

Climbing the Hill of Carpenters, she saw the gray dome of the church rising against the sky—a smooth, unrelieved ovoid, with a crescent of morning light upon it. Overhead, a flock of gulls hung in the air, wings spread, rising and dipping. They were gray against the light.

She paused on the porch step to look down. From this height she could see the quays and the breakwater, and the sun on the brightwork of the moored launches; and then the long rolling back of the sea, full of white-caps in the freshening breeze; and beyond that, the dark smudge of the land, and the clutter of brown win-dowed stone that was Porto. She stood looking at it for a moment, dry-eyed, then went into the shadowed door-way.

Clabert the Priest rose up from his little desk and came toward her with ink-stained fingers, his skirt flap-ping around his ankles. "Good morning, cousin, have you a trouble?"

"I'm in love with a man who has gone away."

He stared at her in perplexity for a moment, then darted down the corridor to the left. "This way, cousin." She followed him past the great doors of the central harmonion. He opened a smaller door, curved like the end of an egg, and motioned her in.

She stepped inside; the room was gray, egg-shaped, and the light came uniformly from the smooth ceramic walls. "Twenty minutes," said Clabert, and withdrew his head. The door shut, joining indistinguishably with the wall around it.

Mary found herself standing on the faintly sloping floor, with the smooth single curve of the wall surround-ing her. After a moment she could no longer tell how far away the big end of the ovicle was; the room seemed first quite small, only a few yards from one end to the other; then it was gigantic, bigger than the sky. The floor shifted uncertainly under her feet, and after an-other moment she sat down on the cool hollow slope.

The silence grew and deepened. She had no feeling of confinement; the air was fresh and in constant slight movement. She felt faintly and agreeably dizzy, and put her arms behind her to steady herself. Her vision began to blur; the featureless gray curve gave her no focus for her eyes. Another moment passed, and she became aware that the muffled silence was really a continual slow hush of sound, coming from all points at once, like the distant murmuring of the sea. She held her breath to listen, and at once, like dozens of wings flicking away in turn, the sound stopped. Now, listening intently, she could hear a still fainter sound, a soft, rapid pattering that stopped and came again, stopped and came again . . . and listening, she realized that it was the multiple echo of her own heartbeat. She breathed again, and the slow hush flooded back.

The wall approached, receded . . . gradually it became neither close nor far away; it hung gigantically and mistily just out of reach. The movement of air imperceptibly slowed. Lying dazed and unthinking, she grew intensely aware of her own existence, the meaty solidity of her flesh, the incessant pumping of blood, the sigh of breath, the heaviness and pressure, the pleasant beading of perspiration on her skin. She was whole and complete, all the way from fingers to toes. She was uniquely herself; somehow she had forgotten how important that was . . .

"Feeling better?" asked Clabert, as he helped her out of the chamber.

"Yes . . ." She was dazed and languid; walking was an extraordinary effort.

"Come back if you have these confusions again," Clabert called after her, standing in the porch doorway.

Without replying, she went down the slope in the brilliant sunshine. Her head was light, her feet were amusingly slow to obey her. In a moment she was running to catch up with herself, down the steep cobbled street in a stumbling rush, with faces popping out of shutters behind her, and fetched up laughing and gasping with her arms around a light column at the bottom.

A stout Carter in blue was grinning at her out of his tanned face. "What's the joke, woman?"

"Nothing," she stammered. "I've just been to church . . ."

"Ah," he said, with a finger beside his nose, and went on.

She found herself taking the way downward to the quays. The sunlit streets were empty; no one was in the pools. She stripped and plunged in, gasping at the pleasure of the cool fresh water on her body. And even when two Baker boys, an older one and a younger, came by

273

and leaned over the wall shouting, "Pretty! Pretty!" she felt no confusion, but smiled up at them and went on swimming.

Afterward, she dressed and strolled, wet as she was, along the sea-wall promenade. Giddily she began to sing as she walked, "Open your arms to me, sweetheart, for when the sun shines it's pleasant to be in love . . ." The orchestrinos had been playing that, that night when—

She felt suddenly ill, and stopped with her hand at her forehead.

What was wrong with her? Her mind seemed to topple, shake itself from one pattern into another. She swung her head up, looking with sharp anxiety for the brown tangle of buildings on the mainland.

At first it was not there, and then she saw it, tiny, almost lost on the horizon. The island was drifting, moving away, leaving the mainland behind.

She sat down abruptly; her legs lost their strength. She put her face in her arms and wept: "Klef! Oh, Klef!"

This love that had come to her was not the easy, pleasant thing the orchestrinos sang of; it was a kind of madness. She accepted that, and knew herself to be mad, yet could not change. Waking and sleeping, she could think only of Klef.

Her grief had exhausted itself; her eyes were dry. She could see herself now as the others saw her—as something strange, unpleasant, ill-fitting. What right had she to spoil their pleasure?

She could go back to church, and spend another dazed time in the ovicle. "If you have these confusions again," the Priest had said. She could go every morning, if need be, and again every afternoon. She had seen one who needed to do as much, silly Marget Tailor who always nodded and smiled, drooling a little, no matter what was said to her, and who seemed to have a blankness behind the glow of happiness in her eyes. That was years ago; she remembered the sisters always complained of the wet spots Marget left on her work. Something must have happened to her; others cut and stitched for the Weavers now.

Or she could hug her pain to herself, scourge them with it, make them do something . . . She had a vision of herself running barefoot and ragged through the streets, with people in their doorways shouting, "Crazy Mary! Crazy Mary!" If she made them notice her, made them bring Klef back . . .

She stopped eating except when the other sisters urged her, and grew thinner day by day. Her cheeks and eyes were hollow. All day she sat in the courtyard, not weaving, until at length the other women's voices grew melancholy and seldom. The weaving suffered; there was no joy in the clan house. Many times Vivana and the others reasoned with her, but she could only give the same answers over again, and at last she stopped replying at all.

"But what do you want?" the women asked her, with a note of exasperation in their voices.

What did she want? She wanted Klef to be beside her every night when she went to sleep, and when she wakened in the morning. She wanted his arms about her, his flesh joined to hers, his voice murmuring in her ear. Other men? It was not the same thing. But they could not understand.

"But why do you want me to make myself pretty?" Mary asked with dull curiosity.

Mia bent over her with a tube of cosmetic, touching the pale lips with crimson. "Never mind, something nice. Here, let me smooth your eyebrows. Tut, how thin you've got! Never mind, you'll look very well. Put on your fresh robe, there's a dear."

"I don't know what difference it makes." But Mary stood up wearily, took off her dress, stood thin and pale in the light. She put the new robe over her head, shrugged her arms into it.

"Is that all right?" she asked.

"Dear Mary," said Mia, with tears of sympathy in her eyes. "Sweet, no, let me smooth your hair. Stand straighter, can't you, how will any man—"

"Man?" said Mary. A little color came and went in her cheeks. "Klef?"

"*No,* dear, forget Klef, will you?" Mia's voice turned sharp with exasperation.

"Oh." Mary turned her head away.

"Can't you think of anything else? Do try, dear, just try."

"All right."

"Now come along, they're waiting for us."

Mary stood up submissively and followed her sister out of the dormitory.

In bright sunlight the women stood talking quietly and worriedly around the bower. With them was a husky Chemist with golden brows and hair; his pink face was good-natured and peaceful. He pinched the nearest sister's buttock, whispered something in her ear; she slapped his hand irritably.

"Quick, here they come," said one suddenly. "Go in now, Gunner."

With an obedient grimace, the blond man ducked his head and disappeared into the bower. In a moment Mia and Mary came into view, the thin girl hanging back when she saw the crowd, and the bower.

"What is it?" she complained. "I don't want— Mia, let me go."

"No, dear, come along, it's for the best, you'll see," said the other girl soothingly. "Do give me a hand here, one of you, won't you?"

The two women urged the girl toward the bower. Her face was pale and frightened. "But what do you want me to— You said Klef wasn't— Were you only teasing me? Is Klef—?"

The women gave each other looks of despair. "Go in, dear, and see, why don't you?"

A wild expression came into Mary's eyes. She hesitated, then stepped nearer the bower; the two women let her go. "Klef?" she called plaintively. There was no answer.

"Go in, dear."

She looked at them appealingly, then stooped and put her head in. The women held their breaths. They heard her gasp, then saw her backing out again.

"Crabs and mullets!" swore Vivana. "Get her in, you fools!"

The girl was crying out, weakly and helplessly, as four women swarmed around her, pushed her into the bower. One of them lingered, peered in.

"Has he got her?"

"Yes, now he's got her." Stifled mewing sounds were coming from the bower. "Hang onto her, you fool!"

"She bit!" came Gunner's indignant voice. Then silence.

"Sst, leave them alone," whispered Vivana. The woman at the bower entrance turned, tiptoed away. Together the women withdrew a few yards, found themselves seats on the old steps under the portico, and sat down comfortably close to one another.

There was a scream.

The women leaped up, startled and white. Not one of them could remember hearing such a sound before.

Gunner's hoarse voice bawled something, then there was a stir. Mary appeared in the entrance to the bower. Her skirt was ripped, and she was clutching it to her lap with one hand. Her eyes were filmed, pink-rimmed. "Oh!" she said, moving past them blindly.

"Mary—" said one, reaching out a hand.

"Oh!" she said hopelessly, and moved on, clutching her garment to her body.

"What's the matter?" they asked each other. "What did Gunner do?"

"I did what I was supposed to do," said Gunner, sulkily appearing. There was a red bruise on his cheek. "Gut me and clean me if I ever do it with that one again, though."

"You fool, you must have been too rough. Go after her, someone."

"Well, then serve her yourself the next time, if you know so much." Prodding his cheek gently with a finger, the Chemist went away.

Up the slope, an orchestrino began playing. *"If you*

*would not be cruel, torment me no more. Do not deny
me ever; let it be now or never. Give me your love,
then, as you promised me before . . ."*

"Shut that thing off!" cried Vivana angrily.

Her ageship, Laura-one, the eldest Weaver, was pacing
up and down the sea-wall promenade, knotting her fingers together in silent agitation. Once she paused to look
over the parapet; below her the wall dropped sheer to
blue water. She glanced over at the blur of Porto, half
concealed in the morning haze, and at the stark hills above
with their green fur of returning vegetation. Her eyes
were still keen; halfway across the distance, she could
make out a tiny dark dot, moving toward the island.

Footsteps sounded in the street below; in a moment
Vivana appeared, holding Mary by the arm. The younger
woman's eyes were downcast; the older looked worried
and anxious.

"Here she is, your ageship," said Vivana. "They found
her at the little jetty, throwing bottles into the sea."

"Again?" asked the old woman. "What was in the bottles?"

"Here's one of them," said Vivana, handing over a
crumpled paper.

" 'Tell Klef the Fisher of the town of Porto that Mary
Weaver still loves him,' " the old woman read. She folded
the paper slowly and put it into her pocket. "Always the
same," she said. "Mary, my child, don't you know that
these bottles never can reach your Klef?"

The young woman did not raise her head or speak.

"And twice this month the Fishers have had to catch
you and bring you back when you stole a launch," the
old woman continued. "Child, don't you see that this
must end?"

Mary did not answer.

"And these things that you weave, when you weave
at all," said Laura-one, taking a wadded length of cloth
from her apron pocket. She spread it taut and held it
to the light. In the pattern, visible only when the light
fell glancingly upon it, was woven the figure of a seated
woman with a child in her arms. Around them were

birds with spread wings among the intertwined stems of flowers.

"Who taught you to weave like this, child?" she asked.

"No one," said Mary, not looking up.

The old woman looked down at the cloth again. "It's beautiful work, but——" She sighed and put the cloth away. "We have no place for it. Child, you weave so well, why can't you weave the usual patterns?"

"They are dead. This one is alive."

The old woman sighed again. "And how long is it that you have been demanding your Klef back, dear?"

"Seven months."

"But now think." The old woman paused, glanced over her shoulder. The black dot on the sea was much nearer, curving in toward the jetty below. "Suppose this Klef did receive one of your messages; what then?"

"He would know how much I love him," said Mary, raising her head. Color came into her cheeks; her eyes brightened.

"And that would change his whole life, his loyalties, everything?"

"Yes!"

"And if it did not?"

Mary was silent.

"Child, if that failed, would you confess that you have been wrong—would you let us help you?"

"It wouldn't fail," Mary said stubbornly.

"But if it did?" the older woman insisted gently. "Just suppose—just let yourself imagine."

Mary was silent a moment. "I would want to die," she said.

The two elder Weavers looked at each other, and for a moment neither spoke.

"May I go now?" Mary asked.

Vivana cast a glance down at the jetty, and said quickly, "Maybe it's best, your ageship. Tell them——"

Laura-one stopped her with a raised hand. Her lips were compressed. "And if you go, child, what will you do now?"

"Go and make more messages, to put into bottles."

The old woman sighed. "You see?" she said to Vivana.

Footsteps sounded faintly on the jetty stair. A man's head appeared; he was an island Fisher, stocky, dark-haired, with a heavy black mustache. "Your ageship, the man is here," he said, saluting Laura-one. "Shall I—?"

"No," said Vivana involuntarily. "Don't— Send him back—"

"What would be the good of that?" the old woman asked reasonably. "No, bring him up, Alec."

The Fisher nodded, turned and was gone down the stair.

Mary's head had come up. She said, "The man—?"

"There, it's all right," said Vivana, going to her.

"Is it Klef?" she asked fearfully.

The older woman did not reply. In a moment the black-mustached Fisher appeared again; he stared at them, climbed to the head of the stair, stood aside.

Behind him, after a moment, another head rose out of the stairwell. Under the russet hair, the face was grave and thin. The gray eyes went to Laura-one, then to Mary; they stared at her, as the man continued to climb the steps. He reached the top, and stood waiting, hands at his sides. The black-mustached Fisher turned and descended behind him.

Mary had begun to tremble all over.

"There, dear, it's all right," said Vivana, pressing her arms. As if the words had released her, Mary walked to the Fisher. Tears were shining on her face. She clutched his tunic with both hands, staring up at him. "Klef?" she said.

His hands came up to hold her. She threw herself against him then, so violently that he staggered, and clutched him as if she wished to bury herself in his body. Strangled, hurt sounds came out of her.

The man looked over her head at the two older women. "Can't you leave us alone for a moment?" he asked.

"Of course," said Laura-one, a little surprised. "Why not? Of course." She gestured to Vivana, and the two turned, walked away a little distance down the promenade to a bench, where they sat looking out over the sea-wall.

Gulls mewed overhead. The two women sat side by

side without speaking or looking at one another. They were not quite out of earshot.

"Is it really you?" Mary asked, holding his face between her hands. She tried to laugh. "Darling, I can't see . . . you're all blurred."

"I know," said Klef quietly. "Mary, I've thought about you many times."

"Have you?" she cried. "Oh, that makes me so happy. Oh, Klef, I could die now! Hold me, hold me."

His face hardened. His hands absently stroked her back, up and down. "I kept asking to be sent back," he said. "Finally I persuaded them—they thought you might listen to me. I'm supposed to cure you."

"Of loving you?" Mary laughed. At the sound, his hands tightened involuntarily on her back. "How foolish they were! How foolish, Klef!"

"Mary, we have only these few minutes," he said.

She drew back a little to look at him. "I don't understand."

"I'm to talk to you, and then go back. That's all I'm here for."

She shook her head in disbelief. "But you told me—"

"Mary, listen to me. There is nothing else to do. Nothing."

"Take me back with you, Klef." Her hands gripped him hard. "That's what I want—just to be with you. Take me back."

"And where will you live—in the Fishers' dormitory with forty men?"

"I'll live anywhere, in the streets, I don't care—"

"They would never allow it. You know that, Mary."

She was crying, holding him, shuddering all over. "Don't tell me that, don't say it. Even if it's true, can't you pretend a little? Hold me, Klef, tell me that you love me."

"I love you," he said.

"Tell me that you'll keep me, never let me go, no matter what they say."

He was silent a moment. "It's impossible."

She raised her head.

"Try to realize," he said, "this is a sickness, Mary. You must cure yourself."

"Then you're sick too!" she said.

"Maybe I am, but I'll get well, because I know I have to. And you must get well too. Forget me. Go back to your sisters and your weaving."

She put her cheek against his chest, gazing out across the bright ocean. "Let me just be quiet with you a moment," she said. "I won't cry any more. Klef—"

"Yes?"

"Is that all you have to say to me?"

"It has to be all." His eyes closed, opened again. "Mary, I didn't want to feel this way. It's wrong, it's unhealthy, it hurts. Promise me, before I go. Say you'll let them cure you."

She pushed herself away, wiped her eyes and her cheeks with the heel of one hand. Then she looked up. "I'll let them cure me," she said.

His face contorted. "Thank you. I'll go now, Mary."

"One more kiss!" she cried, moving toward him involuntarily. "Only one more!"

He kissed her on the lips, then wrenched himself away, and looking down to where the two women sat, he made an angry motion with his head.

As they rose and came nearer, he held Mary at arm's length. "Now I'm really going," he said harshly. "Good-bye, Mary."

"Good-bye, Klef." Her fingers were clasped tight at her waist.

The man waited, looking over her head, until Vivana came up and took her arms gently. Then he moved away. At the head of the stairs he looked at her once more; then he turned and began to descend.

"Dear, it will be better now, you'll see," said Vivana uncertainly.

Mary said nothing. She stood still, listening to the faint sounds that echoed up from the stairwell: footsteps, voices, hollow sounds.

There was a sudden clatter, then footsteps mounting the stair. Klef appeared again, chest heaving, eyes bright.

He seized both of Mary's hands in his. "Listen!" he said. "I'm mad. You're mad. We're both going to die."

"I don't care!" she said. Her face was glowing as she looked up at him.

"They say some of the streams are running pure, in the hills. Grass is growing there—there are fish in the streams, even the wild fowl are coming back. We'll go there, Mary, together—just you and I. Alone. Do you understand?"

"Yes, Klef, yes, darling."

"Then come on!"

"Wait!" cried Laura-one shrilly after them as they ran down the stair. "How will you live? What will you eat? Think what you are doing!"

Faint hollow sounds answered her, then the purr of a motor.

Vivana moved to Laura-one's side, and the two women stood watching, silent, as the dark tiny shape of the launch moved out into the brightness. In the cockpit they could make out the two figures close together, dark head and light. The launch moved steadily toward the land; and the two women stood staring, unable to speak, long after it was out of sight.

THIS ONE PRESENTED ITSELF TO ME as a vision, and all I could do was surround it with a suitable progression of events. Other people have explained it, but to me "The Handler" is just what it is.

18

THE HANDLER

<<<<<<<<<<<<<<<<<<<<<<<<<<<<<<<<<<<<<<<<<

WHEN THE BIG MAN CAME IN, THERE WAS A movement in the room like bird dogs pointing. The piano player quit pounding, the two singing drunks shut up, all the beautiful people with cocktails in their hands stopped talking and laughing.

"Pete!" the nearest woman shrilled, and he walked straight into the room, arms around two girls, hugging them tight. "How's my sweetheart? Susy, you look good enough to eat, but I had it for lunch. George, you pirate—" he let go both girls, grabbed a bald blushing little man and thumped him on the arm—"you were great, sweetheart, I mean it, really great. Now HEAR THIS!" he shouted, over all the voices that were clamoring Pete this, Pete that.

Somebody put a martini in his hand, and he stood holding it, bronzed and tall in his dinner jacket, teeth gleaming white as his shirt cuffs. "We had a show!" he told them.

A shriek of agreement went up, a babble of did we have a *show* my God Pete listen a *show*—

He held up his hand. "It was a good show!"

Another shriek and babble.

"The sponsor kinda liked it—he just signed for another one in the fall!"

A shriek, a roar, people clapping, jumping up and down. The big man tried to say something else, but

285

gave up, grinning, while men and women crowded up to him. They were all trying to shake his hand, talk in his ear, put their arms around him.

"I love ya *all!*" he shouted. "Now what do you say, let's live a little!"

The murmuring started again as people sorted themselves out. There was a clinking from the bar. "Jesus, Pete," a skinny pop-eyed little guy was saying, crouching in adoration, "when you dropped that fishbowl I though I'd pee myself, honest to God—"

The big man let out a bark of happy laughter. "Yeah, I can still see the look on your face. And the fish, flopping all over the stage. So what can I do, I get down there on my knees—" the big man did so, bending over and staring at imaginary fish on the floor. "And I say, 'Well, fellows, back to the drawing board!' "

Screams of laughter as the big man stood up. The party was arranging itself around him in arcs of concentric circles, with people in the back standing on sofas and the piano bench so they could see. Somebody yelled, "Sing the goldfish song, Pete!"

Shouts of approval, please-do-Pete, the goldfish song.

"Okay, okay." Grinning, the big man sat on the arm of a chair and raised his glass. "And a vun, and a doo— vere's de moosic?" A scuffle at the piano bench. Somebody banged out a few chords. The big man made a comic face and sang, "Ohhh—how I wish . . . I was a little fish . . . and when I want some quail . . . I'd flap my little tail."

Laughter, the girls laughing louder than anybody and their red mouths farther open. One flushed blonde had her hand on the big man's knee, and another was sitting close behind him.

"But seriously—" the big man shouted. More laughter.

"No seriously," he said in a vibrant voice as the room quieted, "I want to tell you in all seriousness I couldn't have done it alone. And incidentally I see we have some foreigners, litvaks and other members of the press here tonight, so I want to introduce all the important people. First of all, George here, the three-fingered band leader —there isn't a guy in the world could have done what he did this afternoon—George, I love ya." He hugged the blushing little bald man.

"Next my real sweetheart, Ruthie, where are ya? Honey, you were the greatest, really perfect—I mean it, baby—" He kissed a dark girl in a red dress who cried a little and hid her face on his broad shoulder. "And Frank—" he reached down and grabbed the skinny pop-eyed guy by the sleeve. "What can I tell you? A sweetheart?" The skinny guy was blinking, all choked up; the big man thumped him on the back. "Sol and Ernie and Mack, my writers, Shakespeare should have been so lucky—" One by one, they came up to shake the big man's hand as he called their names; the women kissed him and cried. "My stand-in," the big man was calling out, and "my caddy," and "Now," he said, as the room quieted a little, people flushed and sore-throated with enthusiasm, "I want you to meet my handler."

The room fell silent. The big man looked thoughtful and startled, as if he had had a sudden pain. Then he stopped moving. He sat without breathing or blinking his eyes. After a moment there was a jerky motion behind him. The girl who was sitting on the arm of the chair got up and moved away. The big man's dinner jacket split open in the back, and a little man climbed out. He had a perspiring brown face under a shock of black hair. He was a very small man, almost a dwarf, stoop-shouldered and round-backed in a sweaty brown singlet and shorts. He climbed out of the cavity in the big man's body, and closed the dinner jacket carefully. The big man sat motionless and his face was doughy.

The little man got down, wetting his lips nervously. Hello, Harry, a few people said. "Hello," Harry called, waving his hand. He was about forty, with a big nose and big soft brown eyes. His voice was cracked and uncertain. "Well, we sure put on a show, didn't we?"

Sure did, Harry, they said politely. He wiped his brow with the back of his hand. "Hot in there," he explained, with an apologetic grin. Yes I guess it must be, Harry, they said. People around the outskirts of the crowd were beginning to turn away, form conversational groups; the hum of talk rose higher. "Say, Tim, I wonder if I could have something to drink," the little man said. "I don't like to leave him—you know—" He gestured toward the silent big man.

"Sure, Harry, what'll it be?"

"Oh—you know—a glass of beer?"

Tim brought him a beer in a pilsener glass and he drank it thirstily, his brown eyes darting nervously from side to side. A lot of people were sitting down now; one or two were at the door leaving.

"Well," the little man said to a passing girl, "Ruthie, that was quite a moment there, when the fishbowl busted, wasn't it?"

"Huh? Excuse me, honey, I didn't hear you." She bent nearer.

"Oh—well, it don't matter. Nothing."

She patted him on the shoulder once, and took her hand away. "Well excuse me, sweetie, I have to catch Robbins before he leaves." She went on toward the door.

The little man put his beer glass down and sat, twisting his knobby hands together. The bald man and the pop-eyed man were the only ones still sitting near him. An anxious smile flickered on his lips; he glanced at one face, then another. "Well," he began, "that's one show under our belts, huh, fellows, but I guess we got to start, you know, thinking about—"

"Listen, Harry," said the bald man seriously, leaning forward to touch him on the wrist, "why don't you get back inside?"

The little man looked at him for a moment with sad hound-dog eyes, then ducked his head, embarrassed. He stood up uncertainly, swallowed and said, "Well—" He climbed up on the chair behind the big man, opened the back of the dinner jacket and put his legs in one at a time. A few people were watching him, unsmiling. "Thought I'd take it easy a while," he said weakly, "but I guess—" He reached in and gripped something with both hands, then swung himself inside. His brown, uncertain face disappeared.

The big man blinked suddenly and stood up. "Well *hey* there," he called, "what's a matter with this party anyway? Let's see some life, some action—" Faces were lighting up around him. People began to move in closer. "What I mean, let me hear that beat!"

The big man began clapping his hands rhythmically. The piano took it up. Other people began to clap. "What I mean, are we alive here or just waiting for the wagon to pick us up? How's that again, can't hear you!" A roar of pleasure as he cupped his hand to his ear. "Well come on, let me hear it!" A louder roar. Pete, Pete; a gabble of voices. "I got nothing against Harry," said the bald man earnestly in the middle of the noise, "I mean for a square he's a nice guy." "Know what you mean," said the pop-eyed man, "I mean like he doesn't *mean* it." "Sure," said the bald man, "but Jesus that sweaty undershirt and all . . ." The pop-eyed man shrugged. "What are you gonna do?" Then they both burst out laughing as the big man made a comic face, tongue lolling, eyes crossed. Pete, Pete, Pete; the room was really jumping; it was a great party, and everything was all right, far into the night.

ONE TIME MY THIRD WIFE AND I were living in Kentucky, next door to an amiable redneck whose back porch was full of garbage on account of a dispute with the garbage collectors. (He wouldn't carry it out to the road until they picked it up; they wouldn't pick it up until he carried it out.) I told him if he wanted to get rid of it, he ought to put it in neat bags out by the roadside, under a sign lettered "GARBAGE, 25¢ A BAG." I'm morally certain he would have sold it at that price.

19

THE BIG PAT BOOM

<<<<<<<<<<<<<<<<<<<<<<<<<<<<<<<<<<<<<<<<<<

THE LONG, SHINY CAR PULLED UP WITH A whirr of turbines and a puff of dust. The sign over the roadside stand read: BASKETS. CURIOS. Farther down, another sign over a glass-fronted rustic building announced: SQUIRE CRAWFORD'S COFFEE MILL. TRY OUR DOUGHNUTS. Beyond that was a pasture, with a barn and silo set back from the road.

The two aliens sat quietly and looked at the signs. They both had hard purplish skins and little yellow eyes. They were wearing gray tweed suits. Their bodies looked approximately human, but you could not see their chins, which were covered by orange scarves.

Martha Crawford came hustling out of the house and into the basket stand, drying her hands on her apron. After her came Llewellyn Crawford, her husband, still chewing his cornflakes.

"Yes, sir—ma'am?" Martha asked nervously. She glanced at Llewellyn for support, and he patted her shoulder. Neither of them had ever seen an alien real close to.

One of the aliens, seeing the Crawfords behind their counter, leisurely got out of the car. He, or it, was puffing a cigar stuck through a hole in the orange scarf.

"Good morning," Mrs. Crawford said nervously. "Baskets? Curios?"

The alien blinked its yellow eyes solemnly. The rest

291

of its face did not change. The scarf hid its chin and
mouth, if any. Some said that the aliens had no chins,
others that they had something instead of chins that
was so squirmy and awful that no human could bear to
look at it. People called them "Hurks" because they
came from a place called Zeta Herculis.

The Hurk glanced at the baskets and gimcracks hung
over the counter, and puffed its cigar. Then it said,
in a blurred but comprehensible voice, "What is that?"
It pointed downward with one horny, three-fingered
hand.

"The little Indian papoose?" Martha Crawford said,
in a voice that rose to a squeak. "Or the birchbark calendar?"

"No, that," said the Hurk, pointing down again. This
time, craning over the counter, the Crawfords were able
to see that it was looking at a large, disk-shaped gray
something that lay on the ground.

"That?" Llewellyn asked doubtfully.

"That."

Llewellyn Crawford blushed. "Why—that's just a cowpat. One of them cows from the dairy got loose from the
herd yesterday, and she must have dropped that there
without me noticing."

"How much?"

The Crawfords stared at him, or it, without comprehension. "How much what?" Llewellyn asked finally.

"How much," the alien growled around its cigar, "for
the cowpat?"

The Crawfords exchanged glances. "I never *heard*—"
said Martha in an undertone, but her husband shushed
her. He cleared his throat. "How about ten ce— Well, I
don't want to cheat you—how about a quarter?"

The alien produced a large change purse, laid a quarter
on the counter and grunted something to its companion
in the car.

The other alien got out, bringing a square porcelain box
and a gold-handled shovel. With the shovel, she—or it—
carefully picked up the cowpat and deposited it in the
box.

Both aliens then got into the car and drove away, in a whine of turbines and a cloud of dust.

The Crawfords watched them go, then looked at the shiny quarter lying on the counter. Llewellyn picked it up and bounced it in his palm. "Well, say!" He began to smile.

All that week the roads were full of aliens in their long shiny cars. They went everywhere, saw everything, paid their way with bright new-minted coins and crisp paper bills.

There was some talk against the government for letting them in, but they were good for business and made no trouble. Some claimed to be tourists, others said they were sociology students on a field trip.

Llewellyn Crawford went into the adjoining pasture and picked out four cowpats to deposit near his basket stand. When the next Hurk came by, Llewellyn asked, and got, a dollar apiece.

"But why do they *want* them?" Martha wailed.

"What difference does that make?" her husband asked. "*They* want 'em—*we* got 'em! If Ed Lacey calls again about that mortgage payment, tell him not to worry!" He cleared off the counter and arranged the new merchandise on it. He jacked his price up to two dollars, then to five.

Next day he ordered a new sign: COWPATS.

One fall afternoon two years later, Llewellyn Crawford strode into his living room, threw his hat in a corner, and sat down hard. He glared over his glasses at the large circular object, tastefully tinted in concentric rings of blue, orange and yellow, which was mounted over the mantelpiece. To the casual eye, this might have been a genuine "Trophy" class pat, a museum piece, painted on the Hurk planet; but in fact, like so many artistic ladies nowadays, Mrs. Crawford had painted and mounted it herself.

"What's the matter, Lew?" she asked apprehensively. She had a new hairdo and was wearing a New York dress, but looked peaked and anxious.

"Matter!" Llewellyn grunted. "Old man Thomas is a damn fool, that's all. Four hundred dollars a head! Can't buy a cow at a decent price anymore."

"Well, Lew, we do have seven herds already, don't we, and—"

"Got to have more to meet the demand, Martha!" said Llewellyn, sitting up. "My heaven, I'd think you could see that. With queen pats bringing up to fifteen dollars, and not enough to go 'round— And fifteen *hundred* for an emperor pat, if you're lucky enough—"

"Funny we never thought there was so many kinds of pats," Martha said dreamily. "The emperor—that's the one with the double whorl?"

Llewellyn grunted, picking up a magazine.

"Seems like a person could kind of—"

A kindly gleam came into Llewellyn's eyes. "Change one around?" he said. "Nope—been tried. I was reading about it in here just yesterday." He held up the current issue of *The American Pat Dealer,* then began to turn the glossy pages. *"Pat-O-Grams,"* he read aloud. *"Preserving Your Pats. Dairying—a Profitable Sideline.* Nope. Oh, here it is. *Fake Pats a Flop.* See, it says here some fellow down in Amarillo got hold of an emperor and made a plaster mold. Then he used the mold on a couple of big cull pats—says here they was so perfect you couldn't tell the difference. But the Hurks wouldn't buy. *They* knew."

He threw the magazine down, then turned to stare out the back window toward the sheds. "There's that fool boy just setting in the yard again. Why ain't he working?" Llewellyn rose, cranked down the louver, shouted through the opening, "You, Delbert! Delbert!" He waited. "Deaf, too," he muttered.

"I'll go tell him you want—" Martha began, struggling out of her apron.

"No, never mind—go myself. Have to keep after 'em every damn minute." Llewellyn marched out the kitchen door and across the yard to where a gangling youth sat on a trolley, slowly eating an apple.

"Delbert!" said Llewellyn, exasperated.

"Oh—hello, Mr. Crawford," said the youth, with a

gap-toothed grin. He took a last bite from the apple, then dropped the core. Llewellyn's gaze followed it. Owing to his missing front teeth, Delbert's apple cores were like nothing in this world.

"Why ain't you trucking pats out to the stand?" Llewellyn demanded. "I don't pay you to set on no empty trolley, Delbert."

"Took some out this morning," the boy said. "Frank, he told me to take 'em back."

"He what?"

Delbert nodded. "Said he hadn't sold but two. You ask him if I'm lying."

"Do that," Llewellyn grunted. He turned on his heel and strode back across the yard.

Out at the roadside, a long car was parked beside a battered pickup at the pat stand. It pulled out as Llewellyn started toward it, and another one drove up. As he approached the stand, the alien was just getting back in. The car drove off.

Only one customer was left at the stand, a whiskered farmer in a checked shirt. Frank, the attendant, was leaning comfortably on the counter. The display shelves behind him were well filled with pats.

"Morning, Roger," Llewellyn said with well-feigned pleasure. "How's the family? Sell you a nice pat this morning?"

"Well, I don't know," said the whiskered man, rubbing his chin. "My wife's had her eye on that one there"—he pointed to a large, symmetrical pat on the middle shelf—"but at them prices—"

"You can't do better, believe me, Roger. It's an investment," said Llewellyn earnestly. "Frank, what did that last Hurk buy?"

"Nothing," said Frank. A persistent buzz of music came from the radio in his breast pocket. "Just took a picture of the stand and drove off."

"Well, what did the one before—"

With a whirr of turbines, a long shiny car pulled up behind him. Llewellyn turned. The three aliens in the car were wearing red felt hats with comic buttons sewed

295

all over them, and carried Yale pennants. Confetti was strewn on their gray tweed suits.

One of the Hurks got out and approached the stand, puffing a cigar through the hole in his—or its—orange scarf.

"Yes, sir?" said Llewellyn at once, hands clasped, bending forward slightly. "A nice pat this morning?"

The alien looked at the gray objects behind the counter. He, or it, blinked its yellow eyes and made a curious gurgling noise. After a moment Llewellyn decided that it was laughing.

"What's funny?" he demanded, his smile fading.

"Not funny," said the alien. "I laugh because I am happy. I go home tomorrow—our field trip is over. Okay to take a picture?" He raised a small lensed machine in one purple claw.

"Well, I suppose—" Llewellyn said uncertainly. "Well, you say you're going home? You mean all of you? When will you be coming back?"

"We are not coming back," the alien said. He, or it, pressed the camera, extracted the photograph and looked at it, then grunted and put it away. "We are grateful for an entertaining experience. Good-bye." He turned and got into the car. The car drove off in a cloud of dust.

"Like that the whole morning," Frank said. "They don't buy nothing—just take pictures."

Llewellyn felt himself beginning to shake. "Think he means it—they're all going away?"

"Radio said so," Frank replied. "And Ed Coon was through here this morning from Hortonville. Said *he* ain't sold a pat since day 'fore yesterday."

"Well, I don't understand it," Llewellyn said. "They can't just all quit—" His hands were trembling badly, and he put them in his pockets. "Say, Roger," he said to the whiskered man, "now just how much would you want to pay for that pat?"

"Well—"

"It's a ten dollar pat, you know," Llewellyn said, moving closer. His voice had turned solemn. "Prime pat, Roger."

"I know that, but—"

"What would you say to seven fifty?"

"Well, I don't know. Might give—say, five."

"Sold," said Llewellyn. "Wrap that one up, Frank."

He watched the whiskered man carry his trophy off to the pickup. "Mark 'em all down, Frank," he said faintly. "Get whatever you can."

The long day's debacle was almost over. Arms around each other, Llewellyn and Martha Crawford watched the last of the crowd leaving the pat stand. Frank was cleaning up. Delbert, leaning against the side of the stand, was eating an apple.

"It's the end of the world, Martha," Llewellyn said huskily. Tears stood in his eyes. "Prime pats, going two for a nickel!"

Headlights blinding in the dusk, a long, low car came nosing up to the pat stand. In it were two green creatures in raincoats, with feathery antennae that stood up through holes in their blue pork-pie hats. One of them got out and approached the pat stand with a curious scuttling motion. Delbert gaped, dropping his apple core.

"Serps!" Frank hissed, leaning over the stand toward Llewellyn. "Heard about 'em on the radio. From Gamma Serpentis, radio said."

The green creature was inspecting the half-bare shelves. Horny lids flickered across its little bright eyes.

"Pat, sir—ma'am?" Llewellyn asked nervously. "Not many left right now, but—"

"What is *that*?" the Serp asked in a rustling voice, pointing downward with one claw.

The Crawfords looked. The Serp was pointing to a misshapen, knobby something that lay beside Delbert's boot.

"That there?" Delbert asked, coming partially to life. "That's a apple core." He glanced across to Llewellyn, and a gleam of intelligence seemed to come into his eyes. "Mr. Crawford, I quit," he said clearly. Then he turned to the alien. "That's a *Delbert Smith* apple core," he said.

Frozen, Llewellyn watched the Serp pull out a billfold and scuttle forward. Money changed hands. Delbert produced another apple and began enthusiastically reducing it to a core.

"Say, Delbert," said Llewellyn, stepping away from Martha. His voice squeaked, and he cleared his throat. "Looks like we got a good little thing going here. Now, if you was smart, you'd rent this pat stand—"

"Nope, Mr. Crawford," said Delbert indistinctly, with his mouth full of apple. "Figure I'll go over to my uncle's place—he's got a orchard."

The Serp was hovering nearby, watching the apple core and uttering little squeals of appreciation.

"Got to be close to your source of *supply*, you know," said Delbert, wagging his head wisely.

Speechless, Llewellyn felt a tug at his sleeve. He looked down: it was Ed Lacey, the banker.

"Say, Lew, I tried to get you all afternoon, but your phone didn't answer. About your collateral on those loans . . ."

I HAD WHEN I WROTE THIS STORY (and still have) the habit of trying to see hypnagogic visions as I fall asleep. Even when I don't see them, it's not a bad way of turning my attention away from things that keep me awake. In 1963 I began to think about what it would be like if you had a gadget that would permit you to invent any vision you liked, store it, and retrieve and modify it at will. In "Semper Fi" I tried to show that although the gadget might be bad for you, that would be hard to demonstrate. Campbell bought the story and published it in *Analog* as "Satisfaction." My title, which I prefer, is Marine slang meaning "Fuck you, Jack, I've got mine."

20

SEMPER FI

<<<<<<<<<<<<<<<<<<<<<<<<<<<<<<<<<<<<<<<

THERE WAS A BRISK LITTLE WIND UP HERE,
flipping the white silk of his trousers like flags against
his body, ruffling his hair. Two thousand feet down past
the dangling tips of his shoes, he could see the mountains spread out, wave after brilliant green wave. The
palace was only a hollow square of ivory, tiny enough to
squash between thumb and forefinger. He closed his
eyes, drank the air with his body, feeling alive all the
way to the tips of his fingers and toes.

He yawned, stretched with pleasure. It was good to
get up here sometimes, away from all that marble and
red velvet, the fountains, the girls in their gauzy pants
. . . There was something about this floating, this complete solitude and peace.

An insect voice said apologetically, "Pardon me, sir."

He opened his eyes, looked around. There it was, the
one he called the "bug footman," three inches of slender
body, a face half-human, half-insect, wings a blur—flying
as hard as it could to stay in one place.

"You're early," he said.

"No, sir. It's time for your therapy."

"That's all I hear from you—time for therapy."

"It's good for you, sir."

"Well, no doubt you're right."

"I'm sure I'm right, sir."

"Okay. Get lost."

The creature made a face at him, then veered away on the wind and diminished to a drifting speck of light. Gary Mitchell watched it until it was lost against the sunlit green background. Then he tilted lazily in the air, closed his eyes and waited for the change.

He knew to the second when it would happen. "Bing," he said lazily, and felt the world contract suddenly around him. The wind was gone; mountains and sky were gone. He was breathing a more lifeless air. Even the darkness behind his eyelids was a different color.

He moved cautiously, feeling the padded couch under him. He opened his eyes. There was the same old room, looking so tiny and quaint that he snorted with amusement. It was always the same, no matter how often he came back to it. That struck him so funny that he rolled over, closing his eyes again, shaken with silent laughter.

After a minute he lay back, emptying his lungs with a grunt, then breathing deeply through his nostrils. He felt good, even though his body ached a little. He sat up and stared at the backs of his hands with amused affection. Same old hands!

He yawned hard enough to crack the cartilage in his jaw, then grinned and heaved himself up out of the hollow half-egg shape of the couch. Wires and tubing trailed from him in all directions. He pulled the cap off his head, breaking it free of the tiny plastic sockets in his skull. He dropped it, let it swing at the end of its cable. He unfastened the monitoring instruments from his chest, pulled off the rest of his gear, and strode naked across the room.

There was a click from the master clock on the control board, and Mitchell heard the water begin to hiss in the bathroom. "Suppose I don't want a shower?" he asked the clock. But he did; all according to routine.

He rubbed his palm over the stubble on his cheeks. Maybe he really should try to work out a gadget that would shave him while he was under the wire. A housing fitted to the lower part of his face, feedback to regulate the pressure . . . But the damned thing might be more trouble than it was worth.

Staring at himself in the mirror, he saw a glint of delighted irony come into his eyes. Same old thoughts! He got out the razor and began to shave.

The clock ticked again as he came from the bathroom, and a tray slid out of the conveyor onto the breakfast table. Scrambled eggs, bacon, orange juice, coffee. Mitchell went to the closet, took out pale-blue slacks and shirt, dressed, then sat down and ate, taking his time. The food was food—nourishment; that was about all you could say.

When he was done, he lit a cigarette and sat with half-closed eyes, letting the smoke spurt in two streams from his nostrils. Vague images drifted through his mind; he did not try to capture them.

The cigarette was a stub. He sighed, put it out. As he walked to the door, it seemed to him that the couch and the control panel were staring at him reproachfully. There was something abandoned and pathetic in the empty egg-shape, the scattered wires. "Tonight," he promised it. He opened the door and stepped through.

Pale, yellow-tinged sunlight came from the big picture window overlooking the Hudson. The philodendron in the ceramic pot had unfurled another leaf. On the wall across from the window hung an enormous abstraction by Pollock, upside down. Mitchell gave it an ironic grin.

Reports in their orange plastic binders were piled on one side of the long mahogany desk, letters on the other. In the center, on the green blotter, lay a block of soft pine and an open jackknife.

The red light of the intercom was blinking steadily. Mitchell sat down and looked at it for a moment, then touched the button. "Yes, Miss Curtis?"

"Mr. Price wants to know when you'll be available. Shall I tell him to come in?"

"Okay."

Mitchell picked up the top report, glanced at the sketches and diagrams inside, put it down again. He swiveled his chair around, leaned back and gazed sleepily out over the haze-yellowed landscape. A tug was moving slowly up the river, trailing puffs of yellow-white smoke. On the Jersey side, housing units stood like a child's building blocks; sunlight glinted from the tiny rows of windows.

Curious to see all that still here, still growing; on the other side, he had leveled it years ago, filled it in with jungle. There was something quaint about it now, like an old, yellowed snapshot. That was a little disturbing: coming back like this was always like re-entering the past. A faint sense of wrongness . . .

He heard the door click, and turned to see Jim Price with his hand on the knob. Mitchell grinned, waved a hand. "Hello, boy—good to see you. Knock 'em dead in Washington?"

"Not exactly." Price came forward with his heron's gait, folded himself into a chair, twitched, knotted his thin fingers together.

"Too bad. How's Marge?"

"Fine. I didn't see her last night, but she called in this morning. She asked me to ask you—"

"Kids all right?"

"Sure." Price's thin lips compressed; his brown eyes stared earnestly at Mitchell. He still seemed about twenty years old; to look at him, he had not changed since the days when Mitchell-Price, Inc., was an idea and a back room in Westbury. Only the clothes were different— the two-hundred-dollar suit, the perfectly knotted tie. And the fingernails; once they had been bitten to the quick, now they were manicured and shiny. "Mitch, let's get down to it. How is that deep probe gadget coming?"

"Got Stevenson's report on my desk—haven't looked through it yet."

Price blinked, shook his head. "You realize that project has been dragging on thirty-six months?"

"There's time," Mitchell said lazily. He reached for the knife and the block of wood.

"That's not the way you talked fifteen years ago."

"I was an eager beaver then," Mitchell said. He turned the block in his hands, feeling the little dusty burrs along the unfinished side. He set the blade against one edge, curled off the first long, sensuous shaving.

"Mitch, damn it, I'm worried about you—the way

303

you've changed the last few years. You're letting the business slide."

"Anything wrong with the earnings reports?" Mitchell felt the cut surface with his thumb, turning to gaze out the window. It would be fun, he thought absently, to drift out into that hazy blue sky, over the tops of the toy buildings, still farther out, over the empty ocean . . .

"We're making money, sure," Price's thin voice said impatiently. "On the mentigraph and the randomizer, one or two other little things. But we haven't put anything new on the market for five years, Mitch. What are we supposed to do, just coast? Is that all you want?"

Mitchell turned to look at his partner. "Good old Jim," he said affectionately. "When are you ever going to loosen up?"

The door clicked open and a dark-haired girl stepped in—Lois Bainbridge, Price's secretary. "Mr. Price, sorry to interrupt, but Dolly couldn't get you on the intercom."

Price glanced at Mitchell. "Push the wrong button again?"

Mitchell looked at the intercom with mild surprise. "Guess I did."

"Anyway," the girl said, "Mr. Diedrich is here, and you told me to tell you the minute—"

"Hell," said Price, standing up. "Where is he, in reception?"

"No, Mr. Thorwald has taken him down to Lab One. He has his lawyer and his doctor with him."

"I know it," Price muttered, prying nervously into his pockets. "Where did I put those damn— Oh, here." He pulled out some notes scrawled in pencil on file cards. "Okay, look, Lois, you phone down and tell them I'll be right there."

"Yes, Mr. Price." She smiled, turned and walked out. Mitchell's mild gaze followed her. Not a bad-looking girl, as they went. He remembered that he had brought her over to the other side, three or four years ago, but of course he had made a lot of changes—slimmer waist, firmer bust . . . He yawned.

Price asked abruptly, "Do you want to sit in?"

"Want me to?"

"I don't know, Mitch—do you give a damn?"

"Sure." Mitchell got up, draped an arm around the other man's shoulders. "Let's go."

They walked together down the busy corridor. "Listen," Price said, "how long since you've been out for dinner?"

"Don't know. Month or two."

"Well, come out tonight. Marge told me to bring you for sure."

Mitchell hesitated, then nodded. "All right, Jim, thanks."

Lab One was the showcase—all cedar veneer and potted plants, with the egg-shaped mentigraph couch prominently displayed, like a casket in a mortuary. There were half a dozen big illuminated color transparencies on a table behind the couch, to one side of the control board.

Heads turned as they walked in. Mitchell recognized Diedrich at once—a heavy-set pink-and-blond man in his early forties. The ice-blue eyes stared at him. Mitchell realized with a shock that the man was even more impressive, more hypnotic than he seemed on television.

Thorwald, the lab chief, made the introductions while white-coated technicians hovered in the background. "The Reverend Diedrich—and Mr. Edmonds, his attorney—and of course you know Dr. Taubman, at least by reputation."

They shook hands. Diedrich said, "I hope you understand the terms on which I am here. I'm not looking for any compromise." The pale eyes were intent and earnest. "Your people put it to me that I could attack the mentigraph more effectively if I had actually experienced it. If nothing changes my mind, that's just what I intend to do."

"Yes, we understand that, of *course,* Mr. Diedrich," said Price. "We wouldn't have it any other way."

Diedrich looked curiously at Mitchell. "You're the inventor of this machine?"

Mitchell nodded. "A long time ago."

"Well, what do you think about the way it has turned out—its effect on the world?"

"I like it," said Mitchell.

Diedrich's face went expressionless; he glanced away.

"I was just showing Mr. Diedrich these mentigraph projections," Thorwald said hurriedly, pointing to the transparencies. Two were landscapes, weird things, all orange trees and brown grass; one was a city scene, and the fourth showed a hill, with three wooden crosses silhouetted against the sky. "Dan Shelton, the painter, did these. He's enthusiastic about it."

"You can actually photograph what goes on in the subject's mind?" Edmonds asked, raising his black eyebrows. "I was not aware of that."

"It's a new wrinkle," Price answered. "We hope to have it on the market in September."

"Well, gentlemen, if you're ready—" Thorwald said.

Diedrich appeared to brace himself. "All right. What do I do? Shall I take my jacket off?"

"No, just lie down here, if you will," Thorwald answered, pointing to the narrow operating table. "Loosen your tie if it will make you more comfortable."

Diedrich got up on the table, his face set. A technician came up behind him with a basket-shaped object made of curved, crisscrossing metal pieces. She adjusted it gently over Diedrich's skull, tightened the wing nuts until it fitted. She took careful measurements, adjusted the helmet again, then pushed eight plungers, one after the other.

Taubman was looking over her shoulder as she removed the helmet. At the roots of Diedrich's hair, eight tiny purple spots were visible.

"This is merely a harmless dye, Doctor," Thorwald said. "All we are doing here is to establish the sites for the electrodes."

"Yes, all right," said Taubman. "And you assure me that none of them is in the pleasure center?"

"Definitely not. You know there is legislation against it, Doctor."

The technician had moved up again. With a small pair of scissors she cut tiny patches of hair from the purple-marked spots. She applied lather, then, with an even smaller razor, shaved the patches clean. Diedrich lay quietly; he winced at the touch of the cool lather, but otherwise did not change expression.

"That's all of that," Thorwald said. "Now, Reverend Diedrich, if you'll sit over here—"

Diedrich got up and walked to the chair Thorwald pointed out. Over it hung a glittering basketwork of metal, like a more complicated and more menacing version of the helmet the technician had used.

"Just a moment," Taubman said. He went over to examine the mechanism. He and Thorwald spoke in low voices for a moment, then Taubman nodded and stepped back. Diedrich sat down.

"This is the only sticky part," Thorwald said. "But it really doesn't hurt. Now let's just get your head in this clamp—"

Diedrich's face was pale. He stared straight ahead as a technician tightened the padded clamp, then lowered the basket-shaped instrument. Standing on a dais behind the chair, Thorwald himself carefully adjusted eight metal cylinders, centering each over one of the shaved purple patches on Diedrich's skull. "This will be just like a pinprick," he said. He pressed a button. Diedrich winced.

"Now tell me what sensations you feel," said Thorwald, turning to a control panel.

Diedrich blinked. "I saw a flash of light," he said.

"All right, next."

"That was a noise."

"Yes, and this?"

Diedrich looked surprised; his mouth worked for a moment. "Something sweet," he said.

"Good. How about this?"

Diedrich started. "I felt something touch my skin."

"All right. Next."

"Pew!" said Diedrich, turning his face aside. "A terrible smell."

"Sorry. How about this one?"

"I felt warm for a moment."

"Okay, now this."

Diedrich's right leg twitched. "It felt as if it were doubled up under me," he said.

"Right. One more."

Diedrich stiffened suddenly. "I felt—I don't know how to describe it. *Satisfied.*" His cold eyes went from Mitchell to Thorwald. His jaw was set hard.

"Perfect!" Thorwald said, getting down from the platform. He was grinning with pleasure. Mitchell glanced at Price, saw him wiping his palms with a handkerchief.

The cylinders retracted; the technician unfastened the headclamp. "That's all of that," said Thorwald heartily. "You can step down."

Diedrich got out of the chair, his jaw still set. One hand went up to fumble at his skull.

"Pardon me," said Taubman. He parted Diedrich's hair with his fingers and stared at the little gray plastic button, almost flush with the scalp, that had covered one of the purple spots.

Mitchell drifted over to stand beside Price. "Our friend didn't like that jolt in number eight," he murmured. "Careful, boy."

"I know," Price answered in an undertone. Across the room, Thorwald and the technicians had seated Diedrich in another chair and put the cap on his head. One of the technicians began showing him big sheets of colored pasteboard, while another, a pale young man with big ears, read dials and punched keys at the control console.

"This is a pretty big gamble you're taking, son," Mitchell said. "You know if we just make him mad, he can really smear us. How'd you get so brave?"

Price scowled, shuffled his feet. "Don't bury me yet," he muttered.

A technician was passing vials of scent under Diedrich's nose, one after another.

"Something up your sleeve?" Mitchell asked; but he had lost interest, and did not hear Price's reply. The technicians were walking Diedrich up and down, getting him to bend, raise his arms, turn his head. When they finally let him sit down again, his face was slightly flushed. Mitchell was thinking dreamily that he could use Diedrich on the other side—make a Teutonic knight out of him, noble, humorless and fierce. But reduce him to about half-size . . . that would be funny.

"We won't try to calibrate the emotional responses this time, Mr. Diedrich," Thorwald was saying. "That's more difficult and complicated—it takes quite a while. But you've got enough here to give you a very good idea of the device."

Diedrich put up a hand to feel the cap on his head, the cluster of wires emerging from the middle of it. "All right," he said grimly. "Go ahead."

Thorwald looked a little worried. He motioned to the technician at the console. "Input one, Jerry." To Diedrich he said, "Just close your eyes, if you will, and let your hands relax."

The man at the console touched a button. An expression of surprise crossed Diedrich's face. His right hand moved spasmodically, then lay still. A moment later he turned his head aside. His jaws made slow chewing motions. Then he opened his eyes.

"Amazing," he said. "A banana—I peeled it and then ate a bite. But—they weren't my hands."

"Yes, of course—that was a recording made by another subject. However, when you learn to use the other circuits, Mr. Diedrich, you can run that through again and change it until they *are* your hands—or make any other changes you like."

Diedrich's expression showed controlled distaste. He said, "I see." Watching him, Mitchell thought, he's going to go home and write a speech that will blister our tails.

"You'll see what I mean in just a moment," Thorwald was saying. "This time there won't be any primary recording—you'll do it all yourself. Just lean back, close your eyes, and imagine some picture, some scene—"

Diedrich fingered his watch impatiently. "You mean you want me to try to make a picture like those?" He nodded toward the transparencies ranged along the wall.

"No, no, nothing like that. We won't project it, and only you will see what it is. Just visualize a scene, and wherever it seems vague or out of proportion, keep on changing it and adding to it . . . Go ahead, try it."

Diedrich leaned back, closed his eyes. Thorwald nodded to the man at the console.

Price moved abruptly away from Mitchell, strode over to the chair. "Here is something that may help you, Mr. Diedrich," he said, bending close. He looked at the notes in his hand, and read aloud, "And it was about the sixth hour, and there was a darkness over all the earth until the ninth hour. And the sun was darkened, and the veil of the temple was rent in the midst."

Diedrich frowned; then his face relaxed. There was a long silence. Diedrich began to frown again. After a moment his hands moved spasmodically on the arms of the chair. His jaw muscles lost their tightness; his chin dropped slightly. After another moment he began breathing quickly and shallowly, lips parted.

Taubman stepped over, frowning, and attempted to take his pulse, but Diedrich knocked his hand away. Taubman glanced at Price, who shook his head and put a finger to his lips.

Diedrich's face had turned into a mask of grief. Moisture appeared under his closed eyelids, began to run down his cheeks. Watching him closely, Price nodded to Thorwald, who turned toward the console and made a chopping motion.

Diedrich's tear-filled eyes slowly opened.

"What was it, Mr. Diedrich?" Edmonds asked, bending toward him. "What happened?"

Diedrich's voice was low and hoarse. "I saw—I saw—" His face contorted and he began to sob. He bent over as if in pain, hands clasped so tightly that the fingers turned red and yellow-white in patches.

Price turned away, took Mitchell by the arm. "Let's get out of here," he muttered. In the corridor, he began to whistle.

"Think you're pretty slick, don't you, boy?" Mitchell asked.

Price's grin made him look like a mischievous small boy. "I know I am, old buddy," he said.

There were four of them at dinner—Price and his good-looking red-haired wife; Mitchell, and a girl he had never met before. Her name was Eileen Novotny; she was slender, gray-eyed, quiet. She was divorced, Mitchell gathered, and had a small daughter.

After dinner they played a rubber of bridge. Eileen was a good player, better than Mitchell; but when he blundered, once or twice, she only gave him a glance of ironic commiseration. She did not talk much; her voice was low and well modulated, and Mitchell found himself waiting for her to speak again.

When the rubber was over, she stood up. "I'm glad to have met you, Mitch," she said, and gave him her warm hand for a moment. "Thank you for a lovely dinner and a nice evening," she said to Marge Price.

"You're not going already?"

"Afraid I have to—my sitter can only stay till nine, and it will take me a good hour to get up to Washington Heights."

She paused at the door, glancing back at Mitchell. He could well imagine how it might be with this girl—the long walks, the intimate little restaurants, holding hands, the first kiss . . . Price and his wife were looking at him expectantly.

"Good night, Eileen," he said.

After she was gone, Marge brought in some beer and excused herself. Price settled himself in a relaxer and lit a pipe. Squinting at Mitchell over the bowl, he said mildly, "You might have given the girl a taxi-ride home, old buddy."

"And start all over again? No thanks, old buddy—I've had it."

Price flipped out his match, dropped it into an ashtray. "Well, it's your life."

"So I've always imagined."

Price shifted uncomfortably in the chair. "So I'm a matchmaker," he said, scowling. "Dammit, I don't like to see what's happening to you. You spend more time under the wire than out of it. It isn't healthy, it isn't good for you."

Mitchell grinned and held out a hand. "Indian rassle?"

Price flushed. "All right, all right, I know you work out at the gym every week—you're in good shape physically. That's not what I'm talking about, and you know it damn well."

Mitchell took a long pull at his can of beer. It was lighter and maltier than he liked, but it was cold, at least, and felt good going down his throat. What about a green beer for St. Paddy's day? Give it a suggestion of mint—just a touch . . .

"Say something," Price said.

Mitchell's eyes focused on him slowly. "Hmm. Think Diedrich will stop being a nuisance now?"

Price made a sour face. "Okay, change the subject. Sure, I think Diedrich will stop being a nuisance. We're sending him a complete rig—couch, control board, library of crystals. And he'll take it. He's hooked."

"Dirty trick?" Mitchell suggested.

"No, I don't think so."

"You planted that picture of the three crosses, didn't you? Then, just to make sure, you stepped up and read him a paragraph from the crucifixion scene in Matthew. Pretty foxy."

"Luke," said Price. "Yeah, pretty foxy."

"Tell me something," Mitchell said. "Just for curiosity—how long since you've been under the wire yourself?"

Price looked at his hands, clasped around the pipe-bowl. "Four years," he said.

"How come?"

"Don't like what it does to me." He folded his free hand around the one that held the pipe; his knuckles cracked, one after another.

"Made you twenty million," Mitchell said gently.

"You know I don't mean that." Price unclenched his hands, leaned forward. "Listen, the Pentagon turned down that contract for forty thousand training crystals. They decided they don't like what it does to people, either."

"Keeps them from being eager little beavers," Mitchell said. "My back aches for the Pentagon."

"What about the contract—does your back ache for that?"

"You know, James, I don't understand you," Mitchell said. "One minute you're telling me the mentigraph is worse than hashish, heroin, booze and adultery, all put together. The next, you're complaining because we don't sell more of 'em. How do you explain that?"

Price did not smile. "Let's say I'm a worry-wart. You know I keep talking about pulling out—maybe I'll do it some day—but till I do, I'm responsible to the corporation and I'll do my best for it. That's business. When I worry about you, it's friendship."

"I know it, old buddy."

"Maybe I worry about the whole world once in a while, too," Price said. "What's going to happen when everybody's got a private dream-world? Where's the old Colonial spirit then?"

Mitchell snorted. "Have you ever done any reading about Colonial times? I did some research on it years ago. They used to drink a horrible thing called flip, made out of rum and hard cider, and they'd plunge a hot poker into it to make it froth up. You could tell the drunkards just by seeing who had an apple orchard."

Price swung his legs off the relaxer, put his elbows on his knees. "All right, what about this? You've got it made, haven't you—you can spend half your time in a world where everything is just the way you like it. You don't need that sweet kid that walked out of here half an hour ago—you've got twenty better-looking than her. And they're on call any time. So why get married, why raise a family? Just tell me this—what's going to happen to the world if the brightest guys in it drop out of the baby-making business? What happens to the next generation?"

"I can answer that one too."

"Well?"

Mitchell lifted his beer can in salute, staring at Price over the shiny top. "The hell with them," he said.

IN THE SIXTIES, DURING AN EARNEST phase of the Milford Science Fiction Writers' Conference, it came to my notice that things were happening in science and technology that nobody was writing stories about. One of these was modern prosthesiology. I worried over that for several years, read books and articles, and at last, painfully—I was in a slump, and all writing was painful—put "Masks" together. It feels jagged and lumpy to me now because of the way I wrote it.

21

MASKS

‹‹

THE EIGHT PENS DANCED AGAINST THE MOVING strip of paper, like the nervous claws of some mechanical lobster. Roberts, the technician, frowned over the tracings while the other two watched.

"Here's the wake-up impulse," he said, pointing with a skinny finger. "Then here, look, seventeen seconds more, still dreaming."

"Delayed response," said Babcock, the project director. His heavy face was flushed and he was sweating. "Nothing to worry about."

"Okay, delayed response, but look at the difference in the tracings. Still dreaming, after the wake-up impulse, but the peaks are closer together. Not the same dream. More anxiety, more motor pulses."

"Why does he have to sleep at all?" asked Sinescu, the man from Washington. He was dark, narrow-faced. "You flush the fatigue poisons out, don't you? So what is it, something psychological?"

"He needs to dream," said Babcock. "It's true he has no physiological need for sleep, but he's got to dream. If he didn't, he'd start to hallucinate, maybe go psychotic."

"Psychotic," said Sinescu. "Well—that's the question, isn't it? How long has he been doing this?"

"About six months."

"In other words, about the time he got his new body —and started wearing a mask?"

"About that. Look, let me tell you something: He's rational. Every test—"

"Yes, okay, I know about tests. Well—so he's awake now?"

The technician glanced at the monitor board. "He's up. Sam and Irma are with him." He hunched his shoul-

315

ders, staring at the EEG tracings again. "I don't know why it should bother me. It stands to reason, if he has dream needs of his own that we're not satisfying with the programed stuff, this is where he gets them in." His face hardened. "I don't know. Something about those peaks I don't like."

Sinescu raised his eyebrows. "You program his dreams?"

"Not program," said Babcock impatiently. "A routine suggestion to dream the sort of thing we tell him to. Somatic stuff, sex, exercise, sport."

"And whose idea was that?"

"Psych section. He was doing fine neurologically, every other way, but he was withdrawing. Psych decided he needed that somatic input in some form; we had to keep him in touch. He's alive, he's functioning, everything works. But don't forget, he spent forty-three years in a normal human body."

In the hush of the elevator, Sinescu said, ". . . Washington."

Swaying, Babcock said, "I'm sorry, what?"

"You look a little rocky. Getting any sleep?"

"Not lately. What did you say before?"

"I said they're not happy with your reports in Washington."

"Goddamn it, I know that." The elevator door silently opened. A tiny foyer, green carpet, gray walls. There were three doors, one metal, two heavy glass. Cool, stale air. "This way."

Sinescu paused at the glass door, glanced through: a gray-carpeted living room, empty. "I don't see him."

"Around the ell. Getting his morning checkup."

The door opened against slight pressure; a battery of ceiling lights went on as they entered. "Don't look up," said Babcock. "Ultraviolet." A faint hissing sound stopped when the door closed.

"And positive pressure in here? To keep out germs? Whose idea was that?"

"His." Babcock opened a chrome box on the wall and took out two surgical masks. "Here, put this on."

Voices came muffled from around the bend of the room. Sinescu looked with distaste at the white mask, then slowly put it over his head.

They stared at each other. "Germs," said Sinescu through the mask. "Is that rational?"

"All right, he can't catch a cold or what have you, but think about it a minute. There are just two things now that could kill him. One is a prosthetic failure, and we guard against that; we've got five hundred people here, we check him out like an airplane. That leaves a cerebro-spinal infection. Don't go in there with a closed mind."

The room was large, part living room, part library, part workshop. Here was a cluster of Swedish-modern chairs, a sofa, coffee table; here a workbench with a metal lathe, electric crucible, drill press, parts bins, tools on wallboards; here a drafting table; here a free-standing wall of bookshelves that Sinescu fingered curiously as they passed. Bound volumes of project reports, technical journals, reference books; no fiction except for *Fire* and *Storm* by George Stewart and *The Wizard of Oz* in a worn blue binding. Behind the bookshelves, set into a little alcove, was a glass door through which they glimpsed another living room, differently furnished: upholstered chairs, a tall philodendron in a ceramic pot. "There's Sam," Babcock said.

A man had appeared in the other room. He saw them, turned to call to someone they could not see, then came forward, smiling. He was bald and stocky, deeply tanned. Behind him, a small, pretty woman hurried up. She crowded through after her husband, leaving the door open. Neither of them wore a mask.

"Sam and Irma have the next suite," Babcock said. "Company for him; he's got to have somebody around. Sam is an old air-force buddy of his and, besides, he's got a tin arm."

The stocky man shook hands, grinning. His grip was firm and warm. "Want to guess which one?" He wore a flowered sport shirt. Both arms were brown, muscular and hairy, but when Sinescu looked more closely, he saw that the right one was a slightly different color, not quite authentic.

317

Embarrassed, he said, "The left, I guess."

"Nope." Grinning wider, the stocky man pulled back his right sleeve to show the straps.

"One of the spin-offs from the project," said Babcock. "Myoelectric, servo-controlled, weighs the same as the other one. Sam, they about through in there?"

"Maybe so. Let's take a peek. Honey, you think you could rustle up some coffee for the gentlemen?"

"Oh, why, sure." The little woman turned and darted back through the open doorway.

The far wall was glass, covered by a translucent white curtain. They turned the corner. The next bay was full of medical and electronic equipment, some built into the walls, some in tall black cabinets on wheels. Four men in white coats were gathered around what looked like an astronaut's couch. Sinescu would see someone lying on it: feet in Mexican woven-leather shoes, dark socks, gray slacks. A mutter of voices.

"Not through yet," Babcock said. "Must have found something else they didn't like. Let's go out onto the patio a minute."

"Thought they checked him at night—when they exchange his blood, and so on?"

"They do," Babcock said. "And in the morning, too." He turned and pushed open the heavy glass door. Outside, the roof was paved with cut stone, enclosed by a green plastic canopy and tinted-glass walls. Here and there were concrete basins, empty. "Idea was to have a roof garden out here, something green, but he didn't want it. We had to take all the plants out, glass the whole thing in."

Sam pulled out metal chairs around a white table and they all sat down. "How is he, Sam?" asked Babcock.

He grinned and ducked his head. "Mean in the mornings."

"Talk to you much? Play any chess?"

"Not too much. Works, mostly. Reads some, watches the box a little." His smile was forced; his heavy fingers were clasped together, and Sinescu saw now that the fingertips of one hand had turned darker, the others not. He looked away.

"You're from Washington, that right?" Sam asked politely. "First time here? Hold on." He was out of his chair. Vague upright shapes were passing behind the curtained glass door. "Looks like they're through. If you gentlemen would just wait here a minute, till I see." He strode across the roof. The two men sat in silence. Babcock had pulled down his surgical mask; Sinescu noticed and did the same.

"Sam's wife is a problem," Babcock said, leaning nearer. "It seemed like a good idea at the time, but she's lonely here, doesn't like it—no kids—"

The door opened again and Sam appeared. He had a mask on, but it was hanging under his chin. "If you gentlemen would come in now."

In the living area, the little woman, also with a mask hanging around her neck, was pouring coffee from a flowered ceramic jug. She was smiling brightly but looked unhappy. Opposite her sat someone tall, in gray shirt and slacks, leaning back, legs out, arms on the arms of his chair, motionless. Something was wrong with his face.

"Well, now," said Sam heartily. His wife looked up at him with an agonized smile.

The tall figure turned its head and Sinescu saw with an icy shock that its face was silver, a mask of metal with oblong slits for eyes, no nose or mouth, only curves that were faired into each other. ". . . project," said an inhuman voice.

Sinescu found himself half bent over a chair. He sat down. They were all looking at him. The voice resumed. "I said, are you here to pull the plug on the project." It was unaccented, indifferent.

"Have some coffee." The woman pushed a cup toward him.

Sinescu reached for it, but his hand was trembling and he drew it back. "Just a fact-finding expedition," he said.

"Bull. Who sent you—Senator Hinkel."

"That's right."

"Bull. He's been here himself, why send you. If you are going to pull the plug, might as well tell me." The face behind the mask did not move when he spoke; the voice did not seem to come from it.

"He's just looking around, Jim," said Babcock.

"Two hundred million a year," said the voice, "to keep one man alive. Doesn't make much sense, does it. Go on, drink your coffee."

Sinescu realized that Sam and his wife had already finished theirs and that they had pulled up their masks. He reached for his cup hastily.

"Hundred-percent disability in my grade is thirty thousand a year. I could get along on that easy. For almost an hour and a half."

"There's no intention of terminating the project," Sinescu said.

"Phasing it out, though. Would you say phasing it out."

"Manners, Jim," said Babcock.

"Okay. My worst fault. What do you want to know."

Sinescu sipped his coffee. His hands were still trembling. "That mask you're wearing," he started.

"Not for discussion. No comment, no comment. Sorry about that, don't mean to be rude: a personal matter. Ask me something—" Without warning, he stood up, blaring, "Get that damn thing out of here!" Sam's wife's cup smashed, coffee brown across the table. A fawn-colored puppy was sitting in the middle of the carpet, cocking its head, bright-eyed, tongue out.

The table tipped; Sam's wife struggled up behind it. Her face was pink, dripping with tears. She scooped up the puppy without pausing and ran out. "I better go with her," Sam said, getting up.

"Go on, and, Sam, take a holiday. Drive her into Winnemucca, see a movie."

"Yeah, guess I will." He disappeared behind the bookshelf wall.

The tall figure sat down again, moving like a man; it leaned back in the same posture, arms on the arms of the chair. It was still. The hands gripping the wood were shapely and perfect but unreal; there was something wrong about the fingernails. The brown, well-combed hair above the mask was a wig; the ears were wax. Sinescu nervously fumbled his surgical mask up

320

over his mouth and nose. "Might as well get along," he said and stood up.

"That's right, I want to take you over to Engineering and R and D," said Babcock. "Jim, I'll be back in a little while. Want to talk to you."

"Sure," said the motionless figure.

Babcock had had a shower, but sweat was soaking through the armpits of his shirt again. The silent elevator, the green carpet, a little blurred. The air cool, stale. Seven years, blood and money, five hundred good men. Psych section, Cosmetic, Engineering, R and D, Medical, Immunology, Supply, Serology, Administration. The glass doors. Sam's apartment empty; gone to Winnemucca with Irma. Psych. Good men, but were they the best? Three of the best had turned it down. Buried in the files. *Not like an ordinary amputation, this man has had everything cut off.*

The tall figure had not moved. Babcock sat down. The silver mask looked back at him.

"Jim, let's level with each other."

"Bad, huh."

"Sure it's bad. I left him in his room with a bottle. I'll see him again before he leaves, but God knows what he'll say in Washington. Listen, do me a favor; take that thing off."

"Sure." The hand rose, plucked at the edge of the silver mask, lifted it away. Under it, the tan-pink face, sculptured nose and lips, eyebrows, eyelashes, not handsome but good-looking, normal-looking. Only the eyes wrong; pupils too big. And the lips that did not open or move when it spoke. "I can take anything off. What does that prove."

"Jim, Cosmetic spent eight and a half months on that model and the first thing you do is slap a mask over it. We've asked you what's wrong, offered to make any changes you want."

"No comment."

"You talked about phasing out the project. Did you think you were kidding?"

A pause. "Not kidding."

"All right, then open up, Jim, tell me; I have to know. They won't shut the project down; they'll keep you alive, but that's all. There are seven hundred on the volunteer list, including two U.S. senators. Suppose one of them gets pulled out of an auto wreck tomorrow. We can't wait till then to decide; we've got to know now. Whether to let the next one die or put him into a TP body like yours. So talk to me."

"Suppose I tell you something but it isn't the truth."

"Why would you lie?"

"Why do you lie to a cancer patient."

"I don't get it. Come on, Jim."

"Okay, try this. Do I look like a man to you."

"Sure."

"Bull. Look at this face." Calm and perfect. Beyond the fake irises, a wink of metal. "Suppose we had all the other problems solved and I could go into Winnemucca tomorrow; can you see me walking down the street—going into a bar—taking a taxi."

"Is that all it is?" Babcock drew a deep breath. "Jim, sure there's a difference, but for Christ's sake, it's like any other prosthesis—people get used to it. Like that arm of Sam's. You see it, but after a while you forget it, you don't notice."

"Bull. You pretend not to notice. Because it would embarrass the cripple."

Babcock looked down at his clasped hands. "Sorry for yourself?"

"Don't give me that," the voice blared. The tall figure was standing. The hands slowly came up, the fists clenched. "I'm in this thing; I've been in it for two years. I'm in it when I go to sleep, and when I wake up, I'm still in it."

Babcock looked up at him. "What do you want, facial mobility? Give us twenty years, maybe ten, we'll lick it."

"No. No."

"Then what?"

"I want you to close down Cosmetic."

"But that's—"

"Just listen. The first model looked like a tailor's

dummy; so you spent eight months and came up with this one, and it looks like a corpse. The whole idea was to make me look like a man, the first model pretty good, the second model better, until you've got something that can smoke cigars and joke with women and go bowling and nobody will know the difference. You can't do it, and if you could, what for."

"I don't— Let me think about this. What do you mean, a metal—"

"Metal, sure, but what difference does that make? I'm talking about shape. Function. Wait a minute." The tall figure strode across the room, unlocked a cabinet, came back with rolled sheets of paper. "Look at this."

The drawing showed an oblong metal box on four jointed legs. From one end protruded a tiny mushroom-shaped head on a jointed stem and a cluster of arms ending in probes, drills, grapples. "For moon prospecting."

"Too many limbs," said Babcock after a moment. "How would you—"

"With the facial nerves. Plenty of them left over. Or here." Another drawing. "A module plugged into the control system of a spaceship. That's where I belong, in space. Sterile environment, low grav, I can go where a man can't go and do what a man can't do. I can be an asset, not a goddamn billion-dollar liability."

Babcock rubbed his eyes. "Why didn't you say anything before?"

"You were all hipped on prosthetics. You would have told me to tend my knitting."

Babcock's hands were shaking as he rolled up the drawings. "Well, by God, this just may do it. It just might." He stood up and turned toward the door. "Keep your—" He cleared his throat. "I mean, hang tight, Jim."

"I'll do that."

When he was alone, he put on his mask again and stood motionless a moment, eye shutters closed. Inside, he was running clean and cool; he could feel the faint reassuring hum of pumps, click of valves and relays. They had given him that: cleaned out all the offal, replaced it

323

with machinery that did not bleed, ooze or suppurate. He thought of the lie he had told Babcock. *Why do you lie to a cancer patient.* But they would never get it, never understand.

He sat down at the drafting table, clipped a sheet of paper to it and with a pencil began to sketch a rendering of the moon-prospector design. When he had blocked in the prospector itself, he began to draw the background of craters. His pencil moved more slowly and stopped; he put it down with a click.

No more adrenal glands to pump adrenaline into his blood, so he could not feel fright or rage. They had released him from all that—love, hate, the whole sloppy mess—but they had forgotten there was still one emotion he could feel.

Sinescu, with the black bristles of his beard sprouting through his oily skin. A whitehead ripe in the crease beside his nostril.

Moon landscape, clean and cold. He picked up the pencil again.

Babcock, with his broad pink nose shining with grease, crusts of white matter in the corners of his eyes. Food mortar between his teeth.

Sam's wife, with raspberry-colored paste on her mouth. Face smeared with tears, a bright bubble in one nostril. And the damn dog, shiny nose, wet eyes . . .

He turned. The dog was there, sitting on the carpet, wet red tongue out—*left the door open again*—dripping, wagged its tail twice, then started to get up. He reached for the metal T square, leaned back, swinging it like an ax, and the dog yelped once as metal sheared bone, one eye spouting red, writhing on its back, dark stain of piss across the carpet, and he hit it again, hit it again.

The body lay twisted on the carpet, fouled with blood, ragged black lips drawn back from teeth. He wiped off the T square with a paper towel, then scrubbed it in the sink with soap and steel wool, dried it and hung it up. He got a sheet of drafting paper, laid it on the floor, rolled the body over onto it without spilling any blood on the carpet. He lifted the body in the paper, carried it out onto the patio, then onto the unroofed section, opening the doors with his shoulder. He looked over the wall. Two stories down, concrete roof, vents sticking out of it, nobody watching. He held the dog out, let it slide off the paper, twisting as it fell. It struck one of the vents, bounced, a red smear. He carried the paper back inside, poured the blood down the drain, then put the paper into the incinerator chute.

Splashes of blood were on the carpet, the feet of the drafting table, the cabinet, his trouser legs. He sponged them all up with paper towels and warm water. He took off his clothing, examined it minutely, scrubbed it in the sink, then put it in the washer. He washed the sink, rubbed himself down with disinfectant and dressed again. He walked through into Sam's silent apartment, closing the glass door behind him. Past the potted philo-dendron, overstuffed furniture, red-and-yellow painting on the wall, out onto the roof, leaving the door ajar. Then back through the patio, closing doors.

Too bad. How about some goldfish.

He sat down at the drafting table. He was running clean and cool. The dream this morning came back to his mind, the last one, as he was struggling up out of sleep: *slithery kidneys burst gray lungs blood and hair ropes of guts covered with yellow fat oozing and sliding and oh god the stink like the breath of an outmouth no sound nowhere he was putting a yellow stream down the slide of the dunghole and*

He began to ink in the drawing, first with a fine steel pen, then with a nylon brush. *his heel slid and he was falling could not stop himself falling into slimy bulging softness higher than his chin, higher and he could not move paralyzed and he tried to scream tried to scream tried to scream*

The prospector was climbing a crater slope with its handling members retracted and its head tilted up. Behind it the distant ringwall and the horizon, the black sky, the pin-point stars. And he was there, and it was not far enough, not yet, for the Earth hung overhead like a rotten fruit, blue with mold, crawling, wrinkling, purulent and alive.

"DOWN THERE" IS MY UNKNOWN MAS-
terpiece; I am prouder of it than of most
things I have written, but the only reader
who saw what I meant by it was Barry Malzberg. Wake up, America!

22

DOWN THERE

‹‹‹

THE HARD GRAY TILE OF THE CORRIDOR RANG under his feet, bare gray corridor like a squared-off gun barrel, bright ceiling overhead, and he thought bore, shaft, tunnel, tube. His door, 913. He turned the bright key in the lock, the door slid aside, hissed shut behind him. He heard the blowers begin; faint current of fresh cool air, sanitized, impersonal. The clock over the console blinked from 10:58 to 10:59.

He leaned over the chair, punched the "Ready" button. The dark screen came to life, displayed the symbols "R. A. NORBERT CG190533170 4/11/2012 10:59:04." The information blinked and vanished, recorded, memorized, somewhere in the guts of the computer nine stories down.

Norbert removed his brown corduroy jacket, hung it up. He sat down in front of the console, loosened the foulard around his throat, combed his neat little goatee. He sighed, rubbed his hands together, then punched the music and coffee buttons.

The music drifted out, the coffee spurted into the cup, fragrant brew, invigorating beverage, rich brown fluid. He sipped it, set it down, filled his pipe with burley from a silk pouch and lit it.

The screen was patiently blank. He leaned forward, punched "Start." Bright characters blinked across the screen, the printer clattered, a sheet curled out into the tray.

The first one was "WORLDBOOK MOD FEM MAR 5, SET OPT," and the other two were just the same except for length—one four thousand, the other three.

He thought discontentedly of novels, something there a man could get his teeth into, a week just setting up the parameters: but then a whole month on the job, that could be a bore: and Markwich had told him, "You've got a touch with the short story, Bob." A flair, a certain aptitude, a *je ne sais quoi*. He drank more coffee, put it down. He sighed again, pinched his nose reflectively, touched the "Start" button.

The screen said "2122084 WORLDBOOK MOD FEM MAR SET OPT 5," then "THEME: COME TO REALIZE

                VICTORY OVER RIVAL

                ADJUSTMENT WITH GROUP"

He picked up the light pen, touched the first of the three choices. The other two disappeared, then the whole array, and the screen said:

"SETTING: NEW YORK

            PARIS

            LONDON

            SAN FRANCISCO

            DALLAS

            BOSTON

            DISNEYWORLD

            ANTWERP

            OCEAN TOWERS"

He hesitated, waving the light pen at the screen. He paused at "Antwerp"—he'd never done that one—but no; too exotic. New York, Paris, London . . . He frowned, clenched the bit of the pipe in his teeth, and plunged for "Ocean Towers." It was a hunch; he felt a little thrill of an idea there.

He called for pictures, and the screen displayed them: first a long shot of the Towers rising like a fabulous castle-crowned mountain out of the sea; then a series of interiors, and Norbert stopped it almost at once: there, that was what he wanted, the central vault, with the sunlight pouring down.

Sunlight, he wrote, and the screen added promptly *fell from the ceiling as*—and here Norbert's stabbing finger stopped it; the words remained frozen on the screen while he frowned and sucked on his pipe, his gurgling briar. *Fell* wouldn't do, to begin with, sunlight didn't fall like a flowerpot. *Streamed?* Well, perhaps— No, wait, he had it. He touched the word with the light pen, then tapped out *spilled.* Good-oh. Now the next part was too abrupt; there was your computer for you every time, hopeless when it came to expanding an idea; and he touched the space before *ceiling* and wrote, *huge panes of the.*

The text now read:

Sunlight spilled from the huge panes of the ceiling as Norbert punched "Start" again and watched the sentence grow: . . . *as Inez Trevelyan crossed the plaza among the hurrying throngs.* End of sentence, and he stopped it there. Trevelyan was all right, but he didn't like Inez, too spinsterish. What about Theodora—no, too many syllables—or Georgette? No. Oh, hell, let the computer do it; that's what it was for. He touched the name, then the try-again button, and got *Jean Joan Joanna Judith Karen Karla Laura.* There. That had got her— Laura Trevelyan. Now then, *crossed the plaza*—well, a plaza was what it was, but why be so obvious? He touched the offending word with the light pen, wrote in *floor;* and then *murmuring* instead of *hurrying,* appeal to another sense there; and now, hmm, something really subtle—he deleted the period and wrote in *of morning.*

Sunlight spilled from the huge panes of the ceiling as Laura Trevelyan crossed the floor among the murmuring throngs of morning.

Not bad—not bad at all. He sipped coffee, then wrote, *The light.* You had to keep the computer at it, or it would change the subject every time. The sentence prolonged itself: *was so brilliant and sparkling,* and he stopped it and revised, and so on; and in a moment he had: *The light was so yellow and pure, even where it reflected from the floor amid the feet of the passersby, that it reminded Laura of a field of yellow daisies. The*

329

real sun was up there somewhere, she knew, but it was so long since she had seen it . . .

Good. Now a little back-look.

Her first day in Ocean Towers, she remembered unexpectedly, it had been gray outside and the great hall had been full of pearly light. It had seemed so wonderful and thrilling then. It had taken some pluck for her to come here at all—cutting her ties with County Clare, leaving all her family and friends to go and live in this strange echoing place, not even on land but built on pylons sunk into the ocean floor. But Eric's and Henry's careers were here, and where they went she must go.

She had married Eric Trevelyan when she was nineteen; he was a talented and impetuous man who was making a name for himself as a professional table-tennis player. (A mental note: jai-alai might be better, but did they have jai-alai in Ocean Towers? Check it in a moment.) *He had the easy charm and bluff good humor of the English, and an insatiable appetite for living—more parties, more sex, more everything. His teammate, Henry Ricardo, who had joined the marriage two years later, was everything that Eric was not—solid, dependable, a little slow, but with a rare warmth in his infrequent smiles.*

So much for that. Norbert punched the query button and typed out his question about jai-alai in Ocean Towers, and found they had it, all right, but on thinking it over he decided to make it chess instead: there was something a little wonky about the idea of a slow jai-alai player, or for that matter table tennis either. And besides he himself loathed sports, and it would be a bore looking up rules and so on.

Anyhow, now for a touch of plot. Eric and Henry, it appeared, were rising in their field and had less and less time for Laura. An interesting older man approached her, but she repulsed him, and took the transpolar jet back to County Clare (using Eric's travel permit).

The computer displayed a map of Ireland, and Norbert picked a town called Newmarket-on-Fergus, avoiding names like Kilrush, Lissycasey and Doonbeg that were too obvious and quaint. Besides, Newmarket was not far from Shannon Airport, and that made it plausible that Laura had met Eric there in the first place.

Laura was rapturous to be home again (the daisies were in bloom), and although the Clancy cottages seemed crowded and smelly to her now, it didn't matter; but after a few weeks she grew tired of watching the cows every day and the telly every night, and went over to Limerick for a party. But Limerick was not what she was seeking, either, and she finally admitted to herself that she was homesick for Ocean Towers. The register stood at 4,031 words.

Laura took the next jet back to Ocean Towers and had an emotional reconciliation with Eric (but Henry was a little cool), only to learn that they had been offered a three-year contract in Buenos Aires. Walking the promenade over the Pacific that night, unable to sleep, she met the older man again (Harlan Moore) and wept in his arms. The next morning she called Eric and Henry together and told them her news. "You must go on to the wonderful things and far places that are waiting for you," she said. "But I—" and her eyes were suddenly as misty as the dawn over Killarney—"I know now that my yellow daisies are here."

Five thousand, two hundred and fifteen words: pretty close. He became aware that he was hungry and that his legs ached from sitting so long. The clock above the console stood at 2:36.

No point in starting on the next one now, he would only go stale on it over the weekend. He got up and stretched until his joints cracked, walked back and forth a little to get the stiffness out, then sat down again and relit his pipe. When he had it drawing to his satisfaction, he leaned forward and punched the retrieval code for a thing of his own he had been working on, the one that began, "Chirurging down the blodstrom, gneiss atween his tief," and so on. He read it as far as it went, added a few words half-heartedly and deleted them again. *Ficciones* would probably send it back with a rejection slip as usual, the bastards, although it was exactly like the stuff they printed all the time; if you weren't in their clique, you didn't have a chance. He tapped out,

331

"THANK HEAVEN IT'S THURSDAY," and blanked the screen.

At 2:58 the screen lit up again: a summary of his weekly earnings and deductions. The printer clattered; a sheet fell into the tray. Norbert picked it up, glanced at the total, then folded the sheet and put it into his breast pocket, thinking absently that he really had better cut down this week and pay back some of his debit. He remembered the music and turned it off. The soothing strains. He punched the "Finished" button and the screen came to life once more, displaying the symbols "R. A. NORBERT CG190533170 4/11/2012 3:01:44." Then it blinked and went dark. Norbert waited a moment to see if there was anything else, a message from Markwich for instance, but there wasn't. He straightened his foulard, took down his jacket and put it on. The door hissed shut behind him and he heard the wards of the lock snick home. Down the gunmetal corridor. He gave his key to the putty-faced security guard, a crippled veteran of the Race War who had never spoken a word in Norbert's memory. In the public corridor, a few people were hurrying past, but not many; it was still early. That was how Norbert liked it. If you could choose your own hours, why work when everybody else did? He punched for twenty, and the elevator whisked him up. Here the traffic was a little brisker. Norbert got into line at the mono stop, looking over the vending machines while he waited. There were new issues of *Madame*, *Chatelaine*, *Worldbook* and *After Four*. He punched for all of them and put his card into the slot. The machine blinked, chugged, slammed the copies into the receptacle. Moving away, he could hear the whirring of the fax machines making more.

After Four had nothing of his, as he had expected— he did very little men's stuff. But *Madame* and *Chatelaine* had one of his stories apiece, and *Worldbook* two. He checked the indicia to make sure his name was there: " 'Every Sunday,' by IBM and R. A Norbert," the only recognition he would get. The stories themselves were unsigned, although occasionally one of them would say, "By the author of 'White Magic,' " or whatever. He boarded the shuttle and sat down, leafing through the magazines idly. "Making Do with Abundance," by Mayor Antonio, illustrated by a cornucopia dribbling out watches, cigar lighters, bottles of perfume, packages tied with blue satin bows. A garish full-page ad, "Be Thoroughly You—*Use Vaginal Gloss*. The best way to give it to you is with a brush." "Q Fever—the Unknown Killer." "Race Suicide—Is It Happening to Us?" by Sherwood M. Sibley. The medical article had an IBM house name for a byline, but the others were genuine. He had met Sibley once or twice at house parties—a popeyed, nervous man with a damp handshake, but judging by the clothes he wore, he must be making plenty. And it was really unfair, how much better non-fic writers were treated, but, as Markwich said, that was the public taste for you, and the pendulum would swing.

He got off at Fifth Avenue and changed to the uptown mono. The lights in the car were beginning to make his head ache. As the car pulled up at the 50th Street stop, he looked back and saw something curious: a sprawled black figure hanging in midair in the canyon of the avenue. Then the car pulled in, other people were getting up, and by the time he could see in that direction again, it was gone: but he knew somehow that it had been too big and the wrong shape for anything but a man falling. He wondered briefly how on earth the man had got outside the building. All the balconies were roofed and glassed in. The fellow must have been a workman or something.

The farther uptown they went, the more crowded the mono cars were on the other side of the avenue, going south; it was getting on toward the dinner hour. The crowds he could see on the balconies were mostly touristy-looking people in Chicagoland suits and West Coast freak outfits, white-haired and swag-bellied. Some of the women, old as they were, had smooth Gordonized faces. A few Pakistanis, a little younger. Really, he told himself, he was lucky to have such a good job, young as he was, and let's face it, he didn't have the temperament for going out and interviewing people, gathering information and all that.

The man beside him, getting off at 76th Street, dropped his newspaper on the seat and Norbert picked it up. MORE KIDNAP-MURDER VICTIMS FOUND. WILL MARRY KEN, ORVILLE: ELLA MAE. UNIVERSE LESS THAN 2 BILLION YEARS OLD, SAYS COLUMBIA PROF. The usual thing. At 125th Street, a glimpse of the sky as he stepped out onto the platform: it was faintly greenish beyond the dome. He crossed the public corridor to the bright chrome and plastic lobby of BankAmerica. At the exchange window, he presented his card to the blond young woman. "Another twenty-five, Mr. Norbert?"

"That's right, yes, twenty-five."

"You must really like currency." She made a note on a pad, put his card into her machine and tapped keys.

"No, I don't really—I travel a good deal, you see. It isn't safe to carry credit cards anymore." She glanced up at him silently, withdrew his card from the machine. "They kidnap you and make you buy things," he said.

Her beautiful Gordonized face did not change. She counted out the bills, pushed them across the counter. Norbert took them hastily, sure that his cheeks were flushed. It was no use, he would have to change banks; she knew there was no legitimate reason to draw twenty-five dollars in cash every week. . . . "Thank you, good-bye."

"Good-bye, Mr. Norbert. Have a good trip."

In the public corridor of his level a few minutes later, he ran into Art and Ellen Whitney heading for the elevators. Art and he had been roommates at one time, and then when they got married, Art and Ellen moved up to one of the garden apartments on the fiftieth floor. They looked stiff and dressed-up in identical orange plastiques. "Why, here he is now," said Art. "Bob, this is real luck. We were just trying to get you on the phone, then we went and banged on your door. This is Phyllis McManus—" he turned to a slight, pale blonde Norbert had not noticed until now. "And her date stood her up. Well, you know, ah, his mother is sick. Anyhow, we've got tickets to the ice opera at the Garden, and we're going to Yorty's afterwards. What do you say, would you like to come along?" Phyllis McManus smiled faintly, not quite looking at Norbert. Her virginal charm. "You will come, won't you, Bob?" said Ellen, speaking for the first time. She gave his arm a squeeze.

"I'm *terribly* sorry," said Norbert, letting his eyes glaze and bulge a little with sincerity. "I promised my sister I'd have dinner with her tonight—it's her birthday, and, you know . . ." He shrugged, smiled. "I would have loved it, Miss McManus, really I can't say how sorry I am."

"Oh. Well, that's really a shame," said Art. "You're sure you couldn't call her up—tell her something—"

"Sorry . . . just can't be done. Hope you have a good time, anyhow—good-bye, Miss McManus, nice to have met you. . . ." They drifted apart, with regretful calls and gestures. When they were safely gone, Norbert headed for the private corridor. His room, 2703; the telltales showed it was all right. He unlocked the door, closed and barred it behind him with a shudder of relief. The little green room was quiet and cool. He rolled up the closet blind, undressed and hung his clothes up with care. Before he stepped into the minishower, he punched for a Martini and a burger-bits casserole, his favorite. Then the refreshing spray. Air-dried and out again, he ate leisurely, watching the 3D and leafing through the magazines he had bought. By now Art and Ellen and what's-her-name would be sitting in a row at the Garden under the lights, watching the mannequins cavort on the ice-covered arena below. Norbert's thighs were beginning to tremble. He dressed again, quickly, in his "street clothes"—dirty denim pants, a faded turtleneck, a cracked vinyl jacket. He retrieved the wad of bills from his weskit, pulled the closet blind down again. He locked and secured the door behind him. Once out of the building, he took the shuttle crosstown to Broadway, down two levels, then north again to 168th Street. The dingy concourse was echoing, almost empty. Two or three dopes, twitching and mumbling, rode the escalator down with him. He came out into the gray street, slick and shiny under the glare of dusty light panels. Streaks of rust down the gray walls. The spattered pavement, here since LaGuardia; globs of sputum, puddles of degradable plastic. Posters on the walls: PARENTHOOD MAY BE HAZARDOUS TO YOUR HEALTH. DRIP, DON'T DROP. WHAT DID KIDS EVER DO FOR YOU? Rumble of semis and vans on the expressway just overhead; electrics sliding by on the avenue. Hallucinatory red and blue of 3D signs, the faint sound of music. Norbert went into the Peachtree and had a quick shot at the bar; he wanted another, but was too nervous and walked out again. In the window of Eddie's, three or four good old boys were tucking into a platter of pork and mustard greens. Norbert crossed the avenue and turned west on 169th. The doorways were full of 'billies and their girls lounging and spitting; one or two of them gave him a knowing look as he went by. "Hey, yonky," called a mocking voice, just barely audible. Norbert kept walking, past a few closed storefronts into an area of crumbling apartment houses built in the sixties. The front windows were all dark, the hallways lit only by naked yellow bulbs. At the remembered entry, he stopped, looked around. On the sidewalk, beside an arrangement of numbered squares, someone had written in yellow chalk, "Lucy is a Hoka." He went in, under the sick yellow light. The hallway stank of boiled greens and vomit. The door at the end was ajar.

"Well, come awn in," said the lanky old man in the armchair. His blue eyes stared at Norbert without apparent recognition. "Don' knock, nobody else does, walk right in." Norbert tried to smile. The others at the card table looked up briefly and went back to their game. The red drapes at the courtyard window were pulled back as if to catch a breeze. Somewhere up there in the blackness a voice burst out furiously, "You cocksucker, if I catch you . . ."

"Hello, Buddy," said Norbert. "Flo here?"

"Flo?" said the old man. "No sir, she sho' ain't."

Norbert's insides went hollow. "She's not? I mean —where'd she go?"

The old man waved his arm in a vague gesture. "Down home, I reckon." He stood up slowly. "Got us a new gal, just up from the country this mornin'." He put one hand casually between Norbert's shoulderblades and pushed him toward one of the bedroom doors.

"Well, I don't know," said Norbert, trying to hang back.

"Come on," said the old man in his ear. "She do innything. You wait now."

They were standing in front of the door, pressed so tightly together that Norbert could smell the old man's stale underwear. Swollen knuckles rapped the door. "Betty Lou?"

After a frozen moment, the door began to open. A woman was standing there, monstrous in a flowered housedress. Norbert's heart jumped. She was olive-skinned, almost Latin-looking; the folds of her heavy face were so dark that they seemed grimy. She looked at him steadily from under brows like black caterpillars; her eyes were evil, weary and compassionate. She took his hand. The old man said something which he did not hear. Then the door had closed behind him and they were alone.